P9-CRF-553

Praise for Megan Hart

"Hart's beautiful use of language and discerning eye toward human experience elevate the book to a poignant reflection on the deepest yearnings of the human heart and the seductive temptation of passion in its many forms."

—*Kirkus Reviews* on *Tear You Apart*

"*Naked* is a great story, steeped in emotion. Hart has a wonderful way with her characters.... She conveys their thoughts and actions in a manner that brings them to life. And the erotic scenes provide a sizzling read."

—*RT Book Reviews*

Praise for Deborah LeBlanc

"*The Wolven* seamlessly weaves a remarkably well-detailed mythology into the recent history of New Orleans. LeBlanc's dialogue sparkles and the sexual chemistry between Shauna and Danyon is delicious."

—*RT Book Reviews*

Megan Hart is the award-winning and *New York Times* bestselling author of more than thirty novels, novellas and short stories. Her work has been published in almost every genre, including contemporary women's fiction, historical romance, romantic suspense and erotica. Megan lives in the deep, dark woods of Pennsylvania with her husband and children. Visit her on the web at meganhart.com.

Books by Megan Hart

Harlequin Nocturne

Bound by the Night
Strangers of the Night

Visit the Author Profile page
at Harlequin.com for more titles.

STRANGERS OF THE NIGHT

MEGAN HART

WITCH'S HUNGER

DEBORAH LeBLANC

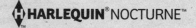

If you purchased this book without a cover you should be aware that this book is stolen property. It was reported as "unsold and destroyed" to the publisher, and neither the author nor the publisher has received any payment for this "stripped book."

ISBN-13: 978-0-373-20860-9

Strangers of the Night & Witch's Hunger

Copyright © 2017 by Harlequin Books S.A.

The publisher acknowledges the copyright holders of the individual works as follows:

Touched by Passion
Copyright © 2017 by Megan Hart

Passion in Disguise
Copyright © 2017 by Megan Hart

Unexpected Passion
Copyright © 2017 by Megan Hart

Witch's Hunger
Copyright © 2017 by Deborah LeBlanc

Recycling programs
for this product may
not exist in your area.

All rights reserved. Except for use in any review, the reproduction or utilization of this work in whole or in part in any form by any electronic, mechanical or other means, now known or hereinafter invented, including xerography, photocopying and recording, or in any information storage or retrieval system, is forbidden without the written permission of the publisher, Harlequin Enterprises Limited, 225 Duncan Mill Road, Don Mills, Ontario M3B 3K9, Canada.

This is a work of fiction. Names, characters, places and incidents are either the product of the author's imagination or are used fictitiously, and any resemblance to actual persons, living or dead, business establishments, events or locales is entirely coincidental.

This edition published by arrangement with Harlequin Books S.A.

For questions and comments about the quality of this book, please contact us at CustomerService@Harlequin.com.

® and TM are trademarks of the publisher. Trademarks indicated with ® are registered in the United States Patent and Trademark Office, the Canadian Intellectual Property Office and in other countries.

HARLEQUIN®
www.Harlequin.com

Printed in U.S.A.

CONTENTS

TOUCHED BY PASSION

Megan Hart

This collection is dedicated to Jeffe Kennedy,
who was there for me
every time I struggled with the words.

Prologue

Collins Creek

Jed doesn't like the sound of the babies crying. He can hear them even from the other building, wailing inside his head. He's too big to be one of them anymore. No more diapers. No more crib. No more giant room that always smells faintly of milk and poo. Now he has his own big bed in the dorm with the other kids, and although he misses his mothers, he knows better than to give in to tears. If you cry here in the dorm, you get a beating.

Instead, he clenches his fists tight at his sides and stares up at the ceiling. His cot is hard and lumpy. The blanket scratches his chin if he pulls it up too high, so he tucks it around his belly. The other kids are sleeping, but Jed can't seem to manage. There's too much noise, too much going on. If he gets up now, he could go to the monitor, who will give him some medicine to sleep, but it makes his head feel fuzzy and his belly hurt. He tries to fall asleep on his own.

Tomorrow is dedication day.

The fathers have been watching them all since they were babies in the nursery. They already know which ones are special. Who will be dedicated, who will be sent away.

This is Jed's first dedication time, but he's heard the other kids talking even when they're not supposed to. Everyone's scared about what happens when you're sent away. The rumor is that you get put into the big fireplace in the barn and made into smoke, and Jed believes it. He's been able to "feel" everyone at the farm for as long as he can remember. The kids who get taken away after each dedication, well…he doesn't feel them anymore.

Before he's even had time to sleep, the lights overhead come on. The other kids shift and squeal, crying out in excitement and fear when the doors to the dorm boom open and the fathers are there in their black robes, their white masks. It's supposed to make them all equal, but it doesn't matter to Jed that they all look the same. They all *feel* different.

The kids are up and in a line, marching into the hallway. One by one, they go into the meeting room. None of them come out. They won't know until later who's still left, though of course, Jed will know before everyone else. That's what he tells the fathers waiting for him in the meeting room when they ask him. He tells them who he can still feel. Who he cannot. They stare at him from behind their white masks, nodding when he points to each and names them.

They feel happy, and that makes Jed feel happy, too. He won't be burned up into smoke. He gets the special pudding for dessert that makes the world spin around in many colors. He gets to go back to the dorm and his lumpy bed, where he can only lie on his back, laughing and laughing at the funny way everything grows and shrinks.

He's still laughing when the doors bang open again. More men in black. No white masks. Guns. They kick over the beds, the monitor's desk. They shout. Most of them feel angry, though one or two feel more scared than anything else, and none of them feel nice.

They take all of the children.

Jed never sees Collins Creek again.

Chapter 1

Samantha Janecek had never liked hospitals in general, but she loathed this hospital in particular.

It wasn't the smells of chemicals and despair, though those clung to her like some stinking perfume she could never quite scrub away. And it wasn't the bright, unrelenting lights that forced everyone inside to adjust to some artificial internal clock, although they messed with her sleep so much that she hadn't been able to get more than four hours at a time since she'd started here. More than anything else, it was this uniform.

No scrubs for the nursing staff here at Wyrmwood. Nope, the women had to wear white, starched dresses with Peter Pan collars and a weird belt thing that hit her too high on the ribs to be comfortable. Thick white support stockings, crepe-soled granny shoes. Worst of all, the mesh cap she had to pin into the thickness of her blond hair, which refused to ever stay neatly in the required bun. The uniform was straight out of the late sixties—fitting, she supposed, since the rest of Wyrmwood seemed to have been arrested in that same era. Including the fact there were no male nurses here, only orderlies. They also wore all white, but at least they got to wear pants.

"Morning, miss," said Nathan through the glass as she showed him her ID card and pressed her fingertip to the panel at the side of the door.

When the green light clicked on, she pushed through the heavy door that slid behind her with a hushed whirr. "Hi, Nathan. How's it going?"

"Same old, same old." Nathan shrugged. "Quiet tonight."

Of course it was quiet. Not only were all the patients on the fourth floor secured in their individual rooms behind soundproof walls, but most of them barely spoke aloud. Some by choice, an elective muteness. Some because they'd lost the capability for speech somewhere along the way. It might've been different on other floors, but as she'd never worked on any of them, Samantha couldn't say.

"Have a good one," Samantha said as she signed in using the electronic keypad at Nathan's station.

She paused for the automatic snapshot that would be added to her file, another level of proof that she was who she said she was. That she was here when she ought to be. She'd often considered pulling a funny face during the picture taking, but had never quite dared. Humor was not encouraged here.

She didn't speak to the armed guards posted at the elevator entrance to the floor. One or both of them might be on her team, but she never knew. Never would know, not unless it was necessary. Vadim made sure of that.

Samantha had been working at the Wyrmwood job for the past eighteen months. She'd never asked what strings had been pulled to make sure she was assigned to the fourth floor. She simply followed the rules she'd agreed to when she took the job. The money from the Crew kept coming in, deposited into an account in no way connected to the one she used for her Wyrmwood salary, and which she checked only once a month, using an encrypted burner phone she then tossed immediately. Money she couldn't spend until she was no longer needed here.

The question was, when would she decide that *she* was finished with this assignment? How much longer could she stand it here before she lost more than a little bit of her own mind? Working in near silence all day long, taking the vitals of men and women who were often little more than chilly mannequins. Forcing her body into an artificial day/night cycle that fucked up her social life, not just her mental state. She was not the first person Vadim had ever assigned to this task. Sooner or later, all of those who'd come before her had ended up leaving, some of their own accord and others because they'd stopped toeing the Wyrmwood line. She'd never found out how many of them had ended up as patients themselves. Stopping for a moment in front of a closed door with nothing more than a small viewport in it, she allowed herself the briefest second to touch the cold metal. A little longer, she told herself. Surely she could last a little longer.

At the desk, positioned between the two corridors

of the L-shaped building, she managed some banal chitchat with the nurse leaving her shift. Patty was nice enough. She did yoga. Had a bland husband, several unremarkable children and a couple of dogs she referred to as "fur babies" in a way that made Samantha supremely uncomfortable. She and Patty would never be friends—Wyrmwood employees were discouraged from socializing outside of work, anyway, even if they'd had anything in common beyond the job. Samantha knew, though, that no matter how normal Patty seemed, the fact she worked here at Wyrmwood meant she had the highest security clearance possible. It meant that, like Samantha, Patty was capable of killing you with a ballpoint pen or her bare hands. Not only capable, but willing.

"Quiet tonight," Patty said in an echo of Nathan's earlier statement. "You shouldn't have any trouble."

"Never do," Samantha said with the bright, sterile smile she'd cultivated over the years as part of her armor against the "normal" world. It had worked well for this stint in Wyrmwood, that was for sure. That smile, she was convinced, was what had finally earned her the job. "Have a good night. Give the pups a squeeze from me."

"Will do!" Patty gathered her things and signed out of the computer, pausing for another of those snapshots, and left.

Alone at the desk, Samantha released a pent-up sigh and allowed her face to fall into an expression that didn't even come close to a smile. She was still being watched, of course. She knew that. But she didn't have to pretend she was here for a party. If anything, the two performance reviews she'd had since taking the assignment had made note of her "professional demeanor" and "consistent attitude."

Signing in, adding another profile picture to the files, she settled into her seat to scroll through the notes left behind by the last shift. Patty preferred crossword puzzles to extensive note taking, which was fine with Samantha, since there was rarely anything important to note. Fourth floor had twenty patients who required varying levels of care, and all of them were her responsibility.

But she was there, really, to take care of only one.

Chapter 2

If there was something about warm, smooth skin and bristly beard stubble that wasn't meant to send a girl straight to heaven, Persephone Collins didn't want to hear about it. The man in the bed beside her had muscles in all the most important places, eyes as dark as midnight, hair like the sweetest Australian black licorice and, more important, a mouth made for kissing that he hardly ever used to talk. Silence was one of a man's best qualities, according to Persephone.

Well, silence and a nice cock.

It didn't have to be huge, she thought as she rolled over to let her hand trail down his firm, hairless pecs to the bit of fur on his belly. Just proportional. A little lower, and her fingers brushed soft flesh. He stirred, thickening under her stroking touch. His groan made her smile.

He put a hand over hers. "Again?"

"Again," she whispered and lowered her mouth to taste him. Warm, sweet skin. Tangy. She closed her eyes to savor his unique flavor.

"Please," he said. "I don't think I can."

She looked at him. "Oh, I think you can."

"We've done it five times, babe." His voice dipped low, almost into a growl that became a drawn-out groan when she again dipped her head to take him between her lips.

She ran her hands over her body, knowing exactly what he would see. High, huge breasts tipped with cherry nipples. Flat belly. Wide, curving hips. And also…

"You don't want this sweetness?" She let her fingertips travel over the thatch of soft strawberry hair between her thighs. The hair was really hers.

Not much else was.

The guy on the bed—damn, what was his name, exactly? It began with an *M.* Mark? Marcus? Marcellus? Whoever he was said, "Of course I do, darlin', but you've about wore me out."

Her fingers curved around his shaft again. Stroking gently. Up over the head and around, until he arched. Cock stiff. The sound of his moan rippled through her.

Oh, how she loved fucking.

Especially men built like working out was their job. Oh, right, she thought as he continued to respond to her touch. It *was* his job. She'd met him at the gym. He was a personal trainer.

It surprised her when he sat up to put one big hand on the back of her neck to pull her close for a kiss. She managed to turn her face at the last second so their lips slid against each other quickly, barely connecting. She urged his mouth along the line of her jaw and down her throat. Lower, to her breasts. He licked and sucked at one nipple, then the other, and although this body that he was worshipping was mostly illusory, it still felt good. More than good. Fantastic.

Desire rose within her, trickling through her veins. Filling her. It swept away everything except the urge for mindless ecstasy.

"Come up here." Strong hands urged her upward to straddle his face.

His tongue slid against her, effortlessly finding her clit. His hands kneaded her ass cheeks—plumper than her own. Softer. Her real body was tight, lean, hard with muscles she's built at the gym where they'd met. The gym where he'd never paid a second of attention to her before today, when her rising need had made her focus on him.

Persephone shook away these thoughts. She needed to come, to lose herself in exploding pleasure. To be swept away by fantasy, not reality. She looked down at his face, his eyes closed as his mouth worked on her.

"There," she murmured, rocking against him. Letting the sensations swirl inside her from deep in her belly. "Oh, yeah. Right there. Right there."

She'd intended to ride his cock one more time before using his shower, helping herself to whatever was in his fridge, perhaps lifting the contents of his wallet before leaving him sleeping in the tangled, sweaty sheets left behind after their marathon fuck session. However, she wasn't going to turn down the delight of his lips and tongue against her. It was better, in fact. Taking this pleasure from him without having to focus on his.

He muttered something against her. The vibrations sent another surge of pleasure, up, up, twisting tight and coiling. She cried out as her thighs trembled. Her cunt clenched, throbbing. His tongue swirled on her clit, sending her over the edge at last.

She rode it, shaking and crying out. The climax eased. She rolled off him and limply fell back on the bed.

Silence.

A low chuckle turned her toward him. Persephone pushed herself up on her elbow to look into his face. "Thanks."

Marcus or Marco or whoever he was smiled. Yawned. "You're welcome."

She glanced down at his cock, no longer hard. "You sure you don't want…?"

"Oh, I want." He rolled to face her and put a hand on her hip. "Just can't right now. Surprised I was able to so many times already, girl. Something about you…"

Well, yeah. There was that. She smiled and touched his face. For the briefest moment she thought about letting the pretense drop. Instead, she let her fingers press the spot between his eyes. Gently. Softly.

His eyes closed. He began to snore. She studied him a moment longer, thinking how much nicer he'd been than she expected. Of course, she wasn't going to be around in the morning to find out if she was wrong about him. And the next time she saw him, he wasn't going to recognize her, so it wasn't as though she'd even have to worry about either an awkward conversation or getting the blow-off.

"Good night," Persephone whispered into his ear.

He didn't stir. She got off the bed. Long slim legs

and big boobs wavered and shifted. When she looked in the full-length mirror, her real, true image stared back at her. Five foot two. A-cup breasts. Thick, muscled thighs and biceps. Her body was strong and fit, and never let her down, no matter if she was running from the cops, breaking and entering or letting some rando with a hard cock have his way with her. This body, she thought as she cupped her breasts and flicked her nipples erect, was no wonderland. It was the real deal.

Without a glance behind her, she got dressed. She did raid the fridge, snagging a piece of cold pizza and a soda, along with a couple bananas from the counter for later. She did not, however, take his wallet. Didn't even sneak a couple twenties from it. He'd been a good lay but more than that, seemed like a pretty decent guy...

Clearly, she was slipping.

Pushing that thought from her head, Persephone kept her head down once she reached the street and headed for home. Light was tingeing the sky when she got back to her place. Maybe she'd be able to sleep now.

The sound of feet scuffling behind her as she stopped to pull her mail from the box didn't make her turn. She knew who it was without looking. She said nothing as Kane Dennis moved beside her to check his own mail.

"Morning."

She pursed her lips. "Mmm."

He laughed, the sound of it low and rich and rippling through her in a way she hated because of how much she liked it. She pulled out a sheaf of junk mail, the only kind she ever got. Pretended it was something important, like she was a real person who paid bills or got postcards from friends. She shot a sideways glance at him.

Six feet of lean, long legs. Broad shoulders. Taut stomach. Faded jeans, form-fitting Henley under a plaid shirt, unbuttoned but rolled up to his elbows to expose his finely muscled forearms. She was such a sucker for forearms, and his completely slayed her.

"Still having a problem with the hot water," Kane said conversationally. "Not trying to be a pain in the ass about it, but if you could take a look?"

"Now?" Persephone tucked the mail into her bag.

"It would be great if I could grab a hot shower before bed," he told her.

She tucked the inside of her cheek against her teeth at the thought of Kane beneath a spray of hot water, sluicing over the perfect body… She shook it off. "Sure. I can come up now."

"Great," Kane said with a smile that tried to get its way inside her, despite her every effort not to let it. "See you in a few?"

"Yeah, sure," Persephone said without returning the smile. "See you in a few."

Chapter 3

There were twenty patients on the fourth floor of Wyrmwood, ten in each wing. Samantha had never been told she had to take care of them in any certain order, but she almost always started at the far end of A wing and worked her way down toward the end of B wing. Dispensing meds. Taking vitals. Her role as a nurse was very limited, which was a good thing, since she'd never had any kind of actual medical training. Her degrees had been fabricated the same as the rest of her history. Still, none of her required tasks were difficult, and she'd been trained to call on other staff if anything did get out of control. It made her wonder, more than once, what the Wyrmwood powers above truly intended her function, and that of the other nurses, to be.

Glorified babysitters, she thought as she loaded the tray with necessary pills and vials of liquids for each room and pocketed her stethoscope and thermometer. Or more likely, part of the experiment, whatever it was. The cameras everywhere, the security. The out-of-date uniforms and strict rules that controlled after-hours behavior. The deathly quiet working atmosphere, no cell phones allowed. No outside reading material. It all seemed designed to drive the staff to madness right along with the patients, that was for sure.

She paused outside A1 to look through the porthole. The patient inside, sixty-year-old Helena, liked to draw elaborate spirals but had been denied the use of a pen or pencil since she'd stabbed an orderly with the point. She'd been allowed soft chalk, though, and routinely covered the walls and floor of her room with intricate designs every day, only to wipe them all away and start over when she'd finished. She never gave Samantha any trouble and was amenable to halting her work long enough to take the drug cocktail she'd been pre-scribed. She didn't make eye contact with Samantha. She answered when spoken to, but nothing beyond that.

"Do you need anything?" Samantha asked the stan-dard question that was rarely answered by any of the fourth floor's patients.

Helena shook her head, already reaching for the thick block of blue chalk. She turned from Samantha without another word. Outside, Samantha took one last peek into the porthole, but Helena was already back to her drawing.

In a normal job, there'd be patient histories. Records she'd have been able to pull to see why the patient had been put here in the first place. She supposed it didn't matter much. They paid her well enough not to ask those sorts of questions; more important, they paid her enough not to worry about it. Since none of the patients were being blatantly abused and all of them seemed content enough in their captivity, Samantha did her best not to care.

Slowly, she worked her way down the A wing. Whatever fight had been inside these patients in their lives had gone dead a long time ago, Samantha thought as she double-checked the next wing's meds and pushed the cart toward B10. She very carefully didn't think about the man in B1. Not until she got to B5, at least, and then, then…

She smelled lavender.

Closing her eyes as she pretended to fuss with the cart and the meds, Samantha couldn't stop herself from smiling. Jed knew it was her favorite smell. She'd mentioned it once, early on. She'd never told him that she noticed how the scent always wafted around her when she got close to his room. Saying it aloud would mean the ones who watched them would be able to hear. It would be proof that Jed was still capable of manipulating his environment. Proof of a connection between them that she didn't dare let anyone know about.

She drew in another slow breath, though, delighting in the scent. As she stood, the meds for B5 in one hand, the door at the end of the hall opened and Dr. Ransom came through it, flanked as he always was by two guards. He nodded at her, stopping in front of Jed's room.

"Hello, Nurse. I'm here to get Jed for a session."

"He hasn't had his meds yet—" The doctor was already gesturing to one of the guards to step forward and take them from her. With a frown, Samantha pulled the small paper cup from the cart but didn't hand it over. "If you can wait a few minutes, I'll be happy to—"

Again, the doctor cut her off with a dismissive wave. "Not necessary, thank you, Nurse."

The scent of lavender faded, replaced by the chemical, hospital stink that burned the insides of her nose, making her cough. The pills chattered a little in the paper cup, and she forced her hands to stop shaking. "It would really only take—"

Dr. Ransom's head swung around and, for the first time in perhaps the entirety of her working here, he looked Samantha in the face. "Is there some reason you feel it necessary to argue with me?"

"No." With that same bright, plastic smile, Samantha handed over the pills to the guard, who took the paper cup without even blinking. "Of course not."

"Get back to work," Ransom told her, already dismissing her and looking through the portal.

Samantha wasn't dumb enough to say another word. She lingered, though, at the cart, until they brought Jed out. Not in cuffs, although the men on either side of him were clearly ready to handle him if he did anything out of line. He hadn't in the past eighteen months, but she knew he had, a long time ago. Watching Ransom's face, she thought the doctor was sort of hoping Jed would pull something now, so he'd have an excuse to order Jed's restraint.

Was this it? The end of things? Were they finally taking him away? Should she react? There'd been no word from the Crew, and nothing from Wyrmwood, either. No changes in the schedule that would indicate that anything had changed.

Jed didn't look at her when he came out of the room. Not so much as a glance over his shoulder.

She was already planning her attack when the softly drifting scent of lavender returned. She didn't think he even knew she was there. She'd never spoken to Jed about the real reasons she'd come to Wyrmwood, but it wasn't impossible that he knew and understood. Not out of the realm of possibility that he would know before she could, before anyone else could, that his time here was over.

Chapter 4

Jed came back as Samantha was finishing her shift. She heard the doors open and stood up from her place at the desk to look. Ransom hadn't come back with him. The same two guards from before were marching him to his room, a hand beneath each of his elbows to hold him up. He looked exhausted.

"Does he need something? Jed, do you need something?" She came around the desk to face them.

"Doctor said he'll be fine, he just needs to sleep." One of the guards gave her an assessing up-and-down look, and then a surprising grin. "I could use a little something, though."

"Shut up, Clement," said the other guard with a scowl. "Get this door open. Get the guy inside, okay? I want to go the hell home."

Samantha ignored both of them and stepped closer. "Jed?"

He shook his head. "No. Just tired. I'll sleep now. That's all."

He looked terrible, but so did most of the patients when they came back from a session with Ransom. Samantha hesitated, once more wondering if now was the time. She could take out the first guard, no problem, and with great satisfaction, considering how he'd leered at her. The second would be harder to topple, warned and ready, but she had no doubts that she could take care of him, too. Her fingers fairly itched to strike out at both of them, but she didn't show any signs of it.

Vadim, the man in charge of the Crew and the one who'd brought her in on this assignment, had told her there'd be times when she felt ready to act, but that she needed to wait. She'd be told when the time was right. Until then, she was to monitor Jed. To foster a relationship with him, such as she could with limited interactions. She would have to trust the Crew, Vadim had said, and she'd have to get Jed to trust her.

Samantha had never been big on trust, either giving or receiving, but she did believe Vadim and the Crew knew what they were doing. So now, instead of going into battle mode and destroying the two dudes manhandling Jed through the door and into his room, she went back to the desk and gathered her things. She signed out, although until the next nurse showed up to cover her shift, there wasn't much she could do.

"Hey, listen, so maybe me and you…" The first guard had come out of Jed's room and leaned over the desk to give her a wink. "Drinks?"

"You know that's not allowed." Without looking at him, Samantha scanned through the security feeds on the camera, searching for any sign that her replacement was at least in the elevator.

"Hey. I'm talking to you." He went so far as to put his hand over the top of the desk and tried to grab her shoulder.

She pulled away before he could touch her, one hand going up automatically to grip his wrist and break it, before she stopped herself. She did not smile. "I'm not interested in getting fired, Clement."

"Yeah, that pussy isn't worth it, anyway," he said derisively, his mouth twisting. In the next second, he was choking, coughing, doubled over so that she had to stand and look over the edge of the desk to see what the hell was going on. The fit lasted only another few seconds, but when he stood his face was red, eyes streaming tears. He muttered a low curse and backed away from her with a scowl.

A dozen retorts leaped to her lips, but as with almost every other action she ever wanted to take while on this job, Samantha held it back. She gave Clement her patented blank smile and enjoyed the way it made him flinch. The hall door opened, letting in the nurse who'd be taking over, and Samantha pushed past him without so much as a look at his face.

The scent of lavender stayed with her the entire way home.

Chapter 5

It was a rare day when Persephone didn't have anything going on. No repairs to make or schedule for the building. No appointments with the small but consistent stable of men who paid her to be the woman of their dreams…or sometimes, nightmares, depending. She couldn't remember the last time she'd woken feeling semi-rested, without even a tinge of anxiety following her around.

It wouldn't last, she thought as she headed out into the morning, taking the concrete steps at the front of the building two at a time so she could get to the bodega on the corner for a cup of coffee and a candy bar. Caffeine and chocolate in hand, she was already tearing open the plastic when she bumped head-on, literally, into a man as solid as brick. She hit him hard enough to bounce off, stumbling back.

"Watch it," she muttered, preparing to push past him.

The guy snagged the sleeve of her sweatshirt, turning her to face him. Persephone was already working, shifting, smoothing the lines and curves of her face to look like someone else. Dark hair instead of bright red-gold. Big tits. Tight top. His eyes went right there, and even if she hadn't masked her face he'd have barely paid attention, so taken was he by the sight of her knockers.

Men, she thought with a sneer. So predictable.

"I'm looking for someone," he said. "You seen her?"

The picture he pulled up on his phone was blurred, but definitely her. Thank god she'd automatically put on the glamour for him. The question was, why did he have a picture of her in the first place?

"Nope. Never," Persephone said. "What'd she do?"

She thought he might say she owed him, or someone he was working for, money. That she was part of a scam. That she'd been caught up in a kinky prostitution ring, and he was part of the sting operation.

"Nothing." Something in his cold, dead eyes left her shivering. "Just looking for her."

Then he backed up and kept walking, leaving her behind. She watched him go, knowing that if he turned to glance back, she would still look like someone else. Uncertain if, in the end, it would matter. If a man like that was on her trail, she might be in trouble sooner rather than later.

He was from Wyrmwood. She felt it. He wasn't one of the soldier guys who'd raided Collins Creek; they were drones that followed orders. This guy was the advance scout, sniffing around to see if he could catch wind of her anywhere.

And if he found out where she really was, Persephone thought, then the other men would come.

Then, they would try to take her away.

Chapter 6

Jed would have liked to really put down that guard who'd been harassing Samantha all the way to the ground, his lungs blowing up, heart bursting from his chest. He'd settled instead for squeezing the asshole from the inside out, just enough to get the guy to back off from Samantha, and even that effort had nearly put Jed onto his hands and knees. There wasn't any blood, though. Whatever damage he'd done to the guard's brain hadn't been bad enough for that.

Ever since he was twelve years old, Jed had discovered the joys of hurting people, especially when the rewards bore merit—video games, chocolate cake, comic books. All he had to do was let Dr. Ransom open the window blinds into the other room and show him the man or the woman in the chair, then he'd have to think really hard and later, not quite as hard and then not hard at all, to make them scream and writhe in agony.

It had taken him only another year to understand that hurting people did not make him feel good. It left him with a sick stomach and an aching head, worse than finishing the puzzles or reading the word cards in the box or any of the other dozens of things they had him do. Hurting people took effort; getting them to behave like his puppet took even more. More than once it left his nose bleeding.

One terrible time, it left him blind.

His sight came back. So did the tests. So did his anger, bigger now than anything else. No more rewards for doing what they wanted. Now he suffered the punishments for refusing. Starvation. Electric shock therapy. When they realized he could no longer be controlled by any of those methods, the drugs began.

At seventeen, he killed a man, but not the one they wanted him to kill. After that, the people at Wyrmwood started to be afraid of him.

Now, at twenty-five, he should still be terrifying them, but he'd spent the last eight years doing his best to convince them that they had nothing to fear.

The testing tonight during his session with Dr. Ransom had been unexpectedly brutal. After years of proving to them he was no longer capable of doing what they wanted, years of taunting them into just disposing of him already, Jed had almost forgotten what it was like when the doctor was convinced he could get a reaction from his patient. Almost, but not quite. His body remembered, anyway, the sting and burn of electricity. The pungent horror of the chemicals they dripped into his veins to make him compliant. There'd been times over the years when it would've taken so little to tip him into death, but they'd pulled him back. So many times he'd have let them—but that had changed when Samantha started working there.

She was not the first person to look him in the eyes, but she was the first to at least try to connect with him as a human being. Small things, nothing that would get either of them in trouble. A gentle squeeze of his shoulder when she took his vitals. A smile. A compassionate laugh at his lame jokes.

He felt it when she left the hospital. If he tried a little harder, he'd be able to feel her wherever she went, but doing that would surely rip something inside his head, so he eased back the small tendrils of thought that had connected him to her in the first place. She'd be back tomorrow, he thought just before he passed out on the hard cot, her face the last coherent thought he had.

Chapter 7

Samantha could not stop thinking about him.

After escaping from the hospital that was a prison, she went home only long enough to change into her workout gear. She hit the street as dawn pinked the sky, and though her body cried for sleep, the only way she'd get any was to exhaust herself. She set off on a route that would take her through the park, where she could test herself on soft dirt paths and boulders, then along the riverfront and back home before the early-morning-rush traffic started.

Since starting at Wyrmwood, she'd shared perhaps a couple dozen conversations with Jed that weren't related to his medication or treatment. The training and rules had been explicit and strict about having as little contact with the patients as possible. She'd rarely bent the rules and never enough to get any disciplinary action. There was no denying that she felt closer to him than she did any of the others, but she'd always chalked it up to the fact she'd been hired to save his life when the time came. Something like that would naturally lead her to be more…*affectionate* was not the right word, not even close. Concerned. Protective. Aware?

She ran harder, leaping a park bench with one foot on the seat and pushing off with the other on the back, then hitting the grass with her fingertips digging into the soft earth before she leaped again. It was ridiculous to think Jed had done anything to the guard. Though there'd been plenty of documentation about what he'd been capable of when he was younger, all the reports Vadim had given her said that Jed's abilities had begun fading in late adolescence, becoming completely extinct over time.

It had happened with other members of the commune where he'd been born. Children born with psychokinetic or telepathic talents had been taken away from the Collins Creek farm under the guise of child protective services, but they'd been sent to places like Wyrmwood, not foster care. They'd been held, tested. Of those that had been released in adulthood, none of them had been reported as maintaining their abilities. Most of the ones the Crew had been able to track had suffered from the years of institutionalization. High rates of suicide and crime had followed. Jed was one of the last of the Collins Creek kids the Crew had been able to find.

She jumped up to grab a low-hanging tree limb and swung out, arching her back. Landing hard. She no longer smelled lavender, but the memory of it wouldn't leave her. There'd been more than a few times when she'd thought she sensed Jed's presence while she was at the desk, always looking up, expecting to see him there but finding only empty space. Sometimes, a joke would tickle its way into her head until she laughed aloud.

Maybe all of that had been Jed. He had come to her defense, not that she'd needed him to, with that moron Clement. Which meant that despite all the information Wyrmwood had been collecting on him, he wasn't telekinetically dead.

But he was going to be physically dead if he didn't reveal that truth to the Wyrmwood team, or if Samantha wasn't able to get him out of there when Vadim gave the go-ahead. It would have to be soon, she thought, thinking of how drained Jed had looked when they'd brought him back to the room.

On the way home, she picked up a burner phone and sent off a text to the number she'd memorized.

How long?

Then she tossed the phone into a Dumpster and continued on home. She didn't worry about how Vadim was going to answer her. He always found a way.

Chapter 8

Persephone had stopped dreaming about Collins Creek a long time ago. If she did think about her childhood, it was only in a series of flashing memories she did her best to shove aside. She and her twin brother, Phoenix, had managed to escape when Wyrmwood attacked and took most of the children away. The two of them had grown up on the streets, running constantly from Wyrmwood's scouts who'd found other survivors and made them disappear. The rumors about what was done to the Collins Creek children had circulated. Phoenix and Persephone had always managed to stay a few steps ahead of them, and in many ways the memories of the things they'd done to survive had been much worse than anything she could truly remember from her first ten years on the farm.

Now, though, she couldn't stop herself from looking

over her shoulder everywhere she went. She couldn't prove the guy from this morning had been from Wyrmwood.

Twenty years had passed since the raid. Why would they suddenly be looking so hard now? Turning over in her bed, she thought of calling Vadim. He'd offered her and Phoenix sanctuary, but her brother had refused, not willing to throw in his lot with a group that, to him, seemed as likely to turn out to be as awful as Wyrmwood. Persephone had not been quite as convinced of that. She had, in fact, done a job or two for Vadim over the years. Never anything serious or long-term. The money was fantastic, but like her brother, she'd never wanted to commit to it.

Vadim would know if there was anything new going on with Wyrmwood, though. Restless, Persephone got out of bed and paced through her apartment, checking as always the exits. One door in, one door out. The only window a single transom on the alley side of the building. She could get through it if she had to, but her real escape was the service elevator, a dumbwaiter, in a closet off the kitchen.

Running through her escape plan calmed her a little, but she was still not going to sleep. She needed something else, and she knew exactly where to find it. She dialed a familiar number.

"Leila? Girl, what are you up to?"

Leila was up to going out and causing trouble, as she almost always was. Persephone didn't hang out with her very often for just that reason—any kind of trouble Leila wanted to get into usually ended up bad. She didn't have the sense of self-preservation that Persephone had, or even Phoenix, who admittedly could be way less worried about keeping his ass out of the fire.

Leila's skill was in counting. Her brain was an abnormally brilliant calculator that could figure the most complex equations with little more than a blink or two. She had not yet managed to use this Collins Creek–created skill for much of anything, though. Maybe she never would.

Still, it was good to get out, go dancing. Get a little drunk. Grind on a handsome guy or two or three. Persephone and Leila hit the town, dressed to…well, not to kill, Persephone thought absently as she scanned the crowed for likely prey. She never wanted to kill anyone ever again.

All at once, there he was from across the room. Kane Dennis, the cop who lived in Persephone's building. He was the one with the hot water problem. He was leaning against the back wall, a cup of beer in his hand. Scanning the room, back and forth, as though he were looking for something. Or someone. It didn't look like he'd seen her yet.

She began to layer herself, homing in on his mind. One at a time, that was the only way she could do this. He would have no idea that he was looking at a different woman from the one everyone else could see.

"I'm glamouring for that guy," Persephone said to Leila with a discreet point toward Kane. "You'll be okay here?"

Leila was already tonsils-deep into a make-out session with a guy she'd picked up a few minutes before, and waved Persephone away. Why, exactly, Persephone was doing this when there was a club full of dudes she didn't have to see in front of the mailbox every morning, she could not say. Only that he was there and she was here, and a curling flicker of need was rising inside her that she wanted to sate.

Maybe it was because he was a cop. She would be safe. If someone broke in and tried to take her, she thought, blaming the booze and the smoke and the little white pill of undetermined origin that Leila had slipped her earlier for this ragged train of thought. If someone broke in, Kane would be able to protect her. Wouldn't he?

By the time she got to him, she wore longer legs. Bigger tits as usual, since that's what most men seemed to dig. Soft, round booty. Dusky skin. Dark ringlets. Red lips, dark eyes.

"Hi," she said. "I'm Maria. Thinking about getting out of here, how about you?"

That was all it took. Persephone had not figured Kane for a guy so easily seduced and was in truth a little put off at how simple it had been, but she supposed it didn't matter as long as she got what she needed from him. Hard cock. Big hands. Sweet tongue. They found a cheap room in one of the hotels lining the street this end of town.

He kissed her mouth as soon as they got inside the door, his hands roaming over her. Fingers playing beneath her skirt, he found her already wet. Slick. Hot. He slipped his fingers inside her, fucking in and out, and she opened for him. His thumb pressed her clit, a steady pace that had her ready to go in minutes.

He let her lead him to the bed and strip him down. He watched her do the same. He rolled her over, nudging open her knees. She thought he would go down on her; she hoped he would, but instead Kane pressed a series of kisses to her belly, up to her breasts. Her throat.

Her mouth. He'd pulled a condom from his wallet while they undressed and sheathed himself so efficiently that he was inside her in moments.

"Oh," she said. "Okay, then."

Kane fucked her slowly at first, making sure to get her going. When she needed a little extra pressure on her clit, he gave it to her, just right. Persephone rarely had any trouble getting off, but tonight it was taking her longer. Because she knew him, she thought, irritated with herself now that the buzz was fading. She ought to have found a stranger.

She didn't have much more time to think about it then because something in the way he shifted had brought her to the tipping point. They moved together, easily, steadily, and she came in a slow rush of rolling pleasure. He followed with a shudder and buried his face against the side of her neck.

When her phone rang, she was happy to shift out from underneath him so she could grab it. "Hey, girl."

"I didn't go home with that guy," Leila's drunken voice crackled through the phone, a bad connection. "I'm back at my place. You okay?"

"Yes, fine." Persephone glanced at Kane, who'd sat up to look at her. She'd been holding on to her illusion as a matter of habit, a good one, but tightened it now to be sure he had not even a glimpse of her true self. Leila had disconnected.

"I have to go," she said. "Sisters before misters, am I right?"

"Sure. No problem." He yawned and fell back on the bed. "You need a cab or anything?"

"I'm good." She paused as she gathered her clothes to look at him. "Thanks for tonight."

He rolled onto his side to crack open an eye and grin at her. "You're welcome."

It was on the tip of her tongue to offer him her number, which of course would be ridiculously stupid, even if she did use the fake side line she kept for these very occasions. Instead, she dressed quickly and let herself out of the hotel room.

Chapter 9

Jed studied the wooden puzzle in front of him. It was more suitable for a five-year-old than a twenty-five-year-old, but since he'd been given puzzles identical to this one or nearly so since he had been five, he guessed they'd never seen any reason to change. A rectangular wooden base with different sized, shaped and colored holes, meant to hold the brightly colored matching pieces. Unlike a toddler puzzle, this one had more complicated shapes and smaller pieces. The goal: fit the pieces into the slots as fast as possible. He'd been using this same one for so long, the paint had worn down to bare wood in many places. It didn't matter. At this point, the exercise was more of a self-soothing device than anything else.

He shook out the pieces, scattering them across the desk like jacks. He set the base upright and leaned back in his chair, closing his eyes. His hands went to the edges of the table, fingertips touching the worn wooden surface lightly. Through the pads of his fingertips, he could taste the harsh sting of the antibacterial cleanser they used in here every afternoon while he was in session with Dr. Ransom. It was a bad taste, yet somehow comforting. It had been the same for twenty years. Just like the puzzle. Like the lights set on timers to keep him on a regular day/night schedule that had nothing in common with the actual movement of the sun. Like everything else here, over time, the hospital had become…home.

Without opening his eyes, Jed began fitting the pieces into the slots. His fingers moved, stroking over the wooden desk, though now the harsh bite of the chemicals had been replaced by the smoother, older smell of colored paint. Blue star. Yellow circle. Red hexagon.

Faster.

Green cross. Black square. Purple triangle.

Faster.

The wooden pieces fit themselves into place with small, clattering thumps and thuds as they rolled across the desk.

When all the pieces had returned to the base, the vibration in the desk ceased and he opened his eyes. He put his fingertips on the edge of the table again and touched the puzzle with his gaze and nothing more. He'd done this forty-seven times already tonight, and would keep doing it until the lights went off when he was supposed to be sleeping—but of course he didn't sleep. He hardly ever did, never more than an hour or two at a time, anyway.

He closed his eyes.

Faster.

Faster.

He could do this another three times, if he was quick, before it was time for Samantha to bring him his meds. He'd have to be finished before she got here. She had no idea what he was, what he could do. But out of all the people who'd worked here over the years, all the doctors, nurses and orderlies, all the guards, hundreds of people who'd taken care of him—Samantha was the only one who'd made it seem like it mattered. How she saw him. What she thought of him. She was the first person since he'd been sent here to make Jed care about anything.

A scant few seconds before he heard the click of the door lock, Jed had finished his last round of the puzzle and pushed it aside. He was already on his feet, standing behind the red line painted on the floor well away from the door. He smoothed his hair, suddenly self-conscious. He should have quit the puzzle sooner. Brushed his hair, his teeth. Changed his shirt, as if any of the four he owned were not identical.

"Hi, Jed." Samantha's grin urged his own. "How's it going?"

"Good, good. You?" He always sounded such like an idiot when he spoke to her, but she never seemed to notice.

"Oh, I'm dandy." She waited for the door to lock behind her before stepping toward him.

In the past eight years, Jed had never once moved over the red line before that solid click. In eight years, never given anyone reason to fear him. For a brief period of time when he was a teenager, they'd upped his meds to keep him from trying to escape, testing him over and over again to see if he could do with the door lock what he could do with the puzzle, but he'd always failed. It was the type of metal, they said amongst themselves. They had no idea that it wasn't anything to do with that all, but the simple fact that Jed wanted them to stop drugging him.

Not so he could get out. That, he could've done at any time, despite the drugs and the special metal in the locks. His memories of what life had been before had never faded, even through the distortion of childhood. He never wanted to go back to the life he'd known before coming here. If that meant spending his life in this room, so be it. No, he'd simply hated the fuzzy way the meds made him feel. Slow and thick and stupid.

"Is it getting cold outside?" he asked her suddenly, regretting the stupid words the moment they flew out of his mouth.

Samantha frowned and gave him a sideways glance, then another at the corner of the ceiling where the hidden camera lurked. "You know I'm not allowed to talk about that, Jed."

"Right, right. I know." Did they really think he didn't remember there was a world outside these walls? Sometimes, Jed thought, they must. He'd allowed them to think of him as simple for so long, he must've convinced them he was also stupid. "I just wondered."

"Can you sit down, please?" She gestured, and when he had complied, as he always did, always, never disobedient, she made a show of pulling out her stethoscope but leaned over him as she placed the round part of it against his chest. "The leaves are changing. The air smells like snow."

That whisper sent an electric jolt all through him. So did her touch on his wrist as she counted the too-many and too-fast beats of his heart. Samantha looked into his eyes, so close he could see the white specks surrounding the blackness of her pupil. She gave him a small, secret smile and waited a moment or so before she officially took his pulse. Giving him time to relax.

She knew him.

She'd never commented on the embarrassing way his body reacted to her standard routine. Not when she used gentle fingers to press his neck and throat to check his lymph nodes and his heartbeat again raced, and not when she had him lift his arms to his sides so she could pass her hands along his body and he shifted against the rise in his pants. She noticed it. She had to. There was no way to hide the heat of his skin. But she always managed to be standing at an angle to block it from the camera, and she always took her time to make it possible for him to calm down before she stepped back.

Today (it was really close to midnight, though they wanted him to think it was more like noon) she lingered with the exam. Stood a little closer than usual. She dropped her stylus, a soft-tipped rubber utensil that should not have been able to cause any harm, should he decide to take it from her and shove it into a vulnerable spot. It was a sensible precaution, though he wondered why nobody had ever seemed to consider the fact he'd need no weapon if he really wanted to hurt someone.

And they thought he was the stupid one.

She smelled so fresh, so clean, that all he could do was close his eyes and breathe her in. He wanted to cover himself in her scent, to wash away the stink of this room. Of all the years…

"Jed," she said. Warning. "No touching."

He hadn't meant to. The gentle pressure of his fingers against the inside of her elbow had been involuntary. He didn't move them away. Staring into her eyes, Jed let his fingers trace a small circle on her bare skin.

Her lips parted on a small sigh. She blinked rapidly. At the tiniest hint of her tongue pressed to her upper lip, another rush of electricity jolted through him. He was so hard now there'd be no way she could keep up the pretense of this exam long enough for him to hide it from whoever it was that got their jollies watching.

She should move away from, he thought a little incoherently. She had to know what was happening. He should stop touching her, but he couldn't make himself. Another infinitesimal stroke of his fingertips on her skin had her eyes going wide. Dark.

Her smell changed from fresh air to something his brain told him was flowers, though it had been twenty years since he'd even seen a flower; the taste of her like golden honey, sweet syrup, flooded him through the continuing touch. Every muscle in him tensed, straining, though neither of them so much as moved more than the constant, steady motion of her hands as she made a show of checking his vitals.

Pulse. Temperature. One-handed, not moving so he could keep his fingertips on the inside of her elbow, Samantha kept up a running commentary on what she was doing—for the benefit of the observing camera, maybe. Or for him. For herself, Jed thought irrationally as the steady drone of her voice cracked and dipped for a second before she recovered.

He had never kissed a woman. Never made love. They'd started giving him porn when he hit adolescence—an outlet, they thought, so any pent-up desires could be dissolved. Preventing him from what, from violence? From yearning? It had worked, to a point, he thought now, but you couldn't replace human touch with paper pages or digital images. You couldn't replace making love to a woman with your own hand.

He wanted to kiss Samantha. He wanted to touch her. He wanted to make her shiver and shake, not the way the women in those movies did, but from deep inside her core. For real. He wanted to hear her say his name while her body tightened around him...

Samantha put her hand over his, her eyes closing. Her body tensed. She shook, but so briefly there could be no way anyone but Jed would notice. A small moan slipped out of her, covered up so fast by a cough as she turned her head that again, nobody but he could've possibly heard it.

"You have to stop." Her lips moved, in silence he understood, anyway.

Ashamed, he let her go. Samantha took a step back, almost stumbling before she caught herself. Her eyes opened. Gaze focused. A flush had spread up her throat to paint her cheeks. With her back still to the camera, shielding him, she pulled the small cup of meds from her uniform pocket and made a show of dispensing them.

"Take your vitamins," Samantha said.

They weren't vitamins, but at least they weren't hallucinogens or sedatives. He swallowed them with the bottled water she gave him from the small fridge next to the desk. By the time he had, he'd also managed to will his erection back down.

"Careful, you've spilled," she said calmly without

looking away from his eyes, not so much as a glance at the small wet patch on the front of his pants.

Still watching out for him, he thought. Doing what she could. His balls ached, but he didn't dare even to shift in the chair.

They shared a look, lingering as long as they dared. At least he imagined they did, but when she cut her gaze from his, Jed had to admit that perhaps all of this was in his head. Surely Samantha didn't have any romantic feelings for him. How could she? He shouldn't mistake kindness and a sense of duty for anything like affection. In fact, he should be ashamed of using his talent to inflict his lust on her.

"Do you need anything?" she asked him.

He needed lots of things, none of which she could give him. "No, thanks. Is it almost time for my session with Dr. Ransom?"

"Yes. I…think so." Again, her cheeks colored as she checked her watch. "Wow, yes it is. I lost track of time."

"The exam took longer today," Jed said, watching her.

Again, Samantha snagged his gaze with hers and didn't look away. She smiled. "Yes. A little longer."

Behind her, the green light over the door clicked to red. She didn't turn to look at it, but noticed him staring. She straightened, tucking the empty tin back into her pocket and patting it. She smoothed the fine tendrils of pale hair that had fallen over her forehead and cheeks. She cleared her throat and took another step back.

"Everything's fine, though," she said.

Jed smiled without much humor. "Isn't it always?"

"No," Samantha said even as her mouth formed the word *yes*, adding, "Don't forget to buzz if you need me."

I need you. I always need you. His answer, unspoken, could not possibly have reached her. His talents didn't extend to projecting thoughts.

Still, she nodded as though she'd heard him, but that was his own foolishness. His own desire. Without another word exchanged, Samantha left the room and the door locked behind her, and Jed forced himself to get out of the chair so nobody would think something was wrong.

Chapter 10

Leaving her shift in the light of day meant Samantha would be going home to blackout shades and a white-noise machine—but there'd be no easy sleep for her this morning. Not after that interminable five minutes in Jed's room. Not with the memory of his touch lingering.

A cold shower didn't help. She tried it, of course, running the water as frigid as she could stand it until her teeth chattered and her nipples peaked to near-painful tightness—but getting out, drying off, every stroke of the towel's soft fabric against her had Samantha's nerves tingling. Now she lay naked in her bed, the covers tossed off to expose her to the chilly autumn air, her window open to let in the breeze, because after a night's work in Wyrmwood she couldn't bear to be closed in, not even inside her own apartment.

Stretching, letting her naked skin shift on the sheets, she tried not to touch herself but gave up after a few minutes of halfhearted resistance. She'd been on fire since giving Jed his exam—the same one she gave him every shift. A quick check of his temperature, his pulse, his glands, the clarity of his eyes and little more than that. It was required, but useless, since the likelihood of anything being wrong with him that nobody hadn't already noticed was so slim.

It was not the first time she'd murmured to him about the world outside, completely in defiance of the rules. Nor the first time she'd lingered over the exam, if only because of the way he'd pushed himself into her touch the way a cat would, purring, butting at her hand for the barest scrap of affection. Nobody touched him unless they were examining him. She knew that much, not from anything she'd ever been told as a staff member, but from the reports she'd studied, provided by Vadim and the vast reference and research sources of the Crew.

Nobody touched Jed to comfort him, not since childhood. Certainly never to arouse him, though she'd noticed about six months into her stint there that he'd begun reacting to her in that way. She'd never made a fuss about it, at first because she didn't want to risk them pulling her off duty taking care of him, for fear there was any kind of connection between them. Later, to keep him from being embarrassed. Now, she noticed but never acknowledged it because she couldn't admit to anyone, not even herself, how knowing that the simplest touch of her against him got him hard. How he looked at her, hungrier for that ten minutes they shared than he ever was for the trays of bland food they brought him.

Tonight was the first time, though, she'd ever had a similar reaction.

Her hand slid between her legs to cup herself. Fingers slipping inside. She was still slick. Her clit, still sensitive enough that the slight flick of it from her thumb forced a sigh out of her.

He'd almost made her come while barely touching her.

With a low groan of frustration, she stopped. This was no good. She didn't want to admit that she thought of Jed in that way. Jed, the man she was supposed to protect. Not lust after.

Still, the job with Wyrmwood had made it impossible for her to have much of a social life, which left nothing but the touch of her own hand. It had been about a week since the last time she'd pleasured herself, and she was surprised she'd made it this long without taking the time to get herself off. No wonder he'd been able to bring her so close, Samantha thought with a sigh as she rubbed her clit in a slow, steady circle. She was definitely in need of an orgasm.

The scent of lavender. It teased and tickled her nostrils. Memory, she was sure, but caught up in the eroticism of her own touch, she didn't think much about it beyond that. She let the smells wash over her, urging her toward release.

Sometimes she used toys, but tonight the touch of only her fingers was getting her there. That and the memory of standing next to Jed, her fingertips on his wrist and feeling the suddenly swift throb of his heartbeat. His erection, conspicuously thick in his scrubs.

The small wet spot of his precome that had stained it…
all that from doing nothing but sitting near her. The
thought of it was intoxicating and had her slipping over
the edge into a hard, brief orgasm that left her breathless and sated…for now.

She gave herself a few minutes to luxuriate in
the afterglow, which was nowhere near as nice as it
would've been if she had been with someone else, but
it would have to do. She'd already filed her daily report
for the Crew, but now she rolled out of bed and slung on
a silk kimono to sit at her desk and flip open her laptop.
She typed in the web address of the secure reporting
site and scrolled back through all the information she
had on Wyrmwood. On Jed. Her notes were complete
and thorough and said very little because there wasn't
very much to say. She went in. She did her job. She
came home. She waited for word on when it was time
to get him out of there.

And sometimes, she thought with a small pang of
guilt, she made herself come when thinking about him.

She wasn't surprised when her computer rang.
Surely they monitored when she logged in, and what
she looked at. "Vadim."

He smiled at her from the small video chat window
on her screen. "Samantha. What's going on?"

She did not want to tell her boss about the sexual
encounter today. It was an embarrassing lack of self-
control on her part. It might get her pulled from the
assignment, and there were so many reasons she didn't
want that to happen—some she'd own up to and some
she would not.

"Nothing," she said after a second's hesitation.

"Can't sleep. Just trying to refresh myself on the case, I guess."

"There's nothing new in there. If there were, I'd have alerted you." Vadim tilted his head to study her. "You haven't heard anything from the hospital, have you?"

"Of course not. Like they'd tell me anything." She snorted soft laughter and shook her head.

Vadim was no longer smiling. "It's going to be soon. Our source says the paperwork's been filed for his transfer."

The transfer from Wyrmwood to an unknown location. They didn't need to know where they were taking him to understand that he'd be killed wherever he ended up. "Why do they bother, Vadim? Why not just overdose him at the hospital? It's not like anyone would know."

The words were truth but tasted bitter, making her sneer.

Vadim shrugged. "Who knows, other than even their most vetted employees could end up with too much information, and they don't want to risk it? Better to 'transfer' the ones they're no longer interested in using to someplace else and simply dispose of them along the way."

Samantha shuddered at the thought of it, of Jed being put into a white van. A gun to his head, maybe, or a simple injection. His body put into an unmarked grave. Vadim gave her a curious look, even as she quickly smoothed her expression.

"You'll be ready?" he asked. "The only time you'll be able to extricate him is in that small window between him leaving Wyrmwood and before he arrives at where it is they plan to take him."

She'd known that when she took the assignment. Breaking him out of the hospital was an impossibility, no matter her level of skill or how much the Crew could help with computer hacking or other measures to get past security. She'd always known she would have to wait until they were transferring him and move at that time. So why, then, did she feel so suddenly desperate not to wait any longer?

"It's been years." She leaned closer to the computer, staring into the camera. "Is it possible they're simply going to leave him alone? There are plenty of residents at Wyrmwood living out their lives without interference."

"Not a single one of the children captured from Collins Creek have been left to live without interference," Vadim said. "The ones that showed no abilities were, of course, put into the foster care system. The others have either been kept, as Jed's been kept, or exterminated."

"There are some others," Samantha said quietly. "The ones who got out."

She'd read about them in the files. A few obscure references, no more than that, these special children almost as much of a myth as Bigfoot. Sometimes spotted in the wild, but never captured, their existence never proven.

"You know as well as I do that nobody's ever been able to connect anyone out there with Collins Creek. It was swept, the residents removed and most of them died during the raid." Vadim paused. "Certainly we've had many cases of men and women with extraordinary psychic talents, but none of them have been connected with the farm or the cult. And even if they were, does it matter? Your assignment is to protect this one man."

"Of course." She nodded, pulling the robe closer around her throat from the sudden chill sweeping over her.

"Samantha, you should know I have no doubts about your ability to handle this assignment. You're very, very good at what you do." Vadim did smile again, though the effect of it was probably less reassuring than he meant it to be.

Samantha saw no point in false modesty. She'd spent her childhood being trained to survive any situation, including the impossible, like an alien invasion or the rise of the undead. She'd joined the Crew after several stints in government organizations so secret even she wasn't sure who ran them—only that the training she'd had as a kid had been nothing compared to what she'd learned there. Those skills and credentials had been what got her approved to work at Wyrmwood. "Yes. It's not that I'm worried about it… I'll be ready. But…"

"Yes?"

Samantha shook her head, knowing she had to own up to it. "It's the subject. He seems to have formed an… attachment."

"Ah. Can you use it?"

Startled, she recoiled with a grimace. "What? No! Why would I?"

"If it was necessary to gain his cooperation, I would expect you to, especially if it was to help protect him." Vadim shrugged, eyeing her.

"I fail to see how encouraging him to have a crush on me could help protect him." The words came out too sharply. She sounded guilty.

Vadim gave her a narrow-eyed look. "The subject has been kept in near isolation since childhood. Before that, he'd been raised in horrific social conditions. Understandably, he could be expected to form an emotional or sexual attachment to an attractive caregiver. The records show you are likely not even the first…"

That made her feel all kinds of irritable. She'd read the reports, of course, about the nurse who'd been removed from duty when her relationship with Jed had become closer than the Wyrmwood executives decided was appropriate. That had been when he was little more than a kid, though. It wasn't like what was between the two of them. It couldn't be. She kept her expression smooth. "We don't talk about it, of course. I do my job. I leave the room. I wait."

"Ah, yes. The waiting. Well, we're all waiting."

"And why?" she demanded suddenly. "Why not just take him out of there now? There has to be a way!"

"If there was, don't you think we'd have gotten him out of there long ago?" Vadim fixed her with a stern look. "Even with inside help, Wyrmwood is impossible to break into or out of."

"Nothing is impossible. I thought that was the Crew's motto or something like that."

Vadim laughed without much humor, although his dark eyes did twinkle. "If we had a motto, I suspect it would be more like 'nothing is improbable.' As it is, you won't have to wait much longer. All the signs are pointing to his imminent transfer. Be prepared to hear more as early as next week."

"If you can tell they're getting ready to transfer him," she began, but stopped at the look on the older man's face. She'd never made Vadim angry with her, and she wasn't about to find out now what might happen to her if she did. As charming and paternal as

Vadim could be, there was a darkness in him that Samantha recognized…and didn't want to mess with.

"This connection you believe he's begun. Is it something you reciprocate?"

"Of course not," she said steadily, getting his gaze head-on as best she could through the computer screen. "He doesn't deserve to be put down like a dog that's lived past its use, that's all."

Vadim said nothing for a moment or so, studying her. Not for the first time, Samantha wondered what Vadim's talents were. She wouldn't have doubted that one of them was reading minds.

"Be ready," he said finally.

Chapter 11

"How are we feeling today?" Dr. Ransom pushed his glasses up higher on his nose with one hand, tapping his pen against the desk with the other. "Nurse says you didn't eat your breakfast."

"Her name's Patty," Jed said mildly. Dr. Ransom never knew their names. Jed wouldn't have been surprised if the doctor barely remembered Jed's name. He certainly hardly ever used it.

"Was there something wrong with breakfast?"

"I didn't feel like eating today. That's all." Jed used a small push, a tiny one, undetectable, to still the doctor's tapping pen by making it microcosmically harder to move. Just enough to make the other man feel as though he didn't want to make the effort, but nothing close to him feeling that he was being manipulated.

It had taken Jed a long, long time to refine that skill.

Many hours of having to listen to the doctor's relentless fidgeting.

"Not hungry? Not feeling well?"

"I don't like pancakes," Jed said.

Dr. Ransom looked confused. "No? Who doesn't like pancakes?"

"Me. Never liked them." Jed leaned back in the chair, one leg crossed over the other, with a grin. Blank and empty, stretching so wide it felt as though his teeth were the size of dominoes.

"Well. I suppose I can make sure the kitchen never sends you pancakes again."

That wasn't going to happen. If anything, now that he'd made his preference known, he'd be served pancakes three or four times a week, and that was because they liked to mess with him that way. The truth was, Jed preferred pancakes to eggs, but although he knew that lies were the devil speaking with his tongue, he didn't care. He'd stopped caring about that a long, long time ago, about the same time he'd decided to stop playing by their rules. He was simply careful about how he went about it, that was all.

When Jed didn't answer, Dr. Ransom looked concerned. "Nurse said you didn't get out of bed at the usual time, as well."

"Her name is Patty," Jed repeated.

Dr. Ransom put the pen down completely and laced his fingers together. "Patty."

"Samantha is the day nurse. Bryant and Carl are the orderlies. Stephen is the janitor."

"You've never interacted with the custodial staff," Dr. Ransom said.

And the janitor's name was not really Stephen,

but the doctor wouldn't know that. Jed shrugged. He thought about using his talent to take up the pen and bury it point-deep into the wood of the desk, but didn't want to give them the satisfaction or deal with the consequences.

"Is there a reason why you overslept today, Jed?"

The fact he'd been unable to sleep last night, tossing and turning after the interlude with Samantha. He wasn't about to admit that to Dr. Ransom, though. As far as the doctor was concerned, Jed barely knew the nurse, and that was how he wanted it to stay.

When he was fourteen or so, there'd been another nurse. Miss Jean. That was how she'd referred to herself, and how Jed still thought of her. Miss Jean had worn the same uniform as all the other nurses, the same as it had been in all the years Jed had been in Wyrmwood. She'd had pale, short hair and wide green eyes and a smile that reminded him of his birth mother's, when Mother had been happy. Miss Jean had never looked at him the way the others had sometimes. Afraid. No matter what he did or how he behaved, Miss Jean always stayed calm, friendly, kind. And because she never gave him reason to misbehave, slowly, slowly, Jed had stopped always trying to cause trouble.

When it had become apparent to the unseen—whoever was in charge, the ones he'd learned watched and judged, but never met with him in person—that Miss Jean's influence was changing Jed from who they wanted him to be into something else, something less violent, well. Miss Jean went off shift one day and never came back.

That was when Jed had started training himself to unlearn all the things they'd taught him.

Eleven years later, and the daily testing had stopped. His sessions with Dr. Ransom had gone from five days a week to twice, each session only lasting thirty or so minutes, since there never seemed to be much to say anymore. It couldn't be much longer, now, Jed thought. Until they either killed him, or let him go.

"Jed?"

"I was tired, I guess. Had a bad headache." That part was true enough, though it wasn't like his head didn't always throb with the effort of holding himself back from giving them what they'd been after since he was five.

"Your medicine should prevent that. Your vitals haven't changed. Your blood pressure is fine."

Jed had learned to control that, too.

"Maybe it's seasonal allergies," Jed said, deadpan.

Dr. Ransom didn't smile. He did, however, lift up the pen again to scratch a few notes on the pad in front of him. "I'm going to prescribe you something new. For anxiety."

"No! I mean," Jed said in a calmer voice, "I'm not anxious about anything."

He was already on some complicated cocktail of pills designed to keep him under control, but it had been years since they'd felt the need to use anything to keep him calm. He wasn't going to go back to being chemically brain-dead again. He couldn't. He would die first.

"Just a little something," Dr. Ransom said in that soothing tone he always employed. He looked at Jed over the rims of his frameless glasses. "It seems to me that you haven't been yourself lately."

Himself? Ransom had no idea who Jed was. No-body did, including Jed.

"Is it because of the tests?" Jed asked bluntly.

The doctor hesitated, cutting his gaze from Jed's. "Of course not. You know we've always made it clear that our concern is for your well-being. Never any test results."

It was what they said, but never what they'd meant. Jed frowned. "New meds won't make it any easier for me to do what they ask."

For the first time since Jed had entered the room, Dr. Ransom smiled. The effect of it was chilling—a stretching of the older man's lips that in no way resulted in any humor reaching his eyes. Ransom tap-tapped his pen rapidly against the desktop.

"We only want what's best for you, Jed. We're your family."

"The only one I have," Jed replied, sincerely if not gratefully.

Ransom's smile stretched wider, showing his yellowed teeth. "You've been at Wyrmwood a long time. We've worked together for a long time, too. I'd like you to know how...fond...of you I've grown over the years."

Jed shifted in his chair, wondering if the doctor expected a matching response. He couldn't make himself lie, so he stayed quiet. After a moment, the doctor's smile faded. He tapped his pen once or twice more, then closed the folder.

"You can go back to your room now. Our session is finished. Unless you have something you need to talk about?"

Jed shook his head and stood. "Not really. Will there be a test?"

"Oh, no." Dr. Ransom laughed. "No more tests will be necessary."

Relief and terror in equal parts raced through Jed, who did not react in any visible way. He nodded when Ransom repeated that he'd be sending Jed some new meds, but didn't protest again. As he left the room, a guard on either side of him, he considered striking out. Surprising them.

They'd kill him without a second thought—he knew that—and wouldn't suicide by armed guard be a better way to go than waiting, waiting for them to finally decide to end his life by some other method? Wouldn't it be better to go on his own terms? But of course, he only walked meekly between them without a word and stepped through the door into his cell, where he waited for whatever was going to happen next.

Chapter 12

There was always a way to get whatever you wanted, if you knew how to ask. Unlike her brother, who could simply make you do whatever he desired, Persephone had learned the best ways to ask. A quiet word in the ear of the skater kid on the corner who hooked her up with some weed before passing along the word to someone else, who got the news to the contact Persephone needed. Eventually, a woman pushing a stroller took a seat beside her. The woman bent to offer the toddler in the stroller a lick of her ice cream.

"Word is, they're getting a little desperate. Losing funding. Need something to get their grants back." Suburban mom cooed at her child for a second, then pulled a package of baby wipes out of her purse and started to wipe the kid's face.

"Does that mean they're actively looking for us again?"

"If they get one of you, they could make a case for keeping the program open. We've had no word that they're doing anything major, but I'd be careful, yes. They have freelancers working on it."

Persephone sat back on the bench. "Bounty hunters?"

She'd dealt with bounty hunters before. The guy from the other day had sure felt like one. Not a very skilled one, she thought with some relief and a little alarm at how close he'd been to her, even if he hadn't known it.

"They don't have the means to put together any kind of teams like the one…" The mother trailed off, looking around, but they seemed to be the only ones there.

Persephone nodded. "I got it. You don't have to say."

"The reality is, the organization has been privately funded for a long time, but they're on the way out. They're swirling the drain. Without a big benefactor or some kind of breakthrough, they're going to have to close completely. Look, I'm on maternity leave right now, and the only reason I agreed to meet you is that this is really low priority. You know they don't have eyes and ears all over the place, they're not monitoring the entire world or anything. Vadim said to tell you that they've assessed the danger to you as minimal, but that doesn't mean you shouldn't be careful."

"I know."

The woman studied Persephone. "He said to remind you that you have a place with us whenever you want it."

"I'm doing all right. Thanks." Persephone stood.

"Even so, he told me to remind you." The woman

stood, too, and pressed a small square of paper into Persephone's hand. "Call him on this number when you're ready."

Chapter 13

Waking from a nightmare, she realizes all too quickly that this has not been a dream. The ringing in her ears is still so loud all she can do is clap her hands to the side of her head and rock back and forth until it eases. She's alone. Whoever did this to her has left her for dead, she thinks, and risks running a hand over her body, checking for wounds.

The blood covering her is not hers. The bits of flesh and bone and brain, also not hers. Her fingers clench, remembering the feel of the weapon in her hands, but she can't remember shooting anyone. Unsteadily, she holds her hands out in front of her, inspecting the nails, grimy with filth.

She has killed with these hands.

The question, with the answer she can't remember, is has she killed now? Or perhaps not if, because it feels so obvious that she has, but who? She can't even remember who she was fighting. Staring at the tufts of fur beneath several of her fingers, stroking along the slices in her clothes and the torn flesh beneath, Samantha thinks maybe she needs to ask not who.

What.

Blinking to clear her vision, she makes sure she can stand upright before she tries to go anywhere. She's in a safe house, not one she remembers, but she recognizes it without too much effort. Bare floors, bare walls, utilitarian furniture. Nothing to show anyone on the outside that there's anything here but an almost empty house waiting for someone to occupy it. Nothing to stand out to anyone who came to the door.

She hopes nobody does that now. The beige walls are spattered with thick dark fluid that smells of dank earth. The furniture, a brown plaid couch and matching armchair, are overturned, the stuffing torn out. It would be so very clear this house was the scene of something awful.

She doesn't call out. The ringing has faded enough that she can, if she strains hard enough, hear more than the buzz. Her feet are steady, planted shoulder-width apart. Her fingers ache; she forces them to relax and open. She doesn't search for her weapon. She already knows it's gone.

Whatever happened here was recent enough that the blood is sticky, but not dry. Her wounds still seep. She could not have been unconscious for more than twenty or thirty minutes. Listening hard, Samantha waits for some clue to tell her what went on, but she hears nothing but the harsh rasp of her own breathing.

In the next room, she finds him. Eyes wide. Mouth

open. He stares at the ceiling, the ribbons of maroon on his throat evidence of what killed him. A familiar face.

Her father.

She kneels next to him without bothering to check for a pulse. You can maybe survive a wound that leaves your trachea hanging out of your throat, your bones poking through the skin, but only with immediate medical attention. It's very clear that her father went down alone. He won't get up again.

She tries to cry and can't. Later, she thinks she ought to have tried harder. He raised her, after all, in the absence of a mother. He did the best he could. But she thinks he wouldn't have wanted her to weep, not because it was a sign of weakness, but because he'd passed from this life and into the next. The one he'd always taught her was the better one.

The rest of the house is empty. There are signs, left behind by other safe house users. A code—something like the symbols used by transient hobos in the thirties to distinguish friendly homes from those where a man looking for a meal and a hot shave would instead get a serious thrashing. This house, she reads, is no longer safe.

"No shit." The words leak out of her on a tongue sore from being bitten.

In the kitchen, she finds no signs of struggle. In the fridge, a gallon of milk hasn't turned, and she gulps it greedily although she doesn't like milk. Her stomach bucks a protest, but she keeps it down. She spits a few times into the sink. Pink. Again. Clear this time. She puts the jug on the counter and both hands on the rim of the sink, gripping hard as the floor tips and tilts. When she's once more gathered her balance, she uses the sink to wash her face and rinse her mouth. She watches the water swirl away the blood and bits of fur.

She stands there so long, she realizes the light outside has gone from night to day.

She's lost time again, but this time remembers coming into the kitchen. Drinking the milk. Going to the sink. She remembers her father is dead, and that someone before her tried to warn them that this house was not safe, but she still can't recall what brought them here.

She remembers she hadn't spoken to him in months, though. Before this. How they'd had a final falling-out—he wanted her to keep moving with him, and she wanted to find a place, settle down, keep a job. Have a life. They'd parted on bad terms.

With a gasp, Samantha shakes herself awake again. The faucet is still running, the water ice-cold. She turns it off. Closes her eyes.

Did she kill her father?

No, no, that can't be. She runs a fingertip over her teeth, careless of the gore still grimed into her skin. She wouldn't have done that. And it doesn't explain the fur.

She will never fully remember what brought her to this house, or what happened inside it. She will find the text on her phone from her father asking her to meet him at this address. Nothing more than that. But she does learn what happened to him, and that is because several days after burning that house to the ground in the hopes she can prevent anyone from finding out it had been a haven for the people her father had believed in, a man named Vadim approaches her in a coffee shop two towns away. He sits at the table outside, where Samantha is turning a lukewarm paper cup of .

shitty coffee around and around in her hands without being able to drink any of it. He says nothing, not even when she recoils as though she might hit him.

"I know what happened to your father," he says in the calm and steady voice Samantha will come to learn so well. "If you want to know, come with me."

So she does.

Jed was dreaming.

He knew it, of course, because in the waking world he would not be dancing slowly with Samantha. Her head would not be on his shoulder. His hand would not be on her hip. He surely would not be moving with her to the strains of some classical waltz, both of them keeping perfect time as he led her around the floor.

He would not be kissing her.

But this was a dream, and he had them so rarely that he was not willing to give this one up. Aware of being watched, knowing they would be monitoring him, it didn't matter because the press of her mouth on his was too good. The slide of her tongue along his, too sweet.

He groaned when she aligned her body with his. Softness. Breasts and hips and the curve of her ass under his hands. His cock ached. She rubbed herself against him. She slid a hand between them. Stroking.

"Kiss me," she said.

He did. Then again. She shivered and tipped her head back to give him access to her throat. Her collarbones. She was naked, all smooth skin and warmth. She pulled him down onto a bed—where had a bed come from? He didn't know. Did not care. All the mattered was moving his lips and tongue over every part of her body.

He found the salty heat between her thighs. He parted her. Found the small spot that made her writhe and sink her fingers into the meat of his biceps. He licked her, soft and slow and steady. When he felt her body tense, he moved up and over her to sink inside her.

It's a dream, he thought. *None of this is real.*

He couldn't stop it, though. Pushing his cock inside her heat was better than anything he'd ever imagined possible. He pushed deeper, deeper, pleasure consuming him.

In the way of dreams, some of the details were blurry. Her face, though. Her smile. Her body, welcoming him. All of that was clear as anything.

He moved faster, and she moved with him. Everything around them faded away until it was only the two of them. Naked, skin on skin. Mouth on mouth. Heat and wetness and friction, building up and up until he couldn't hold back anymore.

He woke a second or so before his climax. Fingers clutching the sheets, body tense and straining, he gave up to the rush of pleasure. His cock was so hard it had slipped free of the waistband of his scrubs, and hot fluid spurted onto his belly in a series of forceful jets that left him spent and breathless.

Let them watch, he thought, blinking at the ceiling. Let them get their jollies, if they did. Let them monitor him, make their reports.

He was still alive, and his body was still his, no matter what they did to him. They couldn't take that away. And they could never get inside his head.

Chapter 14

"We've arranged for you to switch shifts with the other nurse," Vadim said via video call. "It seems she and her husband were the lucky winners of a weekend in the Poconos, and they haven't had a real vacation in years. She was quite beside herself with excitement."

Samantha had come in from a run, still sweating, drinking from a tall bottle of fruit water. She tipped her chair back to eye the computer screen. "It's happening? You have confirmation?"

"Bentley cracked the encryption on the transfer orders. It's going down tomorrow."

"And if it doesn't? If it's a decoy?" Samantha didn't like the sound of this. Most of the work the Crew handled dealt with the research and occasional hunting of creatures. Sometimes hauntings. Not double agenting for secret private organizations determined to raise an army of telekinetic soldiers. She was confident in her skills, but it all still depended on accurate information.

"Then we'll arrange for you to switch shifts again."

She laughed at that with a shake of her head and swallowed another gulp of water before capping the bottle and setting it on the desk. She leaned forward, wrists on her knees, to look closer at the laptop screen. She swallowed again, this time against a slightly bitter aftertaste that didn't come from the drink. "Do you know how they plan to do it?"

"As the nurse on duty, you will be asked to give him an additional amount of sedatives in order to keep him calm when they come for him." Vadim looked serious.

"And I'll palm it?"

"No. You'll have to give it to him, of course. He needs to be compliant when they take him out. No chance of him using any of his abilities, should they not have gone latent the way they believe. He'll need to be controllable until you can get him to us, where we can keep him safe."

This didn't sound right to her. "But if he knows I'm there to help him…"

"He killed three men with nothing more than a twitch of his fingers, Samantha."

"Years ago," she countered. "And I'm willing to bet they deserved it."

"We can't risk him getting out of control. You could be hurt or even killed."

"He wouldn't do anything to hurt me," she said, thinking of all these last months, of the scent of lavender, the tickle of fingertips at the back of her neck. Of the guard who'd been harassing her, the one who'd been put down so easily by something unseen.

"You can't be certain of that, and we won't risk it."

Samantha frowned. "I don't like the idea of drugging him, Vadim. It will make it too hard to work with him."

"All you need to do is take care of the guards and get the van to the rendezvous point. We'll be there to help."

She still didn't like it, but there was no point in pushing it. "Fine. So I give him the drugs. Then what?"

"They take him. You follow. Dispatch the guards. Take the van."

"I'm ready," she said quietly. It was what they'd spoken about early on, almost two years ago, when Vadim had first asked her if she'd be able to take on this responsibility. What she would be ready to do in order to save this man's life.

Vadim paused. "Samantha, I don't think I need to impress upon you how much we appreciate your contributions to the Crew. How valuable you are to us."

"It's always nice to be loved," she said with a small smile. "But what are you getting at?"

"We've been aware of the Wyrmwood facilities for a long, long time. This is the first time we've successfully infiltrated. This would be our first successful extrication of one of the original Collins Creek subjects. We're counting on your many skills to get Jed Collins out of there as unharmed as possible…"

"That would be the ultimate goal, yes. To get him out without being harmed, without anyone being harmed. Without bringing any attention to the Crew." She studied him through the computer screen. "But that's not what you're getting at."

"You're important to us, that's what I'm getting at."

"More important than Jed?" Samantha asked quietly.

Vadim nodded, looking serious. "Absolutely. If it comes down to it, Samantha, and you feel you've been at all compromised, no matter where you are in the rescue, you get out. Even if it means leaving him behind."

"Leaving him to die?"

"Yes," Vadim said.

"I'm not going to do that." She shook her head. "No way."

"Samantha, Jed's been kept in a high-security facility for almost the entirety of his life. The studies and tests they did on him before his skills began to deteriorate were some of the most highly controversial results ever to come out of a program like the Collins Creek experiment. The Crew's been aware of him for a long time, but we're not in the business of making soldiers. Nor in rehabilitating them…"

"He's not a soldier." She shook her head again, forcing herself not to raise her voice. "I mean, I've read the reports, too, and yes, there were all those tests, all the things they proved he could do…but he doesn't do them. He can't anymore. He hasn't been able to, not in years. That's why they're going to kill him—he's done being useful."

"Samantha, I think you need to ask yourself something." For a moment, she was sure Vadim was going to question her about the inappropriate sexual attraction she'd been fighting, but the older man simply said, "What's more important to you? Saving his life? Or saving your own?"

Saving Jed's life, or saving her own.

It seemed like a simple choice, didn't it? It wouldn't even be the first time she'd had to face a choice like that, and look, Samantha had her damage. Everyone did. Hers was that she'd been raised by a man who'd taught her how to kill someone with her bare hands before she'd ever learned to drive a car. She'd grown up in bunkers and safe houses, surrounded by weapons and preparing every day for the end of the world. If it came right down to it, she'd always known that if there was a choice between saving her own life and that of another, she was going to look out for number one.

That did not mean she was the sort to cut and run, though. She never would've agreed to take on this job if she hadn't believed with everything inside her that not only could she protect and rescue Jed Collins when the time was right, but also that he was worth making the effort for.

As a child, Jed had not understood what a full belly felt like. In the compound, there were no regular mealtimes. Deprivation was constant. Fasting had been considered a way of praying and starvation a blessing.

He'd rarely been hungry since coming to Wyrmwood, but his stomach grumbled now. He'd been avoiding finishing his meals. The bitter undertaste of the drugs had kept him from it. They were trying to sedate him beyond the pills he was regularly given.

Scarier than that was the fact nobody had said a word about the unfinished trays he sent away after every meal. Two days since his last session with Ransom, and Jed had barely nibbled some dry toast and eaten a handful of nuts. He'd expected to be called down to the doctor's office after the first day of not eating.

It was time, he thought. Or would be, soon. The

thought didn't upset him as much as he thought it would.

Still and silent, he closed his eyes. Let his breathing slow and deepen. He was far from sleep, but even if they were still somehow monitoring his brain waves, it wouldn't matter. He didn't have consistent brain waves, nothing that could be called normal, even for himself. It had been one of Ransom's greatest frustrations, that inability to compare and contrast the test results to see if they could re-create what happened when Jed used his abilities.

He sent out some tickling tendrils of thought, creeping like mice along the edges of the room. To the door. Around the frame. Through the cracks. Whispering into the hallway. Inching like a worm in the patterns on the tile, toward the nurse's station.

He stopped, startled enough to open his eyes before forcing himself to close them again, shifting as though he were dreaming. That was silly. He hadn't dreamed in years, though none of the unseen observers would know that.

Samantha was in the chair behind the desk. Playing a game of solitaire with real, physical cards. The edges soft and worn. Her fingers moved quickly, flipping the cards. Matching. Laying them down.

When he sent himself out this way, it had always seemed to Jed as though he were floating. Invisible, even to himself. He could feel himself reach for something, but his body didn't actually move and he didn't see his own hand. Nor his body. If he turned to face a reflective surface, all he saw was whatever was behind him. He could feel, though. The coolness of the tile floor on his bare feet. The hush of the air currents pushing warmth from the vents in the ceiling. He could smell the scent of her soap and the mint gum she chewed.

He'd been "flying" for years. It was the only way he could tolerate being kept in that small room, the only breaks being the walks to the testing rooms or his sessions with Dr. Ransom. When he was younger, he'd gone outside, but it was harder to control himself without walls and a ceiling to keep him anchored in place. When he was a little older, he'd considered letting himself get lost. Never coming back. His body would eventually die, and he would...what?

He'd never figured that part out.

Now, he watched her. This was not her shift, but a quick nudge of the computer pulled up the schedule to see she'd switched with Patty, who was taking a few days off. He did it so fast, opening and then closing the file to return the monitor to its sleep screen, there should've been no way for her to notice.

Samantha, however, paused in the placing of the card in her hand. She looked up, not at the computer, but out toward where Jed would've been standing, if he were physically there. She tilted her head, a small smile quirking the side of her mouth. Without moving her head, she allowed her gaze to cut toward the computer screen. Then flicked back in front of the desk. She gave a low murmur and shook her head, then bent back to her cards.

I'm here, he wanted to say. *I'm right here, and I need you to see me. Really see me.*

He could've pushed those words into her mind, but again restrained himself from crossing that line. He continued to watch her for a while, thinking of the dream. It was the closest he would ever get to her, he thought, unable to make himself move on. He moved in a slow circle around her, taking in the card game. The opened wrapper of her granola bar. His phantom stomach clenched with hunger. She looked up, though there was no way she could've heard the boing-going of his belly from this far away.

Again, she tilted her head. Listening. She put the cards down, sweeping them into a pile and tapping them to get them in place before setting them aside. She looked at the computer, still asleep.

"Jed?" she whispered.

Swift as a blink, he was back in his room. Sitting up on the bed, blinking, gasping aloud. Both hands clutching his guts, his hunger pressed aside for the moment by a spasm of nausea. He swung his feet over the side, letting his shoulders hunch. Not caring if the unblinking and all-seeing eye of the camera watched him.

A minute or so later, the door opened. He lifted his head without moving from the bed. Samantha stepped through with a tray she set on the table without a word.

"You should eat," she said.

"Not hungry."

"You're hungry," she said. "I…"

Felt it.

Jed did not allow himself to react. He couldn't read minds. He could catch feelings, and because people didn't think in sentences and paragraphs, but in images and scraps of emotion, he could sometimes get a handle on what they were thinking. Or maybe he only imagined he could.

"I don't want to eat," Jed said.

Samantha moved closer. Briskly, she pulled out her

stethoscope. "How about I check you out, make sure everything's okay?"

"I'm fine," he said. Too harsh. Too cold. He didn't want her to touch him.

She stopped a few feet from him. "Jed. If you're not feeling well, I can call the doctor."

"I feel fine. I'm not hungry. Just tired. Go away and let me sleep."

She took another step closer to him. He shrugged away from her touch on his shoulder, though he wanted nothing more than to lean into it. To gather her close, to press his forehead against the welcoming softness of her belly. To have her stroke her fingers through his hair...

"You need to let me check you out," she said in a firm, no-nonsense voice that finally made him look at her.

"Or what? You'll call the guards? Have them re-strain me?"

Her pale blue eyes flashed for a moment, but the rest of her expression remained neutral. "I don't want to do that. I just want to make sure you're all right. That's all. Your chart says you haven't eaten in the past couple days, and I have some new meds I'm required to give you. On an empty stomach, they could make you sick."

"I'm not an idiot," Jed said. "I've been on some kind of medication or another for the past twenty-some years. And I don't need anything new, so you can take them and shove them up Dr. Ransom's ass."

He said it to shock her, to get a reaction from her. Not pity. That would've pissed him off. But something. An acknowledgment, maybe, that this situation was as fucked up as a life could be. It might be all he'd ever really known, but he still knew that.

"I know you're not an idiot." Now she glanced upward at the camera. Her expression firmed. She looked at him. Lowered her voice. "You should eat to keep up your strength."

"They put stuff in the food," he said, not bothering to keep himself quiet. He also threw a glance toward the camera and its bland, unyielding gaze. "I told Ransom I didn't need anything for anxiety. He's having them put it in the food. I can taste it. I don't need anything else on top of it."

An expression he couldn't name skittered across her face. Her lips pressed together. "Will you let me examine you for the records? Please. I'll just check your vitals. Same as usual."

He stared at her for a long, silent moment before finally nodding sharply. "Fine. But I'm not going to eat anything. I told him, I don't need anything to keep me calm."

"Of course not." She moved closer. Her fingertips pressed beneath his jaw, probing. She pressed the back of her hand to his forehead in a gesture that surprised him, but swiftly took it away so she could use the stethoscope. Listened to his heart. Took his pulse. The grip of her fingers on his wrist sent his heart beating too fast, the way it always did, but he forced himself not to react.

"They'll come for you." She said it so low into his ear that he couldn't be sure he'd heard her. "Soon. When they do, I'm going to get you away from here. But you need to pretend to take these meds for me. Please."

Then she stepped back, out of reach. "I can't make you eat, but we both know I can call the orderly in here and force you to take the medicine. I don't want to do that. I don't think you want me to have to do that, do you?"

Who was going to come for him? He had heard her say it, he knew it. He hadn't imagined it. And he knew she was right, because he'd been waiting for that to happen. The question was, how did Samantha know it?

"No," he said after a moment at her hard stare. "I guess I don't."

She held up a needle and syringe. Usually they gave him pills. For a second or so when she stepped closer, he was sure she still meant to drug him, and he tensed. Pushing. She felt it, he could tell. Her eyes went a little wide.

"It won't hurt," she said in a bright, false voice, her gaze boring into his. "I promise you."

He knew better than to trust her. She worked for them, didn't she? Yet something made him hold out his arm, bare below the short sleeve of his faded gray scrub shirt. He braced himself for the pinch and sting of the needle, but Samantha kept up a low patter of meaningless small talk as she placed the needle against his skin, but not into it. She dispensed the contents into a small cotton ball she then pretended to use to cover up the puncture.

"There," she said. "You're going to be just fine."

Samantha wanted to linger, but that would be the best way to ruin this whole operation. Instead, she looked closely into Jed's eyes, thinking of the reports that had tested his telepathic talents. When he was younger, he'd been able to choose the circle, square, wavy lines, whatever was on the small cards used in the test kit. He'd been tested for other thought reading, too, without any confirmation that he could do that. Somewhere along the way he'd stopped being accurate. The reports had determined he was incapable of anything beyond the most average of guesswork. His abilities to manipulate physical objects in his environment, that had been substantiated, but they'd never been able to prove he could read minds. One of the doctors had postulated that, even worse, Jed's ability to predict and empathize with the emotions of others was far lower than average.

They'd started assuming he was a sociopath.

Samantha had grown up among sociopaths and didn't believe Jed fit that diagnosis. On the subject of telepathy, she wasn't certain, but right now, she was going to try.

She concentrated, not sure what exactly she was even trying to convey, other than a sense of…comfort? Protection? Reassurance, she thought, though watching Jed scowl, she didn't feel like he was very reassured.

As his caregiver for the past eighteen months, she'd done little more than check his vitals and bring him food once in a while. Their conversations had been necessarily limited. Their physical connection even less so. So why, then, did she feel closer to this man than she'd felt to anyone else in her entire life?

"You're going to feel sleepy," she told him quietly as she put the sharp into the small red box in her pocket. Her eyes searched his for any sign he was on board with this, but there was no way to know what would happen.

"I'll be fine," Jed said.

Something sifted through the air between them like a breeze, moving the tendrils of hair that had escaped around her face to tickle her cheeks. She closed her eyes at the embrace—and it *was* an embrace. A caress. As soft and specific as if he'd reached a hand to cup her face.

She hadn't meant to go off plan, but the idea of sedating him had not settled well with her, no matter what Vadim had said. Jed had not lost his talents. She felt it. She wasn't sure how much control he still had over them, but the last thing in the world she wanted was for him to be left unable to defend himself.

They'd tried to make him into a soldier, she thought. When the time came for it, she might need him to be able to fight.

She risked squeezing his shoulder, a definite no-no on the list of rules regarding the Wyrmwood patients, but what were they going to do? Fire her? Beneath her fingers, Jed's muscles bunched and tensed, although he remained stone-faced. Hands in his lap. Something about it broke her heart in a way she wasn't expecting.

"Are you sure I can't call down to the kitchen for you?"

Jed shook his head without answering. She backed up a few steps. Samantha pressed her fingertip to the door lock and stepped through it. At the sight of the two armed guards, neither of whom she recognized, she quickly shook her head and stepped back into the room, locking the door behind her. Hands flat on it. Facing Jed.

Her heart raced, but she didn't let it show. Instantly she'd begun the mental countdown. The list in her head of every escape route she'd planned since starting here.

That had been her father's training—always be ready with a way out.

"I didn't write down your vitals," she said brightly, with a clap of her hands. She moved toward him with a pasted-on smile. "I'm going to have to check you again."

Jed narrowed his eyes. "You never..."

"They're coming," she said in a low voice. Not caring so much now if whoever was watching overheard her.

They were beyond that now.

She didn't hear any muffled voices outside the door. Nothing like a warning. She wouldn't have—the doors here were thick, lined with metal. Soundproof.

Jed stood. "You should go. I don't want you to see this."

Surprised, Samantha shot him a look. She wanted to reassure him again, to tell him that she had this covered, that they weren't going to kill him right there. She drew in a long breath, then let it out. They had guns. This was it. It was happening.

When the door opened, she stepped in front of Jed, addressing the guards in a loud, hard voice. "What's going on? I didn't get any updates about this."

"Step aside, ma'am. We're here to take the patient for some routine testing."

"You'll have to show me your paperwork." She put her hands on her hips, playing up the irate nurse. "You should know this patient is not to be removed from this room without the appropriate precautions. This is highly irregular."

The shorter guard stepped forward. They were both armed, but their weapons were not in hand. She was going to assume they both had hidden weapons in addition to the ones she'd already noticed, but for now she had to worry about the guns she could see.

"Just send him forward," the shorter guard said. "We have directions to take him."

Let them take him, Vadim had said. *Then follow.*

The plan didn't feel right.

"I'm not going with you," Jed said matter-of-factly, as though he was commenting on the weather.

The guard on the left smiled. "Sure, kid."

The other one wasn't as nice. "Shut up. You, get out of the way."

He jerked his chin at Samantha. She settled him with a steady, imperious look. Wyrmwood had a lot of rules, but taking shit from a pair of goons was not one of them.

"C'mon, kid," said the nicer guard as he stepped forward. "I don't want to have to get harsh."

Before he could get any closer, he let out a loud, long cough and stumbled. He tried to take another step but looked as though he was struggling against a glass wall. The other guard let out a startled noise, a muttered curse.

"I'm not going with you," Jed repeated. "But keep on coming. Let's see what happens."

That's when everything started going wrong. The guards moved, one toward Jed and the other toward Samantha. She slipped a hairpin from the heavy bun at the base of her neck, pulling the edges open. With the pin between her fingers, she stepped forward. Ducking low before either of the guards could say a word, she swept the taller guard's leg, not expecting to send him down, just push him off balance. It worked. The taller guard took a hopping step away from her. Without stopping, Samantha moved again, jamming the hairpin into the meat of his calf and pulling it free to stab upward into the hand reaching to grab her.

The shorter guard shouted and grabbed her hair. Without the pin to hold the bun in place, he got a handful, but the thick length of it slipped free as she twisted. Then she was up, ramming her head into his chin and sending him back against the wall.

She acted without thinking ahead more than a move or two. Anticipating what would come next, but ready to adjust if she was wrong. Punch, kick, jab for the eyes.

The taller one caught her by the throat, hauling her upright. Neither of them had pulled their weapons— a fact she noticed even with the wind being strangled out of her. They might be there to take Jed away, but they had not been ordered to kill him. Not here, at least. As the red spots began dancing in the edges of her vision, though, she had time to think that they'd have no trouble killing her.

Not that she was going to let them, of course.

She let her body go limp, not fighting, and the sudden weight pushed the guard off balance. In the next second she was up again. His gun was in her hand.

He was on the ground. Then his partner. She'd shot both of them in the legs. The other guard had a hand reaching for his weapon, which she grabbed. Her ears rang from the sound of the shots, but she took the time to aim once more, this time at the camera. When the red light went out, she turned to Jed, who'd stood without moving the entire time.

"I'm a little insulted," he said. "You'd think they'd have hired way more competent guards."

Chapter 15

The woman staring back at him, a gun in each hand, had barely broken a sweat. Her blond hair had come loose from the tight bun she always wore. Her shoulders and chest heaved with her breathing, but her expression was calm. She was still Samantha, but somehow she had become a stranger.

"More will be coming, and they will be more prepared," she told him. "We should get out of here. Now. We don't have much time."

Jed didn't move. "The first attempt on my life came when I was twelve. One of the orderlies had managed to bring in a shiv. He cut me with it before I was able to break all of his fingers. Then his neck. I did it without touching him. There've been two 'rescue' attempts since then. I say *rescue* sarcastically, because I'm guessing wherever they wanted to take me would've been worse even than Wyrmwood."

"They weren't here to rescue you. They were going to take you someplace and kill you."

"I don't know that," he said bluntly, eyeing her.

"You have no reason to trust me," she agreed, which was exactly the right answer to ensure that he did trust her.

Jed looked around the room, then down at the guards, writhing in pain and screaming out curses nobody else could hear. She'd shot the camera while barely aiming. She was good.

"Who sent you?" Jed asked.

Samantha shook her head, that glorious fall of golden hair cascading over her shoulders and down her back. "Nobody. It doesn't matter now. Just know that I'm here to get you out of here, and we have to do it now."

He didn't have to be able to read minds to sense a lie, but she was right. There wouldn't be much time. He'd wondered if there really was someone watching the video feed at all times, and now he was about to find out.

"Don't you want to kill them first?" He pointed at the guards.

Samantha looked surprised. "I'm not usually one to kill for the sake of it. They're neutralized. Isn't that enough?"

The shorter guard started to cry softly. To plead. The other guard muttered a string of threats that Jed ignored.

"You have a soft heart," he said to Samantha.

She laughed, the sound giddy and abrupt and out of place here and now, but welcome for all of that. "That's not what my last boyfriend said. C'mon, before some-one else shows up."

He could take care of whoever else might show up. After watching her dispatch the two guards, he fig-ured Samantha could, too. That didn't mean he was going with her.

"You can't make me go," Jed pointed out, already moving toward her. "They'll kill you for all of this, but they're not going to do anything to me they hadn't al-ready planned to do."

"Why would you want to stay for that?" Samantha asked sharply. She pressed the door lock and opened the door, looking out. Apparently satisfied with what she saw, she looked back at him.

"Because maybe it's my time," Jed said. "Time for this to all end."

She shook her head and grabbed the front of his shirt. "Bullshit. I didn't risk my life so you could stay back like a lab rat, one they're aiming to kill. Let's go."

He followed, if only because she'd yanked him so hard that he would've stumbled if he hadn't moved. Samantha moved to the door, pressing her fingers into the lock. The door didn't open.

She muttered a curse and shot a glance over her shoulder at the cameras. "They know."

Jed moved over the red line, tensing for a few sec-onds automatically, although he knew nothing would happen to him. Behind him, the guards groaned and writhed, letting out soft shrieks when he sent a wave of agony to keep them from getting up. "Move away."

"But the metal—"

"It doesn't matter." He took a faint joy in surprising her, but didn't waste time explaining. It needed only a small push, an easy twist of the lock's interior tumblers, and the door was buzzing open.

There were more guards out there, faces obscured by masks. Armored vests. Giant guns. Samantha shouted, but her hands went up. Jed, grateful she hadn't tried to fight them, held out a hand with his fingers spread. The three guards in the front went to their knees, backs arching and booted feet drumming at the tile floor.

It hurt.

He didn't stop. Once it had begun, he wasn't sure he could stop. Too many years of suppressing himself. Too much anger, coming out now.

He curled his fingers into fists. Pushed outward. Feeling each of the guards, the ones on the floor and the ones behind them, still standing. Feeling Samantha.

Then he felt nothing much at all.

Samantha didn't know what happened. First there were a half dozen guards in the hallway, all of them in riot gear and armed. In minutes they were on the ground, writhing and screaming. There was blood, lacy spatters on the tile. Her head ached, and instead of the smell of lavender, her nostrils burned with a bitter stink she couldn't identify.

Jed had done this without so much as a single mutter or gasp. Now he staggered, a hand going to his temple. A thin runner of crimson trickled from the inside corner of his left eye.

She didn't wait. She took him by the elbow and herded him toward the stairs, certain the elevator would be shut down. The alarms in Wyrmwood seemed to be as hushed as everything else in the hospital, no sound, but eye-piercing blue-white lights that lined the corridor had begun to throb and flash. The door to the stairwell was locked, of course, her fingerprints doing nothing to open the lock. Jed did that with a weary sigh and shake of his head.

"Are you okay?" She slung his arm over her shoulders, supporting his weight.

"What are we going to do?" His voice was slurred, but he wasn't sagging against her. He was still moving. "They're going to be everywhere."

"This isn't how it was meant to go." They rounded the landing and kept going.

Incredibly, he chuckled. "So in other words, you have no idea."

They got to the bottom of the stairs, and the door there proved to be no more trouble than anything else. There weren't any guards waiting for them, although the lights were still flashing. Nathan had risen from behind his security station, his eyes wide. His hand went to the gun at his belt.

"Samantha!" His gaze went to Jed, eyes going even wider. "Oh, shit."

"I don't want to hurt him," Jed said.

Samantha didn't want Nathan to get hurt. When he sat back down, she pushed Jed past him, to the front doors. To the parking lot beyond. Then to her car, which she'd parked as usual to the far end of the lot. She slid behind the wheel; Jed was passenger. Her keys were in her purse, which was back on the desk.

It didn't matter. She looked over at Jed and he took care of that, too. The car's engine churned, turning over. Something about it didn't sound right, but when she put it in gear and stepped on the gas, the vehicle shot forward. She drove, fast as she dared, certain that at any moment a fleet of SUVs were going to show up on her tail.

Beside her, Jed's head drooped. Concerned, Samantha poked him. "Put your seat belt on."

He gave her a strange look. "Huh?"

She gestured. "Your seat belt…"

Too late she realized it was entirely possible he had no idea what a seat belt was or how to use one. An eye on the road, she reached, but there was no way she was going to be able to grab the belt. She had to pull over and put it on him, and risk being caught. Or she could keep going and risk killing him if she got into an accident.

"They can't see us." His voice slurred. He drooped forward even more.

Alarmed, Samantha braked slowly to keep from sending him through the windshield. "Jed. Are you okay?"

"They can't. See. Us. Blocking. Feel." With that, he fell forward, hard enough to smack his head on the dashboard with a thud so loud it hurt her head.

Chapter 16

Jed couldn't remember the last time he'd actually slept so hard that when he woke he didn't know where he was. Maybe never in his life. He woke now, disoriented. Dim light, so much darker than the almost constant pale glow he was used to. Pain ripped through his head and he rolled onto this side, thinking he might get sick. He fought the nausea off and sat up.

"Hey." He felt her before he saw her face in the soft glow of a candle she lit. Samantha smiled at him. "How do you feel?"

"Bad." He let his face fall into his hands. "Where are we?"

She cleared her throat. "It's a safe house."

"How safe?" He gave her a sideways look.

"As safe as…it can be. Are you hungry? I have some soup. It's not very hot. But it will settle your stomach."

She leaned forward into the circle of golden light. "Jed, I'm going to touch your forehead. Okay?"

She'd asked permission first. He moved his hands away from his face to look at her. "Why?"

"I want to be sure you don't have a fever. You've been sleeping for the past day and a half, and you were burning up. May I?"

"Why are you asking me?" he said in a flat voice.

In the candlelight, Samantha's blue eyes looked very dark. "Because I think you deserve the right to decide who puts their hands on you."

"You're not really a nurse, are you." He'd suspected as much for some time—she'd never "felt" the way the other nurses had.

"No."

He didn't seem feverish, but that wasn't why he hadn't yet given her permission to touch him. He was more afraid of what he might do now that they were away from the hospital, with nobody to stop him from kissing her. His head ached and buzzed in the aftermath of all the pushing he'd done. His self-discipline would be nonexistent.

"What are you?"

Samantha looked surprised. "I'm…just a person."

She was more than that, but he could tell she wasn't being facetious. "Are you a soldier? Who do you work for?"

"I work for an organization called the Crew that specializes in investigating and proving or disproving the existence of paranormal or other umm…" She coughed lightly. "Oddities."

"Like children bred and raised in a cult designed to create extrasensory mental abilities?" He turned to face her. His headache was softening. His mouth, though, had gone dry, his throat scratchy. If he'd been asleep as long as she'd said, he'd missed several doses of meds. This was going to hurt.

"Yes, like that. Are you sure you feel all right?"

He frowned. "Of course I don't feel all right. I just got busted out of a top secret research facility to prevent my murder. Unless you still plan to off me."

"No!" She looked startled and shook her head, moving closer. "No, look. I know you have no reason to trust me…"

"I can feel if you're lying to me," Jed interrupted in a low voice, very conscious of her body heat and the faint smell of her shampoo.

She studied him for a moment with a curious tilt of her head. A faint smile. "Can you?"

"Yes."

"Can you feel anything else about me?"

Jed looked into her eyes. "Yes. I can tell that you want to touch me. I told you, I don't have a fever. But if you need to check, go ahead."

"I don't need to check you for a fever if you're feeling all right. But I do want to touch you. Yes. Can you feel that?"

He could feel something inside her, but it was so much a part of everything that made Samantha who she was that he couldn't untangle it from the rest. She moved closer to him. He tensed, unsure of what she meant to do. At the brief brush of her fingertips across his forehead, he sighed and closed his eyes.

"What do you feel about me?" she asked quietly.

He tried to show her, but although it was easy enough to make things happen around him, making a person *feel* something was completely different. There was more to it than emotion. Desire. Longing. Anxiety. There was also sensation.

The touch of fingertips on the inside of his wrist.

The smell of her shampoo.

The sound of her voice.

He tried his best to give her all of this, everything that made up who she was, to him. Convinced he'd failed, Jed opened his eyes. Samantha's eyes glistened with tears.

She kissed him.

Chapter 17

Even as Samantha slanted her mouth against Jed's, she wondered if he was manipulating her into this. She knew all too well what his talents could do. Yet, there'd never been anything in her life that she wanted to do more in that moment than to kiss him, and she hadn't even tried to resist it.

His lips were soft and warm. They parted instantly when she put her mouth on his. He was surprised, she thought as she cupped the back of his neck. He wasn't trying to get his tongue inside her mouth. She'd startled him. It didn't matter. The kiss deepened in the next minute, and she couldn't tell and didn't care who'd initiated it. There was an ebb and flow to this kiss she could not deny.

Neither of them could.

She did not break the kiss, but she did ease her

mouth away. She pressed her cheek to his. Her other hand went to his chest, over his heart. Hers was beating so hard she could feel the throb of it at the base of her throat, and after so many months of checking his vitals, she could tell at once that his was beating much faster than normal, too.

"The other day. When you were giving me the checkup," he said.

She remembered. "Yes."

"I'm sorry. I shouldn't have…it was wrong to do that to you."

He was serious. She sat back, frowning. "What?"

"I shouldn't have touched you like that, without asking. Without you saying it was okay."

"You didn't touch me, Jed."

He furrowed his brow. "I did, and you know it. I don't have to use my hands. You know that, too."

"Did it feel like I didn't want you to?" She sat back, but only a little. She let the hand over his heart slip down his arm to circle his wrist. Then to take his hand, linking their fingers. He wouldn't look at her.

She'd never seen Jed react emotionally to much of anything. She'd long assumed it was the meds they kept him on. The years of isolation and lack of normal social contact. Now, though, he pressed his lips together and swallowed hard, blinking away tears.

"Jed." She turned his face gently to face hers. "Did it ever feel to you like I didn't want you to touch me?"

"I don't know!" he shouted, and pushed away from her to stand and pace.

She'd chosen the small, empty bedroom off the safe house kitchen because of its first-floor access, in case they needed to get out the windows, which had been covered with blackout curtains. It was little more than the size of a walk-in closet, barely big enough for the sagging twin mattress on the floor, so he didn't have much room to move. He spun on his heel when she stood, moving in front of him so he had no choice but to face her.

"You know how I feel. If I had ever once thought or felt like you were manipulating or hurting me in any way, you'd have known it." Samantha wasn't positive if this was true. There'd been hundreds of tests done to research what Jed could do. Nothing about how it affected him emotionally or mentally. "Right?"

Reluctantly, he nodded. "Yes."

"You didn't hurt me. You didn't do anything to me that I didn't…want." It was her turn to swallow hard.

"But why?" he demanded. "Why would you want anything like that from me?"

She shook her head. "I don't know."

"Pity," he said with a sneer that hurt her to see. "Curiosity."

She couldn't deny that at least a little bit of that was true. But not all of it. "Why does anyone ever want something like that from another person? Who knows why two people connect? I've never been able to figure it out. And you know what, I'm not sure I care, to be honest. I haven't been with anyone for a long time. Sex feels good—"

He snort laughed, half choking. "Sex!"

"It feels good," she continued. "Especially with another person, especially with someone you care about. So maybe it wasn't right, what you did. It wasn't right for me to allow it or enjoy it, then. I was your caregiver.

It was crossing a line. But it felt good and I didn't stop it. So, who's the one in the wrong?"

"It made you feel good?"

Heat crept up inside her as she lifted her chin. "Yes. Very good."

"It wasn't sex," Jed said. "Not real sex."

He was a virgin, Samantha thought suddenly. All those years locked up. She wanted to take a step back, but his expression told her he knew what she was thinking. She didn't move. She reached for him instead, snagging his wrist to tug him a step closer to her.

"You didn't do anything to me that I didn't want, even if I didn't know until you did it that I wanted it. And I won't…" She coughed lightly, unsure how to go on without embarrassing them both. *Screw that*, she thought. They were on the run from people who wouldn't hesitate to kill them. She'd gone off plan and had no backup from the organization who'd hired her to protect him. They were in a tiny box of a room with nothing more than a candle and a mattress on the floor. If she couldn't be honest with him about this now, there wasn't going to be any better time. "I won't touch you unless you want me to."

"How could you think I wouldn't want you to?"

Because it was crazy, she thought as Jed moved toward her. Because there wasn't time for this here or now. When he kissed her, there was no more thinking. No more excuses. Jed kissed her as though he'd been waiting a lifetime for the chance to put his mouth on hers, and in a way, maybe he had.

At the stroke of his tongue, Samantha gave a small moan. His hand tightened in her hair while the other found her hip and anchored there. He pulled her against him, and the heat of his erection nudged her through the thin fabric of her nurse's uniform. Somehow they were on the mattress, Samantha straddling Jed's lap as he tugged and tore at the white tights she'd hated since the first day she'd been assigned them. His fingers found her heat beneath; her white cotton panties were about as far from romantic as she could imagine, but he didn't seem to care.

"Oh, my god," Jed whispered into her mouth. "You're so hot, Samantha. So wet."

He'd boldly slid two fingers inside her before she could say a word; all that came out after that was a gasping sigh that spiraled up into a low cry when he began to slide them in and out. Something nudged at her mind, a feeling she remembered from the days in the hospital. Like an inquiry. But this time she knew it was Jed, and she opened herself up to it. Embraced him not only with her body, but her mind.

"Oh…" he said. "Yes. That, there. Now I know."

He might never have touched a woman this way, but it didn't matter. Whatever he was feeling from her showed him exactly what to do. Kissing her harder, he pressed his thumb to her clit, circling as his fingers moved inside her.

Her fingers dug into his shoulder as she pushed herself up a little to slide her hand between them and get at the loose tie of his scrubs. Somehow in seconds after that, he was inside her. She had his face in her hands. Their teeth clashed and she let out a small, surprised laugh that turned into a moan when he sucked her tongue.

Jed's hands slipped under her ass to move her. They rocked together. The sound of their breathing was loud in her ears, harsh in her throat as she gasped with the pleasure filling her.

They should slow down, she thought. Savor this. Make it special…

"It's all right," Jed said. "I don't need candles or rose petals, Samantha, just fuck me."

His words sent shards of icy fire through her. She ground herself against him as her climax rose. Shuddering, she tipped over the edge with her face pressed into the curve of his shoulder. For a moment she couldn't move, she could only let her body take over, clenching on him.

It seemed that was enough. Jed said her name in a low, hoarse rasp and arched. His fingers tightened on her hard enough to hurt, but only for a second before he eased the grip. They moved together for another few strokes before she looked into his eyes, once again cupping his face.

Jed blinked, gaze hazy. He slid his tongue along his lower lip. She'd seen him smile before, but this was the first time she'd ever seen it fully reach his eyes.

"Thank you," Jed said. "Wow. That was amazing. You were right, sex is great."

He didn't have to be able to feel her to know that whatever he'd said wasn't quite right. Her quickly shuttering expression did that for him. Samantha made to get off him, but he held her hips and waited until she'd looked at him.

"Wait."

"We need to clean up and get some sleep. We need to be out of here when it gets dark," she said matter-of-factly. "I need to get you to a rendezvous point where they can take you to someplace really safe."

"Samantha...didn't you...want to?" Again horrified at the thought that somehow he'd manipulated her into having sex with him, Jed let her go.

She got up, rearranging the clothes they hadn't even taken off. Was that the problem? Should he have undressed her all the way? They should've been naked. Had he misread her?

"I wanted to. Yes. I told you, sex feels good. And you obviously wanted it, too. So we're both good. That's all. I'm going to the bathroom."

He followed her, waiting outside until he heard the water running in the sink before nudging open the door. "You're angry."

"No. Look." She turned. "I was assigned to take care of you, to protect and watch over you and to get you out of there when it was time. Not to fuck you. This complicates things, that's all."

Jed had watched hours of daytime television, enough to know that what she said could be true. But... "Does it have to be?"

She stepped aside to let him into the bathroom, where he used the toilet unselfconsciously until he noticed she was looking away with a strange expression. He finished and turned to the sink to wash his hands. It hadn't occurred to him to be modest about it—he'd spent his entire life being observed through cameras.

"I'm sure you've watched me pee before," he said.

She shook her head. "That's not... Jed. We can't..."

"Can't what?" He shook his hands as dry as he could and took her by the upper arms. "Samantha, talk to me."

"Can't you just feel what I'm thinking?" she said, sharp and fierce.

Angry? Disappointed. No…something else he couldn't quite name.

"It doesn't really work that way," Jed said. "You should just tell me."

In answer she left the tiny bathroom and headed back to the small bedroom, where she kicked off her shoes and stripped out of the shreds of her tights. She tossed them in the corner, then put her shoes back on. He watched her from the doorway for a few seconds before coming into the room to stand near the mattress.

"You can have it," he said, pointing. "To sleep."

"Don't be ridiculous. We can share it."

"It's not much better than the floor," he pointed out. "And I don't want you to feel like you have to."

She drew in a long, deep breath. "C'mon. Let's just get some sleep, okay? When it gets dark, we'll get out of here."

Together, they stretched out on the hard mattress. There wasn't much room, but he put his back against the wall to make sure there was space between them, which she seemed to want. Without the candle, the only light came in through cracks around the closed door and the rooms beyond.

He listened to her breathing slow. She was dozing, not fully asleep. Because she was making sure to be ready in case she needed to protect him, he thought.

He didn't want to need protection.

Jed put a hand on Samantha's hip, urging her back against him. She woke, everything about her going tense and alert and aware, but she softened after a second and shifted to let him hold her. He wasn't entirely sure why she'd gone distant from him, but if this was the last chance he ever had to hold her, he was going to take it.

"You're not like anyone else," he said against her shoulder, his voice muffled.

Samantha drew a breath and turned her face a little. "No?"

"No."

"You don't really know anyone else," she said.

Jed closed his eyes, breathing in her scent. "I know you."

"Yes," Samantha said after her heart had thumped four or five times. "You do know me. I'm not entirely sure how, but you do."

"I'm sorry if I upset you."

She didn't say anything for long enough that he'd started to drowse. Her voice was quiet enough not to fully wake him, but he knew it wasn't a dream. "Is it crazy for me to feel like I know you, too?"

Jed nuzzled the back of her neck. "Nobody else ever has."

Her shoulders rose and fell; she gave a hitching half sob that made him open his eyes and frown. He hugged her, marveling in this simple contact that meant so much. Felt so good.

"You're going to have a whole, huge world to learn. New people to meet. This won't be… I will just be the first," she said. "I won't be the only."

He wasn't sure how to answer her. He could feel her confusion and the rest of her tangled emotions, but that didn't mean he understood them—because she didn't. "Do you want to be the…only?"

"That wouldn't be fair." She didn't turn from his embrace, though something in the way she tensed made him feel as though she wanted to.

Jed laughed. "What's fair? I can't think of much of anything in my life that's ever been fair."

Samantha sat, twisting on the mattress to look down at him. "But this should be."

He sat, too. "What are you saying?"

"Never mind. We should rest. Are you feeling okay?"

He wasn't, but it had nothing to do with his efforts during their escape. As she settled back onto the mattress, once more putting a distance between them, Jed tentatively tried to reach toward her with his talents. To figure her out.

But no matter how he tried, he couldn't get inside her.

Chapter 18

The safe house had running water, but it was cold. That turned out to be fine. They didn't have time to linger over anything, and the frigid water slapped some sense into her. Yesterday had been a mistake, there was no question, but it didn't have to be irreversible. In a few hours, they'd reach the pickup spot where Vadim's Crew members would take Jed somewhere safe.

In the kitchen, she found him at the sink. "You shouldn't stand by the window."

He looked at her. "It's fine. I can't feel any of them around here."

"Could you? If they were close enough?"

"Yeah." He shrugged. "I could feel if someone meant harm. Maybe not who it was or where they came from, but yeah."

"We need to get going. It's about a five-hour drive."

"I'm not going," Jed said.

Samantha shook her head. "Yes. You are. Please don't make me—"

"What?" Jed asked calmly. "What can you do to me, Samantha? I know you're trained. You've used weapons. I know you've killed a man."

She tensed, stepping back involuntarily. "It was the job. He—"

"He made you afraid. I know. I can feel that. But do you think you could kill me? I know you felt like you might have to," Jed said. "I know you weren't sure if you could. Do you think you could now, to stop me from getting away?"

She could not, and he had to know it. She shook her head, her eyes meeting his. "Why do you want to get away? I'm trying to help you. The Crew is trying to help."

"I spent almost my entire life locked away while people tried to get inside my head. Do you think, now that I'm out, that I'm going to allow anyone to lock me away again?"

"They won't," she began, but stopped herself. In truth, she had no idea what Vadim planned to do with Jed.

"There came a time when I knew I could get away from Wyrmwood at any time," Jed said. "When there was nothing they could do to keep me. I could've killed them all, Samantha. Or just hurt them. I could have walked out of there at any time without anyone getting hurt at all. I didn't for a long, long time because I had no reason to believe that anything beyond the walls would be any better. Until you came along."

"Let me take you to people who will help you," Samantha said. "You don't have to do this alone."

He shook his head. "I'm not going with you."

"Where will you go?" she demanded. "You don't know how to drive a car, you have no money, no identification, nothing…"

Jed shrugged. "You know what I can do. I'll make my way. Maybe I'll travel. See everything I only ever watched on television."

"I can't let you go," Samantha said.

She didn't mean only that she could not let him run away from the Crew. She meant more than that. He had to know it, she thought as the scent of lavender came up to surround her. She couldn't let him go, because he'd come to mean too much to her.

He had to feel it, didn't he?

"You don't want to hurt me," she said in a low voice. Time had slowed and the world around her had gone a little blurry.

"I'm not going to hurt you, Samantha."

She woke up on the bare and lumpy mattress. Darkness outside. He had not hurt her, no.

He'd left her.

Chapter 19

Persephone hadn't seen her brother in months, but that didn't mean much. Phoenix had a wanderlust and an inherent distrust of anything resembling settling down. The last she'd heard, he was somewhere in Europe, playing with a minor princess from some small country she didn't remember the name of. So when she opened the door to a knock, seeing him on the other side was a surprise.

She ought to have known better, because a day later, he'd managed to get her to write down all the login information for her bank accounts, all of them, even the hidden and secret one she kept for her shady business deals. Then he'd made her forget she'd done it, so when she woke up and found him missing along with a note of apology, he'd already wiped her out.

He'd left her a gift card to the coffee shop, though.

What a prince, she thought as she used it to pick up a coffee and a muffin. What a fucking prince.

"Hi, Persephone."

She turned, already feeling a flush of heat in her throat because she knew that voice. Kane. He smiled at her. She couldn't manage to give him one in return.

He lifted his cup toward her. "This place makes the best coffee, huh?"

"Yes." She couldn't stop herself from thinking about kissing him. She never saw any of the other men she went to bed with, and this was why, she reminded herself. It made her want to kiss him again, and that was too dangerous with anyone, but especially with him.

Somehow they ended up sharing a table and he was making her laugh. Making her forget that Phoenix had screwed her over, or that her life was a long string of bad decisions and shady situations. With Kane, she didn't feel like she had to put on a show...except of course she did, Persephone reminded herself with a shock when she looked at the clock to see that an hour had passed.

They walked out together. On the sidewalk outside, a man wearing jeans and a coat too heavy for the late fall day watched them from the corner. A cigarette in his mouth. Assessing. Keeping her attention seemingly focused on Kane, Persephone created an illusion of a much older woman, heavier and dowdy, for whoever that guy was. When she looked again, he was gone.

It didn't mean he'd been looking for her, she thought. It could've been anyone. Or maybe he wasn't working alone, and even though she'd sent the illusion his way, someone she hadn't even seen might have been able to match her to a picture.

"You okay?" Kane paused at the top of the concrete front steps of their apartment building. "You got quiet."

Persephone shrugged, knowing she seemed distant now and not liking it. But what could she do? Giggle and coo with him? Tell him she'd already seen him naked but he had no idea it was her?

"Fine. Just need to get some things done." She left him and went down into the basement to her own place.

She should pack her shit and go. She had cash hidden away for that very reason, a stash her brother hadn't seen, so hadn't been able to steal from her. It would be enough to get her settled someplace else. Get her away from anyone who might've tracked her here, who was watching.

Or she was being crazy, overreacting, she told herself and forced a breath, then another. She thought again of Kane's touch, his mouth, but now she thought also of the way he'd made her laugh. He was more than good-looking—he was smart and funny, too. And, for whatever reason, he seemed to be into her.

She should go, Persephone thought as she pulled out her laptop and started scrolling through her contacts to see what kind of financial business she could get going for herself, and quick. Run. Leave this behind.

But the lingering flavor of coffee was nothing like the way Kane had tasted, and so even though she knew she was being crazy, she was still going to stay here for a while longer.

Chapter 20

Six months later

It was time to stop looking for him. Jed had vanished as completely as any human being could, and considering the vast extent of the Crew's reach, that said something about how insistent he was on not being found. Samantha had taken jobs that sent her all over the country and none of them had brought her close to finding him.

He was not coming back.

At first, she'd told herself it was because she was worried about him making it out there in the world, but she knew he'd have found a way to be okay. Later, when the search had continued, she had to admit there was more to it than her concern for him. She missed him. She…wanted him.

It hadn't been love, she told herself now, sullen and cranky as she dropped her bag on a chair in the Crew cafeteria. She wanted food first. Then a shower. Then her bed. She'd finished investigating the possibility of a werewolf attack in the middle of Montana, a gig that had meant a lot of long hours in the wilderness. She'd been cold. Hungry. A few times, scared. Whatever creature had been killing hikers, though, she had not confirmed it was a werewolf.

The job had brought up a lot of her past. The final night with her father. The blood, the fur, her lack of memory. She'd return to Montana soon, but Vadim had called her back before the case had been completed, and she didn't know why. Didn't care, so long as the money came in.

Now, all she cared about was getting something in her stomach.

But there he was, standing in front of her. Eyes a little anxious, but a smile on his face. He'd put on some weight and muscle, and a bristly scruff of reddish beard covered his chin. He looked tired.

"Jed!"

He kissed her, and she let him even though she knew she really should pull away. Her arms went around his neck. Their teeth clashed; she laughed. He sighed. His hands buried themselves in her hair. People were staring, but she didn't care. There was this, only this.

"Shhh, shhh," he said against her mouth. "I didn't want to startle you. I was going to wait until you went to your room, but I couldn't. I saw you, and I couldn't wait. Samantha…"

She broke the kiss then, breathing hard. "Where have you been? Never mind. It doesn't matter."

"I'm here now," he said. "I'm sorry it took me so long."

"I'm so damned angry at you," she said.

She kissed him again. Harder. His tongue stroked hers. She could not get enough. She wasn't crying, not really, but the world had blurred with the force of her emotions.

"You should be. I was wrong to ditch you. I just had to…"

She cut him off with another kiss. Looked into his eyes. "I understand. I get it. You had to."

"I'm here, though," he said. "I didn't want to keep moving on around in the world without you. All the things I saw and did, everything I thought I wanted to do all those years in the hospital, none of them seemed to matter very much without you next to me."

Samantha drew in a slow breath, aware that everyone in the cafeteria was carefully pretending not to eavesdrop. Not caring what they heard. "That's the nicest thing anyone has ever said to me."

"I don't know a lot of things. It's going to take me a long time learn them. But one thing I already know is there's nobody else in the world I want to be with. First, last, only, Samantha. That's what I want."

His expression made it clear he thought she was going to argue with him, and she knew that would've been the wise thing to do. She couldn't make herself do it. Whatever they would have to deal with, the two of them could face it together, she thought as she kissed him again, this time to the slow round of applause from the people around them.

"Yes. All right, then," she said into his mouth. "Me, too. All of that, and anything else that comes along. I'm in."

* * * * *

PASSION IN DISGUISE

Megan Hart

Chapter 1

Staying up all night meant sleeping late the next morning, at least for most people. For Persephone Collins, it meant waking up when the light hit the sky even if her eyes were still gritty and her body aching, even if she wanted nothing more than to be lost in dreams for another hour or six. That was the price you paid for a life of crime, she told herself without even trying to stifle the jaw-cracking yawn. She needed coffee.

She needed a lot of things.

Last night's haul had included enough cash to get her through the next few weeks, if she was careful, but Persephone hadn't spent her life being careful. She counted it out carefully, though, separating the bills and tucking away the largest, a rare fifty, inside the hardbound copy of *The Complete Ray Bradbury Collection* that she kept on the top shelf of the basement apartment's built-in bookcase. She'd picked up the book at a yard sale for a quarter, but it now contained easily several thousand dollars' worth of paper money. Any time she found a bill bigger than a twenty, she tucked it inside. It was the only thing she'd be sure to take with her if she ever had to run.

For today, though, she didn't think she'd have to run. Today she was content to start the coffee brewing while she dispensed with the rest of the cash. At the stove, she made herself an egg and put it onto an English muffin before settling at the table with her laptop and a huge mug of steaming black coffee. She had a lot of leads to follow up on, more than a couple scams to continue.

She wasn't expecting a knock just before eight in the morning, but as the superintendent of a building that hadn't exactly been lovingly tended over the past decade, she also wasn't surprised by the rap of knuckles on her door. Mug in hand, she opened the door to find Kane Dennis on the other side.

He grinned and held up two big cups of what smelled like perfect coffee from that place down the street. When she didn't move forward, he held one out to her. "Here."

"I have some," she said with a lift of her mug. "But thanks. Wow. What's it for?"

"For fixing my hot water…again." Kane's grin softened as he sipped, still holding out the insulated cup. He let out a long sigh. "Mmm. Man, I do not know what they do to that coffee there, but it's so, so good. You sure you don't want it?"

Persephone knew that was true without taking a drink. That coffee shop was like magic. Her own mug, which had been filled with perfectly adequate brew, was no longer quite as appealing. She stepped aside to let him in, waving him toward the table even as she was thinking of excuses to get him out of her apartment without seeming too obvious that she was trying to get rid of him. "You didn't have to do this. Fixing your hot water is my job."

"Does that mean I can't show you my appreciation?" Kane set the cup he'd brought her on the table and looked around her apartment, those gray eyes noticing every detail.

Because that was what he did. Paid attention. Put the pieces together to figure out the truth.

Persephone put her mug on the counter to take a sip from the other cup. "God. So good. So fucking good." She glanced up to see him looking at her. "What?"

Kane shook his head with a small smile. "Nothing. Glad you like it. I figured you would."

For a moment, a long, long moment, she considered tossing the coffee into the sink and tossing Kane onto the table to have her wicked way with him. She could start at the bottom and work her way to the top, she thought with a glance at his heavy black work boots, then those long, long denim-clad legs, those muscled thighs… And she stopped herself before she could get herself into trouble. If Kane had seen her looking, he didn't show it, but that small grin of his had widened.

"Well, hey, thanks for the coffee," Persephone said abruptly, guiding him by the elbow back toward the door.

Kane paused in the doorway. His smile faded. He studied her. "Persephone…"

"What?" Irritated and also a little flustered now at

his perusal, she sipped. The coffee burned her tongue, and she winced. Scowling, she lifted her chin. "What?"

"Is there something about me that you don't like?"

She paused, choosing her answer cautiously. "What do you mean?"

"Have I done something to make you think I'm a jerk?" Kane shook his head before fixing her with a steely gaze. "Because it seems like no matter what I do, you look at me like I've somehow done you wrong."

Staring at him now, all she could think about was the way his bristly chin had felt against her throat when he was on top of her. Heat rose up her neck to paint her cheeks. She cut her gaze from his, not wanting him to see her blush—although, of course, he would. Kane saw everything about her.

Everything but the fact she'd been fucking him, randomly on and off, for the past six months.

"I don't think you're a jerk," she said when so much silence had lingered that not saying anything had become awkward. "But…"

"But what?" He eyed her over the rim of his cup.

"We aren't friends."

Kane's mouth twisted. Not quite a smile. "Why not?"

Because she got free rent for being this beat-up old building's superintendent, but she paid her bills through a variety of grifting, scams and outright thievery. Kane was a detective who spent his days and nights putting people like Persephone in jail. Because every other week or so, Persephone used the twisted powers of her brain to make him think she was some other woman so she could pick him up at the local dive bar, take him home and have her wild, wicked way with him. Because she didn't want to have to explain to him where she'd been born and raised and what had been done to her to make her into the freak she was.

Without answering him, she took another sip of the coffee he'd brought her and tried to give him a hard stare. It didn't work very well, because doing that meant she lost herself in the soft gray depths of his eyes, and then she was remembering about the last time he'd been on top of her. How he'd felt inside her. How he'd made her come…and again, she forced herself to get her shit together.

At the sound of Kane's sigh, she waved a hand toward him. "I'm pretty sure your life isn't going to suffer much harm if we aren't besties."

Kane's laugh sound a little stung. "What if I think that having you as a friend would make my life better?"

At this, she took a step back with a lifted brow. "Right, and clearly, whatever you think or feel or want takes precedence over what I think or feel or want. Right? Because you're a guy?"

"Hey, that's not what I—" Kane broke off at the sight of her expression. "Fine. Sorry. I'll go. Thanks for fixing the water heater."

"Thank you for the coffee," Persephone said crisply, leaving no more room for conversation.

She waited until he'd let himself out before she flattened herself against the back of the door and closed her eyes. She listened for the sound of him moving away. For a hesitant, heady moment she imagined him on the other side of the wood, listening for her exactly the same way. Waiting for her to open it, to ask him inside. To take him to bed.

Or to be buddies, Persephone thought with a small

curl of her lip. Friends. Maybe they could kick back with a couple of beers and catch some type of sports on TV.

There weren't many things Persephone felt guilty about in her life. The scams? If anyone was stupid enough to fall for them, they deserved to be bilked out of the contents of their bank accounts. The stealing? Okay, so maybe she wasn't quite Robin Hood, but she never took more from anyone than they could clearly afford to lose. And as for using men for their bodies to get her off so she could occasionally sleep longer than twenty minutes a night? None of them had ever complained.

She did feel bad about the way she'd treated Kane, though. He was never anything but nice to her, and she did treat him like she thought he was a jerk. The coffee in her hand was far from the first kind gesture he'd made. It shouldn't have mattered, but something about it did.

She tossed it in the trash.

She went to her bed and slipped beneath the sheets naked, knowing already that no matter how much she tried, she was not going to be able to get enough rest. For that she needed to be worn out from fucking, orgasm after orgasm, and that would require leaving her apartment and trying to find a pickup, and while it wasn't impossible, it didn't seem likely to be easy at nine in the morning.

Persephone closed her eyes. Her hands moved over her body, finding all the secret places that brought her pleasure. It wasn't working, not easily. Not the way another person's touch would have worked.

Not the way Kane touched her.

* * *

His hands move over her hips, fingers digging a little into the flesh as he pulls her a little closer to the edge of the bed. Her knees skid on the soft hotel sheets. Her fingers, too. She is facedown, ass up, as the saying goes, and her breath comes swift and rasping in her throat as she opens herself to him.

He's a bit too tall to enter her from behind, but when his thick cock slides inside her, it hits at the perfect angle to make her cry out. Her cheek presses the mattress. Her mouth open, lips wet from the tip of her tongue.

Earlier he kissed her hard enough to bring the taste of blood, and it was this roughness that she thinks of now as he fucks into her. His fingers squeeze her harder. One of his hands slips around to stroke her clit in time with every thrust. It's exactly what she needs, exactly where she needs it.

It's even better when he starts to talk. Urging her in that low, growling voice to let him make her feel good. To give her body to him. He demands her pleasure, and this urges her body to respond exactly in the way he's asking her for.

Muscles tense, tight, her thighs shake as her hips buck. He fucks deeper into her, but not faster. Each stroke of his cock inside her heat is echoed by the circling of his fingers on her clit. Ecstasy builds inside her. Higher and higher, until, finally, she explodes.

Quivering in the aftermath of her orgasm, Persephone let out a small moan and buried her face in her pillow. She'd been thinking of the last time she'd seduced Kane. Of all the men she'd slept with in her life, why was it this man was the one her mind turned to when she needed sexual release?

It was dangerous, she thought as her eyes drifted closed. And she was drawn toward danger, always. She strained toward sleep. Kane was dangerous to her, because she liked him.

Chapter 2

Kane Dennis hadn't fallen off the turnip truck yesterday, as the saying went. Not that Kane ever said it, not aloud. It was something his grandfather, the man who'd raised him, would've been likely to say, though, and in situations like these it seemed appropriate.

Persephone from the basement apartment was hiding something. It was in the way she rarely met his gaze, even when he caught her staring. It was something in her posture, how her head went up and back so straight every time she saw him, as though he'd surprised her into a fight-or-flight reaction and she was just barely resisting the urge to either kick him in the junk or run away.

The question was not, however, what she might be hiding, but why on earth he gave a damn. Whatever it was, it didn't affect him in any way. In the beginning when he'd started getting that vibe from her, he'd been on the lookout for any signs of the usual—drug dealing, prostitution, fencing goods. Anything he would have found impossible to look beyond because it was going on literally right under his nose.

There'd been none of that. Only the subtle, persistent feeling that she knew more about him than he could ever discover about her, and that was what had gotten under his skin like a sliver. That's what he told himself, anyway. That it was curiosity. That she seemed interesting, a woman with stories to intrigue him, a woman who might not be repulsed by the ones he had to tell. It had nothing to do with her body, Kane told himself as he avoided the cranky elevator for the stairs, up a flight to his apartment directly above hers. Nothing to do with her soft strawberry blond hair, cut short to emphasize her giant dark brown eyes and the smooth expanse of her pale throat...

Nothing to do with that at all, he told himself grimly as he went inside his own apartment and dumped his now cold coffee down the sink. How had bringing her a cup of coffee made him into an asshole? Or had it been the fact he'd had to ask her why she didn't like him that had made the corners of her mouth turn down the way they had? Worse than that, what the fuck was wrong with him that seeing her clear discomfort and distaste only made him think about her more? *We chase what runs from us*, Grandpa Charles would've said, and Kane had to agree.

Persephone Collins was running from him, and it drove him crazy with desire because he couldn't figure out why.

* * *

"I'll give you a hundred." Chuck gave Persephone a glance over the rims of his reading glasses and shrugged at the sight of her disgruntled expression. "It's the best I can do. Look, you know I can't move this shit very fast. Bring me something I can actually sell, I'll pay you more."

Persephone eyed the array of slightly less than brand-new cell phones and flash drives she'd brought him. She'd known it wasn't likely Chuck would cross her palm with much more than a few pieces of silver, but for the past two weeks she'd kept her sticky fingers to herself—unless someone was foolish enough to walk away from their laptop or phone in a hotel lobby or a coffee shop long enough to get a refill.

"They're all wiped," she pointed out. "Unlocked."

He shrugged again. "Yeah, yeah, but look, you can pick up a refurbed phone for pennies on the dollar anymore. In the box. With a charger."

Persephone frowned. "Fine, I'll take the Benjamin."

It was better than nothing. She pocketed the cash and ducked out of the used electronics shop, glancing out of habit from side to side as she headed down the street. Chuck ran a mostly clean place, hadn't been the target of any raids or anything like that, but you never knew. Maybe it was time to get out of the sticky-fingers game, she thought as she grabbed a bottle of water and a candy bar from the small newsstand on the corner—paying for it with cash from her pocket, not stealing it, although there'd been times in the past when she'd lifted food to keep from starving. She was well beyond that now.

Her phone buzzed in her pocket as she tore the wrapper from the candy. Chewing nougat and chocolate, she answered without looking at the name or number on the screen. Only one person was allowed to get through to her directly on this line.

"What," Persephone said. The liquid male chuckle tickled her eardrum through the distance, and she held the phone away from her face for a second before putting it directly against her mouth to amplify the chewing noises.

"You're disgusting," Phoenix said.

Persephone swallowed the bite of candy. "What do you want? Let me guess, you've run out of funds and you don't have a sugar daddy or mama waiting in the wings."

"Cold, sister mine. So cold."

She pressed her lips together to fight off a smile. He was going to try to charm her, but damn it, she was mad. Phoenix had blown through town a few months ago and emptied her bank account by simply reaching into her brain and forcing her to give him the account numbers and passwords he'd then used to legitimately transfer all her funds to him. Sure, she could've taken it to the authorities, but that would've opened up investigations on her, and he'd known that.

"I would've just given you the money, you know," she said as she hopped the four concrete steps to the front door of her apartment building. "Why do you get to wipe me out?"

Her brother's chuckle went a little darker, enough to raise the hairs on the back of Persephone's neck. Like she could ever forget that behind the laughter and jokes, the put-upon front of laziness and congeniality, her twin brother was as fucked-up as she was. Perhaps more, because Persephone liked to tell herself she maintained some level of morality, no matter how gray, and Phoenix had no such pretense.

"Because I knew you'd be fine," he said simply. "You always are."

"You don't get to come back around into my life and make like you didn't totally fuck me over." Her tone was as cold as his. "What do you want?"

"Can't a baby brother check in with his big sister to make sure she's all right?"

Four minutes had passed between her entrance into this world and his. Persephone unlocked her door and went inside, closing it after her. She tossed her bag onto the couch.

"Forgive me for assuming you have an ulterior motive," she said. "I guess I'm just not a fucking idiot."

Phoenix burst into laughter that urged her to join him, although she kept herself from it. "No. I would never say that about you."

"What do you really want?"

His laughter and his voice softened. "I really did want to make sure you're all right. I wanted to make sure they hadn't taken you."

"You would've known that right away, Phoenix. You didn't have to call me." Her voice was softer, too. She couldn't feel the same connection to her brother that he had with her—Persephone's talents affected other people's perceptions, while Phoenix was able to actually manipulate them into action. No matter how far apart they were, he was always able to sense her, even if he couldn't pinpoint her thoughts.

"You felt upset a few times."

She flopped onto the couch and propped her feet on the table. "Everyone feels upset a few times."

"I never do."

"You don't have to brag about it," Persephone said. Phoenix *could* feel. He just didn't do it the same way most people did. Then again, she thought, did anyone ever feel the same way anyone else did?

"Are you okay?"

"Nobody took me," she said in a kinder tone. Maybe she had only four minutes on him, but that still made him her baby brother.

Phoenix didn't speak for a few seconds. "They took Leila."

"What?" Persephone sat up straight. "No. How do you know?"

"She sent me an email telling me she thought someone had been watching her. Following her. Then nothing, for months. Yesterday she texted me that she was in a safe place. That she was happy there. That I should consider changing my mind."

Persephone fought a wave of guilt. She hadn't talked to Leila in months, not since the last time they'd gone out dancing and drinking and picking up men. That wasn't unusual. Leila could be difficult to be around, because she was constantly screwing up her life.

"So…that's not a bad thing," Persephone said, thinking of the several times she'd felt like she was being watched. Nothing had happened in months. She still had Vadim's number and the knowledge that she had a place with the group he worked for called the Crew. It wasn't unbelievable that Leila might have taken him up on the offer. "She's safe and happy."

Phoenix made a noise low in his throat. "Of course

she would say that to throw off any suspicion. They took her, and they've brainwashed her."

"Phoenix…" Persephone sighed. "You can't be sure. Did you text her back?"

"And have them figure out where I am? No way. I'm not giving them the key to the castle. Fuck that."

Persephone thought a text was the least likely way anyone would ever be able to track them, but what did she know? "She said she was safe and happy. Don't you think if they were really trying to lure you in that she'd have asked you for help, tried to trick you into going to her? I'm sure she's okay, Phoenix."

"You think she went willingly? She allowed that guy to just take her in? You think she's really all right with them?"

She shook her head. "I don't know."

"You wish you'd gone with him when he asked you to," Phoenix accused in a flat voice.

"No," she said. "I don't wish that. But I don't worry that they're going to come along and drag me off to lock me up somewhere. I believed him when he said I would have the choice. That you'd have a choice. You even said you didn't feel anything in his head that meant he was lying."

Phoenix made another of those noises. "Not about that. About everything else, though. His whole head was a lie."

She sighed. "You know if you go to work for him it means room, board, salary. You know Leila was never able to get her shit together. If she went somewhere that helped her out, who are we to judge?"

"You want to be someone's pet?"

"Of course not," she told him, even as her thoughts

flashed against her will to Kane, which was ridiculous since she didn't want to be kept by any man. Especially not him.

"Something's going on with you. I'm not close enough to know it…"

"I'm fine," she said, her tone harsher. "And I'm still pissed at you."

"Nah, you're not. I knew that before I called." Her brother laughed. "But I have a mind to pay a visit, anyway."

"I don't have room."

Phoenix snorted. "You'd make a place for me."

"On the floor," she told him flatly. "On a set of jacks."

"You love me," Phoenix told her calmly, which was the truth, of course, no matter what he'd done. "And I love you. I'm sorry I cleaned out your bank account. I put it all back, by the way. Plus some."

She wanted to ask him how he'd managed to do that, but he'd disconnected before she could. Shaking her head, Persephone tossed her phone onto the table and got up to head for the kitchen in search of a meal that would fill her belly better than a candy bar. She put a frozen pizza in the oven while she flipped open her laptop at the kitchen table and scrolled through her emails, searching for any from Leila. She found one from months before, updating Persephone about her latest series of misadventures. She hadn't outright asked for money, but the subtext had been there.

Frowning, Persephone did a quick search, but that was indeed the last time she'd heard from the younger woman. She sat back in her seat, thinking hard. No texts had come in from Leila, but she probably didn't have Persephone's direct number. Opening one of the apps she kept for sidelines, Persephone scrolled through requests for pictures of her feet, tribute photos from men who'd already sent in their financial donations without even waiting to hear if she was going to accept them, junk and scam emails.

I decided to go with them, the message said. Tired of struggling. Want to be with people who understand. It's good here. You'd like it. Text me.

With a soft mutter, Persephone checked the date. Late yesterday afternoon, which meant she'd texted Phoenix first. That made sense. Leila had always liked him better. Most women did.

It didn't mean that Leila was in trouble, or that she'd been brainwashed the way Phoenix believed. The only way to find out would be to reply to Leila's message and see what she said. Typing in a swift reply, Persephone hit Send and waited. It came a minute or so later.

He is nothing like we were afraid of.
    You should come.

Chapter 3

"*It* would be nothing like Collins Creek." The man who calls himself Vadim has a kind voice, although his eyes are a little scary. He smiles, but something in the rest of his face makes him feel dangerous. Or that he could be, anyway. If you pushed him too hard.

"I don't know why I should go anywhere with you," Phoenix says belligerently with a toss of his long hair over his shoulders. He's pushed his way between Vadim and Persephone. It's a sweet gesture, but Persephone doubts it would do much good if Vadim really wanted to bring them harm.

Vadim spreads open his fingers and shrugs. "I'm offering you a roof over your heads. Food in your stomachs. Safety."

"Your safety sounds a lot like prison to me," Phoenix says. "C'mon, Persephone. Let's get out of here."

"Wait." She puts her hand on her brother's wrist. He shrugs off her touch with a scowl, but she ignores it. She focuses on Vadim. "Why? Why should we trust you? How did you find us?"

"We've been tracking all the children from Collins Creek," Vadim says. "So many of you have been lost, Persephone. So many of you we can't help. But you and your brother..."

"Fuck off," Phoenix snarls. "Come on, Persephone. Let's get out of here."

But she can't. Not yet. They've been running too long. She's hungry. She's tired.

"Where would we go?" she asks.

Vadim smiles. This time it's a little more believable. "We have facilities all over the world. Where would you like to go?"

"What would we have to do?"

"Work with us. That's all. People with your unique skills are always valued in the Crew."

The Crew. The first time she heard the name, Persephone had laughed, thinking he must be joking. A group of people who investigate the strange and extraordinary has such a plain and unassuming name? It was ridiculous.

"And if we decide we want to leave?"

"It's a contract. Like anything else. You're free to leave according to the terms in the contract. We don't keep anyone against their will. We don't make you do anything you don't want to do. We train you to use your skills, and we give you assignments based on what you're best suited to do. You're compensated for it. Very nicely."

Phoenix fixes her with a long, hard glare. "We've

done well enough on our own. There's no reason why we should sign anything with you. And I don't need you to teach me any damned thing."

"You can always learn something new," Vadim says calmly with barely a glance at her brother. He's got her in his sights. She wonders what he sees.

Persephone thinks that might be what is agitating Phoenix so much—that Vadim is paying more attention to her. And there's not a sexy vibe from it, either. They've dealt with that, living on the streets for the past few years. She's done her share of using sex as currency. Phoenix has done his, too. But she's definitely not getting that feeling from Vadim right now, not for either of them. Whatever he wants from her, it's not her body, and that's why she trusts him but her brother does not.

"What if we still say no?" Phoenix challenges.

Vadim shrugs and gestures at the sparsely furnished motel room where he found them. "You walk out of here."

"And if we change our minds?" Persephone asks.

"Then you contact us."

"We won't change our minds," Phoenix says and grabs her by the hand. "Come on, Persephone. Let's get out of here."

She's the one who looks over her shoulder as they leave. Vadim is staring. He mouths something at her just before the door closes off the sight of him.

"You will be safe."

Chapter 4

The Slaughtered Lamb had been sold and bought several times over the past ten years, each owner adding or taking away something to add their individual touch to the place. The pub had suffered for it. Kane could recall when the dark atmosphere had been kitschy, not merely worn-out, and when the drinks had been cheap and the food good. Now he sat beneath a set of flickering sconces made to look like gaslights and a portrait that from one direction showed a beautiful young woman in a historical gown, but from the other showed a werewolf.

He should call it a night. He hadn't been planning on hooking up with anyone when he got in here, but funny how a beer or two could get a man thinking about it. Especially when faced with a tiny-waisted brunette with curves that wouldn't quit. She'd been eye-fucking him from across the bar since she arrived about twenty minutes ago and slipped into the spot he'd been heading for. He'd considered sending her a drink, but that would mean he'd have to have a conversation with her, and unless he really wanted to take her home…

Shit. She'd seen him staring and now she was getting up to cross the room. He hadn't meant to make eye contact, and why? Because he was stupidly hung up on someone who clearly thought he was a douchecanoe. Kane looked up at the brunette, who'd tossed the fall of her heavy dark hair over her shoulder and was giving him a slow, easy smile.

"Hey," she said with that subtle twist of her body that emphasized her hips and breasts, that trick women did when they wanted you to not just look but also touch. "I'm Jena."

"Kane," he said. "Hi."

"So look, Kane," she said as she leaned closer so he could hear her without problem over the noise from the rest of the pub, "here's the thing. I'm about ready to head out for the night, but I was wondering if you'd like to come along with me? Or better yet, I could go home with you."

It was not the most blatant offer he'd ever had, but it ranked right up there. The funny part of it was, it was exactly what he needed in this moment. A no-frills, no-effort-needed, straight-up hookup. If she'd played at seduction, he'd have sent her on her way.

Instead, he gave her a thorough up and down perusal, making sure she knew he was checking out every bit of her before he fixed his gaze on hers. Smiled. Stood. "Sure. Let's go."

* * *

Persephone had spent longer than usual on what she thought of as "the glamour." It was not truly physical, because her body never actually changed. It was all illusion, a short-range manipulation of whatever parts of the brain controlled vision, smell, touch. Everyone else in this place would see her for what she really was, but Kane, the man upon whom she'd set her ravenous, manipulative sights, would be enthralled so long as she kept up the effort of the illusion.

She'd considered asking him to take her to a hotel, but she knew he didn't have money to toss away on something decent enough not to give her the shudders. Besides, in the morning when she slipped out of his bed, it would take only a few minutes to get back to her place, where she could get between her own sheets and hopefully drift off to sleep with a body worn out from a few rounds of amazing sex. She'd done it before.

When he led her into the building's lobby and toward the elevator that broke down more often than it worked, however, she hesitated. Fucking in an elevator was one thing, especially if it was the kind lined with mirrors so you could watch yourself reflected into infinity. This elevator didn't have any mirrors, it smelled vaguely and constantly of cat pee, and the last thing in the world she wanted was to get trapped inside it with Kane while she wore a fake face. They'd have to wait for hours before someone could get them out, and that person was most likely to be her, and that would quickly become a clusterfuck of epic proportions.

"Um…" she said, holding back. "How about the stairs?"

She jerked at thumb toward the small hallway next to the mailboxes set into the wall. Kane gave her a curious look she couldn't interpret, but nodded. He glanced over his shoulder as he led the way, holding open the heavy steel fire door so she could go first.

"What a gentleman," Persephone, a.k.a. Jena, murmured with an extra swing of her hips as she started up the stairs. Let him admire the badonk in her donkadonk, she thought with a small smile that faded when she got to the landing and looked over her shoulder, intending to give Kane a sexy, come-hither look.

He was frowning.

"Something wrong?" Persephone hesitated, a hand on the railing, to study him.

"Have we met before?"

She started back up the stairs. "I don't think so."

He followed her through the metal door at the top of the stairs, but she held back to let him lead the way to his apartment. Once inside, she also held back to let him make the first move. Sure, she'd put on this face, this body, this hair, all designed to get Kane's hormones roaring. And sure, she'd gone after him in the bar the way a wolf would take down a deer with a broken leg.

That didn't mean she didn't like to be pursued.

She didn't have to wait long. In a few long strides, Kane had her in his arms. His mouth slanted along her own in a perfect, sensual pleasure that always made her wonder how he knew exactly how to touch her, every single time.

He broke the kiss to brush her lips with the tip of his tongue, his eyes searching hers as she shivered. "What did you say your name was?"

"Maria." Shit. Shit. No, she'd said—

"I thought you said it was Jena."

Persephone straightened her shoulders and gave him a tipped, coy smile and a flutter of her lashes designed to send a man straight to his knees, which was the perfect position for him to get between her thighs with his mouth. Kane didn't kneel, but his gaze did go heavy lidded. Dreamy. His eyes lost their usual sharp, fierce focus.

This was glamour of a different sort.

"Maybe you meet so many girls whose names you don't ask that you got me confused with someone else," she said with a practiced pout. She put herself into his arms, offered her mouth, pushed her hips forward to rub her belly against his hard crotch.

It worked, of course. There was a reason cats butt your hand to get them to pet you. Persephone's pussy knew how to do the same thing.

She knew where his bedroom was. Even if she hadn't been here a dozen times in the past year, it mirrored her own, immediately below. She waited for him to take her there, though, letting him grip her by the upper arms and turn her. Still kissing, they moved across the L-shaped living room and through the small arched alcove between the kitchen and hallway, then a few steps more and into the bedroom.

Persephone breathed in the familiar, strongly male scent of the space where Kane slept and dreamed. She wanted to bury herself in his pillow but settled for letting him push her gently onto the bed, where he climbed up her body and fit himself between her legs. One hand hooked beneath her knee to tug it upward; she hooked her foot behind his calf.

The kisses deepened. His mouth moved over her

chin, down her throat, along the sloping curves of her high, big breasts spilling out of the tank top. As always, the strange juxtaposition between the flesh he appeared to be stroking and his touch upon her actual, real body was jarring and arousing and strange and exciting. Sometimes, when she allowed herself to dwell too long on the fact that she only fucked men when she looked like any other woman but herself, it was melancholy.

Not tonight. She wouldn't allow herself to feel anything now but rising desire, slightly violent. Consuming her. Filling her. She needed him to strip her bare and wear her out. She needed him.

She needed him…

Persephone sat up hard, backing out of Kane's embrace before she could stop herself. Her head knocked the painted concrete wall. No headboard. It didn't hurt, but the noise was loud enough that she gave a startled "oh!"

"You okay?" Kane had pushed onto his knees, head tilted as he stared at her.

She arched her back, shaking off the sudden rush of unwanted emotions trying to flood her. "Oh, yeah, baby. Just…eager."

She kicked off one high heel and let her naked toes run up over his belly to press his chest. Men went wild when she did that. She could never figure out why. Something about the push and pull between them dominating her and yet somehow submitting at the same time. Some kind of illusion of power and control. All of this was illusion, she thought as she watched him look over the lithe, curving body she'd presented to him.

For a terrible moment she thought he'd changed his

mind about her. There'd been two times with Kane that had ended up with them back here in the morning's wee hours but not engaged in sex. Both times, he'd started off strong and eager, but something had changed his mind and he'd asked her to leave before they fucked. She'd never been able to figure out what had tipped him the other way, but tonight looked as though it might be heading that direction.

No, no, she couldn't let it. It was too late to go out trolling for another hookup, but more than that, Persephone didn't want to. The sex with anyone else, no matter how adequate, could never compare to the nights she spent with Kane, and it had been too long since the last time with him. She needed this right now—for more reasons than she cared to admit.

She pushed outward with the small and curling tendrils of her will to shape herself in his gaze. "Kiss me."

He did, for a second or so. Kane hissed in a gasp when her fingers slid beneath the edge of his shirt and against his bare skin. She put a hand behind his neck, fingers curling, nails digging a little deep. They worked quickly after that, stripping down at the same time until she lay back on the bed with him kneeling over her. He wasn't fully erect yet, but she let her hungry gaze linger on him before she looked up at his eyes. She'd meant to say something sexy, alluring, seductive, but at the sight of his look Persephone's words clipped themselves short against the backs of her teeth.

Again, she wondered with some alarm if he meant to tell her she had to leave. Again, she eased the tickling swirls of her senses to shadow and shape his. It should've been freaky for him to see the long dark lengths of the hair she'd conjured getting shorter, to hit her just above her shoulders, or to see her breasts becoming smaller, her ass more rounded, yet because all of this was hallucination, all Kane would see was her becoming his ideal. He wouldn't even know she didn't look the same as she had earlier in the night. And in the morning, when he woke to an empty spot in the bed beside him, he would have only the vaguest memory of what she had looked like at all.

"Kiss me," Persephone whispered again with a crook of her finger to get him to lean down and take her mouth with his. She meant to say more after that, but the taste of him chased away her words again so that all she found was silence and sighs.

When he ran his hands up her sides to cup her breasts, she arched into the touch. Her knees fell apart of their own accord so her body could open to him. He surprised her again when he slid his mouth down her throat and over her breasts, to her belly, to her hip and then oh, yes, fuck, right there. Right to her core, and he fastened his tongue and lips on her clit and began to lick and suck in a steady but delicate rhythm that had her lifting her hips to meet every stroke within moments.

He'd never gone down on her before. She'd had his cock deep in her throat, and they'd fucked in every position either of them had ever thought to try, but he had never had his mouth on her pussy. Persephone had never asked him for it—she never asked any man for it, though she never turned it down if were offered. She gladly gave herself up to it now, letting pleasure fill her up and wash over her until she was muttering his name from between clenched jaws, unwilling to completely give him everything inside her.

He hummed, sounding delighted. The thrum of it sent another slow, rolling wave of desire coursing through her. Her clit pulsed on his tongue. His hands slipped beneath her ass to lift her closer to his kisses. He murmured again, wordless noises of approval and desire that pushed her closer and closer to the edge.

He blew a soft gust of breath across her as he replaced his tongue for a moment with his fingers. A different pressure, but the same pace. She wasn't going to hold out much longer and didn't want to. The idea of asking him to hold off so she could come with him inside her crossed her mind, but greedily, Persephone didn't manage to keep herself from taking just…a little…more.

As always, her orgasm teased her for what felt like forever before finally she could no longer crest. She had to fall. Plummeting, she writhed and shook and shuddered. Again, she cried out his name. She also looked down at him to find him looking up at her.

She expected an arrogant smile, pride in the way he'd just gotten her off, but confusion blurred his gaze. His mouth was open and wet, and the sight of it continued to arouse her. At least until he blinked rapidly and pushed himself up onto his knees to look down at her.

Before Persephone had learned the extent of her talents in manipulating the way others perceived her, she'd often stuttered in holding on to the glamour. There'd been times when she'd altered her appearance based on whatever she sensed the other person desired, but she hadn't lost the ability to hold on to the illusion. Not in years.

Now, panicked, she reached to touch the soft, red-gold feathers of hair above her ears that had been dark brown and to her shoulders moments ago. Her breasts had shrunk yet again, filling her palms with a familiar weight. How long had she been looking more like herself than an image? It took her only seconds to return to the projection, and by the way Kane was frowning she was relieved to see that her change could've been no longer than that. Long enough for him to notice and be shocked, but not long enough for him to have truly seen her.

Not her real self, not Persephone. Never that. It would be her downfall.

"I thought… I must be drunker than I thought." He shook his head and wiped his mouth with the back of his hand. His cock, despite his consternation, had gone thick and hard. Ready for her.

"Not too drunk to fuck, baby," Persephone purred, putting on her persona even as her heart thumped unsteadily and she had to take a few seconds to center herself. "Come here."

Kane shook his head. "Listen, you're sexy as fuck, and any other time I would be already deep inside you, but…"

She sat, closing her legs self-consciously. Her pussy still throbbed with aftershocks, and when she shifted, she could feel slickness on the insides of her thighs. With a shiver, she covered her breasts with her arms.

"But you want me to get out?" she asked.

Kane ran a hand over his dark hair, rumpling it. "I think it would be best. I can call a car for you, or…"

"No. It's all good." Persephone got out of the bed and began to search for her clothes. Very aware of Kane's eyes on her ass as she bent over, she considered putting a little shimmy in it to tempt him, but didn't. It was awkward enough that he was kicking her out. The last thing she wanted was to try to seduce him only to be utterly rejected.

He walked her to the door and kissed her there, but on the corner of the mouth. Almost the cheek. Bemused, Persephone patted his arm and kept her mouth shut. She wasn't going to offer to see him again, for sure, but she did wonder what on earth had changed his mind about fucking her. She glanced over her shoulder as she headed for the stairs to find him watching her with a narrowed, focused gaze.

Oh, shit.

Chapter 5

Kane had gone for a run before work. Using his muscles, pushing his endurance. He'd spent the rest of the day on paperwork and following leads. Funny how television and the movies showed detectives almost always in the street chasing down the bad guys. They never showed all the work it took to find them first.

Now he was at home with a takeout carton of Chinese and a six-pack of beer, his laptop open on the kitchen table in front of him. He had more work to do. He'd already done a search for his hookup from the other night, but nobody matching the name she'd given him or the description had popped up. There was no reason for him to think she was any kind of criminal or anything, but something about her had set off an alarm bell in his head.

Going down on her had been incredible. She'd tasted

like the sweetest honey. Her body had softened and bloomed under his tongue and lips. When she came, he'd been able to feel every tremor, every flutter. Kane loved cunnilingus, but he rarely opened with it—that wasn't something for a first encounter, and he hadn't had more than a first encounter with anyone in close to two years. He wasn't sure what had prompted him to get his mouth between her legs, only that everything about the evening had been a little off, a little strange... a little extraordinary.

It hadn't been the booze, he knew that. But something screwy had been going on when he sat up to look at her and it seemed for half a second that there was an entirely different woman in his bed. Just for a blink he'd seen Persephone writhing beneath him, her body arched and shaking from the orgasm he'd given her. Only for a blink, and Jena or Maria or whatever she claimed her name was had been back again, and he'd gone all wiggy and sent her home. So what the hell, he thought, was up with that?

He'd done a search on Persephone before but had also found nothing. No criminal record at all. Not even a parking ticket, which wasn't so odd considering that as far as he could tell, she didn't own a car.

Swigging beer, Kane tapped his computer to wake it up, then let his fingers rest on the keyboard. If he kept digging, he was going to find out who she was and where she came from. The question was, did he really want to know? What would happen when she was no longer a mystery? And what would he do, he thought, if he found out something he'd feel compelled to take action on?

So many questions, and he wasn't usually the sort of guy to dwell on this kind of thing. Damn, the woman had gotten deep in his head and under his skin. It had to be more than just that she didn't seem to want to give him the time of day. Sure, he'd had more than his share of women who'd been eager to jump his bones, but there'd been a number whose heads hadn't even turned, just like any guy. He'd always considered it part of the game and moved on.

Until Persephone.

Now, while he dug into his lo mein and sipped at his beer without noticing much of the flavor, Kane started searching again. A friend of his who'd gone into private detective work had taught him some tricks about finding evidence of people who didn't seem to have left any tracks, and he put them into play now. Finally, just before he meant to give up and turn on a movie instead, something popped up.

The article was brief, the mention that had been linked to his searching no more than a sentence or two. It was the photo that caught his attention. A group shot of a bunch of children dressed identically, boys and girls with the same haircuts, all long hair past their shoulders, so it made it difficult to tell them apart. Most of them were smiling—at least there was that, considering the accompanying text told a horrific story about the cult at Collins Creek.

Kane hadn't heard about this group before, but that meant nothing. Cults were far from his area of expertise. Collins Creek turned out to be a fairly obscure cult as well, more mythical than anything according to the article. It said that rumors of the atrocities at Collins Creek were widespread and pervasive but had not been substantiated.

At Collins Creek, it had been all about the children. Pregnant women had purposefully exposed themselves to chemicals, drugs, sleep deprivation, while the men had also undergone voluntary exposure to environmental and mental stressors designed to not only affect the unborn babies but change them at conception. What the leaders had been trying to do was the subject of some controversy, but it seemed as though they'd been attempting to force mutations. To create psychic powers. The success rate was unknown, although there were plenty of rumors about that, too. Mostly, though, the only truth anyone could corroborate was that at some point about twenty years ago, a private group had invaded Collins Creek and taken away as many of the children as they'd been able to. At least the ones that had survived. And after that? All signs of the place had disappeared. Like Area 51, Collins Creek existed, but nobody would admit it or talk about what had gone on there.

Kane did not believe in aliens. He understood conspiracy theories only as the workings of people who had too much time on their hands and big imaginations. Looking at this article, he would usually have scoffed at the idea that there'd been a large farm full of psychically enhanced children running around it only a few hours' drive away. But looking at the photograph, seeing the smiling faces of all those children, something like a chill skittered up and down his spine. He recognized the smiles on the faces of not one of those children, but two, and there in the fine-print caption below the picture, he saw the list of names.

One of them was Persephone.

Chapter 6

Meeting a horny businessman for cocktails and domination was not exactly the worst way to spend the afternoon, Persephone thought. The hotel was upscale, the food was good and he was paying for it.

He'd ordered room service, as she'd told him to do in advance, along with a bottle of very nice champagne that she hadn't requested. She eyed it as she took a seat on the desk chair. "Celebrating?"

"Every date with you is reason for celebration," he said.

Persephone paused to look at him. "Are you falling in love with me, Werner?"

Werner looked uncomfortable for a second before nodding. "Yes. I think so."

"Don't." She raised a finger when he made to speak. "We talked about this right up front. What did I say?"

"You said that it would never be emotional, that it was purely business. It's what I said…" He coughed, cutting his gaze from hers. "I said that was what I wanted."

"Which is why I agreed to it." She frowned, running a finger along the champagne bottle. For Werner, she wore her body older, taller, strong. Dark pageboy hair streaked with silver. She turned to him, still frowning. "You know this is only business, Werner."

"I know. But it's so difficult…" Incredibly, his voice hitched. He closed his eyes. Everything about him turned inward, away from her.

Persephone had seen Werner behave as though he was ashamed many times. It was part of his kink. One thing she had never seen him do was be genuinely distraught by anything they'd ever done. She took a step toward him in concern.

"Hey."

His fists clenched. "It's hard to find someone. Someone who gets it. Who…likes it. Well, who at least doesn't make me feel like some kind of creep for liking what I like. Do you know how hard it is, Chelsea? To find someone who doesn't make you feel like a freak?"

She sat next to him on the bed, aware that he was completely naked but not bothered by it. He'd been naked so many times in front of her, after all. Never quite like this. Nude skin, yes. This was different.

She took his hand. "Yes. I understand how hard it must be to find someone."

Hell, it was hard enough to find someone just to go out with on a date, much less who didn't mind making you beg for orgasms. Men like Werner could pay for sex, but the companionship also came with a price, and he'd always known it. She understood how it could finally have started to pale.

His shoulders hitched, and he still turned away from her. "I'm sorry. I know this wasn't the agreement. You can leave. The money's on the table by the door."

"I'm not going to take your money, Werner." Persephone stood, for one moment taking his chin in her hand the way she'd done many times before. This time not to chastise, scold or humiliate him. This time she held his face still when she brushed her lips over his cheek. "You take care of yourself. Okay?"

He'd closed his eyes at her kiss. She felt him straining toward her, but she didn't kiss him again. He didn't open his eyes. She stepped backward, for an instant catching a glimpse of herself in the wall mirror. Her own self, not the one she'd presented to him over the months of their acquaintance. If he looked at her now, he would still see Chelsea, but that was how it should be.

Without saying goodbye, Persephone ducked out of the hotel door. She paused to shuck the heels and replaced them with a pair of flats she had in her bag. She didn't take the time to do anything with the tight, cleavage-baring dress that hit her midthigh, but she did shrug into a long loose-fitting cardigan.

She'd made it all the way through the hotel lobby and to the sidewalk beyond without so much as turning a head before a male voice stopped her short. She turned, certain she must not have heard him say her name. Surely it would have to be a stranger calling out to someone else.

Certainly, she thought with a sinking stomach as she faced him, certainly it could not be Kane.

"I thought that was you," he said cheerfully enough. He'd been leaning against the hotel near the smoking area, though to her knowledge he didn't smoke.

"Yep, it's me." She rocked a little on her heels and jerked a thumb toward her chest. Heat flooded her throat and painted her face scarlet. She coughed and pasted on a smile.

"What's up?" He glanced at the hotel entrance, then gave her a long, slow going-over that did nothing to relieve her rising blush.

"What's up with you?" she asked boldly. The best way to get out of a sticky situation was by confronting it head-on. She'd learned that long ago. Something told her, though, that Kane was not going to fall for it.

He grinned. "Just hanging out. Meeting a friend."

"Have fun." It was code for a stakeout or something—she knew that by the sly way his mouth twisted. She'd never talked with Kane about his work, but of course she knew exactly what he did.

"Hey, hey," he said as he stepped toward her. "Maybe I meant you?"

The moment he said it, he seemed to regret it. The expression was so comical that Persephone almost laughed. If ever a man wished he could take back what he'd just blurted out, that man was Kane just then.

"You're not waiting for me," she said crisply.

"No. We're not friends. Right?"

She eyed him, then gave a begrudging smile. "Nope."

"Not buddies, not pals, not chums."

"No, no and definitely not." She took a few steps backward before turning to walk away with a little wiggle of her fingertips over her shoulder.

Maybe being bold was going to pay off, she thought. God knew she'd played the same game with security officers at the mall with a bag full of lifted merch. Confidence and walking away without looking back had saved her ass a hundred times.

Not this time. Kane caught up to her in three or four long strides, falling into pace beside her. She could feel him looking at her.

"It's a free country," she said at last without so much as a glance his way. "I'm allowed out of the building, you know. I'm allowed to do whatever things I want to do during the day, and I don't need to explain myself to you, either."

"Was I asking for an explanation?" Kane paused, allowing her to move a few steps ahead before he jogged to catch up.

"What were *you* doing hanging around outside a fancy hotel at two in the afternoon?" Persephone whirled to walk backward for a few steps. "Loitering!"

Kane laughed. "Yep, loitering."

"Hmm." She faced forward again, walking, although not quite as fast as before.

Kane fell into step beside her again, this time not poking her with words. Just walking. She hadn't intended to walk all the way home, but somehow hailing a cab now felt awkward, like he might try to jump in the car with her. Without saying anything, she turned into the park entrance to cut across it. Kane did, too.

It was a nice enough day for walking, at least. Sun bright but not too hot. Clear blue and cloudless sky. Walking the curving path through patches of flowers, Persephone let herself for briefest of moments imagine what it might be like if Kane took her hand.

Sappy, she scolded herself with a sideways glance at him. Even if she did want to risk getting involved with him beyond the anonymous sex, they would never be the sort of couple to skip through fields of flowers holding hands. Well, she wasn't, for sure. Too late, he'd caught her looking.

"What?" Kane said.

"Nothing," Persephone answered.

He smiled as though he knew she was full of it. "Uh-huh."

With a sniff, she went back to ignoring him. Fifteen minutes later they were back at their building, the neighborhood very different from the one where they'd met up earlier. She was definitely overdressed, but that wasn't what made her suddenly anxious.

It was the sight of Vadim sitting on the front steps, waiting for her.

Chapter 7

Kane knew at once something was wrong. Not so much by the look on Persephone's face—she would definitely be a winner at the poker table. It was something subtler than that. A shift in her posture. The soft hiss of a drawn-in breath. Without thinking twice, he stepped between her and the man now standing on the concrete steps to the apartment building.

"Persephone," the guy said in a deep, rich voice with a hint of an accent. "So good to see you again. I've been waiting for you."

"Clearly," she said. "Well, I guess you'd better come on inside."

"Kane Dennis," he said, stepping forward with a hand out for a shake. He kept his voice light. Easy. Nonthreatening, even as he mentally ran through a checklist of what he'd do if the guy showed one second's thought toward harming Persephone.

"Nice to meet you," the guy said without offering a name. He smiled, but it was obvious he was not going to give Kane a damned thing. His attention turned back to Persephone. "That would be most appreciated. Thank you."

Kane touched her shoulder. "Everything okay?"

For a moment it looked as though she meant to say no. Her mouth pursed, her brow furrowed. He couldn't tell if she was annoyed with him for asking or if she was trying to tell him that no, she was not all right.

"Sure. Fine," she said. No shake in her voice. She met his gaze without hesitation. A faint smile, maybe the nicest she'd ever given him, tipped the corners of her mouth. "Thanks, Kane, but I'm fine."

Kane gave the nameless guy a narrow-eyed stare but didn't pursue it. No matter how much he wanted to go all caveman and leap to Persephone's defense, it was clear she didn't want him to. Instead, he nodded and stepped back. He gave the guy another steady stare that didn't seem to affect the other man very much at all.

Persephone didn't look over her shoulder as she went inside and down the stairs to the basement. Kane waited until the door closed behind them, then another few minutes before he went down after them. Persephone's apartment was down the hall from the storage space, and he conveniently needed to look for something that he'd packed away.

Fifteen minutes later, her door opened. The murmur of voices didn't sound alarming, but Kane listened, anyway. When the sound of a single pair of footsteps moved away and her door closed, he came out of the storage space. Quickly and quietly, he followed the man up the stairs and through the lobby, but stopped short at the sight of Persephone's mysterious visitor waiting for him on the sidewalk.

The other man grinned. "She has a good friend in you, I see."

"According to her, we aren't friends."

"You shouldn't let that deter you." The man shrugged. "Miss Persephone is a wary soul, and I would say she has a right for caution."

Kane studied the guy, assessing. "How well do you know her?"

"I don't know her very well at all. I am not a rival for her affections, if that's what worries you." The man's expression was smooth. Neutral. "I am not her friend, either. She'd be the first to tell you that. But I assure you, neither am I her enemy. I want only what's best for Miss Persephone."

"She's in trouble," Kane said flatly. "What kind?"

"I would think such a question might be best asked of her, not me. As for me, I must say goodbye. I have other appointments." With that, the guy turned on his heel and stalked away down the sidewalk, looking neither left nor right and definitely not behind.

After that meeting, Kane had done more searching, but he wasn't surprised to find nothing about Persephone's mystery guest. Still, he couldn't shake the feeling something was very wrong about the whole situation, even though he believed the guy when he said he wasn't interested in Persephone romantically and also that he wasn't her enemy.

He had done more digging into the Collins Creek situation. All of it rumor or urban legend. Nothing concrete. He'd found no more photos of Persephone, but he had dug up a couple reports about the children who'd survived the raid. Some of them had allegedly been put into research facilities. A few others were reported to have grown up on the streets.

It made sense now. The sense of wariness she had about her. Her sharp wit. The way she could either stand out from everyone else around her or blend in so completely you'd never know she was there.

As for the rest of it, the allegations that the children of Collins Creek were all somehow like that chick from the Stephen King flick, the one where she offed everyone at the prom—none of that seemed believable, though he could absolutely believe the cult leaders had thought it was possible.

He had no intention of mentioning any of this to her, of course, except that he did want to tell her that he would be there for her if that guy who'd been waiting for her was indeed going to bring her some kind of harm, even if it was just the painful kind of being reminded of things she'd rather not think about. She'd laugh or mock him; she might even get a little put out by what Kane knew was going to come off as patronizing. He didn't care. He wanted her to know that he would be there to protect her, if she needed it.

As it turned out, he was too late.

Chapter 8

Since Vadim had shown up on her doorstep, Persephone had been lying low. She ventured out of her apartment only to take care of repairs, but beyond that she'd been holed up doing nothing but binge watching television shows. She'd even sprung the extra few bucks for grocery delivery so she wouldn't have to go out.

Vadim had offered her a job. The first time around he'd found her and Phoenix at age sixteen, living on the streets. He'd offered them shelter and training then. This time he'd simply asked her if she'd like to work for him. She could keep her life here if she wanted. She didn't have to give up her other activities, as he'd called them, but for the first time in a long time, Persephone thought she might like to. The grifting was getting old. The petty thievery less profitable. And the sex work…she thought again of Werner, and how even though their arrangement had been meant to be only business, in the end she'd hurt him, anyway.

Also, there was Kane.

It wouldn't be long before he figured out she didn't make her living in any honest way, if he hadn't already. Once he did, even if he didn't arrest her, there'd be no way for her to keep living here. Not seeing him every day and knowing that he thought she was a criminal… well, she totally was a criminal, Persephone reminded herself as she gave Interflix the go-ahead to keep playing episodes of a '90s sitcom she'd never seen the first time around.

Thinking of Kane now made her shift and squirm a little on the couch. It had been over a week since she'd tried to seduce him and been summarily turned away without so much as an inch of him inside her. She hadn't been able to stop thinking about his mouth on her, though. How his tongue had lapped, slow and steady, pushing her closer and closer to the edge.

Damn, she needed him. She wanted him, anyway, and for Persephone that had to count as the same thing. Didn't it? Leaning back against the couch, the mindless TV show blaring in the background, she closed her eyes. Her hands drifted over her body. Her fingers slipped beneath the waistband of her jeans, the fit tight and not giving her much room to maneuver. She was already slick and hot, and she let out a small sigh of pleasure as she found her clit.

Kane is above her, his gaze intense. He moves his hands over her body, finding all the places that make her respond. When he dips his mouth to taste her flesh,

Persephone arches into the embrace. His lips find her nipples, one and then the other, tugging each until they stand up in tight points that ache to be caressed further.

Lower, lower, he moves, tongue tracing wet patterns on her skin as he pauses for a moment to nibble her hip. She laughs at the tickle and his hot breath puffs out on skin dampened by his mouth. When he moves between her legs, she lets out a long, low moan of pleasure that he echoes, and his hum against her pushes her higher.

Higher.

With a gasp, Persephone paused in her self-love, listening for the sound of the knock she was sure she'd just heard. Shit, it was someone at the door. Quickly she pulled her hand out of her jeans and got off the couch, running her fingers through her hair and trying to shake off the swell of arousal still surging through her. She absolutely did not want to answer the door to find Mrs. Cohen in 3B needed her toilet unclogged while she looked like she'd been happily getting herself off to fantasies of Kane.

Mrs. Cohen was not on the other side of the door.

It was Phoenix.

"You're being an asshole," Persephone said through gritted teeth even as she kept walking.

Her brother laughed, which only made her angrier. "Keep moving."

"You didn't even let me pack a bag!" Or grab her book full of cash, and that was the real shame. But every time she thought about stopping, she took another step.

That was Phoenix's talent. Persephone could make other people see what she wanted them to see, but her brother could make them do things he wanted them to do. As with her talent, it was limited. He couldn't command an army, for example, but then, he didn't really have to. Not when he could focus his will on one person who was helpless not to resist.

"You're being—"

"An asshole. You said so. Come on. I have a car."

Persephone chortled. "Oh, yeah? Where did you get a car?"

"I made a woman give it to me," her brother said with a cat-eating-the-cream grin that Persephone refused to admit she'd missed. Once in the passenger seat, she made sure to buckle up. Phoenix was a terrible driver. They both were. No parents to teach them. She didn't even have her license. He probably didn't, either, but he wouldn't care. There wasn't much to worry about if you got pulled over when you could tell the cop to simply walk away and let you go.

"Where are we going?" Persephone asked. "If you tell me to rob a bank, I'm going to punch you in the junk."

"I'll stop you."

"I'll do it so fast you won't have time," she countered. "And I notice you didn't say we weren't going to rob a bank."

Phoenix shot her an amused look as he put the car in gear and pulled out of the parking spot without bothering to look. "We're not going to rob a bank. We're going to save Leila."

Persephone groaned. "Phoenix, no. Why? What on earth do you want to do that for?"

"Because she's our friend, and I think she's in danger!"

For a moment she considered not telling him that Vadim had approached her about taking a job. She wasn't in the habit of keeping secrets from her brother, not exactly, even though there'd been plenty of times when she hadn't told him the entire truth. He always sensed it, though, and all he had to do was tell her to give up the story, and she would.

"Vadim came to see me. He said he had a job for me."

Phoenix didn't look surprised. "Yeah. Me too."

"Then why are we doing some kind of, what, secret mission? Leila said she was fine. Vadim approached both of us… Holy shit, Phoenix! Look out!" Persephone screamed hoarsely as her brother nearly got in a head-on collision with a delivery truck because their car was lumbering down the wrong side of a one-way street.

With a laugh just short of maniacal, Phoenix swerved to avoid the truck, which let out a long, angry bleat of its horn. He took the corner too fast. Persephone closed her eyes.

"This is not how I want to die, Phoenix!"

Another laugh. "Oh, come on. It's going to fine."

She risked a peek, relieved to see that he was at least going down the street the right way now. They drove in relative silence for the next half an hour, with Phoenix changing the radio station every few minutes and singing along, badly, with all the songs. No conversation beyond that. Frankly, Persephone didn't have anything to say.

When they pulled up in front of a truly disgusting-looking roadside motel that looked like something out of a horror movie, she finally found her voice. "No.

Oh my god, I'm getting hives just thinking about the bedbug bites."

"We're not living here. We're just staying here to meet someone on the inside."

"The inside of what?" Persephone twisted in her seat. "Damn it, Phoenix, since when did you turn into, what, an international spy? What the hell is going on? Who are we meeting here?"

"Her name is Samantha. She's got information I want about the Crew."

"And how did you figure this out?"

"Met her on Connex," he said easily with a wave of his hand before he turned off the ignition and gave her a smug grin. "She tries to beat me at WordPals, but she hasn't yet."

"What makes you think she's going to give you some kind of secret information about the Crew so that you can bust in and 'save'—" Persephone used air quotes "—Leila?"

"I didn't tell her that's what I wanted." Without waiting for her, Phoenix got out of the car.

Of course, Persephone followed, because he was manipulating her like a marionette. It showed when she stumbled on the cracked piece of concrete that kept cars from driving straight through the window of the craptastic motel. She didn't fall, but she did let out a muttered curse that had him laughing at her as she managed to keep her feet. He was already holding open the door to the room, ushering her inside, then shutting and locking the door behind them.

It wasn't any better in there than it looked from the outside. Sagging double beds covered in plaid bedspreads that didn't quite match. Faded watercolors on the stucco walls. Through an open door she could see a white-tiled bathroom from which the faintest stink of air freshener wafted.

"Does she think she's meeting you here to fuck?" Persephone asked, since her brother hadn't answered.

He gave her a glance over his shoulder as he went to the window on the far side of the room to twitch the curtains and peek out. "I don't think so. It's not like that."

"So why, then, would she come and help you?"

Phoenix shrugged. "She thinks I can help her find someone who's missing."

"Why on earth would she think that?" Persephone put her hands on her hips. "That's not your skill."

"No, but I can connect with you. And with the rest of them, if I try," he said.

The rest of them. The other kids from Collins Creek. Persephone knew her brother could sense her general location, even when they were far apart, but this was the first she'd heard that he could do that with anyone else.

"He's our brother," Phoenix said at her look.

Persephone's mouth opened, gaping. Her eyebrows rose. "But we don't have—"

"He was younger. He'd just been tested when they raided. But same mother, same father."

"That doesn't make him our brother," Persephone said after a moment.

Phoenix shrugged, expression neutral. She studied him. In childhood, it had been the two of them. For so long after that, they'd been everything to each other, the only other person they could trust. She loved her brother more than anything in the world, but she didn't always like him.

"When is Samantha getting here?"

"I said I'd call when I got here. You hungry?" He leaned to pull a sheaf of what looked like takeout menus from the drawer in the nightstand. "You got the app on your phone that lets you call for delivery?"

"Yeah." She was hungry as well as disgruntled, and she knew that a well-fed Phoenix would be easier to deal with. "What are you in the mood for?"

"Chinese." He settled further onto the pillows with his own phone, tapping out some messages.

Persephone took care of the food order and checked out the bathroom, grimacing at the condition of it. She'd rather be dirty. She washed her hands, though. Catching sight of herself in the mirror, she took a few minutes to swipe away the smears of mascara that had crept down her cheeks. Her hair needed a trim. With a sigh, she leaned on the sink and closed her eyes, wondering what the hell Phoenix had gotten them both into.

"You want to hate me," her brother said quietly from the doorway. "But I know you can't. I know you want to help Leila."

"If you see her and she tells you to your face that she's all right, will you lay off this ridiculous idea that she's been kidnapped or something?" She looked at him in the mirror, then turned to face him. "Will you?"

Phoenix shrugged. "If it feels like she's telling the truth, yes. If I ask her to be honest and she tells me that she's really happy there with them, yes. I'll lay off."

There was more to this than his concern for Leila. Persephone knew it, because she knew the way her brother operated. She also knew she wasn't going to be able to figure it out right away.

The food arrived and Phoenix made the guy leave it without being paid, something that annoyed Persephone even though she'd done her share of cheating people out of food before. Still, they both fell on the fried rice and lo mein with the same appetite and polished off the order within minutes. Then they turned on the television, and despite her disgust with the room and the situation overall, Persephone found herself drifting to sleep.

"Who is he?" Phoenix's voice curled out of the darkness toward her, across the space between the beds.

Persephone yawned. "Who is who?"

"There's someone. I can feel him in there. He's taking up space in your head."

She didn't answer right away. He could make her tell him the way he'd made her give him the bank account information, the way he'd made her get in the car. For a second she thought about forcing him to make her, but then, what difference did it make? No matter how annoying he was or how angry she got at him, Phoenix would always be her brother. The only family she really had.

"His name's Kane."

Phoenix snorted soft laughter. "What the hell kind of name is Kane?"

"What kind of name is Phoenix?" she asked flatly. "Or Persephone?"

"The man and woman who genetically produced us were messed-up people," her brother said.

The description of the people who had indeed created them but had never been parents made her laugh. "Maybe his parents were messed up, too."

"Is he a mess?"

"No," she said quietly after a few seconds had passed in silence. "I don't think he is. I mean, everyone has their damage, right, but no. I don't think Kane's messed up the way we are."

"Nobody's messed up the way we are," Phoenix told her. "Not in this whole world."

Chapter 9

Kane had found Persephone's apartment empty, which wouldn't have been alarming except that her door had swung open at his knock. Unlocked. A chair had been knocked over at the kitchen table. Her laptop was open, the screen dark but coming to life when he tapped the keypad. Aside from that, nothing else seemed out of place, but that was more than enough for him.

Someone had taken her. He knew it in his gut, and he knew it was somehow related to the stranger. With a quick call to the department and his partner to tell them he'd be working on following up some leads and wouldn't be in, Kane started figuring out how to find Persephone.

First, the obvious choice. Her laptop screen had gone dark again, but a quick tap of the keys brought up her screen. She did not have it lock protected, something that was going to make his job so much easier, even though it surprised him. It shouldn't have. In his experience more people didn't password protect their laptops than did. He gave her files a quick glance, not bothering to read any of them, not even the ones with super bland and therefore intriguing titles, like Accounting Receipts.

He found what he was looking for after a minute or so. The Find My Phone app was, as he'd hoped, connected to her phone, and also not password protected. All it took was a quick few taps of the keys to bring it up and he was looking at a map with her phone's location pinpointed with a small blue peg. She wasn't moving, there was that, but what she was doing in the Sentinel Motel was going to be his next task to figure out.

It was possible she was meeting someone, he thought. A lover? A client, more likely, Kane thought with a grim press of his lips together, thinking of how he'd seen her coming out of that downtown hotel dressed for something more than a midafternoon business meeting.

Grabbing her laptop, he slipped it into the soft fabric case patterned in skulls and roses that she'd left on the table. He'd need to get on the internet to access her location again, but that wouldn't be a problem. It would take him over an hour and forty minutes to get to the Sentinel, and if he found after assessing the situation that she didn't need his help, he'd discreetly leave without her ever knowing he'd turned into a creeper. But if she did need help, he thought grimly, whoever was hurting her better hope they knew how to run, because he was going hunt them down and make sure they paid for bringing her harm.

Slowly, slowly, he runs his fingertips up her arms. Then down. Tickling touches across the slope of her belly between her hip bones. Over her thighs. Pausing, he touches the backs of her knees as he pushes her legs up, opening her to his view. She is caught in his gaze, muscles tight and trembling, waiting for his touch.

He teases her.

Long minutes pass beneath this exquisite torment while she writhes and moans; his name on her lips is like candy. Sweetness. Magic.

The softness of his hot breath on her slick flesh makes her wriggle and cry out again. Body straining. She wants to thread her fingers through his hair and push him against her but satisfies herself with twisting her grip into the crisp white sheets.

That first touch of his tongue against her is so good, so fucking good, that all she can do is whimper. Arch. Roll her hips up to get more of him, get herself against him harder, get his tongue to press on her clit and lick and lick and lick...

Pleasure controls her. No words. Nothing but this aching and brilliant desire flooding every inch while she shudders and says his name over and over and over again.

"Kane." Persephone woke with a start, her body flooding with embarrassed heat when she sat up and saw Phoenix giving her a bemused look.

Her brother gestured with the TV remote. "You didn't tell me you had a boyfriend."

"He's not my boyfriend. He lives in my building. That's all." She got out of bed and went to the bathroom. She desperately wanted a glass of cold water, but the tap gave her only lukewarm and she wasn't sure she trusted drinking it, anyway. She settled for wetting a cleanish-looking washcloth and putting it on the back of her neck as she studied her face in the mirror. Through the door, she called out, "How long was I asleep?"

"Only about twenty minutes. You weren't snoring."

"I wasn't worried about snoring." She rolled her eyes. She was more worried she'd been moaning or something really embarrassing.

A knock at the door had her turning. She was expecting the mysterious Samantha, but when her brother opened the door, she saw a familiar face. Framed in the doorway, Kane looked taller and broader than she remembered him being, or perhaps that was because he looked so menacing. His head swung back and forth, gaze sweeping the room and taking in Phoenix, the pair of rumpled beds.

She should've been surprised to see him, perhaps even angry at this interference in her life, but instead relief swept over her in a wave so strong she had to put her hand on the bathroom door frame to keep herself from hurtling forward, across the room and into Kane's arms.

"Kane," she said.

Phoenix's head went up at once, his eyes narrowed. He took a step back as Kane moved forward, not trying to keep the other man from entering the room. He didn't have to do that physically. All he had to do was take control. He could only handle one person at a time, though.

"Persephone," Kane said without giving her brother so much as a second glance, clearly dismissing the threat. "Are you all right?"

She was all right, at least so far as she wasn't being harmed. But was she okay? Not really. Phoenix had forced her to come with him on this trip, and although he hadn't continued to control her every move, she wasn't here by choice.

"Tell him you're all right, sister mine."

"I'm all right," she said at once. No matter what she might have wanted to answer, her brother's words came out of her mouth.

"She's fine. You can leave now, whoever you are." Phoenix didn't say it as a command, which meant he was still bent on controlling Persephone.

Kane ignored Phoenix. "I went to your apartment. I was worried."

A flicker of heat lit inside her, low in her belly but growing upward beneath her heart. She'd known this man for a little over a year. She'd spent hours with him naked, but for all of them she'd been wearing the faces of other women. She'd cold-shouldered him with her own face, but here he was.

He'd come to save her.

Then she was stepping forward, one hand out, her mouth open. What she meant to say, she wasn't sure. She wanted to thank him, maybe. To be grateful that even though she wasn't in any true danger, he'd been worried enough to come after her and find her.

"Sister mine, it seems strange to me that this guy would have figured out where you were. You should ask him how he found you."

"How did you find me?"

Phoenix had not said aloud that she ought to stop moving toward Kane, but he didn't have to speak in order to control her. Her feet wanted to move but would not. She wanted to struggle, actually. To call her brother out and tell Kane what was really going on—but what stopped her from doing that was nothing her brother was doing. She didn't want to tell Kane that her brother could manipulate other people with his mind. He might think she was crazy.

Worse, he might believe her.

She didn't want to tell Kane that she and Phoenix had been conceived by a pack of insane cultists. She wanted him to keep looking at her the way he was now, as though she was exactly the treasure he'd been hunting. He wouldn't, if he knew the truth. Not only about her or about Phoenix, but the other truth, that she'd been sleeping with him for months without letting him know it was her.

"I looked on your computer," Kane said with a twist of his lips as though he knew the admission should embarrass him, but he was owning it, anyway. "I tracked your phone."

Phoenix curled his lip. "That sounds a little creepy."

"Yes," Persephone said because the tickling tendrils of her brother's control were twitching in her brain.

"Super creepy. What the hell? I told you, we're not friends."

I hate you, she thought at Phoenix. He couldn't read her thoughts exactly, but he would get the feeling of what she was trying to convey.

"We don't have to be friends for me to be concerned about you," Kane said.

"So you drove almost two hours to find her? My sister's fine," Phoenix said. "If you ask me, you going all alpha-male caveman on her isn't cool. Not at all."

Kane flicked a glance toward Phoenix, who was probably more angry that the other man had been ignoring him than by the fact he'd shown up in the first place. "I was concerned."

"You need to go," Persephone said. "I'm fine. I'm taking a road trip."

Kane fixed her with a look, then a stare around the room before fixing his gaze back on hers. "A road trip without your computer, without locking the door behind you? Without luggage?"

"We're free spirits. Damn you, Phoenix," she manage to bite out when her brother's mental puppet strings sagged for a split second. "We don't need to answer to anyone. I was tired of working in that building—damn it, Phoenix, why do you have to be such a…good… damn it…brother." *Asshole*, she thought vehemently even though her face betrayed no hint of her anger.

"That's fine," Kane said mildly. "I didn't mind the drive. I like road trips, too."

Another ripple of heat trickled through her. She knew Phoenix would feel it. He rolled his eyes at her. Truthfully, she felt a little exasperated with herself.

After so long fending off even the barest hint of interest Kane directed at her—at Persephone, not when she was in another guise—she didn't want to start getting all gooey about him now. Hell, the man had not only been concerned that something had happened to her, he'd tracked her down to rescue her. It might've made a girl cry, if she'd allowed herself to give in to emotion that way.

It might've made a girl fall in love.

"You can go. I'm really okay," she told him without needing any prompting or mental coercion from Phoenix. Kane needed to get the hell out of here before she lost her shit. "I'm sorry if I worried you. My brother came and got me and I just booked out of there because I... I didn't have anything there I cared enough about to take along."

Including you was the unspoken addition to that sentence, and she could see that Kane understood it. His lips pressed together, hard, and he nodded. He took a step backward, putting himself in the doorway again. He did not look at Phoenix. He looked at Persephone. That steely glare, the one that took in everything, that noticed everything, swept her up and down.

"I wanted to make sure you were safe," Kane said steadily. "I would do anything to make sure you hadn't come to harm."

Offer or threat, she wasn't sure and didn't care. The sentiment was enough to threaten to buckle her knees. The heat beneath her heart flashed upward to paint her cheeks. Her fingers curled, making fists at her sides. She swallowed hard, words fighting to break free but kept inside the prison of her mouth by her brother's insistence she remain silent.

"If you need me, all you have to do is call me," Kane said. "I'll be there."

Phoenix snorted. "How romantic. You can leave now."

The way Kane did immediately without so much as a single word more, even closing the door behind him, told Persephone her brother had something to do with it. Before she could move or say anything, though, Phoenix had the lock on her thoughts again. He didn't let her move.

"I'll hold you here until you convince me you're not going after him," he said calmly.

Persephone frowned. "I'm not going after him."

"I can smell it on you," her brother said. "You're way into him."

"I'm not," she protested.

The hold on her released. She did not go to the door or even the window next to it. She wanted to run after Kane and tell him to wait for her, but that wasn't going to do her any good. Besides, as angry as she might be about Phoenix forcing her to go with him, he wasn't wrong about everything. She did like road trips. She did like adventure. And there really wasn't anything to keep her in that apartment—except for Kane.

"Do you want to go after him, Persephone?" Phoenix sounded confused and a little upset. "Oh my God, you… You're in love with him!"

"Don't be stupid. I barely know him!"

Phoenix shook his head. "That's not how you feel about him."

"You know as well as I do that it doesn't matter," she retorted. "It's not going to happen. Anyway, he's a cop. A detective. What do you think he'd do if he knew about all the things I've done over the years?"

"It doesn't matter," Phoenix began, but there was no time for him to finish because the motel room door broke inward, splintering.

It was not Kane.

Chapter 10

Six of them, six against one. They weren't odds in Kane's favor, although that wouldn't have stopped him from trying. At least not if he'd had the chance, but he'd seen five of them heading toward him and had turned. Another had come up behind him and hit him over the back of the head while he stood in front of the motel room door wondering why the hell he'd immediately gone out, no protest, when Persephone's brother had told him to, and why it had felt like his brain was itching when he tried to resist.

He came to with more than an itch in his brain. His entire head felt like it was on fire, throbbing and aching. His fingers came away bloody when he felt the giant lump on the back of it.

"Shit." He spat, tasting copper. They'd rolled him,

all right. Taken everything in his pockets. Smashed his phone on the concrete. His keys were gone.

It hadn't been a gang attack, though. Those guys were military or at least something close to it, both by the way they'd been dressed and how efficiently they'd dropped him. Feeling like an idiot, Kane got to one knee on the cracked asphalt of the parking lot behind the dumpster where they'd dragged him. His head swam, but he pushed away the nausea and the pain.

He rounded the dumpster and came up short at the sight of a woman with blond hair pulled into a tight bun just coming out of the room Persephone and her brother had been using. Kane was already drawing his weapon. The way the woman came at him, he might have killed her if they both hadn't backed off at the same time, each of them breathing hard and on the defensive.

"Where did they go?" he barked.

The woman backed up a few steps, hands raised to show him she wasn't going to make any wrong moves. "I don't know. I'm Samantha. I was going to meet with Phoenix."

"I came to find out to make sure Persephone was all right." Kane lowered the gun. "The next thing I know, I'm standing outside the door and those goons are coming at me, and one of them hit me."

"You couldn't have known." Samantha put her hands on her hips and shook her head.

Kane's lip curled. "I should have known. I should've done better, anyway. Did they take them?"

"Yes. They would have." Samantha hesitated, eyeing him. "You have no idea who 'they' are, do you?"

"Not a one. You gonna tell me?" He gave her a small

grin. "I have no idea what the hell's going on, other than she's in some kind of trouble."

"You don't want to know. You should just walk away." Samantha gestured with a sigh, then frowned. "Damn it."

"I'm not walking away. I want to know who those guys were, why they took Persephone and her brother, where they took them, and how I can get her back."

Samantha eyed him. "Is she your girlfriend?"

"No."

"Huh." Her eyebrows lifted. "You have a savior complex?"

"No, not that. She was the super in my building and I…" Kane shrugged, meeting Samantha's gaze steadily but not returning her knowing grin. "We were friends. I wanted to be friends."

"You wanted to be more than friends," the woman told him with a shake of her head and a rueful chuckle that led him to believe she knew far more about the situation than she should have. "Take my advice. Get out of here and forget about Persephone. Definitely forget about her brother—he's even more trouble. Just get in your car and go far away. This isn't for you."

Irritated, Kane spat to the side. "No."

"Don't like being told what to do, huh? Can't say that I blame you. But this is a real true mess. Beyond your scope—"

"Try me," he said.

Samantha fixed him with a steady look, studying him. Whatever she saw must've convinced her, because she nodded. "I don't suppose you've ever heard of Wyrmwood?"

* * *

One of them had gone to his knees with his gun to his head before another had come up behind Phoenix and grabbed his arms. Persephone remembered that another had hit her brother on the head with the butt of a gun, knocking him out. It was the only reason why they'd been able to take him. She had been much easier to grab.

Persephone didn't know where they'd taken Phoenix, but she didn't think it had been far. She knew he wasn't dead, at least. That would've left an absence inside her that would've been impossible not to feel.

She was in the back of a van. Bars on the door. Plain benches on the inside. Manacles attached to the metal wall, although fortunately they hadn't shackled her. She was a little insulted they hadn't felt the need.

They'd been driving for what felt like an hour or so, over bumpy roads. She had to pee, desperately. Her stomach was growling. She could smell her own stink, sour breath and armpit sweat.

Kane wouldn't want her so much now, she thought and was surprised at her ability to laugh aloud. The chuckle swiftly became a sigh, and then a half-strangled sob. Not grief, exactly. Not sadness. A combination of both, for the opportunities lost to her. She was never going to see him again; she knew that as surely as she knew the set of armed brutes that had grabbed them were taking her someplace where the only reason there wouldn't be any bars on the windows would be because there weren't going to be any windows.

They were the same men who'd broken down the doors and come through the windows in the dining room where she and Phoenix and a dozen other of the

Collins Creek kids had been eating their daily dose of porridge laced with hallucinogens and other drugs. They'd come from the same place, anyway, even if they weren't likely to be the same exact men.

The table overturns. People are screaming. Persephone freezes, spoon in her hand. Phoenix is beside her. He takes her hand. He pulls her, making her do what he wants her to without tickling her brain the way he usually does. He doesn't have to—she's willing to follow him. Behind the table, a narrow space between it and the wall, they crouch and hide, quiet, so quiet.

The men have guns.

There is screaming and the stink of something like fire that burns her nose, makes her cough, makes her want to throw up. The table is shoved hard against them, trapping them. It bruises her ankle before she can pull it back. She's not crying, because Phoenix has her hand. As long as he's with her, Persephone isn't going to be afraid.

A man is there, wearing black. A mask. She's not scared of masks. The grown-ups here wear them all the time. She can wear one, too, whenever she likes. She's afraid of the gun in his hand, and the way he grabs at them both over the top edge of the overturned table.

"Go away!" Phoenix is pushing, pushing, he's not good enough yet, but he's afraid and this makes him stronger.

Persephone puts on another face. She is small but makes herself bigger, makes a beard and an old man face. The men with the guns want the kids, they're taking all the kids, so she makes herself something else. The man with the gun stumbles back.

*"Get out of here, leave us alone, tell the others
there's nobody back here!" Phoenix says in a voice
so hard Persephone thinks it could break bricks.*

*The man leaves them. Somehow, they're all right.
More screaming. Shooting. They find a way to run,
to get out. There are cars with lights, there are men
and women, there is lots of fighting, but they get out.
They get away.*

They run away.

Yet here she was now in the back of a van, being
taken someplace that would make the very worst days
on the street seem like a picnic. Persephone and Phoenix had heard stories over the years of what happened
to the ones from Collins Creek who were taken away,
and of those who were rounded up and also taken.
Phoenix didn't trust Vadim or the Crew, but Wyrmwood would be so much worse.

With a shudder, she shifted on the hard bench as
the van bounced. She had to grab one of the manacles
to keep herself from falling off. Wherever they were
taking her, they were doing it fast and without much
care about avoiding the potholes.

She let herself think of Kane again. He'd promised
he would come for her, but it was beyond stupid to
think he'd be able to. He would have no clue she'd really been taken this time. No way to find her.

He would not be coming to save her, yet somehow
Persephone clung to the hope that he would find a way.

Chapter 11

"They took my keys. We'll go in your car," Kane said, making it clear to Samantha that he had no intention of taking no for an answer.

She didn't argue, there was that, but she did insist on driving. "You have no idea where we're going "

"Do you?"

"I know where they're taking her, and I can drive fast enough to cut them off. I think," she said grimly as she slid into the passenger seat of the black sedan nobody would ever have been able to remember seeing. "Buckle up."

Kane did, securing a heavy-duty three-point belt over his lap and across his chest. He gave her a look as she put the car in gear. "Racetrack?"

"No. But I do drive fast." She gave him a sideways look and a laugh. "This car is made to go off road. It doesn't look like it, but it's been tricked out for defensive driving. Pursuit."

"Can you talk and drive without running us off the road?"

She nodded, casting a sharp but quick glance at him. "Yes. You want to know about Wyrmwood."

"Talk," Kane said.

She talked. She told him about the hospital whose patients never got better and left only when they were dead. The security precautions. The studies, the tests.

"And Collins Creek?" Kane asked as Samantha maneuvered the car along the winding backcountry roads with impressive skill that still had his heart jumping into his throat. "That's all real?"

"It's totally real. Those kids are real, but they're not kids anymore," she added, shifting.

Faster.

Darkness whipped past the windows. The road curved and dipped; they didn't slow down and caught some air on a small hill, the car landing with a thud that rattled his teeth, but Samantha didn't waver, and the car handled as smoothly as if they were puttering along going thirty on a highway as wide and flat as paper.

"I was trying to get some information from Phoenix about a… About someone I care about. He was one of the Collins Creek kids. They took him during the raid and kept him in Wyrmwood for years. Testing him. Using him. They almost broke him," she spat, voice cracking. "I was assigned to get him out of there."

"Who assigned you?" Kane thought he already knew.

"Guy named Vadim. He runs an organization called the Crew."

"Bald guy? Older? Speaks with an accent?" Kane asked.

"Yes. That's him. They help people like Persephone and Phoenix. Like Jed."

"Your friend."

"Yes." She shot him another glance and took a turn, tires squealing. The road here was gravel, and rocks flew up hard enough that Kane was sure the glass was going to break.

"But you didn't get him out?"

"I did," she said. "But I lost track of him. I thought Phoenix would be able to help me because—"

Before she could answer, Kane caught sight of headlights in the distance. Three vehicles, what looked like two unmarked black vans and a third car, also nondescript. Running parallel with them, trees between them, all he could glimpse was the flash of the lights. Samantha stomped on the gas pedal, gaining on them. The road they were on curved again. No longer parallel, they were on a direct course to collide with the first van.

Samantha didn't slow down.

One minute Persephone was bouncing around in the back of the van. The next, the entire world shrieked and clattered, and Persephone went flying upside down to land in a sprawl of arms and legs. The van rolled. Glass shattered, though none of it fell inside. Safety glass. The metal walls shuddered but didn't bend or break. She ended up on her side, the bench above her head, a swinging metal cuff narrowly missing her face.

Another crash jolted her. The van skidded, no longer on its tires. It slid with a squeal of metal on asphalt. Another crash—something else hit them. She tumbled, ending up on her hands and knees with a ringing in her ears so loud she wasn't sure she'd ever be able to hear again.

The door opened. Light spilled in, hurting her eyes. She managed to put a hand up to block it, seeing only a silhouette. A man stood over her, and she swatted at him knowing it wasn't going to be enough.

"It's me, Persephone. I'm here."

"Kane?"

"Can you get up?" Big, strong hands shifted under her elbow to help her.

She was already pushing upward. "Yeah."

"How bad are you hurt?"

"Bumps, bruises. Nothing's broken." She let him help her toward the door. Outside, the long, low bleat of a car horn droned. "How can nothing be broken?"

"Those vans are so armored nothing much could bust them up. The only thing I could do was knock them into each other." A female voice turned Persephone's face toward the sound. "I took a chance that you'd be okay."

There seemed like there should be a smart-ass answer to that, but Persephone couldn't quite manage it at the moment. She let herself sag in Kane's grasp as he helped her out of the van. She didn't think she meant to kiss him, but that was what happened. Hard, almost an assault rather than an embrace, but on the mouth.

"Can you run?" he asked when he pulled away. "We have to run."

"Yes. I think so."

The three of them took off across the rural highway,

but when they reached the edge of the woods, Persephone hung back. "Phoenix!"

"He's not in there," the woman said. "We checked. He wasn't in the car, either. And the gas I used on them won't last much longer. We have to run. I've already called for a pickup."

This had to be something out of a sci-fi movie, right? One of the cheesy ones about killer octopuses in hurricanes or something like that. The woman had just said she wrecked vans full of solider guys with guns and then gassed them, and someone was coming to pick them up?

"In a spaceship?" Persephone's words were suddenly slurred. She must've knocked her head harder than she thought.

"I got you" was the last thing she heard before it all went dark.

Kane caught Persephone before she could fall. Behind them, the noises of the wreckage were getting fainter, but there was no way they could keep up running this fast for much longer, especially when he had to carry Persephone. Samantha pointed to a small dirt trail in the woods ahead of them.

"There."

"You have to be kidding me." Kane shifted Persephone's slight weight, certain he was causing her some kind of permanent damage. No way had she come out of that crash without some serious injuries, maybe internal bleeding. Something.

Two black cars were waiting for them. Samantha got behind the wheel of the second one, waving him toward the backseat. He laid Persephone gently inside then followed, closing the door as Samantha pulled away. A man sat in the front seat, and he twisted to look behind them.

"Vadim," Kane said as he buckled Persephone into her seat, then focused on his own belt. "The Crew. Right? This is all insane."

"It is a methodical madness, I can assure you. Samantha, are you sure you can drive? You didn't get hurt in the crash?"

She shook her head. "Nothing too bad. That car was like a tank, and we hit that first van like a freight train. Thanks, Vadim. Everything worked like we'd planned."

"Wait, wait, what the hell? You planned this?" Kane was ready to reach across the front seat and throttle someone, but that would've meant one more wreck, and he wasn't so sure he'd make it through another.

"Not this whole thing, but the possibility of it. The eventuality of what might happen. We didn't plan for Persephone to be taken, nor her brother. So you can rethink threatening me." Vadim glanced into the backseat. "It's always been a possibility that Phoenix and his sister might be found. They both knew it. They're fortunate he'd already arranged a meeting with Samantha tonight, or else there would've been nobody to go after them."

"She had me," Kane said. He couldn't see if Persephone was bleeding anywhere, he didn't have enough light, but he had to hope that they were taking them somewhere to get medical help.

"Ah yes. She had you." Vadim's voice held a smile. "Lucky girl."

Kane leaned back into the seat. "I still don't know what the hell is going on. All of this."

"And you don't trust me. Nor should you, I suppose. I wouldn't if I were you. All I can tell you is the same thing I said the first time we met. I intend no harm to Persephone. You and I are on the same side. In fact, based on how you reacted during this entire situation, I think it might benefit us to offer you a position on our team."

"The Crew." Kane didn't want to close his eyes, but the pain was making him see double. Samantha had been right about the car she'd been driving; it had been enough like a tank that they were hardly affected by running straight into the side of a van. Still, it had been a long damned night and everything hurt, including his brain from trying to process all of this. "Whatever the hell that is."

"We'll tell you all about it when we get to a safe place."

"Isn't Wyrmwood or whatever the hell it is going to be after us? Shit," Kane said wearily. "Did you just piss off some kind of secret government facility? Am I on the run now, too?"

Vadim chuckled. "I daresay your name has indeed been put on a shit list of some kind. So the answer is yes. This is not to say that you can't return to your normal civilian life, of course. I supposed you could try it. See what happens."

"You're not worried about yourself?"

Another chuckle. "Oh… Wyrmwood has its methods, and it would not be impossible for them, certainly, to find us. Harm us. But to be honest, Mr. Dennis, the amount of bureaucracy and paperwork required to put together a group even as small as the one tonight is fairly enormous. There've been budget cuts. The economy isn't what it used to be. Wyrmwood is a privately run organization that answers to a board of directors."

"They're afraid of us," Samantha put in.

Kane opened his eyes. She still followed the other black car, but they were both driving on a regular highway at normal speed. He looked behind them, but nothing was back there except the night.

"I can see that," he said.

Vadim laughed. Their eyes met in the rearview mirror, and his gaze softened when he looked at Persephone. "She'll be all right. We'll take care of her."

Somehow, Kane believed him.

Chapter 12

Safety and comfort. The warmth of a body beside hers, not for a few hours but for the night. Waking up next to someone who would make sure she was all right.

It had to be a dream, Persephone thought without opening her eyes. Her entire body ached. She remembered the shitty motel. Men with guns. The van.

She remembered Kane.

It hurt to sit, but she did, noting that she wore the same dirty, torn-up clothes she'd had on the last time she remembered anything. The bed was big, soft, covered in a plain dark blue quilt. Kane was beside her, but he wore a pair of flannel pajama pants. No shirt.

His bare chest, she thought with something like wonder, her fingers uncurling to touch him before she stopped herself. How many times had she already run her hands over that skin? Those places that made him sigh? The scars, she remembered as she forced herself not to move in case she woke him up.

She felt the warmth of his gaze on her before she looked into his eyes. "Hey."

"Hey." Kane sat up with a wince. "How are you feeling?"

"Bumped up. But okay, other than that." She tested her arms and legs gently, but aside from a lot of achiness, nothing seemed too messed up. She drew her knees closer to her chest as she looked at him. "You?"

He yawned. Winced. Stretched. "I'm good, all things considered."

"You kept your word," Persephone said quietly.

Kane nodded. "I did."

"That has not been my previous experience with humans of the male persuasion," she said. Trying to be light about it. Funny, even. The fact that her voice cracked a bit on the words didn't help.

Kane reached to draw a fingertip along her arm, stopping at the back of her wrist before he took his touch away. "I'm sorry."

She closed her eyes. "Where's my brother?"

"We don't know. Vadim thinks he got away before Samantha ran into the side of the van."

She didn't look at him but nodded. "That could be true."

"He wasn't in the van with you when we got you out, or the other one, either." Kane shifted, dipping the mattress.

She opened her eyes then. "He got away, though."

"They're pretty sure he did. Yes."

"But he left me behind."

"I'm sorry," Kane said again, this time with a frown

and a furrow of his brow. "But yeah. It looks like he did."

She could've been upset about it, if Phoenix had not in the past proven himself to be totally capable of ditching her to save his own skin. She shrugged. "It wasn't the first time."

"Still." Kane looked as though he meant to touch her again, but didn't.

She wanted him to.

Suddenly it was all she could think about. She ran her tongue over her teeth, wincing at the sour taste. She glanced around the room, which was neat but sparsely furnished. It had no windows, but nothing about it felt oppressive. Through a half-open door she spotted a bathroom.

"I need a shower," she said.

"They left clothes for you." Kane gestured at the dresser in the corner. "Towels and everything are in there. They thought of everything."

"Are they keeping us here?" She could see another door, but it was closed. Could be locked, for all she knew.

"No. We don't have to stay. I did to make sure you were all right."

The question rose to her lips, but she kept herself from asking it. The shower was gloriously hot and the water pressure fantastic. She found an array of soaps and shampoos and spent the time scrubbing up quickly but thoroughly. She even shaved.

She thought he might be gone when she came out of the bathroom, but Kane had lain back down on the pillow, his eyes closed. Persephone wore only a towel when she went around the bed to his side. She waited for him to look at her.

When he did, she let the towel fall to her feet. She lifted her chin, meeting his gaze straight on, even when his dropped from her eyes to her body. Hers, not some illusion or mirage. The desire to change herself to be thinner, have bigger boobs, be prettier…she fought it. She kept herself as she was.

Kane reached for her, and she let him. He pulled her onto the bed and rolled them both so he was on top of her, bare skin to skin above, the thin flannel of his pajama pants a teasing barrier below. He rocked against her, already getting hard.

He kissed her, and Persephone breathed a small cry into his mouth. His tongue stroked hers. Their teeth bumped, and she laughed. He kissed her again, softer this time. His big hand came up to brush through her still-wet hair. The other cupped her breast, flicking her nipple expertly until she moaned. At the sound of it, Kane buried his face against the side of her neck and shifted to get his hand between them.

It should've been too fast. She should've needed something more than this, but she was already cresting when he slid his fingers against her. Then inside her, dipping into her ready wetness and pulling out to use them on her clit.

Persephone muttered a curse. Then his name. Without thinking, she put a hand on his head, desperate and eager for his mouth between her legs. With only the briefest hesitation, Kane slid lower.

She was wordless at the stroke of his tongue against her. Inarticulate, groaning, Persephone lifted her hips to press herself harder to the tantalizing pressure of his lips and tongue. She arched, giving herself up to this pleasure.

He hummed against her, then stopped. She looked down at him, her vision a little blurry with lust, but not so hazy that she couldn't see his look of surprise. He bent again to sample her, again with an appreciative hum. Kane slid both hands under her ass to pull her closer. He feasted, licking and nibbling and sucking until she couldn't stop herself, couldn't hold back. Desire consumed her. Kane waited for the aftershocks to fade, his mouth still covering her, then slid up her body to kiss her mouth.

Somewhere along the way he'd shed his pajama bottoms and now pressed against her. Heat and hardness. The head of his cock brushed her inner thigh, and Persephone shifted to open for him. She looked up to see him looking down at her. She had never been the sort to cuddle after coming. Never the girl to tenderly touch her lover's face. She was now.

"What?" she whispered.

"I don't have anything."

He meant condoms. Of course. Why would he, here? And she knew him well enough to remember that he never, ever went without one.

She reached between them to take his cock in her fist. "Let me use my mouth."

He shuddered when she said it. Closed his eyes. His lips parted on a moan. "Oh, fuck, yes…please."

She was more than happy to slide down his body, turning them both so that she was on top. Gently, she took his length inside her. The head of his cock nudged the back of her throat before she released him as slowly as she'd taken him in. She savored him. Pleasured him.

At the touch of his hand on the back of her head, not pushing but encouraging her, she took him deep again. Her own desire grew again, an ache spreading throughout her body. With one hand on his shaft as she sucked him, Persephone slipped her other hand between her legs.

She was so wet her fingers slid without friction over her clit, which was still swollen and sensitive. She wasn't intent on getting herself off, because she wanted to concentrate on him, but still, it felt so good that she found herself rocking her hips as she circled her clit.

It took Kane only moments to reach the edge. His cock throbbed hard in her mouth as she eased off. She meant to make it last, but at his desperate groan, Persephone smiled and bent back to him. He began thrusting into her mouth. The sweet-salty flavor of his honey urged her own moan as she tasted how close he was. It pushed her closer to her own climax. They moved together. Pleasure overtook her. She couldn't do anything but ride it, the sweeping waves of orgasm shuddering through her and the tense pulsing of his cock into her mouth. She swallowed, and again, craving every single drop of his desire.

His hand fell away from her hair. Spent, Persephone rolled onto her back to stare up at the ceiling. She wiped her lips with her fingertips, her other hand still feeling the aftershocks of her orgasm.

Silence.

Kane rolled toward her, tugging on her shoulder until she moved up the bed to face him. She thought he might say something, but instead he studied her face with a small frown. Persephone waited, content to watch him looking her over as though it was the first time he'd seen her. Maybe, in a way, it was. It sure felt like she was looking at him with new eyes.

"Are we friends now?" he asked finally.

She smiled. "Yeah. We're friends."

Chapter 13

There hadn't been much for Kane to leave behind, which said a lot about his life. There were people who would miss him, but Vadim had assured him someone from the Crew was working on explanations for everyone. It wasn't like going into the witness protection program or anything. He wouldn't have to miss going to his mother's house for Christmas.

He did need to decide if he was going to stay on and work for this group, though. It seemed like a no-brainer, based on the salary Vadim had offered. The benefits. The work itself didn't seem much different than what he'd been doing before. Researching cases. Putting pieces together. Proving or disproving things. It was just that now, instead of figuring out who done it, Kane would be tasked with figuring out *what* done it.

He'd never been a man to believe in aliens or werewolves, but that didn't mean he hadn't ever thought about the possibilities. If anything, he was more likely to accept the existence of what he'd always thought of as monsters and Vadim had called cryptozoological creatures. Chupacabra, Kane thought with a small laugh. Sasquatch.

Still, he hadn't yet confirmed he was going to sign on. He wasn't scared of the danger. He wasn't worried about not being able to talk about his real work, or living with secrets. No, the only thing holding him back was her.

Persephone.

He was so far from understanding all of her, but at least he'd gotten a good look at the background. Vadim had given him access to all the files they had on Collins Creek. The rumors and stories Kane had found on the internet had been only half-true. What had gone on there had been horrifying, from the active use of psychedelic drugs and other tortures in order to create what they thought would be superchildren… It had turned his stomach, but it explained so much about the woman who'd so intrigued him for the past year.

Kane didn't like thinking that Persephone had gone to bed with him out of some misguided sense of gratitude, but he knew it was the most likely explanation. She'd been a little distant since then, and because she'd been cleared by the staff doctor in this Crew facility, there had been no real need for him to continue sharing her room when he'd been given his own. He might not know her entirely, but he did know her well enough not to push the offer of his protection.

He wanted her to want him. He wanted her to need him. He did not want her to feel obligated to him.

Phoenix had disappeared, no trace, but Persephone didn't seem worried. She said she could sense that he was still alive, at least. Vadim had said they were tracking him down, trying to find out if he'd been taken to Wyrmwood or had indeed managed to get away.

There was one set of files Kane had not yet read, and they belonged to Persephone, personally. There were a few dozen documents labeled with her name, but although Vadim had given him permission to view them, it hadn't felt right. He wanted to ask her if it was okay.

He didn't find her in the cafeteria or the rec room, and she didn't answer her door when he knocked. He went to the library next, a vast room lined with floor-to-ceiling shelves and more books than anyone could ever read in a lifetime. She was curled up in an overstuffed leather chair with a hardbound volume on her lap, her brow furrowed in concentration and the pink tip of her tongue peeking occasionally from between her lips. She was so beautiful it made his heart hurt.

"Hey," he said.

She looked up, her gaze at first wary and then softening when she saw him. "Hey."

"Can we talk?"

She frowned, probably thinking he was going to try to have some big-deal discussion about "them" or something, he thought and almost laughed. Having been on the receiving end of a number of those talks, he understood her trepidation. She put her book aside, though, and sat up.

"Sure," she said hesitantly. "Here?"

"Here's fine. I just wanted to know if it would be all right with you if I read the files Vadim has on you."

Persephone's strawberry blond brows rose to meet the edges of her hairline. "I guess so?"

"You knew he had them, right?" Kane lowered his voice out of deference to being in the library.

"I figured, but I just thought you'd have already looked at them." Persephone's lips pursed and her eyes narrowed for a moment before she blinked rapidly and looked away from. Her shoulders lifted and fell, and she cleared her throat before looking back at him with glistening eyes. "I assumed you would have already looked."

"I didn't want to do it without your permission. All of this has been weird. I didn't want to make it any stranger," Kane said.

She got to her feet then, the book forgotten. She had to stand on her tiptoes to get to his mouth, but the soft kiss she brushed over his lips made him smile. She smiled, too. She touched his cheek for a second or so, her gaze searching his, but what she saw inside it didn't seem to reassure her.

"Sure. Read the files," she said. "I'll be in my room when you're done."

She kissed him again, a little harder this time, and on the corner of his mouth. She pushed past him, her book in hand, and left him in the library. He watched her walk away without looking back. Then he went to one of the computer kiosks and typed in the credentials Vadim had provided for him. In seconds, Persephone's files were on the screen. He started to read.

The criminal activities didn't surprise him. Neither did the sex work. It didn't bother him, even if it should have because his job had been arresting people who broke the law. None of that seemed to matter now, and besides, with a history like hers, he was surprised she hadn't turned to worse vices.

When he learned what she could do, however, he sat back in his seat with a thick feeling of unease in his throat. He'd felt firsthand what it had been like when Phoenix had used his talents to send him out of the motel room, so he could believe everything he'd read in the files was true. He didn't want to believe it of her, but he knew Persephone had also used her talents on him.

The knock at her door had her heart leaping into her throat, and Persephone considered pretending she hadn't heard it. That wouldn't make him go away, though. She opened her door to let Kane step through it, then closed it behind him.

"It was you—all of them were you," he said in a low voice. Not looking at her. "For how long?"

She didn't try to lie about it. "Almost a year. The first time was at a dance club. I'd gone out with my friend Leila and saw you there. And I…"

"You what?" His voice deepened, hard. So did his gaze, turning intense and cold, spearing her. "You thought I'd be another mark? You targeted me? Were you disappointed when you found out I don't have any money or anything to steal?"

"It wasn't for that reason," she told him. "I hadn't been to bed with anyone for a while and I was… I liked you. I liked the way you look."

Kane's lip curled a little bit. "But why trick me? Then and every time after? It was a dozen times, wasn't it? My God, was it you every single time?"

"I have no idea," Persephone snapped, knowing

she had no real right to be irritable with him but feeling defensive, anyway. "I didn't keep track of all the women you brought home. I'm sure there were more than just me."

"Maybe. But at least none of them lied to me."

She snorted derision. "They *all* probably lied to you, Kane."

"Not the way you did." He said the words as though he meant them to sound angry, but they came out rich with disappointment.

That was worse. Fury she could deflect. Looking into his eyes and knowing that she'd hurt him was a much heavier burden to bear. Persephone swallowed the lump of emotion trying to strangle her.

"How did you know?"

"It was the way you tasted. Here, in your bed. You were the brunette that last time. I remembered."

"The one you kicked out," she said, remembering how his mouth between her thighs had made her lose herself so hard she'd let the mirage waver. So he *had* seen it. "Why?"

"Because I wanted her to be you," Kane said. "Damn it, Persephone, from the first time I saw you, I wanted it to be you."

"It was me!" she cried. "No matter what face or body I was showing you, Kane, they were all me."

"But why trick me? Why lie? Why not just…you knew I wanted you. And you just kept shoving me away!"

She backed away from him to pace. "I couldn't trust you. I don't expect you to forgive me, but I hope you can understand why."

"Damn it," he said and trailed off.

She looked at him. "I'm so sorry, Kane. That first time was on a whim. I was lonely and horny and you looked so good to me. Every time I saw you, I wanted to see more of you."

"Do you still feel that way?"

She drew in a breath, one after another, until she could answer him without her voice breaking. "Yes."

"Do you trust me now?"

Her laugh glittered with sobs. "Yes. Of course I do now. You know everything about me. I wouldn't blame you if you didn't want to have anything to do with me."

"That's just it. I want to have everything to do with you. All of it. I should be angry with you," Kane said. "I should feel like you played me for a fool. I should walk away from you and never bother with you again."

"You should," she agreed, risking a step closer. "I wouldn't blame you if you did."

With a low growl, Kane reached for her. She let him grab her, gladly. She let him kiss her. When he scooped her up and took her to the bed, she let him do that, too. They were naked in minutes.

"I have condoms in the drawer," she gasped when his hand moved between her legs.

"Not just yet," Kane said with a wicked grin. "I'm going to taste you first."

She groaned, arching beneath his touch. "So you can be sure it's me?"

"I always knew, somehow," he said against her skin, his lips teasing. Tongue tasting. "I'm not sure how I knew, but I think I must have always known it was you, every time."

Persephone arched, writhing in his embrace. Her fingers threaded through his thick dark hair, tugging his head until he looked up at her. She pulled him up to kiss her mouth. "I can be whoever you want, Kane, you know that? Any time you want. It will still always be me."

"Good," he said as his fingers continued to work the magic his mouth had begun. "Because you're the only one I want."

* * * * *

UNEXPECTED PASSION

Megan Hart

Chapter 1

Willa Ambrose was absolutely not in the mood for crap from anyone. She'd spent the first twelve hours of her day on her feet at the library and the last forty minutes trying to get home through terrible traffic, construction and the sheer stupidity of people who couldn't figure out how to drive in bad weather. By the time she got to the grocery store, she'd had it up to her eyebrows with humanity. Therefore, of course, she'd bumped into—literally—someone guaranteed to set her teeth on edge.

Babs Miller. Perfectly coiffed, exquisitely attired, particularly bitchy. She stood blocking the cereal aisle while she scrolled on her phone. Babs needed to move her sculpted butt cheeks out of the way or Willa was going to have to throw down in the middle of Pappy's Market, and it was not going to be pretty.

"Excuse me," Willa said.

Babs didn't notice. She laughed at something on her phone and took her sweet time typing out a reply, all the while still with her cart completely blocking the way for anyone who needed to get to the Captain's Cocoa Bits. Typical Babs, who probably wouldn't have been caught dead eating sugary cereal, Willa thought as she eyed the contents of the other woman's cart. Bunch of pricey grains and flavored coffee creamers in there, but not much that looked like it would taste very good.

"Excuse me," Willa said again, louder this time.

Babe glanced up. "Just a sec."

"No more secs," Willa said. "I need to get past you!"

Babs looked up then, gracing Willa with a glare that showed she was clearly disgruntled at being asked to consider the needs of someone else. Willa braced herself for the cutting comment the other woman looked ready to deliver. Before Babs uttered a word, she let out a small, surprised *oof.*

She moved the cart.

"I'm so sorry, so sorry," she said in a strained voice not at all like her usual tone. "I'll get out of your way right now. And here, I have this gift card in my purse, why don't you take it. It should cover the cost of your order, plus some extra. You're not buying that much. Let me give it to you as an apology for being so inconsiderate."

Willa was stunned into silence as Babs did indeed reach into her bag to pull out a small plastic card emblazoned with the Pappy's Market logo. "You don't have to—"

"I do, I certainly do, I've been blocking the aisle

here for the past twenty minutes while I answered messages on this dating app," Babs said. "Not that it's working. The only guys who message me are losers. I'm going to die alone, with nothing but a dozen cats and a collection of vibrators that do strange things to my ass."

With that, Babs stepped aside to give Willa room to pass. There seemed to be something Willa ought to say to all of that truth tea Babs had just spilled all over the place, but words escaped her. She gave the other woman a firm nod and pushed her cart toward the bins of bagged cereal. She gave a glance over her shoulder as Babs pushed her cart away, muttering. With a shake of her head, Willa plucked out a bulk bag of Captain's Cocoa Bits to toss into her cart.

When she looked up, a tall, lean man with a mass of red-gold hair tied at the nape of his neck was smiling at her. He looked into her cart. Then at her.

"It's the last one," Willa said. "But they have plenty of Snappy Crisps or Cinnamon Squares."

The man laughed. "I don't really need any cereal, thanks. I was just getting what's-her-face out of your way so you could get what you wanted."

"Uh-huh." Willa eyed him, ready to back up quickly if she had to. "You did that? Sure."

"I did," he said in a low voice, leaning a little closer. "You're welcome."

She laughed, strangely not put off by him even though she should've been. "How'd you manage to do that?"

"I have a way of getting people to do what I want them to." He looked into her cart again. "You could give me those Captain's Cocoa Bits, if you wanted to."

Her hand was on the package and lifting it before she stopped herself with a self-conscious laugh. "And if I don't want to?"

"Then you won't, obviously." The man smiled again, although this time it seemed more as though he were studying her. Like she'd done something interesting, and he was trying to figure her out.

The sensation was a little unsettling. She studied him right back, noticing again the red-gold fall of hair, longer even than her own shoulder-length dark brown cut. He had greenish eyes with dark lashes and crinkles at the corners, and a slightly crooked front tooth. Broad shoulders. Lean build. He wore a pair of faded jeans and a long-sleeved thermal shirt. No coat. Lace-up leather work boots, battered. She hadn't seen him around town, and in a place the size of Penn's Grove, that meant he was from out of town. A stranger—unusual. Intriguing.

"You're one who pays attention," he said, catching her eye when she looked up at him.

Willa laughed. "Yeah. Sorry. You're not from here."

"Passing through, that's all. Stopped here at Pappy's to stock up on toaster pastries and granola bars. The usual food for bachelors." He shrugged and held out a hand. "I'm Phoenix."

"Willa." His fingers were strong, his grip firm. Despite the flirty way he'd been addressing her, there wasn't anything creepy about the way he shook her hand. "Phoenix is an unusual name."

"So is Willa," he said with a grin. "Aren't we a pair?"

She realized he was still holding her hand, and she

took it gently away. "It was nice meeting you. Thanks for getting Babs out of the way."

"Sure. My pleasure." He took a couple steps back so she could move around him.

He was watching her as she got to the end of the aisle; she could feel it. Something made her turn before she rounded the corner. He was still there.

"Let's say you *could* make people do what you want them to do," she said lightly. "Why on earth would you have done that for me?"

"I heard you say 'no more sex,'" he said with a tilted grin, "and I knew there was no way I could let that happen for you."

In a world of catcalls, lewd gestures and unsolicited dick pics, his words were still verging on the edge of unacceptable—and yet Willa laughed. Loud. Hard. A short, sharp burst of hilarity wiped away all the anger and annoyances she'd had that day, leaving her with a grin that almost but not quite matched his.

"Thanks for looking out for me," she told him, and with a tip of her chin, she headed off to the register to pay for her groceries.

Penn's Grove was not quite the armpit of America, but it was close. Phoenix had heard of one-stoplight towns before, but he'd never actually believed they existed. Penn's Grove was such a place, one traffic light in the center of Main Street. It had a grocery store. It had houses and farms and a school. It didn't have much else, but that's what made it a perfect place to hide.

He wasn't going to last here much longer, though. Not without losing a large portion of what remained of his mind, and there wasn't that much there to begin with. Not for the first time since running from the men who'd tried to kidnap him and his sister, Phoenix wondered if spending the rest of his life always looking over his shoulder was better than signing up with the Crew the way Persephone had.

Yeah, he knew she'd done it. They had a connection that went beyond the talents they'd each been born with. Maybe because they were twins. Whatever it was, he knew if she was in trouble, and although he'd had a few waves of emotional upheaval from her over the past few months, it had more to do with the fact she'd fallen head over heels in love with the cop from her apartment building, not because she was in any kind of personal danger. Phoenix could've tried to save her from a lot of things, but he couldn't save her from love.

He knew she worried about him. He'd risked contacting her, just the once, a couple months after leaving her behind. He knew she'd forgive him for it—she'd had the cop with her, and Persephone had never hated the idea of joining the Crew as much as Phoenix had. She was all right. He was going to be all right, too, he told himself as he looked out the window at the falling snow covering the narrow alley behind the house he'd been renting.

The woman he'd met in the market earlier tonight was struggling with her trash can. Willa, he remembered. She'd been having a rough day. That irritating woman Babs had been in her way. He'd nudged Babs to move. Okay, so he'd done more than nudge. He'd mentally shoved her hard enough to leave her numb for a few hours, but damn, she'd been so absorbed in herself that he'd had to push that hard. He'd added the urge to spill her guts just so she'd embarrass herself.

It was far from the worst thing he'd ever had someone do, and besides, Phoenix had always thought people that irritating deserved to be manipulated into doing stuff that made them look dumb.

He'd already known Willa, of course, even though he was a stranger to her. He'd seen her from this window every single day, morning and night, for the past four months. She'd never spotted him because he'd barely come out of the house. Bumping into her in the market couldn't even be considered a coincidence, since Pappy's was the only place in town to buy groceries, so seeing her there was no shock.

What had surprised him was the way she'd been able to resist him when he'd nudged her to give him the cereal. He hadn't wanted it, not really. He'd done it as a test to see what he could poke her into doing for him.

Willa had resisted.

It wasn't the words he used that turned people into puppets, it was something different, something deep inside his mind that Phoenix had never and probably would never understand. Like flexing a muscle—you didn't think consciously about it. You just did it.

However, Willa had not done as he'd nudged her to do. She'd been about to, her hand on the cereal bag and her intention to follow his desire obvious. Yet at the last moment, she hadn't done it. Nobody had ever resisted him before. He supposed it was possible there were lots of people in the world who'd be able to, but Willa was the first person who ever had.

He watched her now, struggling with the metal trash pail she was trying to empty into the dumpster. She wore a pair of fleecy pajama bottoms beneath a heavy parka, her feet shoved into oversize winter boots that nevertheless were slipping in the mess of slushy ice. Before he'd quite decided to do it, he was ducking out the back door and down the alley. She looked up, startled and wary at the sight of him. He couldn't blame her. If she knew who he was and the things he'd done, she'd have run screaming.

"Sorry," he said smoothly, with a jerk of his thumb toward the house. "I live next door. Saw you might need a hand."

"I'm fine."

He watched her struggle with the pail again, her boots slipping in the muck. There was no way she was going to get the leverage to lift it into the dumpster. "I'm happy to help you, Willa."

She looked at him, eyes narrowed. Mouth thin, nothing like the smile she'd given him earlier in the market. "I said I'm fine."

"You should really let me help you," Phoenix said with a nudge.

Willa tensed visibly. Her frown deepened. "Look, I said I was fine. I don't need you to—"

With an easy reach, he snagged the can from her and lifted it, using his other hand to flip open the dumpster lid. He emptied her pail into it and handed it back as he closed the lid. Grinning, he waited for her to thank him. Ladies almost always did when he pulled that he-man trick. They went all fluttery lashes and heaving bosoms and usually invited him back to their boudoirs to show their gratitude. Not that he was going to go to bed with her, he thought, since they were neighbors and he was in Penn's Grove to hide out—not to get involved with someone he couldn't leave behind the next morning.

Willa didn't. "Wow."

"Wow?" Phoenix hesitated. He hadn't thrown on a coat before running out here, and he was starting to get cold. The hems of his jeans were soaked. And she was looking at him like he'd handed her a package of dog poop.

"I don't need a knight in shining armor." Willa looked him up and down, but instead of her eyes glowing with desire, she was barely concealing a sneer of disdain. Strike that. She was absolutely not concealing it—she was full-on sneering.

Phoenix, stung, tossed up his hands. "I was being nice!"

"You're being...weird!" Willa said with a glance over his shoulder toward his house, which was connected to hers. "I've never seen you here before."

"I haven't lived here very long."

"I've never seen you anywhere before tonight at Pappy's. Penn's Grove is a very small town." She took a step backward, keeping the pail between them.

"Hey, I'm sorry." He backed up a few steps, making himself less of a threat. "Really, I was only trying to help."

"Were you spying on me?"

"No, I was just looking out my window and I saw you, I thought you could use a hand. That's all. Truly." Contrite, uncertain what had made her react so strongly, he consciously made himself smaller and less of a threat. Without thinking, he nudged her again, trying to get her to trust that he meant no harm.

The nudge had the opposite effect. Willa winced again, her expression darkening further. "I didn't. I don't. I'm fine."

"Okay. You're fine." Phoenix didn't try to argue

with her any further. He turned and walked away, hopping up the steps of his rented house with a backward glance at her. She'd already gone inside.

He'd really screwed that up, he thought, not sure how. Not sure why it mattered. Only that suddenly, it did.

Chapter 2

Willa had had the whole world to live in, but she'd chosen to stay here in Penn's Grove. She wasn't a fan of regretting life choices, but on days like this, she did allow herself to think about what her life might've been like if she'd gone away. She would be too far from her parents to help take care of them. Too far from her nieces and nephews to go to their school concerts and soccer games. She wouldn't run into her old elementary and high school acquaintances who'd grown up and had families of their own.

She wouldn't run into *him*.

She could have run away from Penn's Grove, but she'd stayed, and that had been braver choice. It didn't even bother her that much anymore when Brady Singer came into the library with his kids, or that his gaze skated over her behind the checkout desk without so much as a flicker of recognition. It was better than the times when he paid attention to her.

Today, with the snow falling thick outside, she hadn't expected a lot of patrons in the library. The early dismissal for the kids had brought a number of people to grab books and movies to keep them entertained, but that had been before the storm really began. She'd been looking out the window of her office, noticing the darkening sky and considering closing early, when the familiar SUV pulled into the parking lot and Brady got out with the three mini versions of himself. The kids had spent the past twenty minutes searching the stacks for books while their father waited impatiently at one of the computer desks, drumming his fingers.

Kathy hadn't made it in to work today, and Willa had already sent Tom home in advance of the bad weather, so it was up to her to check out their books. She waited in her office for them to come to the desk, greeting each of the boys with a smile and a comment on their choices. It wasn't their fault their father was an asshole.

"Come on," Brady said from behind the youngest boy, Tyler. "Move it. I want to get home before the roads get any worse."

His pale blue eyes flicked in Willa's direction, but she made sure not to meet his gaze head-on. They'd long ago come to the unspoken but mutual agreement that neither would acknowledge the other unless it was absolutely necessary, and even then it had become like speaking to a stranger. She checked out what Curt, the oldest boy, had chosen and handed them back. When she got to the middle boy, Parker, however, she frowned.

"Sorry, there's an outstanding fine for you, kiddo. You can't check out any new books until this has been taken care of." She tilted the computer screen so he could see the book and the amount.

"Son of a bitch," Brady said. "Damn it, Parker. How much is it?"

She cleared her throat, showing him the screen even though he wasn't looking at it. "It's twenty-seven dollars. Is it possible you maybe lost the book?"

"Did you lose it?" Brady cuffed the back of Parker's head.

The kid winced away from the slap. "No, Dad. I turned it in."

Brady fixed Willa with a cold stare. "Kid says he turned it in. Take off the fine."

"I can't just…" She could, of course, just remove the fine from the system. That it had gotten so high in the first place was a surprise, but Brady and the boys hadn't been in to the library in months, so there wasn't any way she'd have seen it before today.

A shift of motion behind them caught her attention. The front doors had swung open, admitting that guy from the market. Her neighbor with the white knight complex and the unusual name. He looked as surprised to see her as she was to see him.

Brady snapped his fingers in her face. "Eyes on me, hello. I told you to take care of this fine so we can get out of here."

"I can't just take the fine off, I have to list the book as lost, and if the price of the book is more than the fine you'll have to make up the difference before he can check out more books," Willa said calmly. Under other circumstances, she might have agreed to help. The finger snapping had done it for her.

"Are you fucking kidding me?"

Phoenix had been standing quietly behind Brady, but now he tapped the other guy on the shoulder. "Hey. Watch the profanity. There are kids here."

"They're my kids, and I'll say whatever the fuck I want in front of them," Brady said. "Or you. Back off."

Before Willa could say a word, Phoenix let out a low chuckle and shook his head. Snow was still melting in the red-gold lengths of his hair, which today tumbled over his shoulders and halfway down his back. He sported a few days' growth on his cheeks and chin, too. Dressed in a plaid flannel shirt, jeans and work boots, and again no coat, he was rocking the lumberjack look.

To Willa, he said, "If they pay the fine, the kid gets to take out books again?"

"Yes. And if they find the book, they keep it."

"Just pay her and be done with it, man," Phoenix said to Brady. "Why give her a hard time about it?"

Because he could, she thought with a glance at the man who'd made her life hell. Brady was looking back at her, gaze steely. She waited for him to go off, but instead he pulled out his wallet and flipped a couple of twenties over the counter toward her. Willa took the money before it could fall.

"Keep the change," Brady said.

I can make people do what I want them to do.

Phoenix's words echoed in her head as she scanned the rest of the library books and watched Brady and his sons exit the library. That left her alone in here with Phoenix. He wasn't looking at her; he was watching Brady leave. When he did turn his gaze to hers, he smiled at what she was sure was not a welcoming expression.

"You're welcome," he said.

"The library is closing," Willa said.

Phoenix looked around the empty space. The Penn's Grove library was small, cozy, and on a day not over-cast with storm clouds, it would've been full of light from the bank of large windows along one wall. The shelves had been set up to maximize the space and provide plenty of areas for patrons to sit and read or work at small wooden cubicles or in the computer center. With the storm predicted to last for the next day or so, he'd intended to grab a stack of reading material to keep him occupied.

"I'll be quick," he promised.

He could tell she was hesitant, but on the other hand, it was a public place and her job was to provide services. She nodded after a second or so. She looked as though she might say something, but didn't. Phoenix made good on his promise, choosing a pile of books at random from the new and recommended-reads shelves right there by the desk. He could feel her watching him from her office, where she'd retreated while he browsed. He was careful not to look back.

Phoenix was willing to bet that she had a history with the man who'd been hassling her and that it had a lot to do with why she'd reacted so strongly to him showing up unexpectedly. When he set his choices on the counter, Willa came out of her office to reach for the books. She looked at him.

"You don't have a library card," she said.

"I was going to get one now."

"Of course," she said with a nod. "You'll need a bill with your name and address on it."

Phoenix frowned. "I don't have one."

"Driver's license?"

He didn't have one of those, either. He had credit cards in other people's names that he used sparingly because these days it only took a time or two of un-authorized use before the cards were revoked. He had his charming smile. He had his talent. Neither of those was working on her.

"I walked out without anything. Can you give me a break?" He tried again to nudge her. Again noticed the soft flinch she probably didn't even realize she'd made, but he did. Intrigued, he tried again, gentle but persistent.

Willa shook her head. "I shouldn't. It's against library policy."

"It's a blizzard. I don't have anything to read. Give a guy a break, please?" Phoenix had wooed women with less effort than this for greater rewards than a to-be-read pile.

Willa's smile curved the tiniest bit, not reaching her eyes at all, but it was better than a frown. "How about I take the books out for you, and when you have what we need to get you set up with a card, you can come back and get one. But if you run off with the books, you'll regret it."

"Yeah?" He leaned on the counter with one hand.

"Yeah," she said and started checking out the books quickly and efficiently.

Phoenix waited for her to pause and look at him before he said, "I won't run off with the books. They're safe with me. You can trust me."

"Oh, I'm sure I can't trust you at all," she told him lightly, but with no doubt in her tone that she meant every word.

"But you're letting me take the books."

Her smile widened, more like the one she'd given him in the market and not the way she'd looked at him in the alley. "Like you said, it's a blizzard. What kind of horrible person would I be if I left you without books to read?"

By the time they got to the parking lot, the snow had fallen shin-deep on top of the layers of ice from earlier storms. It covered the two cars there. Hers, an impractical black-and-red Challenger that she'd bought used but loved and treated like a baby. His, a four-wheel-drive pickup truck that had seen better days, the best of them long ago.

"You're not going to get home in that. You should let me give you a ride." He pointed with the hand not holding the library tote she'd lent him to carry his books in.

Willa frowned. Her car was not the best in the snow. "It's only a few miles."

"Fine. Risk wrecking your baby. I'll be at home sipping bourbon and reading books in front of my space heater." Phoenix opened his car door and tossed the books inside. "Suit yourself, Madame Librarian."

"Wait." She shuffled in the snow, her feet already going numb although she'd stopped to change from her black pumps into her winter boots. "Fine."

Phoenix grinned but didn't push the issue. He gestured toward the passenger side door, and she got in, shifting on the bench seat to make room for the tote of books and her own bag, which she'd also filled with reading material meant to last the length of the storm. Phoenix started the truck, which came to life with a coughing roar that made Willa laugh, startled.

"It's not pretty and it's not fast, but it won't let us sit on the side of the road," Phoenix said. "It can go off road, cross-country or get out of a ditch, should we find ourselves in one."

"Let's hope that doesn't happen."

He shot her a look. "I'll be careful."

Pulling out of the lot, he was indeed careful, looking both ways up and down the street even though there weren't any other cars out. The plow had come through some time before, but enough snow had fallen since then that the truck slid a bit despite the heavy tires and four-wheel drive. Not enough to be scary or anything, since they were going only a few miles an hour, but enough that she had the chance to watch him handle the vehicle with skill.

She didn't want to distract him with talk while he navigated the few miles toward home, but it wasn't like they were barreling down the street, and the silence felt strained. "Thank you."

"My pleasure."

She chewed the inside of her cheek for a second at that. "I mean, for everything."

"Again, my pleasure." He shot her a look. "No ulterior motives, despite what you seem to think."

Willa's chin went up. "You don't know what I think."

"I know that you don't like to rely on someone," he said.

She frowned. "That's not true."

Phoenix didn't answer. In another minute or so he

was pulling in front of the house next to hers. He turned off the truck and turned to her on the seat.

"If that guy bothers you again…"

"You don't know me, and you don't know him," she said crisply, cutting him off before he could say more.

"I don't need to know him to see he was a major asshole."

Again, her chin lifted. "Yeah, he is that. But I can handle him."

"I take it you've done it before?"

She hesitated. To deny it would be stupid, but there was no way she was going to start in on that story. "It's cold. I need to get inside. Thanks again for the ride."

He waited until she was on her front porch before he called her name. He was still standing on the sidewalk, the tote slung over his shoulder and his hands in his pockets. "Are you hungry?"

"It's only the middle of the afternoon."

"That's not what I asked you," Phoenix said with a smile she imagined he'd used many times on many women.

"Are you offering to cook for me or something?" She fit her key into the lock and turned it, opened the door but didn't go inside.

"Cook? Me? Oh, no." He laughed and tipped his face up to the sky to let the fluffy white flakes catch in his eyelashes before he looked at her again. Melting snow glistened on his lips, and he licked it away. "I was thinking maybe you would cook for me."

There was a small desire there for her to invite him in, to make some pasta with the tomatoes and basil sitting on her counter. A little olive oil. She *was* hungry, Willa thought. But cook for him?

"You're crazy," she called down to him.

Phoenix grinned. "I've heard that a time or two."

There'd been a time when any man who'd approached her had been shut down immediately. Even fiercely. There'd been a time when she'd allowed fear and rage to consume her. To keep her a prisoner of her emotions. Time had muted that response, but it had not entirely gone away. She was cautious, not coy.

"I have no reason to invite you in," she told him. "Other than because you want me to."

His expression became serious. He nodded. "True."

"Thanks again for the ride." She kicked her boots on the door frame to clear them of snow but paused to look back at him before she went inside. "Maybe I'll make you dinner another time."

Phoenix took a hand from his pocket and pressed it to his heart as he made a little bow. "Another time."

Chapter 3

The storm they'd predicted to end within a few hours had continued through the night. The power had stayed on, at least. Phoenix didn't have a job to go to. He had a fully stocked fridge and thanks to the library trip the day before, plenty to keep him occupied for the next few days while Penn's Grove dug itself out. He also had a laptop and the internet and a curiosity about his prickly next-door neighbor.

When he searched Willa's name, dozens of entries came up at once. The benefit of having a unique name. If he'd searched his own name, there would also be plenty of hits under his various aliases, he was sure, but nothing that could be tied directly to him. Willa had several social media accounts, both her own and the ones for the library. Her posts avoided religion, politics and sex, and told him nothing about who she was. He dug deeper.

A yearbook photo. "Best Smile." Beside her in the picture was a younger but no less douchey-looking version of the man from the library. Brady Singer, read the caption. His arm slung casually around her shoulders told Phoenix a lot, though far from everything. Phoenix sat back in the uncomfortable desk chair that had come with the house the way all the furniture had. He typed again after a moment or so, but he wasn't getting quite the results he wanted, so he picked up the phone and dialed a familiar number. He hadn't called his sister in months, but she answered the way he knew she would.

"So you're not dead."

Phoenix laughed. "Not yet."

"Neither am I, thanks very much for being worried about me."

His laughter softened as he propped his feet on the desk and closed his eyes. "I knew you were fine. How's Officer Friendly?"

"Kane is fine. He's great. We're great together." She sounded defensive, and he couldn't blame her. "Where are you?"

"Somewhere safe. Somewhere nobody would think to look for me."

Persephone sighed. "Come back to me, Phoenix. Come work for the Crew. They're not the enemy."

"I don't want to work for anyone, not ever again." The words bit out of him, harsh and bitter on his tongue. "Maybe they wouldn't have me working the streets, but I guarantee you, I'd end up getting fucked again."

"Oh, Phoenix." His sister sighed.

"I'm not calling to chitchat, sister mine. I have a favor to ask." He opened his eyes, knowing his voice had gone a little harsher, so he added, "Please."

"What do you want?"

He told her quickly, outlining the searches he needed and spelling Willa's full name for her. Persephone's voice was muffled again. He heard the sound of typing.

"Who is she?" his sister asked after a minute or so. "What do you want with her?"

Phoenix thought before answering. "She's my neighbor. That's all. And I'm curious. I looked her up online, but I feel like there's more to her."

"Yeah. There's more."

"Like what?" He put his feet down with a thump and leaned to look at his laptop, as though magically whatever Persephone was finding would show up on the screen.

"I'm not going to tell you."

"Persephone," Phoenix said like a warning.

His sister, however, wasn't intimidated. "It's not any of your business. Why do you want to get into her secrets? Are you trying to get something out of her?"

"No. I just..."

"You have the hots for her," Persephone said flatly. "Well, maybe trying talking to her instead of creeping on her. I'm sure you could pull everything right out of her, whatever you want. Isn't that how you do it?"

Okay, so she was still pissed off about what he'd done to her before. "It doesn't work on her."

Persephone's scalding laugh burned his ear through the phone. "Oh, for sure. Right. You want me to believe that?"

"It doesn't," he repeated, "work on her. I don't know

why. I tried to nudge her, but she won't do what I want her to do."

"Sounds to me like you're screwed, brother mine." Persephone's laughter cycled up, sounding less bitter and more delighted. "Get ready for it. You're about to fall in love."

"You shut your mouth," Phoenix shot back without a second's hesitation.

Persephone guffawed, then went quiet. "If you want to know about her, you really need to get to know her. You could make me tell you, of course. We both know that. But it won't be any good for you to know if she's not the one to share it."

"It's bad?"

"It's hers," Persephone said fiercely. Harsh. "You don't understand what it's like, Phoenix, when you nudge someone. How it can feel after. You ought to know, since—"

"Shut your mouth," he told her, already knowing what it was she meant to say. "Stop."

"Get out of there, wherever you are. Come home."

"I don't have a home," Phoenix said.

"Your home is wherever I am. That's all we need." She sounded as though she might be on the verge of tears.

Phoenix shook his head, even though she couldn't see him. "I am not all you need. Not anymore."

And she could not be all he needed, either. They weren't kids anymore. They were adults, and she was starting on her own, real life with Kane. She didn't have to say it for Phoenix to know it was true.

"Come here, anyway, to us. We have a place for you. You don't have to take the job—"

"I'm good where I am. Thanks." He held the phone away from his ear for a second or so before putting it back. "It all ended up okay, you know. For you."

She didn't answer him for a bit. "That doesn't make it okay."

"Nothing is ever okay," Phoenix said and disconnected the call before she could say something more.

Chapter 4

Willa had exhausted her patience for bingeing on streaming television shows, a feat she might have thought impossible if not for the past day and half of official road closings and a governor-mandated state of emergency that meant the library had remained closed. She'd run through everything she had an interest in watching alone, and without someone to watch with, she didn't feel like starting something else. That left books, of course, and the internet, but something about the steady, softly falling snow was making her restless.

It was because it made everything so quiet.

Snow made silence in the world. No cars passing outside. No voices from the sidewalk beneath her window. The occasional rumble of the passing plows was loud, but infrequent. The quiet was getting to her, making her pace and run her hands through her hair over and over again until it tangled around her fingers.

She needed…something. There was an aching in her chest, an emptiness that echoed throughout her body. Lower. She could pace and stare at the walls and eat cookies until she thought she might explode, but none of that was going to help her. It had been a long time since she'd felt this urge, this desire, and back in the days when she had sought the comfort of a stranger's touch to help her get past everything that had been happening, she'd always made sure to go away. Out of town, at least two or three hours' distance. She didn't have that option now.

"Breathe through it," Willa said to herself, muttering although there wasn't anyone here to overhear her talking to herself like some kind of deranged lunatic.

They used to put people in asylums for this, she thought as she ran her hands over her arms, and then across her belly. One moving between her thighs even as she walked, cupping herself briefly. Sexual hysteria. Masturbation. They'd have tossed her in a cell and thrown away the key.

She didn't want to admit it was because of the man in the house next door. She didn't want to think about the waves of red-gold hair, the green eyes, the strong jaw with that delicious stubble. Not the jeans or the work boots or the way he went out in the cold without wearing a winter coat, not about his crooked smile or the fact he liked to read so much he'd checked out fifteen library books. Certainly not how he'd insisted, several times over, that he wanted to help her.

She didn't have his phone number, thank whoever looked out for horny women who really ought to know better. She did, however, share a wall with him. He was right next door. Which was exactly why she wasn't going to take a shower and shave everything that needed to be presentable, she told herself. He was within literal shouting distance, which was why she was absolutely not going to twist her hair into a tangled braid with sexy tendrils hanging down around her face. Why she wasn't going to dress in fresh, matching panties and bra, the kind that showed off her curves, why she wasn't going to line her eyes and mouth and dip a finger into her slick heat to tuck a bit of her own scent at each pulse point. Pheromones. No perfume had ever smelled as good on her as her own arousal.

Phoenix was a stranger, but not one she picked up in club or on the internet and met in a cheesy hotel hours away. He was her neighbor. Which was why she was not going to put this casserole in a thermal carrier along with a loaf of bread she'd baked in the machine while she blew through two dozen episodes of an obscure '90s teen comedy she barely remembered minutes after finishing.

He lived. Next. Door.

Which was why she had not added a bottle of red wine and some glasses, and why she was not knocking on his door.

"Hi," she said when he answered. "I thought you might be hungry."

It had been a while since Willa had done any kind of seduction. The men she'd gone with had been found on the internet, screened ahead of time, the parameters of their arrangement laid out well in advance of any meeting. Watching Phoenix look her up and down now, though, she thought how easy it could be to make a man want a woman.

"Thanks for dinner." He'd polished off two big plates of the casserole she'd brought over, along with half the loaf of bread and most of the bottle of wine.

She'd limited herself to one glass, craving the warmth of being tipsy but not drunk. "You're welcome. I thought it was the least I could do."

"Neighborly," Phoenix said with a smile.

She smiled, too. "Yes. Neighborly."

"So," he said, "you're not going home."

"No."

Phoenix stood and held out a hand. She took it, although he hung back when she headed for the stairs so she could lead the way. This house was the mirror of her own, and she found her way without problem to the biggest bedroom, the one she assumed he'd taken as his. The rest of the house had been decorated in a style she could only figure was early American rental home, but here in the bedroom, at least, Phoenix had asserted his own taste.

"Wow," Willa said. "This is...amazing."

Phoenix closed the door behind them and locked it, something she noticed at once was strange, since they were likely to be the only ones in the house. Strange and yet oddly comforting, to her surprise, because she also locked her own bedroom door as a matter of habit. She watched him look around the room as though trying to determine what, exactly, she'd found so amazing.

"You like?"

She nodded. "It's not what I expected."

"You put some thought into what you might find in my bedroom, Willa?" Phoenix laughed, low, and came up behind her to put his hands lightly on her hips. His breath tickled the exposed nape of her neck, making her shiver.

She didn't answer that, but stepped out of the embrace to move toward the king-size bed. Covered in white sheets with a solid black comforter and black-and-white-striped pillowcases, it was also draped with a skein of netting that could be drawn around it to curtain the entire thing. No headboard, but the wall behind it had been painted with briars and roses. Small white lights were strung around the ceiling.

"Did you paint that?"

Phoenix didn't reply at first, not until she glanced at him. "Yes."

"You're very talented."

"I have good hands," he said. "Good with my fingers."

It was a totally cheesy line, but it made her laugh. "Uh-huh."

She turned slowly and found a seat on the edge of the bed. She didn't beckon him closer. She waited, each breath rising and falling and her heart starting to thump a little faster in her chest when he stood and stared.

She wasn't expecting him to tug his shirt off over his head and toss it to the floor, or to open his belt buckle and push his jeans down over his hips, to step out of them and leave him entirely naked. Willa's breath caught at the sight of him, long legs and lean muscle. Around one hip curved a lick of red and orange and gold, a ribbon of flames. She gestured, a crook of her fingers.

"Come here."

He did, standing in front of her. She studied the tattoo, very aware of his nakedness. She drew a fingertip over the inked skin, over his hip and around to his back.

"Turn."

He did that, too, without protest. A scar feathered out from the edges of the flames, pale against his golden skin. Fine golden hairs glistened. He shivered when she touched him on the scar, then on the twin dimples at the base of his spine. He shifted, moving his feet apart so she could glimpse a hint of his sac between his thighs.

"What happened?"

"Someone cut me," Phoenix said without turning.

Willa ran her hands up the backs of his strong thighs, covered in more of that same red-gold hair. She traced the curves of his ass, hearing his low, soft groan. He shifted again, widening his stance even further. Granting her access to his body. Heat rushed through her as she slipped a hand between his thighs to run her thumb along the seam below his balls. She cupped them for a second.

"Turn around," she whispered.

He was already hard when he did, and she drank in the sight of his erection. Greedy for him, she put her hands on his hips and pulled him closer so that she could drag her tongue along his length. He shuddered. How gratifying to have such a reaction, she thought as the tip of her tongue teased the small divot beneath the head of his cock. She didn't take him inside her mouth, but she licked him again as her hand cupped him.

"Who?" She breathed the question against his inner thigh as she nuzzled him.

"It doesn't…matter…"

She licked the soft skin there, bare of fuzz. When she nipped, his hips jutted forward. She pressed her face to his skin, her eyes closed as she drank in his scent.

"Someone you trusted," she whispered.

The muscles beneath her lips jumped and tensed. "…yes."

She looked up at him as she took his shaft in her fist and brought the head of his cock to her mouth. "I'm sorry."

"We all have scars."

Willa took him inside her mouth then. His moan encouraged her to take him deeper, as deep as she could. His cock nudged the back of her throat before she released him, adding a brief extra bit of suction on the head. He was already slippery with sweet precome.

When she pressed her teeth to his sensitive flesh, Phoenix cried out, but not in protest. He fucked against the scrape of her teeth. One hand went to her hair to urge her on. Gripping his shaft hard, Willa looked up at him. Warning without words. He understood her at once, taking away his hand. Holding them at his sides, muscles bunched and taut with the strain he was obviously feeling in not touching her.

Again, she pressed him inside her mouth and gave him the edge of her teeth. Her hands ran up the insides of his thighs, finding heat and the sweet spots she knew just how and where to pinch. Lightly, enough to make him jump but not to leave a mark. She let his cock slide free of her mouth, slick with her saliva.

"You should tell me to stop," she said.

Phoenix looked down at her with glazed eyes. "I don't want you to stop."

An electric jolt sparked through her. Every nerve. Every muscle. Right to the center of her. Her cunt clenched, clit throbbing. Her head fell back a little, lips parting on a sigh.

"Get on the bed," she said. He did obediently, on his back. She watched him for a second, then tapped his foot. "Wider."

He spread himself for her, showing her everything. The small red spot from where she'd pinched him sent another thrill through her. She stood, shedding her clothes swiftly, not a striptease even though he watched her as though she were putting on the sexiest of shows. Naked, she moved up the bed between his legs, running her hands up and over him to rest on his hip bones.

She had been with men who proclaimed they wanted to obey, and a lot of them meant it, at least as long as she was asking them to do what they wanted to do. She'd been with men who'd said they wanted her to hurt them, but only so long as she did it in the way they wanted her to. Most of the time it didn't matter. She met with them for a night, never more than two, and she did what she wanted to them and got what she needed, and never much cared if she'd left them unsatisfied.

There was something different about this man. The way he responded to the simple commands and to the small but precise pains she'd deliberately inflicted. It made her want to hurt him, but it also made her want to please him.

When she climbed over him to straddle his face, Phoenix was already waiting with his mouth open, tongue out. His hands cupped her ass, bringing her closer. She cried out from that first slow, exploratory lick and put her hands on the wall. Fingers curling. She rocked her hips into his kiss.

For long minutes, the only sounds were the softness of his tongue on her and Willa's murmured instructions to him of exactly where she needed it. Phoenix's rising hum of arousal. The room had not been warm when they entered it but she was hot now, straining and tense with desire that rose and teased and softened under his expert caresses. Sweat slicked beneath her thighs on his chest, and sometimes she could not stop herself from squeezing her thighs against his head, from grinding on his mouth before she relaxed and allowed him to keep working her flesh.

There were many times when she took this sort of pleasure hard and fast, fierce. When she'd used a man's mouth and tongue to get off by orchestrating every motion, fingers in his hair to tug his head where she wanted and needed it. Now, although it was taking her a very long time to reach the pinnacle, she felt no desperation to get there. No lingering feeling that she needed to finish soon or he would be bored or give up on making her come, or that she needed to finish quickly so they could get to his part of the pleasure.

Willa rode him leisurely, making it clear when she wanted or needed something different but also when he was doing it exactly right. She let him set the pace. Slow, slow, then speeding up with flickering strokes of his tongue. Dipping lower to slide in her folds and sample her sweetness, something that made her cry out and press her forehead to the wall as her body jumped under the sudden sensations.

Then, finally, there it was. No going back. Nothing stopping this rising crash of pleasure that overtook her and made her shake. A wordless stream of sounds slipped from her mouth. Her eyes had been closed while she concentrated, but now she looked down between her thighs to watch him bring her to orgasm.

He looked at her in that last moment when even though her eyes were open, she was not quite seeing the real world. She lost herself in his gaze, her hand going gently to his bright hair but not to tug or yank or move him. Her touch was reverent, recognizing this moment between them even as she lost the ability to focus on anything else.

Ecstasy burst inside her. She cried out again, something more like his name this time. Shuddering, she let the climax rocket through her. Phoenix pressed his lips against her, feeling the ripples of aftershocks. After another moment or so, Willa rolled off him and onto the pillow beside him. She felt light-headed and drained, empty, almost aching in the aftermath of the explosion of desire.

Now he would roll on top of her, she thought, knowing she would allow it. She wanted it, even, to feel the thickness of his cock inside her still-throbbing cunt. It would be a different kind of pleasure, one she was willing to grant him since he'd been so, so fucking good with his mouth.

Phoenix did not roll on top of her. He turned his face to look at her. She looked at him. They studied each other in silence, until she propped herself on her elbow to look into his eyes.

"What do you want?" she asked quietly.

Phoenix closed his eyes. "I want you to hurt me."

She was like something out of a dream…or one of those movies he looked up on the internet when the night was late and his cock was hard without anyone around to help him relieve it.

Phoenix could not ever recall being the target of such a seduction. Women liked him. Men, too. He'd never had any trouble getting laid, and he'd never had to nudge anyone toward it.

"Please," he added when she made no move toward him. He could still taste her and swept his lower lip with his tongue to get every drop of her flavor. His cock was still so hard it cast a shadow. A silver string of precome had left a puddle on his belly.

Willa sat up. "That's what you want? Really?"

"Yes." He wanted to touch himself. He could come within a minute or so, the way he felt right now, but he wanted something more than an orgasm at the moment.

She straddled his hips in a second. The flash of her hand cracked across his face, rocking his head. Fuck, yes, that was it. The bright flare of pain sent an answering shock of pleasure straight to the base of his cock. Something deep inside him pulsed and throbbed. She smacked him again, then grabbed his chin to force him to look at her.

"You want that?"

"Yes. Please."

Her gaze never leaving his, her lips pressed together, Willa dug her knuckles into his sides. Harder. Harder. She ground them between his ribs until he bucked and writhed and gasped out a plea; it was not for her stop, but she did. He hadn't realized he'd closed his eyes, but now he opened them.

She was looking at him with something like wonder.

"This," she breathed, raking her nails over his belly

and his thighs so that her fingers slipped between his legs and she dug her nails into the soft skin there.

He arched, groaning. "Yes, yes, yes…"

She began to work him, then. Pinching fingers. Scratching nails. When she bent to take a mouthful of his flesh between her teeth and bite him, just above the hip on the opposite side of the flames, his cock leaped. The throb of orgasm swelled inside him, but he didn't spill. He muttered her name.

"Oh my god," she breathed over the marks of her teeth. Her voice shook. She licked the pain, then kissed it. "Oh my god, Phoenix…"

Gripping his cock in her fist, she spit on it to wet him. Again, he almost came, but the clutch of her fingers was too tight. She smiled when she stroked him, and he lost himself in the wickedness of her glee.

She worked his cock, up and down, sometimes twisting around the head while he bucked. She shifted, kneeling at his side so that she could keep stroking him as she used the other hand to dig her nails again into all the places she was discovering made him leap.

"You want to come?" she asked him.

It was hard to find the words, but he managed. "Yes."

"Please?"

"Yes, please…fuck!"

Without letting up the steady stroking, she also slapped his face again. Again. The crack of her hand on him was bright and shining—the truth was that she was not actually hitting him hard enough to do more than sting. He could take so much more, and yet something in the deliberate way she held back from using full force was as erotic as anything had ever been.

She bent to kiss him—the first time her mouth had been on his. Her hand kept up the steady pace. He was thrusting, aching, writhing. Her other hand went to the back of his neck to dig her nails into him there. He gave her his tongue, and she bit it.

It sent him over the edge. He jetted into her fist, incredibly feeling every spurt. His orgasm boiled out of him, wrenching every drop from his balls and spilling into her hand. Onto his belly. She had not let go of his tongue with her teeth, and the pain sent wave after wave of pleasure shuddering through him until, at last, he was spent and she sat back with his softening cock in her fist.

"So pretty," she said, and Phoenix thought if love were a thing he might ever have found it possible to feel, he'd have fallen into it right then.

Chapter 5

The orgasm he'd given her had left her sated and weak, but what had just happened had coiled her up inside again, tight. Not so much that she needed another climax, Willa thought, although she would not have refused one. It was something else, a feeling that pricked her like the painted thorns on the wall behind the bed would have if they'd been real.

She'd gone to the bathroom and brought back a warm damp cloth for him, pleased and amused that he'd allowed it without protest. She thought it was more that he hadn't managed to rouse himself enough to get up rather than any expectation on his part, but it satisfied her to take care of him that way, after what he'd allowed her to do.

She thought he would sleep and she would leave, but Phoenix had not yet closed his eyes. They weren't cuddling, but she sat with one hand on his chest, feeling the slowing beat of his heart. She caressed him, touching the scarlet marks her nails had left.

"You'll bruise here," she said quietly, touching him in one spot. Lower, to the place where she'd bitten him. "There, too."

"That's all right."

She ran her hands over him some more, not trying to arouse him. Exploring. Marveling. At the light touch of her hand on his side, Phoenix shuddered. Willa stroked his tattoo. She generally had no opinion one way or another about ink, but it was obvious whoever had done this piece was a true artist. The design was simple but elegant, not cartoonish. The shading magnificent. It looked like real fire.

At this angle, she couldn't see the scar, but she let her fingers drift around his back to touch the edge of it. "Was this…?"

He closed his eyes, remembering. "It wasn't meant to cut so deep. She didn't want to. I thought I knew what I was doing. It was bad. There was a lot of blood."

"Look at me."

He did with obvious reluctance but responded to the quiet command in her voice. He sat up when she gestured and put his back against the wall while she knelt between his legs. Willa studied him. She'd come next door in the hopes of getting laid, because over time she'd learned that satisfying her body could sometimes—although not always—lead to quiet in her mind. The scene with Brady in the library had left her restless and out of sorts, so she'd sought the comfort of a seduction.

"Tell me about what happened," she said.

At first Phoenix shook his head. She would have let

it go. After all, it wasn't like she owned him. He was not required to obey her, not that Willa had any idea of what it would've been like if any of those untruths had been fact. She'd had lots of sex with men who got off on pain, because she'd learned she got off on giving it. She'd never actually been in a relationship with one. It had been a long, long time since she'd been in a relationship at all. She was just about to get up and start getting dressed when he spoke.

"I didn't love her," he said. "Maybe that's why it went wrong."

Curious, Willa leaned a little closer. "Did she love you?"

"She said she did. I didn't believe her. I should have." He shrugged, looking away. "She said she would do anything for me. She meant more than just fucking me, I'm sure, but that was all I had for her. She said it would be enough."

"It's not usually enough," Willa said.

Phoenix gave a low laugh. "Not for most people."

"So, she said she wanted you enough to settle for sex. And then what?"

"I told her what I wanted. What I needed. At first she thought I was joking. I mean, who would think—"

"That a guy like you would want a woman to hurt him? That he'd get off on it?" Willa shook her head.

Phoenix nodded with a smile and leaned his head back against the wall. He lifted one hand over his head to touch the painted wall behind him, tracing a line of briars with his fingers even though he couldn't possibly see them to know where they were. "Yet there are so many people who get off on hurting others."

She wondered for a moment if he was digging at

her, but decided he was not. In the short time she'd known him, he'd proven to be rough yet charming, and roguish. Something of a storyteller. She thought of his proclamations about being able to get people to do what he wanted. She hadn't seen him be deliberately nasty without provocation.

"So…she did it?"

"Yes. Not very well," he said, again without sounding mean. "She didn't like it. She didn't really, in her heart, want to hurt me. Because she loved me."

"Sometimes," Willa said in a low voice, "you hurt someone specifically because you do love them."

Phoenix didn't answer for a moment. His pale eyes narrowed as he looked at her. Something passed between them, a tension, something dark that didn't linger but left a stain behind.

"I was frustrated by her, and I was cruel. I put the knife in her hand. I told her to use it on me. She didn't want to, but I made her. I made her," he repeated with a curl of his lip. "I pushed her too hard, and she cut too deep."

Willa again traced the line of the tattoo covering the scar. "How bad was it?"

"I nearly died."

"Oh." She frowned and let her fingers curl around the back. "Why didn't you cover the whole thing?"

"I left a small piece of it to remind me what would happen if I pushed someone too hard who loved me too much again. What I would have to live with."

She nodded at that. It made sense. "Scars are memories. Reminders of what we've lived through."

"Something tells me you have scars, Willa, even if they're not anywhere I can see them."

Now it was her turn to leave without saying anything. She owed him no more of herself than she'd already given, but Phoenix had told her his story. She supposed there wasn't anything so bad about sharing hers.

"Brady and I were a couple in high school," she said. "On and off. He was possessive. Obsessive. I went away to school, and he followed me there. We broke up again. He wouldn't let it go."

Phoenix frowned. "He hurt you?"

"Nothing that left marks. Nothing that showed, especially if you weren't inclined to believe a good boy from a nice family could ever possibly be a nasty son of a bitch who thought taking what he wanted was always okay. I was working at a bar in the next town to help pay off college, before I got the librarian job. He'd show up. Wait in his car to be sure I wasn't going home with someone else. He said he loved me," Willa said. "He said he would do anything to be with me."

"Did you ask him to let you hurt him?" The question might've been snotty or patronizing, but Phoenix only sounded curious.

"No. I didn't know, then, that I liked it. That came after." Willa closed her eyes for a moment or so, thinking about the paths that had led her to this place. This room, this man. This life. "He got out of hand."

"And you didn't tell anyone?"

"There was nobody to tell, really. Everyone in this town had known us both forever. As a couple. Even when we broke it off, there were people who were just waiting for us to get back together. And he wasn't doing anything I could report," Willa said. "He wasn't hitting me. He wasn't threatening my life. He was just making me miserable. Finally, he said he would kill himself if I didn't get back with him."

"Shit."

"I did not get back with him," Willa said. "He tried to hang himself, but didn't manage it. Everyone knew why he did it. The sympathy was mostly for him."

"Fuck." Phoenix waved a hand. "Why stay? Why didn't you move away from here? Get away from that asshole forever."

"My parents were here. My sister. And I carried a huge burden of guilt for a long time," Willa said. "Thinking it was somehow my fault."

"You know that you can't be responsible for someone else's mental health issues," Phoenix said. "God knows, I have my share of baggage—"

Willa cut in, "Like everyone else in the world."

"—but you can't unpack someone else's bags for them," Phoenix finished.

She knew that, of course. She had for a long time. Yet somehow here she was, this was the life she'd chosen, and for the most part it wasn't a bad one.

"So…what about…this." Phoenix touched the bruise she'd left. "When did you figure that out?"

"It wasn't easy getting a date in a town this size when everyone thought I was the big bad wolf who'd done her best to blow Brady's house down. Even when he got married, which he did almost exactly a year later, people didn't forget what had happened. So, I tried online dating. I met someone. We went on a date or two. Things went well. I agreed to meet him the next town over in a hotel. He asked me to slap him when I came."

Phoenix quirked a brow.

"I couldn't come," Willa admitted. "Too much pressure. Too soon. I wasn't used to casual sex, despite all the accusations Brady had thrown my way. I didn't see that guy again after that, but I thought about him, and that, a lot. I started to seek it out. Men who were into pain. It's both easier and more difficult than you might expect to find someone."

"I believe it." Phoenix shook his head. He leaned forward, offering his mouth, which she kissed briefly before sitting back again. "But I have to ask you. About me. How…how did you know?"

Willa's brow furrowed as she thought how best to answer that. "I didn't."

"So I guess that makes us lucky, then," Phoenix said.

He looked as though he meant to say something else, but from downstairs came the shatter of glass and the thud of the front door breaking open.

Chapter 6

It could've been anything—a strong gust of wind from the storm. A home invasion. The landlord forgetting his keys. Phoenix was up and out of bed in seconds all the same. Moving. Grabbing his clothes and throwing them on as fast as possible while he shoved the heavy dresser in front of the door.

"Get dressed," he shot at Willa without looking to see if she was going to.

Whoever was coming for him would have no interest in her, unless she had some hidden talents she hadn't shown off, and not the ones of the bedroom sort. That didn't mean she wasn't going to get hurt when whoever was thudding up the stairs burst through this door and tried to take him. Dressed, shoving his bare feet into boots, Phoenix backed her up toward the window.

"You're going to have to go out there," he said.

"Drop to the roof of the back porch. From there you can climb the trellis to the street."

"What the hell is going on?"

Already the thunder of feet in the narrow hallway was trying to drown out her words. There wasn't time for her to argue with him. He needed her to get out the window, and now. He nudged.

"Out."

Willa moved toward the window, tearing wide the curtains and pulling up the sash, but she did not do as he'd told her. She looked outside. "They're out there, too, whoever they are."

"Go out, anyway," he said. "They're going to come through that door in a minute and they probably have guns."

She ignored him, moving into the long, narrow closet that he barely used. "No. This way. Come on."

He nudged her harder. She stumbled as though he'd pushed her, a hand to her head, but she did not go to the window the way he was trying force her to. Phoenix pulled back, not wanting to hurt her, his attention torn between Willa and the bedroom door shaking as someone tried to get in. The glass in the window shattered inward after that.

"Up here." She'd pulled down the set of folding stairs into an attic he hadn't known existed. Already halfway up, she turned to gesture at him. "Our two houses share an attic. I can get us into mine. From there we can get out."

He didn't argue but followed. They took the time to pull up the stairs after them, and without a second's hesitation she grabbed an extension cord coiled next to some boxes. She looped it through the folding stairs' metal hinges, securing it from being pulled down, at least easily.

"I read a lot of books," she said when he looked at her. "I learned things."

With an easy, loping step, she navigated the attic's center line where the beams were high enough to let her pass without ducking. At the door in the center, she pushed hard, and after a moment it opened. The attic on her side was brighter, cleaner, with boxes and discarded furniture and racks of out-of-season clothes neatly placed in rows along the side. She had identical folding stairs. In moments they were in her bedroom.

"Will they have surrounded this house, too? Will they be trying to get in here? Quick," she cried, snapping her fingers in his face until he answered.

"I don't know. I don't think so. They try not to engage civilians."

It was the wrong word, because he was a civilian as well. Words were failing him, though not because of the sudden attack on his house. It had been only a matter of time before Wyrmwood caught up to him, he'd thought, but he was left stunned and reeling by how swiftly and with such prowess Willa was reacting.

"Your truck's parked in the alley. If we can get to that, we can get out of here."

"You don't need to get anywhere," he put in. "You can stay here in your house. They're interested in me, and if you're over here—"

Willa cut him off as she grabbed a winter coat hanging from a coatrack. She found a pair of boots and slipped them on as she answered. "You really think they won't come over here asking for me? We left two plates on the table. Two glasses of wine. The thermal bag has my name on it and my address. If they don't figure out we were together just now, at the very least I think they'll come over to ask me some questions."

She was right, although it still knocked him for a loop that she'd reacted so quickly. So smart. He nodded, feeling in his jeans pocket for his keys. Thanking all the gods and goddesses or whoever watched over those who'd royally fucked up their lives that they were in there.

"Let's go," Willa told him as she slung a bag over one shoulder.

Years ago, Willa had gotten into the habit of keeping a go bag near the back door. In case she needed to run away. In case there was a natural disaster that required evacuation. Just in case. She grabbed it now and slung it over her shoulder with a look at Phoenix. There'd be time for him to tell her what the hell was going on, but it didn't seem to be now.

She was doing this. Running out of her house with a man she barely knew, as strangers with guns pursued them. Why? Because he'd let her hurt him? Because she was afraid of what might happen if she stayed? Because it was a chance to get out, she thought as she let Phoenix go out the door ahead of her, onto her slightly sloping back porch and down the rickety stairs she always meant to get repaired but never had.

Screw those stairs, she thought as he took them two at a time, landing on the snowy sidewalk with a grace she admired even in this hyped-up state of fight or flight. There was a man in a black uniform, wearing a mask, holding a gun, but he was looking the other way. He turned as Willa also leaped the stairs of the porch. She slipped on the ice, going to one knee as the gun swung up. She didn't see what happened next, but the soldier or whatever the hell he was fell to his hands and knees in the piled snow.

Eating it?

Chowing down on it like a dog with a bowl of meat and gravy. Tossing his head from side to side. He got right down to pavement while she watched.

Phoenix yanked her arm. "C'mon."

"What the—"

She took another look over her shoulder as Phoenix pulled her toward the truck parked in one of the shoveled-out spots in the alley. From upstairs in his house, lights flashed in the windows. Shadows moved behind the glass. They were quiet, whoever they were. No shouting. No gunfire, thank god.

Another of them stepped out of the shadows as they approached the truck.

A minute after that he, too, was on his hands and knees gobbling at the snow and ice. Willa looked a few feet down the sidewalk to the first guy, who was now getting to his feet and trying to find his gun from where he must've tossed it into a snowbank when he decided to make a meal out of the slush.

"Get in." Phoenix sounded grim, but there was a glee in his eyes, and his mouth had stretched into a tight, wide grin. He opened the driver's side door so she could slide across the bench seat. He followed.

Keys in ignition. Truck in gear. Lights off. He could do nothing about the roar of the engine, but the truck's wide tires took the curb and jumped it without effort. Willa put her seat belt on.

Men came out of both houses. She had a moment to think about how much of a mess they must have made, how much it would cost to fix the door they'd broken on the way out. How much she didn't give one good goddamn, she thought as Phoenix put the pedal to the metal and flew down the alley, over the snowbanks and piles of ice that had built up because of the storm.

There was a bad few seconds at the end when the wheels were spinning, but with a shift of gears he put the truck into four-wheel drive and they got over the barrier. Incredibly, Phoenix was laughing. Even more astoundingly, so was she.

"Are we going to die?" Willa cried out, hanging on to the roof handle as the truck got air from a pile of snow and came down hard enough to rattle her teeth. "Are they going to chase us down?"

"They've been chasing me down for years, and I haven't died yet." Phoenix shot a glance into the rearview mirror, still grinning, as he guided the truck onto Elm Street and kept going, taking turn after turn until somehow they ended up on the main highway out of town.

The roads had been closed for the past day or so, and although plows and salt trucks had come through, more icy snow had fallen and the road was not even close to clear. The truck, battered as it was, took the road without trouble, sliding now and then but recovering under Phoenix's guidance. Willa wisely kept her mouth shut to allow him to concentrate. She kept her eyes on the rearview, but so far, nothing seemed to be following them.

The body can only sustain tension for so long, and she found herself nodding off. Every time she felt her head droop forward she managed to wake herself back up, but soon enough it was a losing battle. She piled a sweatshirt from the bag between them on the seat against the window and let herself drift off. She woke when the truck stopped.

"I need to eat. And sleep," Phoenix said, peering through the windshield at the flickering neon sign of the roadside motel. "This place looks okay."

Dubious but figuring they didn't have many options, Willa also looked. "I have cash in my bag. I don't know how much, but I figure you won't want to use your credit card? I don't have mine, anyway. I left my purse at home. Shit."

"I don't have my wallet." He shifted on the seat to look at her. "Tell you what, you stay here and keep warm, I'll go get us a room. Unless you need your own."

"Safety in numbers," she said, thinking how ridiculous it would be to balk at sharing a bathroom with a man she'd already had an orgasm with. "Right?"

Phoenix laughed. The light from the neon highlighted his red-gold hair and cast shadows on his face. "Be right back."

"Wait, the money."

"I won't need it."

Before she could ask him why not, he was out of the truck and striding across the lot toward the motel office. Inside she could see a gray-haired woman wearing a sweater festooned with Christmas presents, although it was the middle of January. *Well, fa-la-la-la-la*, Willa thought and burst into a scattered flurry of semihysterical giggles. She hadn't quite managed to calm herself by the time Phoenix came out of the office, holding up a key—an actual metal one—hanging from a red plastic key ring.

"I got a room with two beds," he said. "But there's a fridge and a microwave, and the guy at the front desk said there's free coffee in the lobby all day long."

The room turned out to be cleaner than she expected, and if the furniture was worn and the decor outdated, the bathroom had a brand-new shower and the pillows were fluffy. The radiator ticked and tocked as she checked everything out, tossing her bag onto the bed closest to the bathroom.

"I'm hungry," Phoenix said. "There's a diner across the street. Let me go get some food and bring it back."

The last thing Willa expected to want was food, but at the idea of it her stomach rumbled. She put a hand over it. "I'll go with you."

"I can bring it back," he said.

"And leave me here all by myself?" She tilted her head to study him. "Or maybe you're planning to ditch me here."

The startled look on his face told her she'd been spot-on. Frowning, she put her hands on her hips. Phoenix shrugged.

"It would be safer for you if I weren't with you," he said.

"I'm not convinced of that. I don't think I want to take that chance. Do you want me to?"

He shook his head. "No. I guess I don't."

"Good." She paused. "Look, it's not like I expect you to marry me now or anything like that."

He burst into a choking laugh. "Oh…fuck, no. Sorry, but…no."

"No?" She laughed, too. "Never thought about getting hitched?"

"Let's talk about that with our mouths full."

"I can think of something I want in your mouth," Willa said, "and it's not eggs and toast."

His reaction was immediate. Intense. He shivered, visibly. His fingers curled into fists.

Oh, she thought. Oh, so it was going to be like this.

Oh, yes.

Yes.

Chapter 7

Phoenix could not stop himself from devouring the sight of her as quickly as Willa was consuming the platter of food in front of her. The diner across the street was the sort open twenty-four hours, breakfast all day, and she'd ordered the hunter's special. He hadn't thought she'd be able to finish it all, but damn if the girl wasn't putting it away like a trucker.

"I need to keep up my strength," she said now, noticing his stare. Deliberately, she ran her fingertip over the corner of her mouth to catch a drop of syrup that had lingered. She licked it.

He got hard.

There was no way she could see that, not with the table between them, but something in the way she looked at him told him she knew. He'd finished off his meat-laden omelet already and now sat back with a mug of coffee, casually, as though nothing in the world was making him think about how sweet she'd tasted. How hard she'd made him come.

This was not the time to be thinking about this. Not with Wyrmwood probably still on their trail. Still, the gleam in her eyes was as intoxicating as if he were drinking a fine whiskey, straight up without stopping to breathe.

"So," she said as she dug into hash browns drizzled with hot sauce, "what's the story? What is all this? Can you even talk about it here?"

He looked around the diner, deserted at this time of night aside from them, the bored waitress tapping away on her phone and whoever was in the back. "I suppose it's possible this place is just a front for a pseudo-government organization and we're about to be hauled away in the back of a black SUV to an undisclosed location where they will definitely perform experiments on us. But it's probably just a diner. So yeah, I can talk about it here."

"Is that what's going on?" As if defeated by the amount of food, Willa pushed back from the table and lifted her coffee cup to sip.

Phoenix saw no point in lying. She was going to believe him or she was not, and it shouldn't much matter to him either way. It did, somehow. But there was nothing he could do but tell the truth.

"Yes," he said. "They've been after me for years."

"Why?"

"Because I can make people do things." It was not the first time he'd said it to her. It was not, in fact, the first time he'd said it to anyone—most of the time he opened with it as truth, because hardly anyone ever believed it was true until he showed them. He only did that when it mattered.

"You've said that." Her eyes narrowed. She shook her head. Laughed a little, looking away, then back at him. "What does that mean?"

Here was the part of the story that he didn't usually tell. At nearing three in the morning, adrenaline fading, stomach overfull from too much food, it was not a story he wanted to start unless he could finish it. He drank coffee instead, draining the mug and setting it down with a *thunk*.

"You realize it's a hard thing to believe," she said. "Without any kind of explanation."

"You're a librarian," he said. "Isn't it your job to have faith in all sorts of stories?"

She laughed. "Sure. Fictional ones. If you're trying to convince me this is nonfiction, though, you're going to have to be a little more forthcoming."

"I was born to a woman who'd had seven previous pregnancies. So far as I know, the only children to survive were me, my sister and a younger brother I've never met that I can recall."

"I'm sorry," Willa said.

Phoenix shook his head. "It's nothing to be sorry about. She allowed herself to get pregnant by a series of men, all of whom were engaged in the use of various drugs and other things that she also took. There were other things, too. Everything was meant to affect the unborn children. Make monsters."

"I don't understand."

"Collins Creek was a ranch owned by a guy named Harrison Collins, who believed the next step in evolution was the ability of the human brain to do… things."

"Telekinesis? Stuff like that?"

"Yes," Phoenix said, and watched her expression of incredulity. "He and all the people in his cult did their best to create offspring with talents. Mine is the ability to influence people to do things against their will."

Willa's brows rose for a second before her eyes narrowed. "The lady in the grocery store. Brady."

"Yes."

She looked uncertain. "Me? Oh my god. Did you… did we because you…?"

"No," he said. "Not you."

Willa shook her head. "How can I believe that? If what you say is true, how would I even know? I mean, not that I can believe you—it's just crazy."

Without saying a word, with no more than a glance in her direction—and only that to show off to Willa what he was doing, since he didn't need to see the person in order to nudge them, he just needed to be aware of their presence near him—Phoenix had the waitress come to their table.

"I hate my job," she said. "I would like to pour this coffee all over the register and walk out. Can I get you something else?"

"Just the check," Phoenix said at Willa's startled expression. "Which you will have comped. Then you'll forget us both, and if anyone asks, you never saw either one of us."

The waitress grinned. "Sure thing, no problem. Here you go, you have a nice night."

Phoenix waited until she'd wandered back to the counter, where she pulled out her phone and started tapping away again without so much as a glance toward them. Then he looked at Willa. "Ready to go?"

She'd seen it happen, but that didn't mean anything. Did it? Willa didn't even look at him as they crossed the highway to get back to the motel.

In the Penn's Grove library, there was an entire section on the occult and paranormal. Willa had acquired titles and shelved them in that section for years and had never once picked one up. She didn't watch horror movies or read scary books. She didn't hold on to superstitions. Yet she'd seen the waitress respond to something, and it had clearly not been free will.

In the room, she excused herself to use the bathroom. A long, hot shower. Tooth brushing. She put on a pair of soft sweatpants and a T-shirt from the go bag since she hadn't packed pajamas. She swiped away the steam from the mirror to take a long, hard look at her reflection.

"So who were those men?" she said without preamble when she came out to find Phoenix with his head propped on a pillow and watching something on the TV with the sound turned so low he couldn't possibly hear the dialogue.

"They come from a place called Wyrmwood," he said without pause. He sat, back pressed against the headboard. "It is exactly what I said it was in the diner. They found out about Collins Creek years ago and raided it. They took some of the children."

"You?"

"No. My sister and I got away. We ran. We lived on the streets for years."

Willa sat on the edge of the second bed, facing him. "How old were you?"

"Ten. On the farm, all the children lived in the nursery until they turned five, and then we were tested to see if we had any talents. If we did, we got to move into the dorms."

Willa frowned. "If you didn't?"

"You went away. I don't know what happened," Phoenix said, voice free of inflection. No hint of emotion on his face. He might've been talking about the TV show still playing.

"So you and your sister, at age ten, were on the streets and on the run, after years of mental and physical trauma?"

Phoenix said nothing. His steady stare didn't waver. He looked at her, but that was it.

Without thinking of why, without holding back, Willa got up and knelt on the bed in front of him. She pulled him close, his face pressed to her neck. She stroked the length of his hair. When he tried to resist her by pulling away, she tightened her grip, and he sent still. He sighed against her.

"I'm so sorry," she whispered into his ear. She held him tight, not understanding what had pushed her to this offer of comfort. She was not the sort to hug, and while she'd never thought of herself as being unkind, she wasn't totally a warm and fuzzy personality, either.

This time when he made to pull away, she let him. He didn't meet her gaze. Her fingertips rested on his shoulders, no longer holding him, but the connection was still there.

"It was a long time ago. Decades. And I made it through. I'm fine."

Willa had gone through her own hell, but she was sure not one bit of it compared to whatever Phoenix had endured as a child. Being on the streets had to have been awful, too.

"How did Wyrmwood find you this time?"

"I called my sister. She's been..." He paused, then shook his head. "There's another group, kind of the opposite of Wyrmwood. Run by a dude named Vadim. Group of people, some of them with abilities like mine, most just able to do other stuff like computer hacking or whatever. It's called the Crew. They research stuff like this, or they're paid to prove or disprove the existence of this sort of thing. When someone sees a chupacabra, they end up going after it."

"A chupa... I don't even know what that is." Her fingers curled a bit more on his shoulders until he looked at her face.

"So why would calling your sister bring down Wyrmwood on you?" she asked, mind whirling, trying hard to put the pieces together.

Phoenix shrugged. "It's the only thing I can think of. The Crew uses encryption and all that shit, I'm sure. But I was on a phone that might've been monitored. I don't know."

"All of this is crazy," she said.

He smiled and touched a strand of her hair that had curled, damp from the shower. "Totally bat shit."

"I don't like thinking you made me do something," she said bluntly. "How do I know you haven't? How do I know that I'm not here right now because of something you forced me into?"

Phoenix closed his eyes. Said nothing. Beneath her

hands, his muscles shifted and bunched, tensing, before he relaxed.

"I tried with you," he said. "It doesn't work."

She sat back then, putting distance between them. "What?"

"It doesn't work with you," he repeated, opening his eyes. The pupils had gone wide and dark. "I've never met someone I couldn't nudge, but you just won't be nudged. I don't know why."

Something twisted inside her at those words. That look. A slow and spiraling heat began low in her belly, spreading upward.

"You expect me to believe that out of all the people in your life you've ever met, I'm different, somehow?"

Phoenix let his tongue slip out to dent his bottom lip for a second. "Yes."

"I don't think I can believe that," Willa said.

"I can't prove it," he said finally. "You'll always wonder if I'm making you do something. You'll never be able to fully trust me, because you won't be able to trust yourself."

It sounded like he'd been down that road before, but she wasn't going to go there right now. Now she was tired, her stomach full, and at least for the moment it seemed as though they were safe. She stifled a yawn.

"I need sleep," she said.

Phoenix nodded and used the remote to turn off the TV. "Sure. That's a good idea. I'd like to get out of here first thing in the morning."

"It's already first thing in the morning," Willa said.

He smiled. "We don't have to leave at dawn or anything. You can sleep for a few hours."

"What about you?"

"I'll be fine. You sleep," he said, and whether it was because he'd told her to or she could no longer fight the exhaustion, Willa crawled into bed and was asleep almost as soon as her head hit the pillow.

Chapter 8

They'd been driving for an hour before Willa said more than a few grunted words. Apparently she was not a morning person. Phoenix didn't blame her. He didn't love mornings himself.

"So…where are we going?"

He glanced at her. "I'm taking you to meet my sister."

"What?" Startled, she did a double take. "Where is she?"

Phoenix focused again on the road. "Not sure. But I know how to find her, or how to let her find me, anyway."

"You're taking me to the Crew?"

He nodded. "Yes. They'll be able to keep you safe."

"So you do think I'm in danger."

"Because you were with me," he said. "Yes. They

wouldn't keep you, I don't think. But the things they'd do so that you didn't remember them or your time there wouldn't be good."

Willa made a face and looked back out the passenger side window. Without turning back to him, she said, "I don't have anything to go back to, really."

"Your family," Phoenix told her at once.

She nodded, still looking out the window. "Will they be all right?"

"I don't know."

She turned. "Could the Crew protect them?"

"Yes. I think so," he said. "To be honest, though, I doubt Wyrmwood would go after them. I heard they have money problems."

She laughed. Hard. "Are you kidding me?"

He hadn't realized how much he'd been hoping to see her smile until she did. "Nope. Everything takes a budget. Do you know how much it costs to get all those black uniforms?"

She was giggling then, rolling her eyes. It lifted something in him that had felt very heavy for a long time. She waved a hand at him.

"Imagine the dry-cleaning bills," she said.

Then both of them were guffawing, the cab of the truck filling with their laughter. He couldn't recall ever losing himself to humor the way he was in this moment. Maybe once or twice, but not for a long time.

Willa looked at him with shining eyes. "This all feels so surreal, you know?"

"I know. I'm…sorry." He was not used to apologies, but one felt necessary now.

Willa shook her head, her smile softening but not disappearing. "What are you sorry about?"

"Everything." Carefully he navigated the truck off the rural road they'd been following since this morning and onto a smaller road that had not been plowed. There wasn't as much snow here as there'd been in Penn's Grove, but it was enough to make driving difficult.

"Oh," she said.

He glanced at her. "You wouldn't be in this mess if not for me. You'd be at home now, safe."

"Don't be sorry about everything," she said after a second or so. "I'm not."

Again, her look. Her voice. His cock thickened, pressing the front of his jeans. He wanted to answer her but had no words. He wasn't used to that. It made him a little angry but did nothing to release the pressure in his crotch. If anything, it got his cock even harder.

She didn't say much after that, and neither did he. They drove for another half an hour, slow going on the dirt road even with the four-wheel drive. The snow and ice had not been plowed, and it required almost all of his concentration to keep the vehicle on the road. By the time they got to the clearing in the trees and the small wooden cabin there, his fingers had cramped a bit from clutching the steering wheel. He pulled up through the snow to park in front of the cabin and turned to her.

"We're here."

She'd told him in the truck that all of this felt surreal, and that hadn't changed. If anything, several times Willa had stopped herself to make sure she was indeed living this adventure and not dreaming it. Even so, she kept waiting to wake up.

Phoenix had brought them to what he said was a safe house for the Crew. A hunting cabin deep in the Pennsylvania mountains. Fully stocked with food, beverages, with heat provided by a wood-burning stove. Comfortably furnished with everything a hunter might need…or a pair of people on the run from what she was still not certain was a real thing.

"How'd you know about this place?" she asked, watching as Phoenix moved from the stove to the counter and back again. He was cooking something for her from things he'd pulled from the pantry. She wasn't going to argue about it. She liked watching him move.

Phoenix glanced at her as he sliced some onions and set them sizzling in a pan. "Vadim brought me and my sister here a long time ago. He said if we ever needed anything, we should find a way to get here and someone would be along to get us shortly."

"Is that what we want?" Willa frowned at the thought of this. "I get the idea you don't like the Crew."

"I don't want to ever be beholden to anyone," Phoenix said sharply. "I don't want to ever be put in a place I can't get out of. I don't want anyone to tell me what I should do with my abilities. I don't want to be controlled."

She could understand that, for sure, although she couldn't help thinking about the night in his house. "You let me tell you what to do."

He'd been turned toward the stove when she said that, and his back straightened. He half turned. "That was different."

"I'd like to know why," Willa asked quietly.

He didn't answer her. She didn't push. He kept cooking, a simple dish of pasta with sauce made from canned tomatoes, onions and garlic. He put it on the table in front of her and didn't take a seat.

She looked up at him. "Thank you."

"I didn't let you tell me what to do," he said after a second. "I let you do things to me. That was different. I chose it."

"Fair enough." She didn't push. Instead, she picked up the fork he'd given her and twirled it full of pasta. She tucked the bite into her mouth, murmuring with pleasure at the flavors. She chewed. Swallowed.

He watched her, waiting until she'd finished the bite and looked up at him before he put his own plate on the table and took a seat. They ate in silence. She didn't stare at him, although she felt him looking at her a lot. When they'd finished, she cleared the table and started washing the dishes, waving him away when he tried to help.

"I got this," she said. "You made dinner. I'll clean up."

"How domestic," Phoenix said.

She glanced at him as she rinsed a plate and put it in the drainer next to the sink. "How long until someone comes?"

"I don't know. Could be hours. Could be a few days."

"How do they know we're here?" She asked.

Phoenix shrugged. "I don't know."

"Well," Willa said as she finished the last dish and turned to face him. "I guess we'd better make the most of the time we have, huh?"

She'd been testing him, not entirely sure how he was going to react. But there it was again, that fine shiver, the brief flutter of his lashes as his eyes closed and he forced them open immediately. The slick pink point of his tongue on his lower lip before it disappeared.

"Go upstairs," she said, her breath catching and her heart beginning to pound even though she was doing her best not to show it. "Take off your clothes and wait for me."

He didn't move at first, and she thought he was going to refuse. Or make a comment, a joke, maybe even a cheesy retort. There was a second when a hard light flared in his gaze when she thought he might flat-out tell her to fuck off.

He didn't.

He got up from the table with a scrape of the chair on the faded linoleum. Silently, he left the kitchen. She heard the tread of his footsteps on the narrow set of stairs leading up to what she'd already seen was a gabled attic room lined with several beds.

She finished with the dishes, not because she had any sort of cleaning fetish but so she could make him wait. The creak of the floorboards above her had ceased after the first minute or so. She imagined him waiting for her, and her breath slipped out of her on a small hissing sigh as she fought to keep herself from shaking. Desire and need made her fingers tremble so much that she dropped the pot in which he'd cooked the pasta. It hit the sink with a clatter so loud she was sure he'd be down the stairs in an instant, but there was only silence.

Willa gave a breathless laugh at her foolishness and got herself together. They were doing this, she thought with something like wonder, and that idea—that she would climb those stairs and find him waiting for her— was as surreal as anything else had been for the past couple of days. She let the water from the faucet run cold for a half a minute so she could dab it at her throat and over her forehead.

Then she went upstairs.

"Oh," she said at the sight of him. "Oh my god."

He had done as she'd told him. Naked. Stretched out on a sagging double bed. His cock was hard. His eyes were closed, lips slightly parted as she moved to stand over the bed. He let out a small sigh when she ran a hand up one muscled thigh and over his hip to rest on his belly, close to but not touching his erection.

Swiftly, Willa undressed. The cabin was warm downstairs, but up here it was chilly enough that she could see her breath. Her nipples peaked at once. So much for heat rising, she thought, and nearly let out another burst of those semihysterical giggles that so plagued her when she was faced with a situation she couldn't quite believe was happening.

She didn't want to think of this as a dream or a fantasy, though. She wanted it to be real. This man and the things he'd allowed her to do were all too real. Too precious, too sexy, too delicious…too rare, she thought as she dug her fingernails into the taut skin of his stomach and watched him arch beneath her rough touch.

"Open your eyes."

He did.

"Tell me," Willa said in a voice so low and rasping she wasn't sure he'd heard her.

"Hurt me," Phoenix said.

She dug deeper. She would leave marks. She would bring blood. He didn't protest; in fact, his cock swelled, thicker and harder and going a sweet, dusky shade of red that pushed a soft moan from her throat. He groaned when she softened her touch and bent to press a kiss to the gouges.

She let her mouth drift over his hip, where she bit him. Slowly at first. Then harder. He cried out, something between a prayer and a curse, and she laughed as she let go and sat up to look at him.

"We could be interrupted," she murmured.

Phoenix's gaze had already gone a little starry, but he smiled. "Yeah. At any moment."

"What might they think, whoever shows up? Seeing us naked. Fucking." She dipped her head again, this time to fasten her teeth to the tender inside of his thigh. She took the tiniest bit of flesh between her teeth, knowing it would hurt worse than a larger bite. She nipped, hard.

He strained upward, not bucking. "Oh…damn… I don't care what they think."

"No?" She licked the spot she'd bitten. "Me neither."

In truth, she wasn't one to crave an audience, but the thought that someone might find them this way did strangely excite her. Someone seeing her with this power over him. Of him giving in to her.

Of watching her bring him to the edge.

She stroked his cock, watching his face as he lifted his hips to her touch. "There are so many pretty ways to hurt you, Phoenix. I hardly know where to start."

"Please start," he said.

She laughed, but it turned into a half-sobbing sound at the sight of him pushing himself into her fist. None of the men she'd been with had moved her the way Phoenix did. She didn't want to think about why. She didn't want to consider what he'd said in the diner, that she was different to him than anyone else had ever been. She could not let herself even contemplate that perhaps he was different to her than anyone else, too.

There weren't any toys or tool to use, but she had her teeth and pinching fingers; she had her hands. She worked him all over, watching the glorious way his skin went pink and then red beneath her touch. His cock, too. Slick, sweet precome leaked from the head of it, and she used that to circle a fingertip on his cock head while he gasped and groaned.

"Sometimes," Willa said, "pleasure can hurt, too."

She began to tease him. She took his cock into her mouth and sucked, stroking his balls. Her other hand on the shaft. He was pumping inside her mouth in a minute or so. She withdrew, laughing at his groan of frustration.

When she straddled him and took him into her, he put his hands on her hips at once. His cock felt so good, deep inside her, that she almost let herself ride him hard but stopped herself to go slow, achingly slow. Up. Down. Grinding her hips. Any time he started to act as though he were getting close, she stopped to feel the pulse and throb of him inside her. She dug her nails into his chest, leaving a pattern of half-moon marks that filled in with crimson.

She didn't think she was going to get off this way. She needed more pressure on her clit. Still, it aroused her to watch the way his eyes went glazed, his mouth lax. How he groaned each time her touch cut into him. When she raked him with her nails, leaving a long swath of marks, she thought she'd tipped him over.

"No," Willa said and gripped his chin to force him to look at her. "Don't you come."

Phoenix breathed out. Grinned. "No."

Again she began to move, letting her clit rub along the ridges of his belly muscles and the crinkling hair there. The pressure wasn't quite enough. She tantalized herself. Then she lost herself in the slowly building pleasure. Her head fell back. She rocked on him.

"Oh, yes, fuck, yes," she breathed. Her knees pressed his hips. As her desire mounted, again and again she dug her nails into his skin.

She opened her eyes to see him watching her, his gaze sharp now. Focused. He'd begun lifting his hips in time to the grinding of hers. The motion pressed her clit just right, and although she hadn't expected it, she was getting closer and closer. *This, this, this*, she thought, incapable of saying it aloud. Wordless noises slipped out of her. They worked together.

"Don't," she managed to say.

"No," Phoenix murmured.

She stopped worrying that he was going to get there before her. She let herself move. Minutes passed, desire building in breathtaking increments. She eased to the edge of orgasm and didn't go over; she could have touched her clit or ordered him to, but this was too delicious to stop. Tension coiled inside her. Her thighs began to shake. She became aware that she was saying his name under her breath, her voice almost pleading, but for what she couldn't be sure. Everything was going tight inside her. Her clit was swollen, hard, brushing him every time she moved. Her ass clenched. When he cried out, she realized she'd again drawn blood from the smooth skin right over his hips.

Willa's eyes wanted to close so she could give herself up to this pleasure, but she forced herself to look at him. Everything else in the room had faded away, a nimbus of light surrounding them. The headboard creaked in a steady pattern that sounded like music.

She moved faster. Harder. She no longer thought about needing an extra touch on her clit—the throb of his cock inside her was enough. Oh, it was so much better than enough. Her hands pressed his chest, feeling the tight muscles of his pecs. She pinched his nipples, hard, twisting them, and at his hoarse shout she almost went over.

She had to kiss him. His mouth on hers, tongues stroking, the clash of their teeth. She bit his lower lip, and he fucked upward so hard and deep inside her that she cried out in pain, not caring even though it was the giving and not receiving of it that got her off. This was sweet agony, a counterpoint to the rising, throbbing tide of ecstasy inside her.

She could think of nothing else.

She could do nothing but ride him.

Closer and closer, she spun, until there was nothing that could keep her from this. She pushed upward on his chest so she could look into his eyes. His mouth was open and she could not stop herself from spitting into it, then kissing him; she could not stop from biting his tongue the way she had two nights ago. His muffled shout was another push toward the edge. Kissing, kissing, kissing hard enough to bruise, she rocked on him so hard the entire bed moved along the floor.

She came so hard she could not draw breath. She tried, shaking, but could only cry out, long and low and guttural. Her orgasm went on and on, waves of it rushing over her only to crash back.

"Come for me," Willa demanded without the breath even to speak.

Somehow, despite that, Phoenix heard her. She actually felt him swell and throb inside her. Felt the flood of him jetting inside her. Heat and slickness kept her moving, writhing on him to get her clit pressed harder on his stomach and sending another wave of contractions through her. She couldn't tell if she were coming again or if her first climax simply had not ended. All she knew was in this moment there was only pleasure.

Only Phoenix, only him.

Chapter 9

Phoenix was so hard he wasn't sure he was even going to come until her breathless command pushed him over. Then he wasn't sure he was ever going to stop.

Shaking, he let himself go. Blinded, deafened, the sound of blood whooshing in his ears, he was sure he would pass out from the rush. His tongue ached from her teeth; it was too much and not enough. He could never get enough. Not of this, not of pain. Not of her.

Then he could think of nothing but this. When he could focus and breathe, he became aware that Willa had fallen forward to press her face against his neck. Her knees pressed his sides, making him notice the sting from the places she'd scoured with her nails. It sent another throb through his cock, which had not quite softened yet.

"Oh my god," she said into his ear. "I can't move."

"Don't." He put his arms around her, holding her tight against him.

She chuckled, perhaps at the syrupy, drunken tone of his voice that should have embarrassed him. Maybe at the echo of the command she'd given him not to come. Either way, her laughter tightened her internal muscles around him in a way that had him shifting a little to push up inside her again.

"Mmm," she said.

After another minute or so, she sat up and disentangled herself from his grip. Sticky, slippery, she slid off him to lie on her back in the lumpy bed. One leg crossed over his so her toes tapped his foot. She turned her face to press a kiss to his shoulder.

He hadn't been cold during, but now the chill in the attic was apparent. He twisted to tug up the comforter over both of them. Willa let out a sleepy murmur as he did, and he lifted his head to look down at her. She was smiling, her eyes closed, her breath puffing out of her lips. Falling asleep.

He was not much of a cuddler, especially not after sex, but right now he couldn't make himself move. He tucked the comforter around her shoulder and shifted her a little bit so that she would have more of the pillow. His arm was going to fall asleep, he thought as he stared up at the ceiling. He should get up and clean off. There were plenty of other beds to use here—he could use one of them. There was no need for him to sleep with her, not even for a few minutes. Certainly not for the night.

Yet somehow, without knowing quite why or how, that was exactly what he found himself doing.

* * *

Willa woke to the sound of a woman's voice. It took her half a minute to struggle up from dreams before she was conscious enough to realize where she was. She still didn't know who was speaking, not at first, but the woman standing with her hands on her hips at the foot of the bed could only be Phoenix's sister.

"What is wrong with you?" she cried, gesturing at Phoenix. To Willa, she said, "Hey. Sorry about the interruption."

Phoenix got out of bed, apparently not caring if he scandalized his sister, who turned with a roll of her eyes. He grabbed his clothes from the floor and started getting dressed. "How'd you know it was me?"

"I wasn't sure, I was just assigned to come here and get whoever it was," she said. "Maybe Vadim knew."

Phoenix's lip curled.

The woman ignored him and looked at Willa. "He probably did. I'm Persephone, by the way."

"Willa."

Willa had clutched the blanket to her chest and now took advantage of the semiprivacy to pull her own clothes on. She'd fallen asleep in a weird position, and her neck creaked. She'd also fallen asleep sated and sticky, she remembered with a glance over her shoulder, but now was cold.

"A shower would be nice," Phoenix said. "Don't guess we have time for one."

Persephone snorted. "Sure. Let me just wait while you take your time, brother mine."

"I'm sure Willa wouldn't mind one, either," Phoenix said mildly.

Persephone looked startled and cast Willa a curious glance. "Right…you're right. Of course. Do you need some time?"

Both of them must have reeked of sex, but Willa shook her head after a second's look toward Phoenix. He had no expression at all. "I can be ready to go. Where are we going?"

"I'm supposed to take you someplace safe," Persephone said. "I mean, safer than this. Phoenix, shit. You're coming with me? Really?"

His sister had crossed to him now that he was dressed. She didn't hug him, but she took him by the front of the shirt until he looked at her. Phoenix shrugged.

Persephone looked at Willa. "Who are you?"

"She's a librarian," Phoenix said in a slightly mocking tone. "She's just along for the ride. She got caught up in it without knowing what she was in for."

Willa paused before answering. "Right… I got caught up in this, that's all it is."

If Persephone wondered what was going on between them, she didn't show it. Probably, Willa thought, Phoenix's sister was used to stumbling across him in bed with women she didn't know, who meant nothing to him, who'd merely been caught up in whatever tragedies he was going through at the time.

"I'm so glad to see you," Persephone said to him.

Phoenix waved a hand. "You don't have to get all gooey about it."

"I'm not…" Persephone stopped herself and gave Willa a look. "What's been going on? He won't tell me. He'll be a smart-ass about it."

"Wyrmwood," Willa said.

"Oh, shit." Persephone gave her brother a startled look. "You called me on an unsecured line?"

Phoenix said nothing but pushed past her and went down the stairs, leaving the women alone in the attic. Willa finished pulling on her sweatshirt. Persephone gave an awkward laugh.

"Wow," she said.

"It's been an interesting few days," Willa answered.

"I bet. So…listen, you're welcome to come with us, of course. Vadim will take care of you, make sure you're okay. I'm sorry you got caught up in this… How did you get caught up in it, anyway?"

"He was my neighbor," Willa said. "I just brought him dinner."

There'd been so much more to it than that, she thought, although apparently it hadn't meant so much to him. It shouldn't mean anything to her, actually, this fuckery her life had now become because she'd allowed the aching in her soul to lead her next door with a casserole and a bottle of wine. She'd screwed up in the past, for sure, but this had turned out to be an epic mistake.

"If he…" Again, Persephone trailed off, clearing her throat. "Look, if you think that you've been coerced or anything, in any way…"

"No," Willa said sharply. "Definitely not. Anything I've done has been totally my choice."

Persephone didn't look convinced. "Because my brother can—"

"I know what he can do." She had not been so sure she believed it, really, not even with all the proof he'd shown her. She wasn't sure, to be honest, that he had not in fact influenced her. He was right about what he'd said. She would never trust him.

"Did he tell you?"

"We should go," she said, which wasn't the answer to Persephone's question but the only one she gave.

Being in this room was like being tossed into a pit full of fire ants. Phoenix continually felt the sting of them crawling on his skin. The prick and tingle of constant anxiety.

"Stop pacing," Persephone snapped. "God, brother, it's like you think someone's going to do something awful to you."

He swiveled on one foot to look at her. "Like they won't?"

"They won't. I promise you. What will it take until you can believe me?" She looked so sad it ought to have made him feel sad, too, that he'd caused her distress.

He didn't. He felt on edge. Ready to roar. He wanted out of here. So why, then, had he not simply walked away, the way Vadim had sworn he would be able to? Why had he suffered the somewhat invasive medical exam that he knew had been meant to catalog everything about him so they could use it to their own purposes? The Crew might not be as nefarious as Wyrmwood, but that didn't mean he would ever trust them.

Why was he still here?

"Look," he said stiffly. "I can see you're happy here. With what's-his-name."

"Kane," Persephone said. "And you knew that."

Again, he should have felt like the asshole he knew

he was being. "Whatever. You're happy here. You like playing gofer for that guy, good for you."

"It doesn't have to be like that. There's so much else you'd be good at."

Phoenix frowned and went to the small counter of the kitchenette. He couldn't complain about the accommodations, that was for sure. The food wasn't as good as the dinner Willa had cooked for him, but it was all right.

"Willa's thinking about it," Persephone told him. "Vadim said he could use help with the library system."

Phoenix turned. "And she said yes?"

"She said she'd think about it, I guess. She's not completely convinced about a lot of the stuff she'd be cataloging, but she said she was still able to put it in order, keep the collection organized. Vadim said it was okay if she's skeptical. He said we need some people who still need to be convinced, now and then."

"I don't need to be convinced. I just don't want to hang around here. I'm going to get back on the road soon." He said it without conviction. The thought of leaving here, hitting the streets, finding a new place to live, dealing with more people he'd have to influence and manipulate…suddenly he felt too tired to deal with it. "Soon."

"You haven't even listened to Vadim. He would absolutely set you up in something that works for you. I don't know why you're so against it."

"You don't have to understand," he told her. "You just need to accept it. Accept *me*, sister mine. We are not the same person. Never were, never will be."

He'd stung her, he saw that. Persephone frowned and shrugged. She got off the chair and went to the door.

"Please don't leave without saying goodbye, that's all. And at least let us set you up with encrypted phones so you can call me every so often. Okay? Can you at least do that for me? I miss you, brother mine, when you're not around. I worry about you."

He looked up at that. "You know I can take care of myself."

"I know you can. But that doesn't mean I don't want to know where you are or what you're doing."

"Fine," he said. "I'll try."

She closed the door behind her with a soft click, and he opened the fridge to dig around inside and see what might make a decent meal. Most people staying in the Crew's Pennsylvania location ate communal meals in the cafeteria, but you could order limited groceries to be delivered from the commissary if you preferred to eat in your room. Phoenix didn't want to go out and deal with the hassle of talking to other people, but this room, as nicely furnished and full of amenities as it was, still felt too much like a prison cell.

He used his new, encrypted phone to thumb a text to Willa but erased it before he could send it. She knew where to find him just as much as he knew where she was. If she'd wanted him, she should have reached out. Instead she was making friends and getting herself settled in here with a new job and all of that business.

He made his way to the cafeteria, which featured a buffet line more suited to a Vegas casino than a business facility. He loaded his tray with small tastes of whatever he thought looked good, then took the plates to sit at one of the heavy wooden tables lined with comfortable chairs.

"Mind if I join you?"

Phoenix looked up at the unfamiliar male voice. The guy in front of him wore a pair of faded blue jeans and a white T-shirt with the sleeves rolled up. His reddish hair had been cut in a vintage style, adding to the '50s *Happy Days* look.

"There are plenty of other places to sit. Why don't you go find one of them?" Phoenix dug his fork into a slippery pile of chicken potpie.

The guy didn't leave. He set his tray down across from Phoenix. "Look, it's time we met, anyway. I'll move if you want me to, but I was hoping we'd have the chance to talk. Get to know each other a little bit. I'm Jed. Collins."

Phoenix paused with his mouth full of soft noodles slippery with chicken gravy. He chewed. Swallowed. He took another slow, careful bite, giving Jed no indication that the introduction meant anything to him at all.

"I'm your brother," Jed said.

"We shared the same parents. That doesn't make you my brother."

Jed nodded. "Fair enough. Does it have to be such a big deal, though? It's not like I'm trying to get good old Mom and Dad to take my side over yours about who gets to pick which television show we watch. We share DNA, Phoenix. And experiences. There has to be something to that."

"Why?" Phoenix gestured around the cafeteria. "Betcha half a dozen people in here have had similar experiences, if not directly at Collins Creek, at least someplace like it."

"Not related to each other." Jed smiled and tilted his head.

Phoenix felt a small, tickling nudge he was quickly

able to ignore, although he did sit back in his chair to stare at the younger man. "What's your thing? Can you make yourself look like someone else, the way Persephone does? Or do you influence people to do things, the way I can?"

"I might be able to do a little bit of both, but mostly I affect things. Not people." Jed began peeling the paper off a blueberry muffin encrusted with sugar. "Persephone said you weren't staying around."

"I don't plan on it. No." Phoenix eyed the other guy.

Jed glanced up. "Yeah, I don't stick around here for more than a week or two at a time, then I'm off in the field working. I spent the first twenty years of my life locked up in a tiny room. I get antsy if I have to stay here for very long."

"…Locked up?"

"Wyrmwood," Jed said. "You've heard of it."

"Hell, yeah, I've heard of it. Bastards have been after me for a long damned time. I don't intend to let them get me, and I don't intend to get stuck here just to avoid having them catch me, either." Phoenix stabbed his fork into a pile of noodles again but didn't bring a bite to his mouth. "You were in there?"

"Yes. They took me from the farm and put me in there until Vadim and the Crew came to break me out."

Phoenix put the fork down without eating. His entire life for the past twenty years had been spent running from Wyrmwood. Every decision he'd ever made, it seemed, had been to keep himself out of there.

"It was bad?" he asked.

Jed didn't answer at first. Then he nodded. He took a bite of salad, crunching it before speaking. "It was very bad."

"And you don't feel like the Crew is just more of the same, maybe the cells are bigger, maybe your walls aren't quite so high, so you can still see the sky, but don't you feel like it's still a prison?"

"No, not at all." Jed gave Phoenix another curious look. "There's nobody here telling me when or where I'm allowed to go, unless I'm on a job, and even then it's my choice to take it or not. I mostly take the jobs. If you don't work in some way, you don't get paid, but that's how it works anywhere, isn't it?"

Phoenix had never had a normal job, not really. "You said you can't stand to stay here longer than a week or so."

"True, but I get to travel all over. I spent years never getting out of a single room, except to be taken into another single room for testing. I want to see as much as I can. I want to stand on the edge of the Grand Canyon and smell the air. I want to swim in every lake and ocean I can. I want to live my life."

"And you're not afraid Wyrmwood will find you, grab you? Get you back?"

"Nope." Jed grinned. "Not anymore. Not with what I can do to keep myself out of their reach. The Crew's helped me with that. Helped me train, learn. With the kinds of resources we can access here, anything is possible."

"But you have to answer to Vadim."

Jed looked surprised. "Huh? No. I mean, sure, he's the boss, but again, you do a job, you get paid. He's the boss—he's in charge of that. But the rest of your life? No, man. He doesn't get involved with that stuff."

"Somehow, I can't believe that's true." Phoenix had lost his appetite, and he pushed away his tray.

"You don't have to, I guess." Jed shrugged and forked another bite of food. He chewed slowly, looking Phoenix in the eyes. "Speaking for myself, though, I spent a long time wishing I had a family, and now I do. You're a part of that, even if you don't want to be. We don't have to arm wrestle or anything. You don't have to teach me how to ride a bike. I just thought it would be great to have someone else around who understands what it was like where we were born, and what it's like to live with what they made us into."

"I want to forget all that," Phoenix answered sharply. "I don't want it following me around all over the place for the rest of my life."

Jed shrugged and took a long drink of water. "Seems to me that it is already following you around, and you can't get rid of it."

Phoenix was not going to give Jed the satisfaction of knowing how deeply he'd dug with those words, so although he wanted to get up immediately, he made a show of finishing his food and tossing the trash before leaving the cafeteria with a casual, deliberately neutral wave in Jed's direction. Once he left, there was no place to go but to follow the winding halls of the complex to find Willa's room. He figured she wouldn't be inside. She was probably off in the library somewhere.

She answered. She wore her dark hair piled on top of her head. A pair of steel-rimmed glasses dangled from a chain around her neck. Her white blouse, form-fitting but unbuttoned to the throat, and the black skirt that hit just above the knee were such a cliché that he laughed. It came out of him on a stuttering sigh, not sounding much like humor.

"Come in." Willa stood to the side to let him pass. "I was just finishing a shift in the catalog room."

"Looking like that?"

She hesitated, glancing down at her clothes. "It's a professional outfit, Phoenix. Do you have a problem with it?"

"No. I love it. It makes me want to tear it off you."

He wanted more than that. He wanted to go to his knees in front of her while she began to work her magic on him the way she'd done every time they were together. He wanted her to thread her fingers through his hair, tip his head back and scour his throat with her teeth.

He did not want to tell her that.

"Really?" She smiled and gave him a considering look. "I suppose that could be arranged."

Chapter 10

Willa hadn't seen much of Phoenix over the past week or so. She'd been busy learning as much as she could about the Crew and the facility here, about the library system and how she could be of use in running it. It was a dream job, no doubt about it. The only strings attached were that she needed to live on-site, but since room and board were included with a very generous salary, including full health benefits, there didn't seem much reason to turn down the offer. With the money they were going to pay her, she could afford to travel during her vacation time.

The only drawback she could think of was that it meant embracing a whole bunch of ideas she'd discounted for most of her life. Even that wasn't insurmountable, she thought as she stepped aside to allow Phoenix to move past her and into the tiny kitchenette she hadn't used much. He went straight to the cupboard to pull down the bottle of whiskey that had come with the place. Glasses. Ice from the freezer. He poured two drinks and handed her one. He downed his at once, grimacing, the set the glass on the counter so hard she thought he might have cracked it.

"Come here," he said.

She did at once, curious about his intentions. Heat already had begun its slow and sensual rise from her belly toward her throat. When she got within reach, Phoenix grabbed a double handful of her blouse. He tore it, buttons flying, and left the thin fabric in shreds. He'd yanked hard enough to rock her forward, and she put a hand on his chest to keep herself from falling.

"Oh," she said.

His mouth was on the slopes of her breasts, exposed over the lacy edge of her bra, before she could make a protest. Not that she had any to make. She wanted his mouth on her. His hands. His lips tugged the points of her nipples through the soft lace. She moaned. His hands moved on her back, unhooking the bra and exposing her bare skin to his teeth and tongue. When he fastened his mouth on one nipple, Willa cried out.

"Take off your skirt."

She reached behind to get at the button and zipper. The motion thrust her breasts harder against him. He bent to the other nipple, suckling and nipping at the soft flesh surrounding it. She let the skirt drop and stood before him in only the matching lace panties.

He touched her at once, his forefinger stroking along the seam between her legs and up, up to center on her clit. Seconds only of pressure before he was slipping his fingers beneath the waistband to dip low and find her slickness. He brought it up to coat her clit, making small but firm circles.

His other hand went to the back of her neck, fingers curling tight. His gaze dug into hers. His mouth thin, grim, his expression bordering on fierce. A challenge.

"I want you to suck my cock," Phoenix said. "On your knees."

She went at once, wincing only a second at the hardness of the floor. He'd unzipped his jeans, freeing his erection. Willa tipped her head back, staring up at him. She opened her mouth. Waited.

Phoenix grabbed his cock at the base and guided it between her lips. He sank deeper than she would've, had she been controlling this, but she took him in as best she could. He throbbed on her tongue. With a small groan, Willa moved to let his cock slide free of her mouth. Then back in, slicking him thoroughly with her spit until he moved easily in and out of the heated cavern of her mouth. It was easy for her to pleasure him in this position, especially when his fingers sank into the back of her hair and he used that grip to guide her.

With her hand in a fist between her thighs, it was also easy for her to rock herself against it, getting herself off. And oh, she was, turned on by the taste of him, by the way he spoke to her, hard and fierce, as though it made any difference at all in the matter of who, in fact, was truly in charge. He could think so, Willa knew that, but in the end she was still the one who decided whether or not she got on her knees.

She shook with her impending climax, but subtly. Quietly. She focused on taking him in deep and letting him out slowly, until he grunted and started urging her to go faster. She let him fuck her mouth, doing little more than keeping her lips wide and her tongue flat.

She thought he was going to climax then, and she was ready for it. On the edge herself, needing only a little more to tip her over. When he withdrew and took a few steps back, Willa needed a second or so to orient herself to the fact he'd moved away.

She didn't try to interpret his expression beyond that he looked distressed. She thought she knew why, but there wasn't time now to dissect anything. She simply got up and went to the bed, where she placed both hands on it and bent at the waist. Feet apart. Ass tipped. She made an offering of herself, at first uncertain if he meant to take it, but when he did she closed her eyes against a sudden rush of emotion she hadn't been expecting.

He pushed inside her, fast and deep. Pounded. His hands gripped her hips, moving her body in time to his pace and rhythm. He reached around once to stroke her clit with his fingertips, but after that he resumed his rhythm. She touched herself, instead. It was enough. Better than. She was on the edge in seconds, riding the waves of pleasure as he thrust into her from behind.

"You feel so fucking good," Phoenix said. "I feel so good inside you."

Willa had words in response but kept them to herself. She answered with only a moan, a sigh, the rolling of her hips to bring him in deeper. She urged him harder with the motion of her body. Her orgasm rushed over her, and she shook with it, knowing he would feel the pulse and clench of her body around him as he moved inside her.

"Oh, fuck, yes…" Phoenix thrust again, covering her back with his body and shuddering as he came.

They stayed like that for a half a minute or so. Breathing getting slower. The pounding of their hearts easing into a normal pace. He pulled out and backed away from her, and Willa turned to sit on the edge of the bed, very aware of the slippery heat of him on her thighs.

"When do you plan to leave?" she said when it became clear he had no intentions of speaking.

Phoenix frowned as he tucked himself back into his jeans and zipped them. "Was my sister talking to you?"

"She didn't have to. I could see it on your face when you walked in here, that you meant to tell me you were going. So go, then," Willa said. "You have no reason to stay here."

"No? You're not going to ask me to stay?"

Her heart hurt a little at the hard tone of his voice, but she refused to allow him to see that. "I can't make you do anything you don't want to, Phoenix, and I would never want to."

"Because you're not like me," he said. "That's what I do, isn't it? Force people to do things against their will, all for my own gain."

Willa lifted her chin to stare into his eyes, trying to make him understand what she wasn't sure she did herself. "You don't do that with me."

"I just did!" he cried, advancing on her so fast, with such ferocity, that she recoiled. He got up in her face. "I just fucking did it with you, Willa. I came in here, and I made you do all of that stuff you'd never have agreed to if I wasn't forcing it on you…"

"That's not true!"

He shook his head. "What we just did? That's not how we are. It's not who *you* are. I did it to prove to you that I was capable of it. That you should never, ever trust yourself with me, because you'll never be able to tell if what you are doing is because you want to."

"I am perfectly capable of knowing that I want you," Willa said and stood, not caring that she was naked and he was fully clothed. "Tell yourself whatever lies you have to, Phoenix, but you don't get to make me doubt my own mind or what I want to do. No, that's not who we are or what we do, but that doesn't mean I didn't allow it. Willingly. On purpose."

He sneered and scoffed. "And you're going to tell me that you want me?"

She crossed to him, hating the way he flinched from her touch. "Do you know how rare and precious it is that we found each other? That we bring each other such pleasure in such a unique way? That's not easy to find. I certainly haven't found it with anyone, not as good as this. And believe me, I've been looking for a long time."

He didn't look at her. "You say that, but good sex—"

"Phenomenal sex," Willa cut in.

"Sex," Phoenix repeated as he looked at her, finally, "is not the only thing that matters. Because, believe me, I've done more than my share of bed hopping over the years, and in the end it doesn't last. No matter how hard you come, someone always, always wants to leave."

"Right now that person is you." She stepped back,

releasing the front of his shirt. "So go, then. Find your way out there in the world, doing whatever it is you think you need to do."

"And you'll just wait here for me?" Derision fairly dripped from his voice.

She shook her head. "No. I haven't decided yet if I'm going to be here. They offered to let me work remotely. I could go home, back to Penn's Grove, but with security measures in place in case Wyrmwood thought they needed to come back around for me. I'd be able to work for Vadim with almost all the same benefits. The money is fantastic. But no, I don't have to stay here."

Phoenix shook his head. "You'll still be answering to him."

"I have to answer to someone," she told him. "Unless I become independently wealthy, I'll always need a job. This one seems to be pretty damned good."

She thought he'd turn on his heel and storm out then, and this would be over. She was ready for that if it happened. She would find a way to move on with her life.

"You're the only person I've ever met who I can't force to do what I want," he whispered.

Willa took a chance and moved forward. She put her hands flat on his chest. She pushed up onto her toes to kiss his mouth.

"I don't ever want to force you to do anything for me," she said. "Whatever happens with us, it's always got to be your choice. I don't want it if it's not good for you, too. I mean any of it, Phoenix, not just the stuff in bed."

"What happens if you ask me for something I don't want to give you?" he demanded in a low voice. When she tried to pull away, his hands on her hips kept her close.

"Then we talk about it like normal people," she said.

Phoenix laughed, low. "I'm not normal people, Willa. I'm so far from normal…"

"Shh," she said against his mouth. "For now, all we should both ask of the other is to listen. To try. Maybe to not walk away when something goes wrong. Beyond that, who knows? It could be nothing. It could be everything. We don't know unless we try."

"I've never had to try at anything. If I didn't get what I wanted, I made someone give it to me."

She smiled, undaunted. "So walk away."

"Damn it," Phoenix said. "I don't want to walk away from you!"

"So stay." She laughed a little bit through a haze of tears at the way he was fighting this. "Phoenix. Baby."

At the endearment, he looked at her in surprise. When she pulled him close and took his chin in her hands, holding him still in a grip tight enough to hurt, should he try to get away, she forced him to look into her eyes. She said nothing, waiting to feel at least some of the tension in him ease.

"You never know when you start something new if you're going to end up getting hurt," she said. "But I promise you, I'm going to hurt you as much as you want. As often as you want. For as long as we both want me to do it."

With a growl, he kissed her hard and lifted her, carrying her to the bed, where they both fell down in a tangle of sheets and pillows. There he leaned over her to stroke the hair out of her face. His expression was serious.

"Please," Phoenix said.

Willa smiled and kissed him again.

* * * * *

Award-winning and bestselling author **Deborah LeBlanc** is a business owner, a licensed death-scene investigator and an active member of two national paranormal investigation teams. She's the president of the Horror Writers Association, Mystery Writers of America's Southwest chapter and the Writers' Guild of Acadiana. Deborah is also the creator of the LeBlanc Literacy Challenge, an annual national campaign designed to encourage more people to read, and Literacy, Inc., a nonprofit organization with a mission to fight illiteracy in America's teens. For more information go to deborahleblanc.com and literacyinc.com.

Books by Deborah LeBlanc

Harlequin Nocturne

The Wolven
The Fright Before Christmas
Witch's Hunger

Visit the Author Profile page
at Harlequin.com for more titles.

WITCH'S HUNGER

Deborah LeBlanc

For Pookie and Sarah.
It's been a long, hard road without you...

Prologue

The triplets had known trouble since birth.

Near the north wall of a vast cavern southeast of Marseilles stood a wide stone table. Behind the table sat the Council of Elders for the Circle of Sisters— Magda, head of the council, Bayonne and Palmae.

Magda, shaking with fury, glared at the three young women standing before them. Esmee, the eldest of the triplets and most outspoken, and her sisters, Lisette and Julianne François. The girls' shadows danced across the stone walls from the multitude of candles that illuminated the dank cave.

They were forced to wear sackcloth and walk the many miles to the meeting area. They stood dirty, sweating and trembling with fear at what they were about to face. They were identical in appearance save for their eyes. Each held a unique color. Esmee's were brilliant blue, Lisette's a shiny copper and Julianne's blacker than any shade of night.

All three pairs of eyes were now downcast, the girls' heads bowed in sorrow and submission. Coal-black hair fell across alabaster skin. The cave smelled of their sweat, burning candles and the earthy scent of the dirt beneath their feet.

Magda, as head of the council, held the staff of judgment so tightly in her right hand her knuckles had turned white. Her fury was undeniable. The staff of judgment was eight inches long, made of thick, polished Elder-wood and topped with a bloodstone the size of a small woman's fist. The staff was the ballast used only in severe cases, of which this was definitely one.

Being responsible for an entire clan of witches spread throughout France, especially in the fifteenth century, was no small feat. She held fast to being firm and fair, and unwavering from protocol. Despite her anger, looking at the triplets made her heart ache and cluttered her thoughts.

This wasn't the first time the sisters had stood before the council. Mostly for misdemeanors on other occasions. Their youth accounted for the majority of the dismissals of those cases.

Magda knew the council granted special favors to the triplets out of pity. Years ago, their parents had left a theater late one evening when a band of thieves shot out from a dark alley and murdered both of them. The triplets had only been two years old at the time, and by vote, the Council of Elders decided that Bayonne would take responsibility for them. They'd had no other choice. It was part of their culture. Neither adoption nor abandonment existed in their code of ethics. The Circle of Sisters took care of their own.

Magda always suspected Bayonne had been too lenient on the girls throughout the years, and today's fiasco seemed to attest to that. At sixteen years old, with a full fourteen years under Bayonne's tutelage, the young women should have known better.

"But, Elders, we beg of you," Esmee said. "Please consider reason. Would you not have done the same? Would you have allowed such boldfaced betrayal to go unpunished? Would you not have sought revenge? How can you judge us when we were the ones wronged?"

"You demonstrated complete misuse of your powers," Magda said gruffly. "Granted, your years may still be tender, and in many ways the three of you still inexperienced with many spells, but you are not naive to our laws. What you did changes the face of the human race. The monstrosities you created will not only kill and destroy other humans, they will breed and mutate, producing subspecies, and their numbers will become endless. Their nightmare will never end. You have executed your revenge, but these creatures will never know peace. They will never have the opportunity to make amends. You chose to be judge, jury and executioner, all of which you had no right. Punishment is due for this atrocity. And the punishment must match the crime."

Magda glanced at Bayonne, whose eyes brimmed with tears, then at Palmae, who sat ramrod straight, eyes wide with shock. "Are we in agreement here, sisters?" she asked them.

Both gave almost imperceptible nods.

"Very well," Magda said. "So shall it be." She held

the staff of judgment outright, its tip poised over the stone table.

Suddenly a sensation caught her attention, and Magda cocked her head slightly to one side to listen intently. She heard water dribbling from somewhere within the cave, the ragged, anxious breathing from the triplets and the other two Elders, but little more. Despite that, she felt certain…no…*knew* that someone was listening to their conversation from the mouth of the cave.

Trusting her instincts, Magda felt that someone was Tenebrus Cray, one of the most self-serving, power-hungry sorcerers she had ever known. Magda thought about storming out to confront him, then considered a better idea.

They might have gotten away with it, but there'd been too much blood. The entire city raged over the incident. It hadn't taken long for the Elders to find out. Stupid girls.

Gnawing on that thought, and the piece of clove he had stuck in his mouth earlier, Tenebrus Cray squatted near the entrance of the cave. He leaned in as close as he dared to the opening so as not to miss one word spoken by the women.

The witches had gathered secretly in the stone belly of a hillside, far from prying eyes in Marseilles. He knew their location because he had spotted Magda, Bayonne and Palmae clomping out of town on horseback, each wrapped in their signature, floor-length capes—black, purple and red, respectively.

The three were master witches and all but recluses. They lived in a hovel away from the bustle of the city.

Tenebrus had only seen them come out to work in their herb garden. To watch them head out of town was a novelty. To have them retreat so hastily, and on horse-back, was unheard of.

Tenebrus knew that Magda had the power of tele-portation. Why have an animal bear one's weight when all one had to do was wave a hand, cast a spell and the three would have immediately teleported to their destination?

Wherever they were going, whatever they intended to do, had to be significant. And Tenebrus was not about to miss the event.

Magda pounded the stick of judgment on the stone table once. Then decided to complete the trial in their tribal language, Kaswah, a language rarely spoken and only understood by those within the Circle of Sisters.

They had been speaking in French until now. Any-one eavesdropping would only hear gibberish, includ-ing Tenebrus. Magda considered casting a silencing boundary, then dismissed the thought. The sorcerer would immediately open it.

She glanced briefly at Bayonne, noticed the tears trickling down her cheeks. Palmae's expression was one of sheer dread.

Sitting arrow-back straight and lifting her chin, Magda scowled at the triplets. "Step forward."

The triplets complied, instinctively grabbing a hand of the sister nearest her.

Magda pointed the bloodstone at each young woman, then looked over at the other two Elders and said, "Sisters…"

With that single word, the three Elders recited in unison.

"Jealous lovers,
Vengeance sought.
Defiling nature,
Havoc wrought.
To chastise thee,
We Elders three,
Bind ye now for eternity."

Palmae and Bayonne slumped back in their chairs but Magda remained straight and focused and let out a sigh.

"From this day forward, you will be responsible for the creatures you have created," Magda commanded, pounding the staff of judgment once on the stone table. "No longer will you have the freedom to live life as you please. Your purpose and your powers will be used to contain these monstrosities so they do not multiply and exceed the number of humans on earth. You will establish boundaries, you will set binding spells for control. You will supply them food, but only from natural sources."

Esmee dropped her head wearily. Lisette and Julianne began to weep.

Magda pounded the staff of judgment on the table again to emphasize yet another consequence for their actions. "You and the generations of triplets to follow shall be called Triads from this day forth. The name will serve to identify your wrongdoing. And because you have altered the human race, you and the triplets of future generations are no longer allowed to marry a human nor live intimately with a human."

Esmee, Lisette and Julianne gasped in unison, as did Palmae. Bayonne let out a sob.

"Magda, this punishment is far too harsh," Palmae said. "We must consult as Elders before casting such a spell upon these young women."

"I will hear no more!" Magda shouted. "Did we not agree as a council that the punishment must fit the crime?"

"Yes," Bayonne said. "But you cannot call this punishment on your own, Magda. Where is your mercy?"

"As head of this council, I am allowed to call the punishment, if punishment is agreed upon, as I see fit. And mercy, you ask? The men whose lives these women have altered are changed forever; who gives them mercy?"

Bayonne lowered her head and Magda immediately turned her attention back to the triplets. "The creatures you have created shall be named accordingly. The one condemned to thirst for blood shall be known as Nosferatu. The one doomed to hunger for flesh yet never be sated shall be known as Loup Garou. And the one you have caused to eternally search for the marrow of bone shall be known as Chenilles. You and future Triads shall protect humans from them, and with the passage of time, as each species interbreeds and mutates, you will assign constables and shepherds to help manage them."

"But—" Esmee said.

"Silence," Magda demanded. "Along with those tasks, you and every Triad generation to follow until the end of time will bear the mark of *absolutus infinitus* on their body as a reminder of this day." She pointed the bloodstone at Esmee, and the cave echoed with the sound of sizzling flesh.

Esmee hissed in pain, lowered the coverlet of the sackcloth to examine her left shoulder and saw the mark of *8*. The *absolutus infinitus*, at first red, faded quickly to black.

Julianne and Lisette huddled closer to Esmee, but it did not stop Magda's mission. She aimed the bloodstone at Lisette, who let out a shriek of pain and clutched her right hip. Julianne came next, only hers Magda placed on her right ankle. Julianne bore the pain through gritted teeth.

"Now," Magda continued, "to minimize the chances of this occurring again, each of you will compile separate tomes. Your tome must include every spell within your knowledge, whether innate or taught. You are to identify each spell, its purpose and the consequences that occur with use of each spell. These tomes will be known as Grimoires. Once they are completed, you will bind each Grimoire in Elder-wood for preservation."

Magda waved the bloodstone over the stone table that separated the triplets from the Elders. Three palm-sized mirrors appeared on the table, one in front of each triplet. "Behind the front cover of your Grimoire, you will notch out an indention in the wood. One large enough to securely hold one of these mirrors. Understood?"

The triplets only stared at her.

"I said, do you understand?" Magda said loudly.

Esmee nodded slightly, and Lisette and Julianne quickly imitated her acknowledgment.

Seemingly satisfied, Magda continued. "You and

every generation of Triads to follow must review your Grimoire daily. The first thing you will see upon opening your tome, however, is the mirror. It will reflect the death and destruction that will befall the world should you or any Triad not live up to her duties."

Signaling the triplets closer, Magda pointed at the mirrors. "Come closer now and look at what your irresponsibility has set into motion, and why the consequences besetting you are so severe."

All three sobbing now, the triplets drew closer until they stood at the edge of the stone table. Bayonne and Palmae leaned over to look within the mirrors themselves.

With another pounding from the staff of judgment, the reflective surfaces began to dance with a myriad of colors, swirls of red, purple, green, black. Within seconds, the colors settled into indescribable scenes so vivid it was as if they were seeing them firsthand.

Reflected in each palm-sized mirror was a sea of blood, dead bodies, some mid-decay, some fully decayed. Men, women and children, all strewn about the land like garbage. Blowflies, maggots and buzzards fed on the little bits of flesh that remained on corpses. From within these images, they heard great wailing and gnashing of teeth.

When Magda waved a hand over the mirrors, erasing the images, the triplets fell to their knees, sobbing. Bayonne and Palmae looked visibly shaken.

The shadows within the cave deepened, casting purple and dark gray lattices over each triplet. They were in shock, lost, a terrified look in their eyes.

Although her position as head of the council made it necessary for Magda to execute such punishment, she couldn't help the pain she felt in her heart for the young women. She had handed down a life sentence that would change not only their lives forever but every generation of Triads to follow.

Still squatting near the mouth of the cave, Tenebrus, frustrated, strained to understand the words being spoken inside. From the occasional sob he heard coming from inside the cavern, Tenebrus assumed the punishment meted out was harsh. That angered him. Whatever limitations had been imposed on the triplets would limit him, as well.

He had known the three sisters since they were babies, and even back then he'd known something was different about the tiny witches. Triplets in any race seemed an anomaly, but in a tribe of witches, they were nearly nonexistent. So it only made sense that the three held special powers.

The day the triplets were born the Elders of the Circle of Sisters seemed perplexed as to what to make of the unusual birth. It was the beginning of a new race within their tribe. From each set of triplets, one triplet would bear triplets of her own, and so it would be until triplets no longer existed, which probably meant until the end of time.

Tenebrus had been right about them having special powers. All three girls had needed little training from a very young age. Most of the spells they conjured as children took many witches years to learn. Each triplet had special gifts in her own right, but he'd often wondered about what might happen if their powers were melded together. Well, he had to wonder no more. He had witnessed it firsthand the other evening.

The night of the incident, the one that resulted in the trip to this cavern, happened at Lord Chermoine's castle. A prenuptial gathering prepared for the intendeds of the triplets—the wedding scheduled for the following day—and Tenebrus had garnered an invitation, which came as no surprise. He'd cast a simple yearning spell to make certain his name appeared on the roster.

An unfortunate delay, or fortunate depending on one's point of view, caused Tenebrus to arrive at the castle late. Just in time to see the triplets standing outside the castle beside their intendeds, screaming about unfaithfulness. Women Tenebrus knew to be of ill repute ran out of the castle and scattered from the estate on foot, obviously not wanting any part of the tumult taking place outside.

Tenebrus hid behind a tree and watched as each triplet pointed to her intended, railing him unabashedly with obscenities.

Then the girls quickly gathered, joined hands and uttered words Tenebrus had never heard before. They swayed and chanted and from where he hid, Tenebrus felt the air thicken and begin to vibrate. Even with so much distance between him, he saw fear in the eyes of the men meant to marry these women.

Suddenly, Esmee pointed to the man she was to marry the next day and proclaimed, "You blame the drink for your actions, for your unfaithfulness. So let it be. From this day forth, you will thirst from your very core. You shall thirst for that which does not come easily and you will never know satisfaction."

No sooner were those words uttered than the man's face began to contort, widen and turn white. The hair on his head fell away as if someone with shears had been working behind the scenes, waiting for this very moment. His scalp was now white and bulbous with a large vein running up from the center of his fore-head then branching out on top of his skull like tree branches. His mouth opened wide as he cried out in pain. His two front teeth became thin and sharp, incisor-like, and grew to unimaginable lengths. His eyes turned ruby red. The tips of his ears grew long and pointed. He stood frozen for only a moment, watching, feeling his own transformation, then ran for the woods behind the castle.

The two other men looked on in bewilderment and fear. Lisette pointed to her intended and proclaimed, "If you want to act like a beast, then you shall be a beast for all eternity. Your nights will no longer be your own. You will crave flesh like an animal."

Her words caused an immediate transformation in the man. Her intended cried out in pain as fur covered his entire face, and his mouth and nose elongated, creating a snout. His body seemed to explode in width and height. His teeth were no longer those of a man but the fangs of a wolf.

The sisters appeared unaffected by the transformations taking over the men.

The man-wolf howled, confusion obvious in his eyes, and he, too, ran for the woods.

Julianne's intended had evidently seen enough for he, too, began to run. Even if he had gained twice the speed, it would not be fast enough to escape Julianne's spell.

She pointed at him, "You claim your excuse for unfaithfulness to the mindlessness that comes with drink, so you shall remain mindless. Always controlled by another. No longer will you have a mind of your own that allows free will, and you shall hunger for the bone marrow of the man you once were before engaging with that harlot."

Instinctively, Tenebrus knew the sisters had no idea about the seriousness of what they had just done.

When Julianna completed her spell, the sisters joined hands. They raised them to the heavens and proclaimed that by the power of three and every element that made up the universe, no witch or sorcerer could break their spell, no matter how powerful he or she might be.

The mutation of the third man did not appear as hideous as the former two. Oddly, he simply grew taller, thinner, but something in his eyes went empty, like the life within him had drained away. Not even fear registered in them.

Tenebrus wanted that kind of power. Absolute control over the elements of fire, water, earth and air. Over all who existed on this planet.

He had studied the triplets for years and for the past ten years, Tenebrus had become obsessed with finding a way to combine their power with his own. A sorcerer could not drain the power from this special breed of witch. But if he studied them, then took what he learned and joined that with his own superior power, he'd be ruler over every being on earth. His power would be supreme. Ultimate.

Sensing Tenebrus's presence even stronger caused Magda's anger to boil in her veins. If for nothing else but spite, she would stop this event immediately. But she couldn't. As head Elder, she had to set an example for the fifteen-hundred plus witches she, Bayonne and Palmae were responsible for.

Magda cleared her throat. "Should you or your siblings, including the generations to come, shirk their responsibilities, that Triad shall lose her powers. And the creatures they are responsible for will be freed upon the earth to kill and destroy at will."

"But you are condemning us to be alone for the rest of our lives," Lisette cried. "If we cannot marry nor live in intimacy with a human, nothing remains. Our lineage will die. Who will we marry? Who will father our children?"

Bayonne nodded in agreement and looked over at Magda. "Who?"

Magda pointed the staff of judgment at Lisette, giving her a stern look. "You will have at your disposal what remains. Fae. Sorcerers who have transcended, or one of the creatures you have created."

Palmae gasped so loudly it sounded like she'd nearly swallowed her tongue. "Magda, no! This is far too harsh and—"

"Enough!" Magda proclaimed. "It is done." She struck the stone table once more with the staff of judgment. "*Isonno, funjusa, orlato*—so it is said, so shall it be done and so shall it ever be!" Then under her breath, Magda recited another incantation, only this one was for that nosy, good-for-nothing Tenebrus, who dared to eavesdrop on such a sacred meeting. After slamming the shaft of judgment on the table for the last time, the bloodstone atop it shattered. Everyone in the cave gasped in shock, and the collective sound reverberated throughout the hollow space.

The shattered bloodstone came as no surprise to

Magda. In fact, she'd half expected it—for she had just done the very thing to Tenebrus that she had placed judgment for on the triplets who stood before her.

Only this time no one but she would ever know.

Chapter 1

Vivienne François stood behind a forty-foot gate that was topped with silver-tipped barbwire, watching blood, fur and some chunks of flesh fly in every direction, and wondered where she'd gone wrong. The air smelled of dirt, blood, urine and musk.

It was mid-October in Algiers, Louisiana, but witnessing this much brutality made her break into a sweat like it was high-noon in August.

Wearing jeans, boots and a light blue pullover work shirt, Viv took a fighting stance. Feet spread apart, fists at her sides. She closed her eyes, gritted her teeth, then said loudly, "I bind thee now, powerless until released by my word. So shall it be. So it is by my command!"

She opened one eye slowly and groaned. The blood and fur still flew.

"I don't understand what the hell is going on," she said to Socrates, who sat beside her right foot. "That's the fifth damn binding spell I've tried and it's like everyone has gone deaf, including the universe. Either that or I have turned into a frigging toasted marshmallow." She kicked angrily at the ground with the toe of her boot.

"Do you always have to be so abrasive and surly when you're upset?" Socrates asked. He was a pompous Bombay with gold eyes and had been Viv's familiar since her birth. He yawned and gave a swish of his tail. "Truly, Viv, can you not see why your spell isn't working?"

"No." She huffed. "The way it works is I do a spell and the recipient responds immediately. This isn't a show-and-tell game or three-card monte. I'll be damned if they're not going to listen."

"Oh, for heaven's sake," Socrates said with an exasperated sigh. "Must I point out every detail to you?"

"With that attitude, buddy, you're lucky if I don't ship you off to Siberia." Not that Viv would really ship Socrates anywhere, but she was so frustrated she didn't know what to do with herself.

She stood out here alone, behind a gate that served as the compound entrance to a fenced-in, five-hundred acre lair. The compound held the North End pack of Loup Garou, whom she watched over herself, since she didn't live far. Just north of the compound was another three hundred acres that served to feed and grow livestock she and her sisters used to feed the breeds they were responsible for.

Viv was one in a set of triplets, the oldest by ten minutes and responsible for the Loup Garou. The middle triplet, Evette, took care of the Nosferatu, and the youngest, Abigail, dealt with the Chenilles. All breeds were netherworld creatures that she'd had to work hard not to resent over the years. For Viv, it was like babysitting a gigantic pack of prepubescent teens.

To feed their factions, they raised cows, goats, pigs and mules specifically for that purpose. Fortunately, Viv had three humans whom she trusted to handle the cattle in the farm area. One of them was Charlie Zerangue, a fifty-two-year-old cowboy who'd worked with her for the past ten years buying cattle. He made sure his two hands sent that cattle through the feeding shoot that led them directly to an area south of the Loup Garou compound. This was the feeding territory.

Once the cattle were sent through the shoot to the feeding area, the Nosferatu were ferried from New Orleans near the river bank to Algiers. There they were loosed upon the cattle to gorge on as much blood as they wanted. The idea was to have each so satiated that they would be easier to manage around humans during their daily or nightly chores.

Once the Nosferatu were ferried back across the river, the Loup Garou from the North, West and East packs were allowed into the feeding area to rip through as much meat as their stomachs could handle for the exact same reason.

And lastly, the Chenilles, Abigail's brood, were ferried across the river to the compound and allowed to feast on the marrow of all the bones that remained.

This maniacal ritual occurred every day without fail between 3:00 and 4:00 a.m., when most of New Orleans was either asleep or too drunk to understand or care about what was going on. They used a family-owned ferry for the transports, something not easily obtained in New Orleans. But it was nothing that a little magic and a lot of money greasing the right political palms couldn't manage.

Aside from tending the feeding shoot, Charlie was also responsible for a thirty-one-year-old, hard working farmhand named Bootstrap from Ville Platte, Louisiana, and Kale Martin, a forty-six-year-old wrangler from East Texas.

The men were paid well and had free housing in a two-story ranch house near the front of the property. The one thing Viv appreciated most about Charlie, Bootstrap and Kale was that they never asked questions. They worked hard and kept their mouths shut. Not once had any of the men asked about the cattle sent through the shoot. Their job was to keep the livestock area full, the cattle healthy and fat, then send whatever was ordered through the shoot each morning.

The North End pack of Loup Garou that lived beyond the gate where Viv stood now clocked over three hundred strong, all of them Originals. Not the watered-down version of werewolves that existed in other areas. Viv was responsible for all of them, but she had worked hard at putting together a strong team of leaders to manage different territories.

Viv let out a heavy sigh. Some job she had. People thought that just because you were a witch, a real witch, not a Wiccan wannabe, all you had to do was snap your fingers and everything became beautiful. You got exactly what you wanted when you wanted it and how you wanted it. Nothing was further from the truth.

"Miss Viv," called Whiskers, a small female Loup

Garou with blond fur. She peeked out from her den, a bramble of bent tree branches that wasn't far from the fight taking place center court. "Please make it stop. Warden and Milan I mean. They're going to kill each other!"

"Aw, let them have at it," said Moose, another Loup Garou hiding fifty feet away. "It's healthy to see a good fight every now and again. Puts a little spark in you, you know?" Moose was one of the largest Loups in the Northern pack, but not the brightest bulb in the lamp.

Yazdee, a female Loup who denned with Whiskers, gave Moose a little growl. "You're sick, you know that? Leave it to a guy to watch two other males fight to the death over a little tail. I mean, I don't get it. It's not like there aren't plenty of females to go around."

"Yeah," Moose said, "but we're talking about Stratus here. Everybody wants a piece of that alpha female when she's in heat. Hot stuff there, baby doll. Hot stuff."

"Pervert," Whiskers barked.

"Prude," Moose shot back.

Yazdee snorted. "Better a prude than pitiful. If you're so hot for it, why aren't you in the middle of that tangle?"

Moose grunted and ducked back behind a thicket of trees.

Amid the chaos, Stratus lay with her head resting on her paws at the door of her den, which sat on the opposite side of the compound in direct view of Whiskers and Yazdee. She watched the fight, her expression flickering from curiosity to boredom.

A growl rumbled so close to Viv it made her jump.

The mauling, biting and clawing were reaching a fevered pitch. She threw a quick glance around the compound. It seemed most, if not all, of the Loups in camp had gathered in a wide circle to watch the fight. Everyone kept a safe distance away.

The two alphas in combat were Warden, the North End alpha, whom Viv had chosen to mate with Stratus; and Milan, who belonged in the East End pack. Evidently, Milan had found a way to sneak in, hoping to get a piece of Stratus's action.

Viv thought about having Socrates go fetch Jaco, who oversaw the East pack, but the last thing she needed right now, leader or not, was another alpha thrown into this mix.

Finally, after attempting another binding then a freezing spell, both of which failed, Viv let out her own little growl. She ran her hands down her arms, mumbling words beneath her breath. Immediately, all that was visible of her was the vague silhouette of the tall, slender, black-haired woman who stood there seconds ago. Invisibility was a hard accomplishment for any witch, yet at thirty years old, she nearly had it down pat. Partial invisibility was better than none at all.

"And just what do you think you're doing?" Socrates asked, suddenly standing at attention. "Do you think you can simply walk in there and physically stop those two alphas from ripping each other apart?"

Viv grabbed a two-by-four that leaned against the gate and said, "Watch and learn how simply, cat."

She reached for the huge latch that bound the gate to a silver pole but before she could pull it up and open, Socrates rammed into her shins and began to hiss. He darted in and around her legs, threatening to trip her if she took a step.

He hissed again, loudly. "Don't be ridiculous, Viv. Some things are stronger than magic. Put your anger aside for a moment and feel what's coming from that lair. You'll see and understand why your spells have been ineffective."

"Get out of my damn way or you'll get a swift kick that'll land you right in the middle of that mess." She put a hand on her hip, knowing full well, as did he, that her threat was empty. For once, she gave in to his suggestion. She reined in her anger and allowed all of her senses to stretch to full alert.

She knew what was going on and for all intents and purposes, there was only one way she could see to stop it. She couldn't call Charlie, Bootstrap or Kale out to help. They had never even seen the Loup Garou. They had never been allowed on this end of the property. Her sisters would be useless, for their spells only worked for their own broods.

Pondering all of it put Viv in an even crappier mood. It was eight o'clock in the morning, when normal people usually sat down for coffee and eggs, and here she was dealing with this. She just wished for a normal life. Often dreamed about what that might be like, feel like. Just as she often wondered why certain people were born a certain way. Some rich, some poor, some white, some Asian. Others Chenilles, another Nosferatu. Or as Socrates had so aptly put it moments ago—a Triad.

It was hard enough having been born a triplet when life seemed to be about "finding" oneself. How did you find yourself when you were a tether of three?

And an odd tether at that; a tomboy prone to wrangling cattle and sharing a beer with one of three cowboys. Her sisters carried themselves with grace and reeked of femininity. She, on the other hand, usually reeked of sweat.

Even as children, Viv and her sisters never dressed alike, each seeking their own identity. Aside from the need for singularity, they had always remained very close. Oftentimes, if one of the sisters wasn't feeling well or even experienced a startle, the other two felt it just as strongly. In fact, she was surprised with all she was going through right now that Abigail and Evette weren't here standing beside her. Surely they had to know something was going on with her.

Maybe the universe had gone deaf. Whatever the case, with her senses heightened, the intense sexual charge in the air didn't help matters one bit. She hadn't had sex in over a year, all because of some stupid curse that had been handed down too many generations ago.

Because of that curse, every mother or Elder responsible for a Triad lived out their days twisting and turning just to keep them chaste. They weren't supposed to be intimate with humans and marrying one was a huge no-no.

Chances were, the other no-goes for a Triad had gotten twisted around so much that their literal meaning had been tweaked in one manner or another as they made their way to the twenty-first century. She knew they couldn't marry a human, but having sex with one was something she considered left to interpretation. Not that she or her sisters had tried it…yet. They were too chicken to tempt fate.

All Viv knew for sure was that every damn morning before she came down to the feeding shoot, she had to look through her Grimoire and face the horrid mirror. That mirror showed the most horrific scenes regarding the devastation of the world if they shirked their duties. The book itself listed spell after spell, consequence after consequence. And if that wasn't enough to shove her tainted ancestry in her face, she and her sisters each bore a birthmark. An *absolutus infinitus*. Viv's was about two inches long and sat on her right hip. An ugly reminder of some big bad no-no done a gazillion years ago by a grandmother thirty times removed.

Taking that into consideration, all that remained for Viv and her sisters when sex came to mind—which was often—were Fae, leprechauns, one of their brood or a sorcerer who had taken the dark side to devilry and had paid for it with his humanity. Fae and leprechauns did nothing for Viv. Both were too short, and short turned her off. As for sorcerers, there were only three that she knew of in the area. Trey Cottle, a weasel and whore-monger, Shandor Black, who always had his nose stuck so far up Cottle's butt, Viv didn't know how he breathed. And there was Gunner Stern, a sorcerer, but a nice old guy. There being the problem. He was old, like seventy-something old. That certainly didn't make Viv's nipples tingle.

When too much time had passed, and it was either have sex or go blind, she'd have a row with one of her Loups. When not matted with fur and fangs, many of the males were quite handsome. Big and muscular, with long, flowing hair, and they knew what to do with genitalia. There was always something missing, though, when having sex with a Loup. The act felt animalistic, which wasn't all bad at times, but she was a woman, damn it, and a bit of romance would be nice occasionally. Romance, however, was not in a Loup's vocabulary. All they knew was get it while it's hot, then sleep it off until it's time to eat.

Sometimes, though, as Socrates said, some things were stronger than magic, and she gave into her urges and had sex with a Loup. She couldn't get attached to any one of them in particular because the other males would see that as a weakness in her leadership abilities. She certainly wasn't going to marry a Loup Garou, much less a sorcerer.

Viv kicked the dirt again, angry she'd allowed herself to jump on that train of thought. Her frustration level now matched Everest's peak.

Here she was watching two alpha males fight over a female Loup Garou just because she twitched her tail. Viv wanted to beat the two males upside the head with the two-by-four to mellow out her own sexual frustrations. Also so she wouldn't have to babysit them.

It was far from easy being on twenty-four-seven watch over a bunch of sniveling, whining, horny wolves. And when Viv François had enough, she had had enough.

She picked up the two-by-four, gave Socrates a little nudge with her boot when he hissed at her, then unlatched the gate. She immediately closed and locked it behind her.

Still partially invisible, she didn't think she had to worry about the warring Loups turning on her. Even if they glanced her way, they'd only see a shimmer in the air, like heat rising from a desert highway. There was the two-by-four that appeared to be floating in midair, however.

Viv walked slowly toward the alphas, realizing she probably could've stepped up to them in full view. They were too wrapped up in which one would go down first so the other could hop Stratus, who seemed unable to care less about who won the fight. Really.

Socrates started caterwauling, weaving through the bars of the gate, going inside of the compound then quickly back out, as if not knowing what to do or how to stop Viv.

Milan was a large black Loup with a mane that reached to the middle of his back. His ears were long and pinpoint straight, and his bared fangs were at least six inches long. He stood upright like a man, though his paws were those of a Loup, and he swiped at Warden with long, sharp, black claws. Warden was a blond Loup and nearly twice Milan's size. Yet he showed the worst of the wear simply because of his color. More blood stained his fur. It was difficult to tell if most of it came from his own wounds or was splatter from his opponent's. Suddenly, Whiskers and Yazdee started whooping and jumping up and down with excitement. Evidently Socrates's noise had caught their attention and they had zeroed in on the floating two-by-four.

Viv dared to move faster, fearing the racket stirred up by her cheerleading squad might capture Warden's or Milan's attention.

It did rouse Stratus. The alpha female lifted her head from her paws, looked past the two-by-four and directly at Viv as if she were in full view. Viv could've sworn she saw Stratus smirk. She hated when that Loup went into heat. It always turned the compound upside down. Throw in a stray male alpha from a different compound, and she had World War Seven.

Viv kept her focus on the alpha males, inching closer, dodging left, back, forward in rhythm with their fight. It felt like an odd war dance as she juggled around the fight, trying to avoid getting clawed, yet get close enough to make impact.

She took aim. Whichever Loup cleared first was the one she planned to whack.

They tumbled, clawed, she dodged left. Blood from one of the Loups sprayed across her shirt and jeans, then again before she felt it splatter across her face and slide down her neck. These guys were really getting out of control, and if she didn't do something soon, one of them was going to die. And that was not an option.

The closer she moved in, the harder they fought. She ducked left, more blood sprayed across her face. She felt it splat onto her head and through her hair, which she kept in a braid that reached the small of her back.

Finally, seeming to gather what strength he had left, Warden leaped out and took a huge swatch of flesh from Milan's chest, turning him in place. Blood sprayed everywhere, especially over Viv, who now looked like she'd bathed in it. Milan's eyes appeared dazed as he whirled about from the blow.

Before he could refocus for the fight, Viv grabbed the two-by-four in both hands and swung at him, whacking him across the head as hard as her tall, slender body would allow. That pitched him off balance and dropped him to the ground.

As Milan scrambled to get upright, Warden had enough time to race over to Stratus and attempt to mount her even before she stood.

Milan mewled when he saw Stratus begin to take all Warden had to offer.

Viv allowed herself to return to full view, tossed the two-by-four aside and snarled at Milan's mewling. "Oh, grow the hell up," she said, then whirled about and headed back for the gate.

En route, Viv pointed at Stratus, making sure she had her attention. "You want to play games with these guys, sistah? Then get ready to play hard because I quit."

Viv stormed off for the gate, her head buzzing with an ache so painful she could barely see.

No sooner did she unlock the gate, let herself through and relock it than Socrates started yelling at her. She ignored him, catching only a word or two from his rampage because of the buzzing in her head.

"You can't just leave, Viv," Socrates yelled after her.

She stormed past him, turning her back on the fortress bound with silver-tipped barbed wire. In the distance, she caught the sound of Whiskers fretting.

"Wait, wait! What do we do? Stop! Yazdee, what do we do now? What? Our leader has absconded!"

Socrates scrambled to the other side of the gate and watched Viv storm off. He knew he couldn't stop her, not when she was this mad, this disgusted. It worried him that her spells hadn't worked. Even under the circumstances, with all that just happened, leaving hadn't been the answer.

If Viv thought things were bad now, she was about to discover a new definition for worse.

Chapter 2

Nikoli Hyland and his cousins, Lucien, Gavril and Ronan, sat in brown leather captain's chairs across from one another in pairs. A small dining table separated them.

They were flying from New Zealand to New Orleans on the family's Gulfstream G200 jet as instructed. They'd received the alert yesterday evening with orders to leave immediately. The orders came from their fathers, who were brothers and retired Benders.

Although involved in the family business for the past ten years, the onset of a mission always settled hard in Nikoli's gut.

He was thirty-five years old, and his cousins only a year or two younger than he. It was still hard for him to intellectualize that they were the new generation of Benders. The tenth generation, to be exact. And, as usual with the onset of a mission, Nikoli pondered what that *something* was. Sometimes it felt like pride—heavy responsibility—purpose.

Tuning out his cousins' banter about the witches they were about to meet, he glanced out of the plane window, soaking in the sight of dawn beginning to light a blue-black sky. A finger snap brought his attention back to his cousins.

"Where'd you go, bro?" Lucien asked, grinning. "Neverland?"

"No, I heard everything you guys said. But it doesn't matter what these women look like," Nikoli said, knowing full well the appearance of each woman. His father had given him pictures to verify their identification. Each one was drop-dead gorgeous. He'd kept that information to himself, knowing how crude a couple of his cousins could be. "We're going over there for one reason and one reason only. Remember our mission creed. Keep your dick in your pants and your eyes and ears sure and mindful."

"Right," Ronan said.

Now it was Gavril's turn to roll his eyes.

"This is our biggest job ever," Nikoli continued. "And from all indications, it'll get even bigger before we land. We've been nickel and diming Cartesians for the past three years. One here, three there."

"Hey, don't forget about the fifteen we knocked off in Brazil last year," Lucien said. "That was no small bite of potato."

"It is when compared to what we're about to face," Nikoli said.

"How many we talking, cuz?" Gavril asked.

"From what I hear, we might be talking a hundred or more."

Ronan turned his attention back to his cousins and let out a low whistle.

Lucian grimaced. "How in the hell are just the four of us going to handle a hundred or more of those monstrosities? Especially if they pile up into one big-ass troop."

"Like we always do," Nikoli said. "We get 'em one at a time, bro. One at a time."

Cartesians were a nonentity to almost every human and many breeds from the netherworld on the planet. Reason being, Cartesians were rarely, if ever, seen. Nikoli didn't understand the entire story about how his family had initially gotten involved with fighting them, but he did know the enemy. He'd seen them.

Massive creatures. Some Cartesians stood eight to ten feet tall. Their bodies were covered with long thick scales like an armadillo's, only a hundred times thicker, and those scales hid beneath a heavy mat of black and brown fur. Six-inch, razor-sharp claws served for fingers and every tooth in a Cartesian's mouth was a lethally sharp, four-inch incisor.

One didn't simply stab a Cartesian in the heart or brain to kill it. In fact, Nikoli didn't think any Bender knew for sure if they could be killed. To destroy a Cartesian, Benders had been taught to shock it back into another dimension. The farther the dimension, the better.

Somehow Cartesians were able to cross over the wrinkles of time and space from one dimension to another through the smallest dimensional tear. And they traveled swiftly, always on the lookout for other netherworld creatures. Their purpose appeared to be total netherworld domination, no matter the kill. Vampire, werewolf, fae, leprechaun, djinn, anything and everything that did not make up the human race. A Cartesian killed any and all it found to absorb its victim's power.

The creatures had a leader, of that Nikoli was sure, but no one knew his name, not that it really mattered. It wasn't like someone could Google him.

What they needed to do was destroy him, by pushing him into the dimension of no return. The eleventh. Vanquish the head, the rest of the body dies. From all accounts, this so-called leader stood nearly twenty feet tall, but Nikoli would have to see that with his own eyes to believe it. All he had to worry about was destroying whatever Cartesians he found in his missions, hoping that luck or fate might hand him that leader one day.

It wasn't that Benders had any particular liking for vampires, werewolves and the like. But the secret society of Benders knew that if the Cartesians dominated the whole of the netherworld and became one sole power, that power would then take on the human race in order to achieve world domination. And with all that power wrapped up in an army of monstrous, furry armadillos with fangs and claws, world domination would be a cinch. Every Bender had sworn a solemn oath to do all in his power not to let that happen.

Not letting on his thoughts to his cousins, Nikoli secretly worried about the mission that lay before them. It was hard enough to destroy a Cartesian, but even with their massive size, they were difficult to spot due to the speed with which they traveled between dimensional folds.

Benders were trained to recognize a Cartesian's proximity by scent. The creatures emitted a horrendous odor, a mixture of sulfur and cloves. And for some odd reason, on occasion, Nikoli had picked up a vibration that ran up his spine right before he caught a whiff of the odor. He thought it might come from the disturbance of a dimensional fold, right before a Cartesian made its way into their world.

A Bender's job was to push Cartesians back through the dimensional rift with a scabior, an odd-looking tool that for all intents and purposes looked like a child's toy. It was an eight-inch-long metal rod with a marble-size bloodstone topping one end of its one-inch circumference.

Harmless-looking, but if held in the right hand and used in the right manner by a Bender, the scabior let out such a strong current of electrical power that it refolded the dimension from which the Cartesian had entered, pushing him back inside. With each dimensional backward thrust, the scabior emitted a loud, sizzling pop, heard only by the Bender. The number of pops told the Bender the number of dimensions he had been able to push the Cartesian through. To date, Nikoli had only managed six, still the highest number among his cousins.

Each cousin sat quietly, staring off into the distance, probably thinking about what lay ahead.

A full five minutes went by before Lucien broke the silence. "Any of you have an idea about how those ugly mother-effers were created?"

Gavril cleared his throat. "All I know is that eons

ago somebody pissed somebody else off, and that somebody else turned somebody number one into a Cartesian. How they multiplied from there, I don't have a clue."

Ronan leaned over and crossed his arms on the small table. "The first one was created as punishment, for what I'm not sure. I don't think any Bender still alive really knows for sure. But Cartesians multiply by kills."

Frowning, Lucien cocked his head to one side. "Huh?"

"Kills," Ronan repeated. "When the first Cartesian made his first kill in the netherworld, it gave him enough power to create another one just like him. That new Cartesian makes a kill, it now has the power to reproduce itself, but only if the original Cartesian allows it. And you can bet he does. Who wouldn't want the biggest army in the universe?"

"You mean they don't breed like everybody else?" Lucien asked.

"No," Ronan replied. "As far as I know, and this comes from two of the oldest Benders I know in Switzerland, Cartesians don't even have sex organs. Not only do they not procreate, they don't even have genders."

"That's fucked up," Gavril said. "No wonder those things are always out hunting, killing, destroying shit. I'd probably be that way, too, if I never had sex."

"But if they're genderless, why are they usually referred to as male?" Lucien asked.

"Probably because they're big sonsabitches," Nikoli chimed in.

Gavril shook his head. "Well, all I've gotta say is

whoever or whatever did the punishing sure screwed up. Bet they didn't count on the bastard wanting and working toward ruling the entire universe."

"Did everyone get the info on why so many suddenly hit New Orleans?" Ronan asked.

"One of the Triads," Nikoli said.

"You mean those witches we're supposed to meet out there?" Lucien asked.

"Yes," Nikoli said, then signaled for the steward standing at the back of the plane to bring drinks to the table.

"Why are they called Triads?" Lucien asked.

Nikoli waited for the steward to place four glasses of cold, sparkling water on the table then head back to his station before he responded. "Because they're triplets."

"Oh, man, sweet!" Gavril said, twitching in his seat.

"Down, boy," Nikoli warned. "Remember the code. No funny business while on a mission."

Gavril groaned and tossed his head back against his seat. "Spoil sport."

"Do these triplets run their own coven?" Ronan asked.

Nikoli shook his head, then took a long, much-needed drink of water. "Triads belong to a sect of witches called the Circle of Sisters. They don't have covens like other witches. The Circle of Sisters is small, comparatively. Maybe fifteen hundred worldwide."

"All of them sets of triplets?" Lucien asked.

"No. There's only one full set of Triads per generation, and each triplet has a specific duty."

"I'd like to give one a specific duty," Gavril said,

then turned his head quickly when Nikoli scowled at him.

"One of them is responsible for the Loup Garou, another for the Nosferatu and the third the Chenilles."

"Wow," Gavril said. "You're talking original breeds there, cuz. Before vampires, werewolves and zombies and shit."

"I know," Nikoli said. "That's why this mission was put together so quickly. Those breeds have never been hit by Cartesians. The Triads always kept a tight rein on them."

"So what happened," Lucien asked. "Who screwed up and how?"

Nikoli shrugged. "No idea. Guess we'll find out when we get there."

Lucien whistled through his teeth. "Must have been a pretty huge screw-up to cause a rift big enough to let that many Cartesians through."

"Not necessarily," Nikoli countered. "All it takes is a miniscule tear. Once one gets through, any number that want to follow can."

"How many of the Originals have been destroyed so far?" Ronan asked.

"By the time we land and get to the Triads, over a hundred Loup Garous."

"Since they're witches," Lucien said, "can't they just cast some hoodoo spell and close the rift themselves?"

"Nobody can mess with a Cartesian except a Bender," Gavril said proudly.

"True, but they don't even know what's about to hit them," Nikoli said. "The tear hasn't been completed yet."

Ronan leaned back in his seat. "Are they ever in for a surprise."

"Sadly, yes," Nikoli agreed. He felt bad for the Triad he'd yet to meet. Chances were she'd created the rift by accident. Probably didn't even know that rifts existed—or Cartesians for that matter.

As they closed in on New Orleans, Nikoli sensed a circling of sorts. Like the four of them were pioneers, traveling out west by wagon and surrounded by a massive tribe of banshees they could not yet see.

Nikoli sensed something big was about to break loose. He feared this fight might be bigger than any Bender generation had encountered before, and there had been many.

He looked over at his cousins, who were talking softly among themselves. Except for Ronan, of course. Mr. Sole Man was staring out the window, probably thinking about the quest ahead.

The four cousins couldn't have been closer if they'd been brothers. And in his heart of hearts, Nikoli trusted each one with his life. They were equally strong, talented and vicious warriors against the Cartesians.

Regardless, a small nagging voice inside his gut warned that four of them were heading to New Orleans ready to fight, but only three would be returning home.

Chapter 3

By the time Viv had ferried to the opposite side of the river, it was almost ten o'clock in the morning. She smelled coffee and beignets from nearby cafes, and it made her stomach rumble. What she wouldn't give for one of Evette's special hickory-blend coffees and chocolate-drizzled beignets right about now. But food had to wait, she realized as she hurried to her home in the Garden District.

She shared the Victorian with her sisters. It sat on the corner of St. Charles and Washington Avenue. The house had belonged to their mother, who'd died in an airplane accident when they were nineteen.

They never knew their father, as was often the case with Triads. For some odd reason, the fathers of each generation of Triads took to the hills as soon as they discovered their wife was pregnant. Wrong men?

Wrong timing? Who knew. Not that it made any difference to Viv.

Although she was definitely heterosexual and struggled with raging hormones from times to time, she didn't need a man to make her life complete. She had enough on her plate. Maybe her ancestors had felt the same way for none of them had remarried, which was why the François name still held strong today. Although exhausted, Viv picked up her pace, anxious to get home. Each sister had a floor with a bedroom and bath to call her own. Evette, whom they called Evee, had the first floor; Viv, the second; and Abigail, whom they called Gilly, had the third.

Evee owned a café off Royal Street called Bon Appétit. She opened at eight o'clock in the morning and closed at two o'clock, right after the lunch crowd dispersed so there was a good chance she wouldn't be home.

Gilly, on the other hand, would be home. She owned a bar-and-grill off Iberville Street called Snaps. It opened at two o'clock in the afternoon and closed at two o'clock the following morning. Those long hours gave Viv some confidence that Gilly would still be sleeping right now, which meant she had a good shot at getting into the house and into her bedroom undetected.

Thinking about her sisters and the broods they were responsible for made the twinge of guilt Viv carried for her Loup Garous grow stronger.

She'd left without tending to those who worked during the day at construction jobs or city maintenance. Certainly by now, especially at this hour, many would be wondering when they would be released from the compound to go about their chores. The only good thing was that Loups were infamously resilient. If no one released them for duty, they'd make use of the day by napping, prowling or watching Stratus get her fill of Warden.

It seemed to take forever for Viv to finally make it home. Just as she pushed open the back door, Socrates ran past her into the house. She hadn't noticed him on the ferry nor on her walk to the house, yet here he was, skittering around the kitchen toward the hallway, where he started caterwauling at the top of his lungs.

Viv released her partial invisibility spell, which was useless around her sisters anyway.

"Stop that!" she demanded in a loud whisper. "What kind of familiar are you, trying to get your own mistress busted?"

Gilly slept on the north end of the third floor, so although Socrates was loud, Viv doubted Gilly heard him. What she didn't count on was Elvis, an albino ferret with ruby eyes and a pink nose and ears. Gilly's familiar.

Viv barely made it to the stairway when Elvis came streaking down the stairs like a bolt of lightning. The moment he spotted Viv, he came to an abrupt stop, flipped over one step, then jumped up and started racing back up the stairs, letting out a shrill chirping sound as he went. She knew he meant to fetch Gilly, and Viv tried to outrun the inevitable by taking the stairs to the second floor two at a time.

She raced into her bedroom but before she had a chance to close the door, Gilly shoved against it and pushed her way inside.

Dressed only in a pink silk sleep shirt, with her

black pixie cut spiked from sleep, Gilly's mouth dropped open when she saw Viv.

Before her sister uttered a word, Viv had a peculiar thought about Hollywood and witches. Had anyone been watching a movie, they would have expected Gilly to immediately cast a spell that would wash the blood from Viv and have any wounds appear in purple neon so they'd be easily detected.

But there was no spell-casting, and this wasn't Hollywood. Witches were human, just a different race, and just as each race had their distinct features and culture, witches were no different.

A witch's potential for power often depended on the clan from which she was born. Viv and her sisters came from the Circle of Sisters, a relatively small, close and extremely secretive group with maybe fifteen hundred witches worldwide at best. Viv, Evee and Gilly were even a subgroup within the Circle, since they were triplets.

"Wh-what the hell?" Gilly said, snapping Viv out of her daydream. All three of the sisters had olive complexions, but right now Gilly's face blanched as she took in all the blood covering Viv.

"What happened?" Gilly demanded. "Who attacked you? Where are you hurt? Heavens, look at all that blood!"

Elvis scurried around his mistress's feet as if trying frantically to weave a web around them. Then in the blink of an eye, he scampered up Gilly's right leg, across her back and came to rest on her right shoulder.

"I'm going to call an ambulance," Gilly said, and Viv grabbed her by the arm before she had a chance to whirl about.

"Stop, it's not mine," Viv said. It took a few seconds for frenzy to leave Gilly's eyes and settle on Viv's face.

"What do you mean, it's not yours?"

Socrates rubbed up against Viv's left ankle then made his way between the sisters and politely sat as if to create a boundary. Elvis leaned over Gilly's shoulder, watching Socrates's every move. Socrates hissed at him, gold eyes blazing. "Just that," Viv said, obviously a little too nonchalant for Gilly's taste. In that moment, she saw her sister's black eyes turn auburn, which meant only one thing. Gilly's specialty was astral projection, and whenever she zoned off somewhere, the telltale sign was the change of her eye color. Right now, Viv would bet dollars to horseshoes that some ghost of Gilly present was at Bon Appétit summoning Evee home.

"Then you'd better start explaining really quickly," Gilly demanded. "Whose blood is it? Where did it come from?"

For the next ten or fifteen minutes, Viv tried to explain what happened at the compound. She kept stumbling over her own words, uncertain how to tell her sister why her own spells hadn't worked against the Loup Garou. Truth be told, she didn't know why they hadn't worked. Back at the compound, she thought her crappy attitude might have played a part in making the spells ineffectual. But after giving it much thought on her way home, the only thing she knew for sure was that the spells *should* have worked despite her mood. And how was she going to tell her sister why she'd whacked Milan upside the head with a two-by-four, then walked away?

Viv had circled the conversation back to Milan in

the compound and how he and Warden had gone to war when Gilly blew out an exasperated breath.

"You covered that already," Gilly said. "Just spit it out. All of it."

Suddenly Viv heard a loud squawking followed by the entrance of Hoot, a copper-and-white horned owl. Evee's familiar. He swooped down, barely missing Socrates's head, then rocketed back up, nearly knocking Elvis off Gilly's shoulder.

"Damn it!" Gilly yelled and swung out an arm to keep Hoot from flying at her.

That sent Hoot into a high-pitched screech, which pushed Elvis's squeal button to top volume. Socrates stood with his back arched, teeth bared, and hissed like a bucket of snakes.

"Y'all shut the hell up," Viv shouted to no avail. The room continued to vibrate from all the hissing, shrieking, squawking and yelling.

The sisters looked at each other, perplexed. Time seemed to stand still in a deafening vacuum that neither of them could quiet. It wasn't unusual for their familiars to snap at one another from time to time, but normally they got along like brothers and sisters. But this was as though each familiar was out to protect their own territory.

Finally Viv held her arms out at her side, hands out, palms up, and said, "Silence is all I care to hear, I command this noise away from here."

Immediately, all three familiars went silent. Gilly blinked rapidly, then said, "Why didn't I think of doing that?"

Socrates meowed, then said to Viv, "If I'm not mistaken, this is our domain. Would you please get that intolerable ingrate of a bird and elongated rat out of this room?"

Viv nudged him with a foot, signaling for him to hush. Fortunately, to Gilly, Socrates had only cater-wauled since only the mistress of a familiar under-stood its voice.

She didn't know how much time had passed after the racket died down, but it felt like only seconds be-fore Evee burst into the room, out of breath, dressed in a smartly fitted, powder-blue pantsuit and black pumps.

"I—I left Margaret in ch-charge of the café and hurried over as fast as I could," Evee said, panting. "What… Look at you! All the blood! What happened? Where did this happen? Did somebody attack you? We need to call an ambulance. We need to call nine-one-one! No, I'll get the car. It'll be faster."

"We don't need an ambulance," Viv assured Evee.

"She said it's not her blood," Gilly added.

Evee's copper-colored eyes grew wide. "Did you kill somebody?"

"Of course not," Viv said, feeling guilt twist a bit harder in her gut. That answer might have been differ-ent had she hit Milan any harder with the two-by-four.

Now that all three sisters were in the room, Elvis, Hoot and Socrates settled down next to their mis-tresses.

Viv's reassurance may have calmed Evee's voice but seemed to do very little for her nerves. Evee reached out to touch Viv with a shaking hand, then quickly drew it back.

"Really," Viv said. "I'm okay."

Gilly grabbed one of Evee's hands and pulled her sister to the edge of Viv's bed, where they sat.

"Okay, enough bullshit," Gilly said. "Tell us what happened."

Viv sighed, glanced around for a place to sit. Then decided to remain standing so as not to get blood on anything and told them what had happened that morning.

"Why didn't you just open the damn ground up where they were fighting and drop the dumbasses into a hole," Gilly huffed after she'd finished. "If they wanted to kill each other, they could have done it in there. Saved you a lot of grief. And a pair of jeans and shirt."

"Oh, please," Evee said with a shake of her head.

Now that Gilly had mentioned it, Viv didn't know why she hadn't thought about opening the ground while at the compound. The shock of that might have stopped the fight. Once again, she blamed the brain pause.

"I didn't want them dead," she said to Gilly. "They were only fighting for some alpha tail."

Gilly narrowed her eyes. "Wait—you mean those two alphas were fighting so close to the gate where you were watching that you got doused in blood?"

Evee nudged Gilly with a shoulder. "Stop interrogating her like you're some kind of detective," she said. "Give her a break. I mean, look at her. Don't you think she's been through enough?"

Gilly nodded slowly and clicked her tongue between her teeth. "Let me guess. You did that partial invisibility thing and went inside the compound to stop them didn't you?"

Viv looked down at the highly polished oak floor beneath her boots.

Evee and Gilly stood up simultaneously.

"My word, please don't tell me that's what you did!" Evee said.

Viv glanced up at them. "I couldn't think of anything else to do."

Gilly stomped a foot. "I told you what you should have done. You had no business being in the middle of that compound. You could've gotten yourself killed. Two big alpha males like that. What were you gonna do, slap some sense into them?"

"What did you do?" Evee asked shakily, as if not really wanting to know the answer.

Viv glanced away, vividly recalling the scene as she described it to them.

When she was finished, Evee suddenly snapped her fingers. "This whole thing about your powers not working at the compound... Did you remember to read your Grimoire this morning before the feeding?"

"Now who's playing detective?" Gilly said with a snort.

Viv glanced down again. "Yeah, well, it's what we do every morning, right?"

"She asked if *you* read yours," Gilly said, her eyes narrowing again.

"Okay, so maybe I didn't this morning," Viv admitted. "But that doesn't mean I wasn't going to when I got back. I mean, we have this routine where we read it before feeding every morning, but that's not like a hard and fast rule."

"Oh, Viv," Evee said. "You know the rules. That particular one may not be hard and fast, but it's one we've stuck to for years. We have to stay sharp with study. Always armed and ready for anything."

Out of nowhere, Viv felt a nudge in her gut, an urgency that they had to look at their Grimoires right now.

As if picking up on the unspoken message, Gilly and Evee suddenly raced out of the room, and Viv knew they were going to get their books. Hesitantly, she went to the top bureau drawer and pulled out her copy. It was nearly eight inches thick, the heavy parchment pages worn, its cover weathered Elder-wood. She placed it on her bed and within moments Gilly and Evee were standing on either side of her, books in hand. They each placed their Grimoire on either side of hers.

Without a word, the sisters reached for the front cover of their book and opened them simultaneously. The three gasped in unison. Recessed in the front cover of each book was a four-inch oblong mirror. Instead of the apocalyptic scene they were used to viewing each day, the only thing reflecting from the mirrors now were swirls of gray, like billowing smoke.

"What does this mean?" Evee whispered.

"I have no idea," Gilly said. "It's the first time I've ever seen it do this." She leaned over and sniffed at her Grimoire, then Evee's and Viv's. "You smell that?"

"What?" Evee copied her sister's motion and sniffed her book. "It's…" She frowned.

"It's what?" Viv asked, following suit. Her Grimoire did smell a little funny. It not only carried its usual aged, worn-wood scent, there was something different, albeit faint, mixed in. "Is that nutmeg I'm smelling?"

"Cloves," Evee said. She put her nose to Gilly's Grimoire, then Viv's. "Definitely cloves."

"When the hell were these books ever around cloves?" Gilly asked. "Did you bring some back from the café?"

"Why would I do that? To stick cloves between the pages of our books?" Evette said smartly. She tsked. "That's absurd. Absolutely not."

Gilly shrugged and sniffed again.

Viv glanced at her sisters. "Do you think the gray in the mirrors has something to do with why my spells didn't work at the compound?"

Gilly gave her a serious look. "It could be because of what happened at the compound. You're the clairvoyant. What do you intuit from this?"

Viv studied the mirrors, the swirls of gray roiling ever faster. "That the future is uncertain because of something that must unfold. That's why we can't see anything. Something must've happened to change the order of what was to be."

Gilly clamped a fist on her hip and turned to Viv. "Tell us exactly what happened when you were at the compound."

"What are you talking about? I already did."

"Do it again," Gilly demanded. "Don't leave anything out. It could have been something you did or something you said without realizing it that made this change."

With a heavy sigh and slow shake of her head, Viv retold the story. Only this time, she included the very end. "So after I whacked Milan over the head, I turned around to leave, pointed at Stratus and told her if she wanted to play games she was on her own because I quit."

Evee gasped.

"Wait. Wait one damn minute," Gilly said, holding up a hand. "You said *what*?"

"How could you say you just quit?" Evee asked. "That's why these mirrors are gray. I mean, did you really mean that, Viv? You're not going to watch over the Loup Garous? You're just going to leave them at the compound?"

"No," Viv said. "I was just pissed off. Was in a real crappy mood. It's not like I really meant I was quitting this whole gig for good. I just had enough for the day."

Gilly closed her Grimoire and held it close to her chest. "Do you think the universe knows the difference between a bad mood and truth when it comes out of your mouth? You might have set something in motion, and we have no idea what that is."

"I said I'd fix it," Viv said, growing frustrated.

"It has to be done immediately," Evee said, closing and picking up her own Grimoire. "Viv, you forget how powerful your words really are. When you said 'I quit,' you rubbed up against the aura that covers the Circle of Sisters. The universe itself. So if you're really going to fix this, you have to go back there now."

"I intend to," Viv said through clenched teeth.

Neither sister responded.

Viv looked from Evee to Gilly. "Look, tell me the truth. Don't either of you get tired of all this sometimes? What we do is not normal, even for witches. We can't even use the spells we know to enrich our own lives. Everything gets sucked up taking care of the broods we're responsible for. We have to babysit them because of something our great-great-times-thirty grandmother did. Why do we have to be punished for it? Don't you get tired of it?"

"Of course I do," Gilly said. "But quit acting like a martyr. We all get sick of it, just like any human gets sick of their job from time to time. But it is what it is. We have big responsibilities, and you can't just throw words around like 'I quit,' then pretend you can just walk into your boss's office the next day and say, 'Oh, I really didn't mean it. I take it back.'"

"Fine. Got it. Enough already!" Viv said, and whirled about, ready to leave the room. She had more than her fill of her sisters ragging on her.

Chapter 4

Any silence was short lived because Hoot, Elvis and Socrates started a cacophony of squawks, hisses, chirps and shrieks.

Amid the noise, the sisters heard someone pounding on the front door downstairs. Pounding hard, as though they meant to break the door down if it wasn't answered right away. The sisters glanced at each other, then ran downstairs as quickly as possible.

Viv made it to the door first. Already angry and half expecting to see a wayward missionary standing on the front porch ready to show them the error of their ways, she yanked it open. "What in the hell do you—"

The words died in her throat when she saw four men standing side by side on the porch. For more than a few seconds, she stood mesmerized. As a clairvoyant, she didn't sense danger. As a woman, she saw trouble times four.

All four men appeared to be in their early thirties, stood over six feet tall and were dressed in black. Black jeans, black T-shirts pulled taut over huge, muscular chests and biceps that rippled when they moved. Their shirts were neatly tucked into their pants and held in place by wide black belta with ornate silver buckles.

Although there were four, Viv seemed incapable of taking her eyes off one in particular. He had gray eyes the color of storm clouds and smoke. Walnut-colored hair fell to his shoulders. A cleft accented his chin, and his beard and mustache were trimmed into a perfect Van Dyke. Had he been ice cream on the lawn, Viv would've gladly licked him away from every blade of grass.

"May we help you?" Gilly asked, stepping up alongside Viv.

Viv blinked quickly, surprised and a bit unnerved by her sudden and blatant hunger for the man. Remembering she was still covered in blood, she darted away from the door and ran for the stairs, leaving her sisters to deal with the strangers.

"Is she all right?" Viv heard one of the men ask as she took the stairs two at a time. She wanted to hide in a closet for the rest of the day from embarrassment.

After showering and washing her hair in record time, she dried off. Although her long black hair was still damp, she whipped it into a braid, then headed to the closet, where she pulled out a pair of white linen pants and a light blue pullover to wear. She slid her feet into sneakers then bounded out of the room and down the stairs.

Viv found her sisters and the four strangers in the

sitting room. It was a spacious area that Evee had tastefully decorated in mahogany and leather antiques. Two Chippendale couches covered in delicate beige fabric needled with gold-and-maroon filigree faced each other in front of a stone fireplace.

Three of the men sat on the couch to her left. The fourth, the one with the storm-gray eyes, sat in a maroon wingback chair beside it. Her sisters sat on either end of the couch on the right.

Six pairs of eyes locked onto her the moment she entered. Everyone looked cordial but grim.

"If you don't mind," Evee said as Viv walked toward her sisters, "would you please start again so our sister can be brought up to speed? This is Vivienne, by the way. You can call me Evee, her Viv, and Abigail goes by Gilly."

On her way to the couch to join her sisters, Socrates suddenly darted into the room and ran between Viv's legs, causing her to stumble. He jumped onto the couch between Gilly and Evee, while Viv flailed to find purchase.

A strong arm caught her mid-stumble, and she held back a hiss. In that second she felt ready to combust. The heat that abruptly shot through her body from his touch made her feel like she'd spontaneously combust. Viv didn't have to see his face to know the arm belonged to Storm Eyes. She glanced up to confirm. Oh, it was him all right.

Regaining her composure quickly, Viv gave him a brisk nod, then hurried over to her sisters. Socrates scurried off the couch to make room for her, then darted out of the room as quickly as he'd entered.

When she sat, her heart thudding in her chest, Viv tried to appear nonchalant.

"Are you all right?" Storm Eyes asked Viv.

"Quite all right," she said. "I apologize for disappearing so suddenly when you arrived. An incident at work… Well, I'm sure you noticed my appearance. I wasn't injured. And as for the stumble just now…" Viv shrugged. "Cats will be cats. They have minds of their own."

"They certainly do," Evee said, tossing Viv an odd, questioning look. She turned back to the men. "Gentlemen, if you would continue…"

Storm Eyes smiled and nodded. "Once again, I do apologize for intruding without prior notice. We came as quickly as possible, directly from the airport. My name is Nikoli Hyland, and these are my cousins." He motioned to the men sitting on the couch and named them from left to right. "Lucien, Gavril and Ronan Hyland."

Each man looked like he deserved a front cover on *GQ Magazine*.

Lucien's hair was the color of gingerbread, shoulder-length, and his emerald green eyes seemed to hold a perpetual sparkle. He had full lips and sported a well-trimmed beard and mustache.

Gavril had collar-length, tousled, soot-black hair. His eyes were violet and set deep into a well chiseled, lightly bearded face.

Ronan sat and moved with the precision of a drill sergeant. His serious black eyes were hooded by long-thick lashes, and his collar-length black hair was neatly groomed. His square-jawed face held the hint of a five o'clock shadow.

"Why are you here?" Viv asked Nikoli bluntly.

"According to them, they're here to help us," Gilly said, not giving him a chance to answer.

Viv felt her blood run cold. "What do you mean?"

"Allow me to explain," Nikoli said. "As we were telling your sisters—"

"It's complicated," Evee said to Viv. "I'm still not sure I understand everything."

Lucien nodded. "It certainly is complex, but we're more than happy to go over everything again with you."

"We're Benders," Gavril said to Viv. "And we've been commissioned to you."

Viv frowned. "What's a Bender, and who do we know that would commission you to us? How do you know us?"

"We're the tenth generation of Benders assigned to keep watch over Triads," Ronan said.

"Ten generations?" Gilly said. "Why haven't we heard of you before? Our Elders would've told us about someone like you."

"Not necessarily," Nikoli said, then looked at Viv. "There are many generations of Triads who never knew we existed."

"That doesn't make sense," Evee said. "If you're supposed to help us, how does anyone get that help if they don't know you exist?"

"They didn't know because they didn't need us," Nikoli said. "Unless there's an emergency, we tend to be more of a blend-into-the-background sort of group." He smiled, and his dazzling white teeth and full lips made Viv shift uncomfortably in her seat.

Gilly shook her head. "You're going to have to start from the beginning because I'm totally lost."

"If we were here to con you," Ronan said, "wouldn't we be asking for something?"

"Yeah, so?" Viv said, in Gilly's defense. "We haven't gotten the whole picture yet, so the bullshit might easily be hiding in the back story, and you just haven't gotten to it yet."

"Good point, Viv," Nikoli said, his smile broadening. "But I know you're a clairvoyant, so you already know we mean you no harm. Isn't that true?"

Viv looked at Gilly then Evee. "Did either of you tell him that?"

Both shook their head.

"We know of the Triads," Nikoli continued. "The Circle of Sisters is a very cloistered group, and they keep knowledge of you close to their chest." His eyes moved ever so quickly down to Viv's covered breasts before he turned away and shifted in his chair. "Just the fact that we know all about you—where to find you, what you can do, what you're responsible for—should tell you something."

"If what you say is true," Viv said, "then what are Benders supposed to help us with?

Nikoli's eyes darkened and his face hardened. "Serious trouble is headed your way. An attack on one of your factions. More attacks will follow."

All three sisters sat staring at him, open-mouthed.

"A-attacks?" Viv said.

Nikoli nodded slowly. "What's expected is total annihilation of each of your sectors."

The sisters moved to the edge of the couch like they were about to spring off it.

"Whoa!" Gilly said, holding up both hands. "What the hell?"

"All of them?" Evee asked, her hands beginning to tremble.

"H-how do you know this?" Viv asked, trying to keep her voice level.

"Because our job is to find, keep tabs on and kill Cartesians, many of whom are planning attacks on your territory," Nikoli said.

Viv got to her feet and gestured for a time-out. "Hidden Benders, too much knowledge of what you should know nothing about, now you throw in these… these Corinthians?"

"Cartesians," Gavril corrected.

"Whatever," Viv said, starting to pace. "What are they?"

"Cartesians are monstrous creatures," Nikoli said. "Many stand ten feet or taller. They have incredibly thick scales that cover their body, and the scales are hidden beneath a dense mat of fur. The scales and fur protect them from any form of human weapon. Even a grenade wouldn't faze them. Their teeth are all massive incisors, made to rip and shred, and their claws are four to six inches long and butcher-knife sharp. They travel through dimensions and get into our world through rifts. Their sole purpose is to destroy the whole of the netherworld so they will have absolute power. Every time they kill a creature, be it a vampire, werewolf, djinn, or anything from the netherworld, they absorb that creature's power into themselves. That power allows them to multiply in numbers."

"That can't be possible," Viv said, her head buzzing with all the information. "If creatures that size were roaming around this planet, surely we'd know of their existence."

"I remember the Elders talking about them," Evee said, biting her lower lip. "When we were little. Much, much younger. Remember? Taka told us. She didn't call them Cartesians, not that I recall anyway, but it sounded like bogeyman-talk to me. You know, something to scare us into being good."

"I don't remember any of the Elders or even Mom talking about that kind of creature," Gilly said. She turned to Viv. "You?"

"No."

"Wait," Gilly said, standing up and whirling on the balls of her feet to face Nikoli. "What's this about traveling through dimensions?"

"The reason Cartesians are not as widely known as others from the netherworld is because they hide between dimensions." Nikoli placed one hand atop the other, indicating layers. "They're able to travel through the folds of time and space, move from dimension to dimension. They attack, then simply vanish into another realm. Like they never existed at all."

"How many dimensions are there?" Viv asked. "How much hiding space do the bastards have?"

"Ten dimensions," Lucien said. "But we've only been able to push them back to six."

"Actually, there are eleven dimensions," Ronan said. "The eleventh is still controversial in today's scientific think tanks, but it exists."

"What causes a rift in a dimension?" Viv asked.

Nikoli slid to the edge of his seat, giving her his full attention. "Anything that produces a large amount of atmospheric, electrical static. Like a tsunami, Category Five hurricane… Words from a powerful Triad. Once the tear is created, one or many Cartesians will plow through it, capture whatever netherworldly creature it can, kill it, then return the creature's power to the Cartesian's leader to do with as he sees fit."

"The creeps have a leader?" Gilly asked.

"Yes," Nikoli said. "He's the one all Benders truly seek. He wants to possess the power of every netherworldly creature in existence. Once he's accomplished that, we fear his ultimate goal is to control mankind. To be the supreme power of the universe. He'd be able to control the very structure of planetary alignment with that much power."

Gilly and Evee looked over at Viv, who lowered her head. She knew they were thinking about her saying she'd quit this morning. She wondered how Nikoli knew.

"Ten—eleven—dimensions, does it really matter?" Viv said, to get her sisters' eyes off her. "How do you kill what you can't see?"

"Oh, we can see them," Lucien said, "but only after we track them by scent."

"What kind of scent?" Evette asked.

Gavril wrinkled his nose. "Like rotten eggs and cloves mixed together."

Evee's head whipped in Viv's direction. "Cloves?"

Viv swallowed hard, eyeing Evee and Gilly. She turned to Gavril then to Nikoli. "We've smelled it. The cloves, I mean."

The cousins looked at each other, appearing puzzled.

"*You* smelled it?" Nikoli asked. "Where?"

"Here, in the house," Evee said. "In our Gr… Our

books. We opened three books and caught a whiff of it."

"Why did the four of you look so…I don't know… out of sorts when we mentioned the scent?" Viv asked.

"Because, normally, humans can only pick up a whiff of that scent at the time of a Cartesian's entry or right after an attack. It concerns me that you smelled it in your home. What kind of books were you referring to?" Nikoli asked Evette.

The triplets cyed each other. No one knew of their Grimoires except the Elders or those within the Circle of Sisters. They were taught from a very young age that the books and their contents were not to be shared with anyone except another Sister.

"Personal books," Viv finally replied. "Doesn't matter what kind of book. The point you're trying to make is that we smelled it in here, right?"

Nikoli stared at her, and Viv saw something in his eyes that made her insides feel hot and quivery. "Right."

Suddenly a loud, frantic pounding came from the front door. Without a word, Viv, Gilly and Evee ran toward it.

Through the side windows that bordered the heavy front door, Viv saw Jaco, her East pack leader, standing at the front door, his face serious and drawn. In human form, he stood over six-four with a massive chest and a long mane of black hair that reached below his shoulders. He wore jeans and a white T-shirt. His eyes, usually a brilliant green, looked faded, dull. The sight of him made Viv's heart stutter to a stop. Even though he had access in and out of the locked compound as one of her generals, Jaco *never* came here.

For him to come directly to her home meant something had to be seriously wrong.

Jaco pounded on the door again and was about to give it another hit when Viv opened it.

Jaco took one look at her and took a step back. "I must speak with you immediately," he said.

She motioned him inside.

He shook his head. "I think it is best if we speak privately."

Viv motioned him inside again. "Whatever needs to be said can certainly be said in front of my sisters."

Jaco nodded. "As you wish." He stepped inside, and Viv closed the door behind him.

"Is there a problem at the East lair?" Viv asked.

"No," Jaco said. He looked uneasily at Gilly and Evee. "May I speak freely?" he asked Viv.

She glanced toward the sitting room, saw the four cousins had remained inside. "Absolutely."

He nodded, then lowered his eyes slightly. "The problem is not at the East lair. The problem is at the North compound, where you were this morning." He hesitated and Viv signaled for him to continue.

This time he looked her square in the eye. "There has been a breach in the North compound. We have at least a hundred and fifty Loup Garou dead. The front and back entries were wide open and there are many gaps throughout the fenced territory."

Gilly moaned and Evee gasped. Viv simply stared at him.

"If a hundred and fifty are dead," Evee said, her eyes wide with panic, "then that means at least two hundred might be loose in the city."

"Or dead farther back on the feeding grounds," Jaco

said. "I didn't have a chance to check every inch of the territory." He looked at Viv. "I had gone there to get Milan as I had been notified he was missing and suspected he would be near Stratus. I spotted the massacre as soon as I arrived. Did a quick check along the entire fence lines, then came here to let you know."

Viv nodded, feeling like someone had thrown a fifty-pound boulder into her stomach. "Go back to the North compound. I'll meet you there and get this figured out."

Jaco nodded, turned on his heels, opened the front door and disappeared in a flash.

As soon as the front door closed, Gilly whirled about and faced her. A cocoon of hot air wrapped tight around Viv. Always an indicator of Gilly's fury.

"Viv François," Gilly said in a low, trembling voice. She took a step closer to her sister. "What the fuck have you done?"

Chapter 5

The first emotion to hit Viv full in the heart when she made it back to the ranch and the compound with Nikoli was shock. A huge sob suddenly locked up in her chest, and she feared if she released it, she'd be changed forever. She didn't know what to think—how to think.

She didn't even remember leaving the house. Somehow in the midst of the scramble to get to the compound, Nikoli appeared to take charge, ordering Lucien and Ronan to go with Evee to check on her Nosferatu, and Gavril to go with Gilly to check on her Chenilles. Gilly had started to protest, but instinct told Viv Nikoli was right and she told her sisters as much.

Viv stood, holding a hand over her mouth. Still a sob escaped. "Who could have... How did... Oh, this can't be. It can't."

Socrates sat between Viv and Nikoli, his head lowered. Then he let out a loud mewl and said to Viv, "I told you not to leave! Oh dear, oh dear. This is so terrible, so horrific." He sounded like an old, fretting, English butler. "What shall we do, Vivienne? What shall we do?"

Reflexively, Viv turned her head away from the scene before her and buried her face in Nikoli's shoulder, never giving a thought to the fact that they'd only met hours earlier. He cupped her head with a hand. "How?" she whispered. "Who?"

"The Cartesians," Nikoli said, his voice hard.

Viv forced herself to turn back. The very gate that she'd opened earlier, and knew she had locked before she'd left, had been torn away from the fencing that held it up. Rips and gouges ran throughout the fencing as far as the eye could see. Far worse were the bodies of her Loups strewn everywhere. Many lay in the area where Milan and Warden had been fighting earlier that morning.

With Nikoli beside her, Viv took a tentative step inside the compound, beyond where the gate should have been. Her tears refused to be held back any longer and started to flow profusely down her cheeks.

When a Loup died, it immediately transformed to its human body. It made her think of all the wars that had been fought by countries around the world and how their battlegrounds must have looked a lot like this. Body after bloody body. The air reeked of blood, urine and feces. A putrid, solid scent that forced her to hold a hand over her mouth and nose.

She whimpered when she spotted Whiskers. Her timid, sweet Whiskers. Death stealing her beautiful blond coat and leaving behind a young woman who appeared no older than twenty with long, blond, blood-matted hair. Her body was so mutilated she was barely recognizable.

"No," she mumbled between her fingers. "Heavens, no…"

To her left, Viv saw Warden, or what was left of him. Stratus lay beneath him, both positioned as if they still copulated. But that was far from the case. They lay in what looked like a swimming pool of blood. Stratus was on her stomach, but her head had been twisted about so it faced the middle of her back.

"Moose," Viv groaned between sobs when she spotted her big, lovable oaf crumpled and flattened beneath a tree. It looked like he'd been run over by a semi.

So many bodies everywhere. Certainly they couldn't all be dead. Not all…

Dropping her hand from her mouth and nose, Viv let out a shrill call to her Loup Garous. The sound wasn't audible to the human ear, but any Loup Garou within a reasonable distance would hear it and recognize the sound as her beckoning call.

When nothing stirred, Viv called again, cupping her hands around her mouth so the sound would travel as far as possible through the five hundred acres. She called and called until her throat hurt.

Still not getting any response, Viv closed her eyes and sent out her own vibration, sent it through the earth, causing the ground to rumble with it. *"Your mistress desires your presence. Your mistress demands your presence."*

Nobody came.

"I really didn't mean it," Viv said, turning to give Nikoli a sorrowful look. "I was just upset, you know?

Tired of fighting with them." Fresh tears poured down her face.

Nikoli put an arm around her shoulders and pulled her in close. "I know. We can't bring these Loups back, but we can damn sure make certain it doesn't happen again. Trust me."

Viv lowered her head, sobbing, and gave a slight nod. She had no other choice but to trust because she and her sisters had no idea about the enemy targeting them.

"Right now, we've got to give these guys a proper burial. If we don't, the stench will only grow stronger, cause people downwind to start investigating." Nikoli lifted Viv's chin. "You up for that?"

The question added starch to her back, making Viv stand taller and lift her head higher. "Yes. They're my Loups, and I won't leave them rotting here like garbage at a slaughterhouse."

Nikoli nodded, and he and Viv walked back to the outside of the compound.

When they stood just past the entrance, Viv closed her eyes and released the same vibrations that she'd sent out to summon her Loups, only stronger. She held her arms out in front of her, hands out, palms up, and pulled from deep within herself, seemingly from her soul, a call to Mother Earth to bring her dead brood front and center.

In that moment, the ground began to rumble and roll like soft waves on an ocean. Within the five hundred acres, the ground rolled gently from North to South, then East to West, then vice versa. Viv opened her eyes and watched as body upon body rolled into a heap near the tree where she'd found Moose. She lost count after ninety.

When no more bodies found their way center, Viv lowered her arms and scrubbed her hands over her face to keep the sobs at bay. Then she held out a hand, gave a quick twist of her wrist and pointed her index finger toward the heap of bodies.

Instantly a spark of fire roared to life in the middle of the pile and within seconds it consumed the entire death toll with a flash of white-hot flames.

The air quickly clogged with the scent of cooking meat.

Viv lowered her hand, and the fire blinked out as quickly as it had started. All that remained was a pile of ashes.

"Do you smell that?" Nikoli asked.

"How can you not? The stench is horrid."

"No, not just that. Something else mixed with it."

As much as she hated to, Viv drew in a deep breath. What filled her lungs nearly gagged her, but she caught on to what Nikoli meant. "It's the same thing we smelled on our Gr—our books" she said.

Nikoli nodded. "Cloves."

"Only it smells stronger here than it did in our books. Where is that scent coming from?"

"I'm not certain yet. Let's finish this so I can find out." Nikoli gave Viv a light rub on her back, which sent electricity and guilt racing through her body.

Viv stepped away from him and held out her arms once more, only this time she held her hands together as if to pray. "Open now by my command," she said aloud. "Let all that's gathered enter this land. *Surah— mobdin—garnesh*." Then Viv opened her hands like a book, and the earth emitted a rumble, then a loud cracking sound. The ground within the compound split open, creating a narrow ravine that swallowed up the entire pile of ashes along with the trees that stood near it.

When Viv closed her hands back into a prayer position, the ravine zipped closed like it had never been there, sealing the ashes and blood far below. With that done, Viv then held out her left hand, palm up, and drew a swirling motion with her right index finger. Layers of dirt within the compound began to churn and flip like a grater had been set in motion. Every drop of blood that hadn't been touched by the fire was soon covered over with fresh soil.

"I was wondering how we were going to clean everything up. Was afraid the smell would get people's attention."

Viv whirled about, startled by the sound of Jaco's voice behind her. "Shit! You know better than to creep up on me like that."

"Forgive me," he said. "I really didn't creep though. The man standing over there saw me walking up. You were just…busy at the time." Jaco's eyes grew hard. "Who's the man?" He motioned to Nikoli standing a few feet away.

"A—a friend," Viv said, for lack of anything better to say. "He's here to help."

Jaco let out a soft snort and turned his attention back to her.

As Viv's heart rate lowered from its shot of adrenaline, she said, "You have no idea who did this, Jaco? You didn't see anything? Anyone?"

"Nothing and no one. I came here looking for

Milan. His lair companion came to me and claimed he'd gone missing. I figured with Stratus in heat, he might have slipped out and found his way here. That's when I saw…well, all that was here. But let me show you something else I found."

He motioned for Viv to follow him as he walked about a hundred yards east of where they stood, outside the compound area. Viv signaled Nikoli to follow. When Jaco stopped, he pointed to the ground.

"See?" he said. "Tracks."

Tracks were there, just as he indicated, but from what, Viv couldn't decipher. They looked more like dog prints than footprints, only the pad markings were five times the size of a man's hand. Above each pad track were claw marks that dug into the ground at least four inches deep.

"Shit," Viv whispered loudly. "I've never seen prints that big before. What is it? Bear?"

"Oh, no," Jaco said. "Even if we had grizzlies down here, their prints wouldn't be that big."

Viv felt fury roiling in her chest. "I'm going to go talk to Charlie and the boys over in the cattle area to see if they noticed anything out of the ordinary."

"You shouldn't be alone out here," Jaco said. "Whatever did this to the Loups is no joke. The Loups are powerful in their own right and for something to take down that many… I can't even imagine a creature capable of that."

"I won't be alone," Viv said. "Nikoli will be with me. I want you to check on your brood. Make sure everything is as it should be. Get a head count. Make sure we're good there. Also let Aaron running the West pack know what's going on if he doesn't already.

Have him do a count, as well. Then meet me back here." Viv pointed to the North compound's entrance. "But make it quick. I've got other things for you to do once I get the all clear on West and East."

Jaco nodded. "I'll take care of it quickly."

Nikoli offered to drive Viv's old blue Chevy pickup, which she kept in Algiers to haul around supplies and to trek from the compound to the ranch. When they were about two hundred yards from the ranch house, Viv signaled for Nikoli to stop.

"It's best you stay here," Viv said to him. "The hands out here aren't used to seeing other people with me. Don't want to get their hackles up."

Nikoli put the truck in Park, shut off the engine and turned to her. "Hackles?"

"Just stay put, okay?"

Viv was making her way to the ranch house when she heard a loud whistle in the distance. She looked toward the sound and saw Charlie Zerangue waving at her from the back of his battered pickup. From the looks of it, he and his two helpers, Kale and Bootstrap, had been tossing salt blocks out of the truck into a cow pasture south of the ranch house.

She sent a wave back and started to walk in their direction but the men scrambled into their truck and headed her way.

"How you doin', Miss Viv?" Charlie said through the open truck window when he drove up. It wasn't until all three men were out of the truck that Charlie did a double take.

"You got somebody with you, Miss Viv?" Charlie asked, surprise in his voice as he squinted at her truck parked in the distance.

Viv threw a quick glance at her truck. "Oh, just a friend from out of town."

"You okay?" Kale, an ex-wrangler from Texas, asked. "Looks like you been crying."

"Did somebody hurt you, Miss Viv?" asked Bootstrap, the youngest of Charlie's helpers. "If'n so, we can take care of 'em quicker than spit."

Viv held up a hand and shook her head. "Nobody hurt me," she said and looked away. "Allergies."

Charlie shook his head. "Must be one hell of an allergy for your eyes to be all swollen up like that."

"Mmm," Viv said and left it at that.

"Odd world we live in today," Charlie said, for the simple sake of saying it. "Lots of crazy people. Odd everywhere you turn."

"Talking about odd," Viv said, "have any of you noticed anything out of sorts out here? Anything or anyone heading to the back compound? Weird noises, people?"

"No, ma'am," Charlie said. "We don't let anybody out this way much less out to the compound. Not even us. We know you don't want us out that way."

"Now that I'm thinkin' on it," Bootstrap said, "I did hear some weird noises coming from back that way."

"When?" Viv asked.

"Early this morning," Kale said. "I heard it, too. A weird high-pitched sound."

"Yeah," Bootstrap pitched in. "Sounded like a bunch of ghosts yelling at the same time."

Charlie gave Bootstrap a shove on the shoulder. "Shut up now, boy. Don't be making up stories like that in front of Miss Viv."

"I ain't makin' it up," Bootstrap said, then held up four fingers. "Scout's honor."

"Sorry, Miss Viv," Charlie said. "Don't know what these boys are talking about. I sure didn't hear anything like that."

"You didn't hear it 'cause you was out picking up those ten head of Brahmas," Bootstrap countered. "I'm tellin' you we heard it, didn't we, Kale?"

Kale gave a quick nod, then tapped his cowboy hat low over his eyes. "Heard something. Could have been a bunch of coyotes, though. Not unusual out in these parts."

"So neither one of you went back there to see what was making the noise?" Viv asked.

"No, ma'am," Bootstrap said. "Seein' how you told us never to go back that side, we did just like you ordered. Nothing."

"Saw your man Jaco head back that way a bit later," Kale said. "Figured if something had gone sideways back there, he'd let us know. Guess he went and told you first though, seeing you're here now."

"You got troubles back there, Miss Viv?" Charlie asked. "Need us to go tend to anything for you?"

"No, just do your job right here, guys. If I need you, I'll give you a call. I just wanted to check in with you. Make sure nothing or no one had been out that way."

"No, ma'am," Bootstrap said. "Hand to God. Been just us three. Well, 'cept when Charlie went out for the Brahmas this morning. We been pitchin' hay and salt most of the day."

"Sorry we couldn't be more help, Miss Viv," Charlie said.

"No problem," Viv said. "But I'd appreciate if you'd keep an eye peeled."

"For sure," Charlie said. "I see anything, I'll make sure you're the first to know."

"Thanks, Charlie."

As Nikoli drove her truck to the landing where the ferry was moored, Viv rode along in silence.

She didn't know what to do, but she vowed to find out and to take back what was hers, even if it meant losing her own life in the process. Whatever was out there causing that much damage was no small ordeal. She might have thrown in the towel during Warden and Milan's fight, but she'd be damned if she'd let her entire city-wide brood of Loups be slaughtered. They were her responsibility, just like they'd been her mother's and her mother's mother's. She wasn't about to let this go without a fight.

She closed her eyes for a moment and saw Whiskers's innocent face. It took all she had to keep her tears from running anew.

As they bounced along the highway in the battered pickup, she felt a searing heartache for all she left burned and buried behind her. Now she was heading back to a city that most people thought existed for one big, continuous party.

Nothing could have been further from the truth.

Chapter 6

"We're going to have to change the time we have lunch. This simply will not work. They give me indigestion," Vanessa Crane said. She crinkled her nose at the three gentlemen who sat four tables away from them in the Bon Appétit Café.

She sat with the other two Elders of the Circle of Sisters, Arabella Matthews and Taka Burnside. They lunched at their usual table at the front window, where they could watch the pedestrians go by.

Arabella, who was spearing a grilled shrimp from her Caesar salad and drinking tea sweetened with marmalade and sugar, turned her head slightly to have a look at what had Vanessa so flustered. She frowned. "They're just eating like we are. Why do you let them bother you so much?"

Taka, who was munching her way through a cheeseburger with curly fries and enjoying a Diet Coke said, "We can't change the time we eat. You know that we have to be here at 11:45 a.m. If we come later or earlier, I'll get indigestion. I have to eat at this time, and we have to come here. They can go and eat somewhere else if something has to change. I'll go tell them myself if I have to."

Arabella, head Elder of the Circle of Sisters, said, "Don't be ridiculous, Taka. Let's enjoy our lunch, and they'll be gone soon enough."

The café was packed with people, everyone chatting in cheerful, low tones with forks clanking against china plates, glasses tinkling against one another and waitresses buzzing about tending to customers. The small establishment was decorated in blues and silver with white linen tablecloths. Whether you chose a cheeseburger or a filet mignon from the menu, the food was always served on china and crystal. Evette exuded class when it came to serving her customers, which was why the café was always so full.

Despite the cheerfulness of the place and the beautiful day radiating through the window, Vanessa kept the sneer on her face as she took a bite of her crab cake and roasted green beans. Every few seconds, she'd throw a look over at the three men and wrinkle her nose.

Arabella shook her head. They had so much more to worry about than the three sorcerers sitting nearby. But once Vanessa got something stuck in her head, there was no reasoning with her.

At sixty-five, she was the same age as Arabella. Today, she wore a black polyester pantsuit printed with red and yellow flowers and pink slippers. It was the only type of shoe she ever wore. She was a constant worrier and often forgetful. She wore her auburn-dyed hair in a chin-length sweep-over, had an aquiline nose, brown eyes and always wore wine-red lipstick. Vanessa loved costume jewelry and a lot of it. Her ears weren't pierced, so she had black-and-white baubles, the same size and color of her necklace, clamped to her earlobes.

Taka, on the other hand, wore an electric blue overshirt on top of a black blouse along with a string of pearls and a turquoise necklace. Her earrings were turquoise, as well, but the size of broaches. She was a week shy of sixty-nine, had snow-white hair that she wore in a tousled pixie cut, blue eyes and a snub nose.

Arabella had chosen to dress a little more conservatively for lunch. She wore a light pink silk blouse and white linen pants, which, when eating at Bon Appétit, wasn't always a great idea, especially when sitting beside Vanessa and Taka. Something was bound to be spilled. She had to work at enjoying her salad and ignoring Vanessa's constant smirks at the sorcerers.

Vanessa called them "the three amigos." Regardless, they were the only real sorcerers in New Orleans.

The trio included Trey Cottle, who looked to be in his late sixties or early seventies, and was someone Arabella absolutely abhorred. He had a bulbous beak, wore thick, black glasses, had a bald head save for a three-inch wrap of hair around the back of it, and sniffled every few seconds. It wasn't his looks that bothered Arabella as it was what he stood for. Arrogance. He used his sorcery for personal gain. He owned the law firm of Cottle and Black, was part owner of a casino, and he drank like a fish. No matter the time of day, you could always count on Trey having a bourbon close at hand.

Across from Trey sat his law partner, Shandor Black. Shandor looked to be in his midsixties, had a hawk nose, wore wire-rimmed glasses and had a badly wrinkled face with thin lips that held a perpetual scowl. He was well-groomed in a new brown suit, but no matter what Shandor wore, it didn't change his face.

Arabella didn't care for Shandor either, but for different reasons. Just two weeks ago at the café, Arabella had noticed him eyeing Evette like she'd been a juicy, four-inch ribeye. What a letch. And even worse, he was Trey's yes-man. Had his nose so far up his partner's butt, Arabella didn't know how he breathed.

Beside Shandor sat Gunner Stern, a handsome gentleman who looked to be near seventy years old. He had a Greek nose, a wide forehead due to a severely receding hairline, a well-trimmed mustache and was always well dressed and well spoken. His bright blue eyes always seemed to sparkle, and the crow's-feet around his eyes gave testament to a man who smiled often.

He glanced over suddenly and caught Arabella staring at him. She blushed and he smiled. She returned the smile and quickly looked away. She didn't have any idea why Gunner hung around Trey and Shandor. He owned his own art gallery, which did quite a brisk business. Maybe it was simply because the three men were sorcerers and like attracted like. For lunch and breakfast anyway.

"We have business to discuss," Arabella said and took a sip of her marmalade tea. She leaned toward

Taka and Vanessa. "The Triads are in trouble," she said, keeping her voice low.

"Again?" Vanessa said. "Who'd they piss off now?"

"Not that kind of trouble," Arabella said. "We're talking serious. Very serious."

Taka's mouth dropped open, revealing chewed-up curly fries.

"For heaven's sake, close your mouth," Arabella told her.

"What happened?" Vanessa asked, then looked about conspiratorially. "Should we be talking about this here? Someone might overhear, like those nosey sorcerers. They'd love to know some of our sisters are in trouble. They'd revel in it."

"I don't have specifics. Picked it up this morning during meditation and wanted to give both of you a heads-up."

"Why didn't you tell us then?" Vanessa asked.

"You've known me long enough to know the answer to that," Arabella said.

"'Cause she wanted to make sure, that's why," Taka said, a bit too loudly. "But if they're in trouble, why aren't we doing something about it?"

Arabella shushed her, then leaned in closer. "Because they have to come to us, you know that. You both know how this works. We can't interfere in their business and control every move they make. They have to stand on their own feet. We can't intercede until they come to us."

"I need to go to the bathroom," Taka said suddenly and got up from the table, clutching her purse to her chest. Arabella watched as she wove her way through the tables to get to the back of the café.

"Surely there has to be some kind of dispensation if the matter is serious like you said," Vanessa whispered.

"There isn't."

Vanessa shoveled more crab cake into her mouth, her brow furrowing deeper. "Did they kill or kidnap somebody?"

"Oh, please. Now you're starting to sound like Taka," Arabella snipped. "I didn't sense anything like that. All that feels certain is that we need to be prepared to help as best we can."

What Arabella didn't tell Vanessa was that she felt the Triads would indeed be coming soon, and she dreaded the hour. Something big was about to go down. She couldn't quite put her finger on it, but she knew the situation was dire. As high-strung as Vanessa and Taka were, she wasn't about to share that bit of information with them until the triplets arrived.

"My word, look," Vanessa said. "Here come the three amigos." Abruptly, she sat up straight. She took the linen napkin from her lap and dabbed the corners of her mouth with it.

Arabella threw a side glance to her right and spotted Trey, Shandor and Gunner getting up from their table and heading over to the cashier's podium. Mid-route, however, Trey turned on his heel with Shandor following closely in step and walked right up to the Elders' table.

"How lovely to see you again, Arabella," Trey said. "Vanessa."

"Hello, Mr. Cottle," Arabella said briskly. "Mr. Black, Mr. Stern." She smiled when Gunner nodded at her with a grin.

"So wonderful to see you, Arabella," Gunner said. "I must say, you look quite lovely today."

Arabella felt her cheeks flush. "Thank you."

"We don't want to interrupt your meal," Trey said. "But we saw you sitting here and didn't want to be rude and not at least say hello." He turned to his brown-noser. "Shandor, why don't you go ahead and take care of the bill?"

Shandor, with his perpetual scowl, simply nodded and left to do as he was told.

"You know," Trey said to Arabella, "since my office is so close to the café, we eat here often. And more times than not, we see the three of you here. The six of us should schedule a lunch date. Catch up on old times and all the new things happening in the city since Katrina. You know, we do have some things in common. We may be on opposite sides of an odd fence, but we both water the same type of lawns."

Vanessa grabbed Arabella's hand under the table, her signal for, *Don't you dare say yes!*

Arabella worked up a smile, knowing Trey to be a snake in the grass. She needed a second to come up with a polite excuse. Chances were if she had caught wind of the fact that the Triads were in trouble and something was about to go down, so had Trey. The reason for his invitation was obvious. He wanted to milk them for more information.

"We'll see what we can manage," Arabella finally said. "Thank you for stopping by. Enjoy the rest of your day.

Trey grinned, and it came across as a sneer. "We hope you can manage something soon," he said. "Have a nice day, ladies." Then he turned and walked away in his black slacks, white dress shirt and pink tie.

Gunner didn't follow Trey right away. He stayed behind and held out a hand to Arabella. She took it without thinking and enjoyed the warmth and strength that exuded from his palm.

He shook Arabella's hand gently, holding her gaze. "Hopefully we'll be seeing you again soon." He released her hand and nodded at Vanessa. "Good day, Miss Vanessa." He smiled, then walked away.

The front door had just started to close behind the men when Arabella spotted Taka waddling back to their table. The timing couldn't have been better. Taka often had trouble holding her tongue, and there was no way of knowing what she might have said with the sorcerers around, especially considering the issue with the Triads.

"He's sweet on you," Vanessa said with a smirk.

Arabella frowned. "Who?"

"Gunner, of course. I saw the way he looked at you and shook your hand."

"Don't be silly, and hush, Taka's coming."

"The hand towels," Taka said, when she reached the table, still clutching her purse to her chest. "There's a shortage of hand towels in the ladies' restroom. That would upset Evette greatly if she knew. We should alert someone."

"Let's finish our meal," Arabella said. "Then we'll let Margaret know about the towels and ask her if she's seen Evette." She said that more to console Taka than anything. She knew Evette wasn't here. She was somewhere with her sisters at this very moment. Arabella could almost feel them roiling in whatever chaos they'd clashed with.

Arabella went back to her meal, eating slowly. She wasn't looking forward to the Triads' visit.

Not at all.

Chapter 7

After parking the pickup under a lean-to near the ferry dock, Nikoli killed the engine and turned to Viv. She sat at the far end of the bench seat with her head back and eyes closed. Dusk had pushed against the sun, causing shadows to play over her face. He wanted to touch her cheek, soothe the weariness on her face, the worry lines from her brow.

The first time Nikoli had seen Viv back at the Tri- ads' home, when she'd yanked her front door open ob- viously madder than a hornet, he'd gone numb. When she'd shot out of sight, Lucien had asked her sisters if Viv was all right, given the blood splattered in her hair and on her clothes. For some reason, Nikoli had instinctively known it wasn't her blood.

In fact, all he'd really seen were her large, cobalt blue eyes, heart-shaped face with high cheekbones, and full lips and small nose, all of it orchestrated over a flawless, olive complexion. When they were offered entrance into the house, Nikoli had caught sight of Viv bolting up the stairs, long, slender legs clad in blood-stained jeans. A Bombay cat with gold eyes had followed at her heels.

Viv looked a lot like her sisters, but they were not identical triplets. All three had black hair and the same basic facial features, but the color of their eyes varied greatly. While Viv's were heart-stopping cobalt, Gilly's were as black as a moonless night sky and Evee's the color of well-polished copper.

When he first caught sight of Viv, Nikoli had felt the air charge with an electrifying energy. His heart began to beat so hard he feared his cousins might hear it slamming against the inside of his chest. Vivienne François was one of the most beautiful women he'd ever seen.

During the time they'd spoken in the sitting room, despite the severity of the conversation, Nikoli had caught Viv's scent. Lilac with an earthy undertone and latent sexuality that seemed ready to explode at any moment.

Not only was she beautiful, but he admired her mind, her wit, her confidence and determination. It took extreme willpower to keep his mind on business whenever she was near.

When they'd met up with Jaco again at the North compound, Nikoli had stayed near, on alert for more Cartesians, while Viv tended to business.

Jaco had told Viv that he'd spoken to Aaron, her West pack leader, and filled him in on what had occurred at the North compound. He also gave her a head count of the remaining Loup Garou as she'd requested.

She told him to put his second in command in charge of his pack and then have Aaron do the same. She wanted Jaco and Aaron to return to the North compound and, using protective gloves that she'd pulled out of her pickup, they were to repair the fence and gate surrounding the compound.

Nikoli knew Loups to be fast and strong, so it made sense for her to issue the command. The gloves made sense as well, for a Loup couldn't tolerate silver. It shocked their hearts into arrhythmia or, depending on the degree of contact, stopped their hearts altogether.

Nikoli shifted ever so slightly, and Viv opened her eyes and sat upright in the truck.

"Sorry, I didn't mean to wake you," Nikoli said.

"Wasn't sleeping," she said, staring out of the windshield. "Worried about leaving the Loups."

"Having Aaron bring his troop to the North compound was a smart idea," Nikoli said.

"Tell Jaco that," she said with a shake of her head. "He wasn't exactly thrilled about it."

When Viv had told Jaco to have Aaron bring his pack to the North compound so all her Loups in the city would be in one place, Jaco had argued vehemently against it. So much so that for a moment, Nikoli thought he'd physically attack Viv. But she'd held her own. Even when Jaco told her, "Why do you want us to bring all the Loups here when you couldn't even protect the ones who *were* here?"

"I thought you were going to punch him," Nikoli said.

"Wanted to," Viv said, then turned to him. "Why

the hell are you here, Nikoli? You and your cousins claim you came here to help, yet a large group of my Loups were slaughtered. What kind of help is that?"

Before he could respond, Viv opened her door and jumped out of the truck. He had to hurry to reach her before she took off on the small ferry without him.

As the engine hummed and water lapped against the sides of the ferry, Nikoli stepped closer to her. Viv turned away from him, which sent an odd, sharp pain through Nikoli's heart. "I was in your home when the attack happened. As well trained as we are, there was no way for me or my cousins to pick up their scent and prevent the attack."

She whirled about to face him, and they were nearly nose to nose. Nikoli gritted his teeth to keep himself in check. Despite the circumstances and the fury on her face, he had an overwhelming urge to kiss her.

"According to your story, the four of you were summoned here. Scent or no scent, shouldn't that have given you a clue that an attack was imminent?"

Reluctantly, Nikoli took a step back to make room for her anger. "What would you have had me do? Go right to the compound without talking to you and your sisters first?"

"To save my Loups, yes!" This time she stepped toward him, and he saw tears trickling down her cheeks. "Look, buddy, if this is the best you and your cousins have to offer, you can get yourself right back to the airport. We don't need you."

"You will."

"Yeah, right," Viv said and moored the ferry on the city-side dock.

Nikoli stepped off the ferry, took the key fob to

the black Camaro he'd rented at the airport out of
his pocket and pressed the unlock button. The car
beeped a welcome just as Viv stepped off the ferry.
She marched past him and the car, never looking back
once.

"Viv, where are you going?" Nikoli asked. "The
car's here."

"I don't need your damn car. I'm walking home,"
she said. "Have a safe flight."

Nikoli forced himself to remain in place. He wanted
to run after her and shake the hardheadedness out of
her. Viv only thought she had a bad incident at the
compound. She had no idea as to what lay ahead.

As he watched her pace quicken to a stoic march,
Nikoli realized just how much trouble he'd walked
into. If he didn't get his head out of his ass where Vivienne François was concerned, they very well might
all end up dead.

By the time Viv reached home, it was late. Gilly had
left a note for her, stating all was well with her Chenilles and she was headed to Snaps to make certain
her managers were in place. Evidently, Evee had other
matters to tend to as well because when Viv walked
through the house, she found it empty.

With exhaustion seeping through every bone in her
body, she couldn't help but feel grateful for the soli-
tude.

Viv climbed the stairs slowly, aching with every
step and feeling sorry for herself. She really had no
business being responsible for anything, much less
having the powers of a Triad. The last thing she should
be doing was managing others. Hell, she couldn't even

manage her own mouth. What was she doing with the responsibility of an entire breed that depended on her for food, direction and safety?

When she reached the bathroom within her master suite, she washed up quickly, trying not to think about all the blood and bodies she'd had to incinerate earlier.

It was impossible. When she looked in the mirror, all Viv saw was the person who let down her Loups.

Her poor Whiskers. She'd seen the fear that death had locked in her Loup's eyes. How her beautiful Loup must have pleaded for help. The scene played over and over in Viv's head—Whiskers—Moose, so much innocence in a massive body. Her heart broke. She'd miss them all—so very much.

Trying to stanch her tears, Viv pushed away from the sink. Tears wouldn't help her Loups now.

She made her way into her bedroom and stretched out on the chaise near her bed. A fierce headache throbbed behind her eyes from all her crying. It felt like the frontal lobe of her brain had split wide open. Viv closed her eyes.

No matter how hard she tried, she couldn't get the images of the dead Loups out of her head. Nor the fact that the binding and calming spells she'd attempted on Warden and Milan had bombed. Something she still couldn't understand. She had cast those spells a thousand times before, and neither had ever failed.

Of course, this was the first time she'd been confronted with two alphas from different packs fighting over a strong alpha female in heat. Still, the spells should have worked, and her clairvoyant abilities should've warned her about the attack.

The explanation Evee had offered regarding her

spells and the sexual energy being strong enough to override a Triad's spell didn't sit right with her. She needed to see the Elders. They might have some answers to help make sense of it all.

Suddenly, Viv felt something jump onto the chaise beside her right hip. Startled, her eyes flew open, and she saw Socrates snuggling up next to her. He pressed his body close to hers without a word, as if to assure her that she wasn't truly alone. She laid a hand on his head and softly thumbed his fur.

Rolling hillsides, meadows free,
I summon your energy to comfort me.
Lazy river, soothing sea,
I summon your energy to quiet me.
Licking flames and warmth of fire—

Before Viv had a chance to finish her spell, her eyes, heavy and burning from exhaustion, closed against the deep ache in her head. Sleep soon caught her unawares, and she allowed herself to fall into the sweet blissful darkness of it. A clean, blank slate.

It was an illusion of course, just like the ones Evee knew how to conjure with a small wave of her hand and a short list of words. The only time a person truly held a blank slate was at birth. And even then, Viv had been screwed out of that deal. Being born a Triad, she carried a curse that had followed each triplet born into the Circle of Sisters for the past thirty generations.

She moved her hip closer to Socrates and thought of Nikoli. The worry in his eyes, the firmness of his jaw, the size and feel of his hands when he'd caught her after she'd stumbled when they first met.

Unable to shake the thought, Viv drifted off to sleep, bringing Nikoli with her.

Chapter 8

He loved it when a plan came together, especially one that hadn't necessarily started out as a plan. Once it got started, all it took was a little push here, a nudge there, and the dam holding back her frustration had cracked. That had been enough to allow the slightest rift in the fourth dimension, where his army had been collecting.

Granted, it had taken some doing. The rift had been small, eye-of-a-needle size. Regardless, it had been enough. He'd picked, tweaked, pulled, nudged until that tiny snag had grown large enough to release a Cartesian. And once one made it through, the rest had been a cake walk.

He wanted to celebrate but felt it a bit premature. Just getting that snag in place so he'd have this opportunity had taken centuries. He could be patient and wait a bit longer to reward himself for a job well done. Better to save the real party for when the entire quest was completed.

Later meant a larger army, which meant more awareness of his greatness and supremacy. Then he'd be able to command the very stars in the sky to dance, to bow at his feet and call him Master... God.

He hadn't decided yet which term he preferred. There'd be time for that later.

Now that the proverbial ball had started rolling, he'd make certain it picked up speed. This moment's priority was to make sure his army, each squadron and its leader knew their position. To make certain they were committed to the fight and, more important, to him. To be at his right hand, ready to inform and infiltrate, to ingest the true purpose of his being in this operation. And that they would do so without question, doubt or reservation.

He played and replayed the day's events in his mind, going over every detail. What had worked and why. What hadn't worked and why. Great leaders did that. Analyzed, strategized, reorganized.

He'd watched the fight between the two alphas from afar, glorying in the frustration that had grown in Vivienne. The sexual tension in the air from the Loup Garous had been so strong it created its own bubble around the entire compound, causing Vivienne's spells to weaken.

But it hadn't negated them as she'd thought. That was one thing she didn't know and would never find out—if he had anything to do with it. Had she pushed a bit harder, she might have broken through.

The alphas had felt the spell hit them, surround

them. They'd fought against it, putting more energy into tearing into each other. His money had been on Milan, but alas, because of her he wasn't able to watch either Milan or Warden succumb to death. By their own hands anyway.

The stupid wench hadn't realized that her binding spells and calming spells had been the reason Warden and Milan hadn't killed each other. She kept repeating them over and over, spewing out her ridiculous, rhythmic words. Her own frustration level had done her in.

And the fact that four Benders had arrived like knights on black horses didn't worry him one bit. Sure, they managed to take out a few of his people with their stupid baton toy from time to time, but that was only a battle or two. No way they'd stop the war.

As commander in chief, he'd had a small taste now of victory with the Originals, and refused to let anything or anyone get in his way when it came to taking them all. And that included the Triads.

He was so thrilled with how well all had gone today, he felt a giggle threaten to rise in his throat. He held it back. Leaders, especially powerful ones, didn't do ridiculous things like giggle. Truly, after waiting so many years, centuries, just being ordinary from time to time wasn't so bad.

All those years ago, he'd known he'd been born for greatness. He'd known from a very young age. His parents had never recognized his potential for supreme power. They'd cared for him as one would a family pet.

Now the time had come to prove his greatness to the world. To the universe.

They would know his army, his goal, his dream. They'd watch as he gathered every monstrosity from the underworld. The Nosferatu, the Loup Garou, the Chenilles and all their bastard subspecies—vampires, werewolves, zombies, leprechauns, fairies, the djinn. Every creature large and small, some immortal, all with unique and dangerous powers. He would take those powers unto himself, meld them with his own and make himself the most powerful creature the universe had ever known.

The netherworld was the key, for those creatures were stronger, offered so much more than humans. Although those from the netherworld feared at times and each bore its own Achilles' heel, they hungered for human flesh, blood and bone. What they feared was the mentality of humans and their resourcefulness in killing not only those of the netherworld, but each other.

For him, there would be no fear. Only greatness. He'd have no worries about whether it was night or day or what he might have to feed upon.

He looked over the small squadron of Cartesians that stood before him, all standing with pride, many still soaked in blood from their recent conquest. How they made him proud.

In the natural world, they were stronger, more terrifying than any netherworldly creature known to man. They stood well over eight feet tall, bodies covered with thick scales that were overlaid with heavy fur. Their fangs were five times the length of any Loups or werewolf, and their claws were razor-sharp killing instruments.

Nothing would stand in their way. Their size, power and talents were all of his making. His first victory dance had been the day he'd discovered his ability to weave in and out of dimensional folds. He taught each of his Cartesians to do the same. Such beauty and wonder to watch them duck and dodge time and space and wreak havoc of monstrous proportions. Then simply vanish as if they'd never existed at all.

He'd discovered over the last forty decades that bending time and space took effort, but with the right amount of determination and focus, it was easily done. He had experimented with each fold, pushing farther each time.

The farthest he'd managed was the sixth dimension and by the time he'd reached it, he'd been so exhausted, it had taken him nearly a decade to return to the third. He allowed and even encouraged his Cartesians to experiment as well, but none were allowed past the sixth dimension. He was unclear as to whether or not they'd be able to return if they went beyond that.

Even restricted to the sixth, what his Cartesians were able to accomplish was far greater than he'd ever hoped. He kept most on standby in the fourth dimension so, should he sense a breach into the third, all he had to do was issue the command. In the blink of an eye, his troops would pounce through the breach and collect their bounty.

For years, it had been one Cartesian here, another there. Two fairies, four or five subspecies of vampires or werewolves, but nothing on such a grand scale as today's slaughter.

The fact that their conquest had been the Loup Garou, one of the original breeds, untainted by another species, made it all the more delicious. No other creature, save for a Cartesian, would have dared cross that line. The protection over the Originals had always been too strong, too consistent. But time evidently changed things. One just had to be patient.

And he had been the victor in that arena over Vivienne. She'd lost patience, and her frustration had taken hold and controlled her. That was not the mark of a great leader. That was the demise of stupid wenches who had been named Triads. How bogus. How superfluous.

No rift in any dimension had produced so much fruit. Not of this magnitude. And for all intents and purposes, it was one to be repeated again very, very soon. He felt it down to his own scale-and-fur-covered bones.

The thought of it made him shiver with delight—with power—with ecstasy. Soon it would all be his for the taking.

With that thought front and center, he raised his monstrous arms and roared in triumph. He was Lord—he was Master—he was God.

Chapter 9

Viv didn't know how long she'd been out, but she must have been sleeping the sleep of the dead. The next thing she knew, Socrates was yelling in her ear, and it was dark.

"Get up!" Socrates yelled again.

Viv swatted at him. "Stop. Let me sleep."

"*He*'s back in the house, Vivienne," Socrates hissed. "All four of them in fact."

"Huh?"

Socrates gave her an incredulous look. "The men from earlier, remember? Or did you leave your brain behind in REM sleep?"

Her brain finally kicking into gear, she stumbled off the chaise, gave her eyes a second to adjust to the darkness, then went to her bedroom door and opened it a crack.

She heard Gilly's and Evee's voices coming from

downstairs along with Nikoli's. She'd recognize the man's silky baritone anywhere. Then Lucien spoke, and Gavril responded.

Furious that Nikoli had the audacity to come back to their home after she'd told him to leave, Viv slapped on the lightswitch and blinked against the harsh brightness. She was about to yank the door open, then realized she had on the same clothes she'd worn since showering that morning.

She headed to her closet, Socrates followed at her heels.

"What are you doing?" he asked. "Those men are back. Why aren't you going downstairs, Vivienne?"

"I am," she said, pulling out a clean pair of jeans and a maroon V-neck blouse.

Socrates sat on his haunches, watching as she stripped off the clothes she'd fallen asleep in and jumped into her clean ones. "My word, this is absurd," he said. "I knew it. I simply knew it."

Viv gave him a warning glance. "Knew what?"

"I tell you those strange men are back and instead of rushing downstairs to rid the house of them, you're changing your attire. The only explanation for such a ridiculous reaction is as I assumed. You're in heat, and for the man they call Nikoli."

"Oh, shut up," Viv said. "You don't know squat." After dressing, she hurried into the bathroom, checked her reflection in the vanity mirror and saw her hair sticking out of her braid like straw from a worn broom. "Shit." She quickly untangled the braid, brushed out her hair, then wove it back into place.

Shoving her feet back into sneakers, Viv headed for the bedroom door. "Stay put, understand?"

Socrates yawned in response.

"I mean it."

With that, Viv left her bedroom and headed down the stairs. She glanced at the antique grandfather clock near the foyer as she followed the sound of the voices. She paused, staring at the time. 10:00 p.m. If the clock hadn't gone on the fritz, it meant she'd slept for almost six hours, something she never did during the day. It unnerved her.

As before, her sisters and the Hyland cousins were in the sitting room, almost in the exact positions they'd been in earlier that day. Except this time, Nikoli stood just inside the entrance to the room, his hands behind his back, head down as he listened to Gilly talk about her Chenilles.

Viv stormed inside, ready to give Nikoli a piece of her mind, when Socrates jumped out in front of her as if he meant to land on the occasional table that stood near the back wall. His acrobatics caused Viv to twist and duck so as not to get clawed in the head. Landing face first on the hardwood floors seemed imminent until an arm snatched her around the waist and stood her upright.

They were Nikoli's arms. And in that moment, her clairvoyant gifts chose to shift into high gear.

She no longer saw the sitting room, her sisters or Nikoli's cousins. She had been mentally transported to a different place—a different time...

Where Nikoli's lips were on hers, full and soft. They kissed hungrily, greedily, his tongue darting into her mouth, devouring it. His lips moved across her chin, down her neck. The width of his broad chest pressed against her breasts, which were bare. She felt her nipples aching, hardening when he stepped back ever so slightly to allow his hands access to her body.

His touch sent fire coursing through her, and she moaned unabashedly for more. He lowered his mouth to her left breast, flicked her nipple with his tongue, his teeth grazing gently across it until she cried out.

At the sound of her voice, he lifted his head, pressed her tightly against him once more, sought her mouth with his own and moved his hand down to the small of her back.

His touch sent heat, passion and something Viv couldn't identify flowing through her like lava. It awakened every nerve ending in her body, opening her up, yet closing her off at the same time, so all that existed or mattered was Nikoli's touch.

As his kisses grew more fervent, his hand slid lower—lower still, until she felt his fingers slide over her buttocks, then between her legs. One of his fingers edging closer to the center of her heat. She felt an orgasm forming in her core, growing higher and higher, like a tsunami of such magnitude it had the power to shift the earth on its axis.

The next thing Viv knew, she heard a whisper in her ear.

"Are you all right?" Nikoli asked.

Viv blinked, embarrassed. She'd just experienced a clairvoyant episode while still in Nikoli's arms. Her legs felt like rubber, and she trembled as she stood upright. She wanted to say something but feared gibberish might pour out of her mouth.

"Sorry," she finally said, throwing him a quick glance. The look in his smoky gray eyes appeared heated, like he'd been in the moment with her and had basked in their passion.

Viv turned away, still shaken. She wiped her sweaty palms against her pant legs and tried not to wobble as she went to sit by her sisters.

"Are you okay?" Gilly asked Viv. "Your cheeks are flushed."

"Maybe she has a fever," Evee said, her brow furrowing with worry. She put a hand on her sister's forehead, and Viv quickly brushed it away.

"I'm not sick," Viv said, then glared at Nikoli. "What are you doing back here?" she asked him.

"Viv," Evee said, her voice filled with shock. "How rude. He told us what you had to do at the compound, and my heart breaks for you, sister, but the attack wasn't his fault."

Now Viv felt heat wash over her face. "They came here saying they wanted to help. Do you call seeing the aftermath of a slaughter of a hundred-plus Loups helping? If Benders are supposedly commissioned to help us… What the hell?"

Gilly reached over and touched Viv's knee. "I feel for you, I truly do, but you've got to cut these guys some slack."

"I don't have to cut anyone anything," Viv said, growing furious. How dare her sisters side with the Hylands.

"You're right," Nikoli said, and all three sisters looked at him stunned. "If given the chance to do it over again, we'd have gone directly into hunt mode and found our way to the compound. I'm to blame for the error. I chose courtesy first. I realize no amount of apologies will ever right the situation, but please accept mine."

Viv didn't quite know what to say to that. Gilly and Evee elbowed her gently on either side of her ribs as if to say, "See?"

Feeling sandwiched between traitors, Viv stood and faced Nikoli. "As I said before, what are you doing here? The damage is done and can't be undone. It's over, so you can leave now."

"Unfortunately, it's far from over," Ronan said from where he sat.

Viv glared at him. "What do you mean?"

Nikoli stepped closer to her, and Viv felt her heart rate jump up a notch. "The attack at the compound was only the beginning," he explained. "Now that the Cartesians know the whereabouts and have had a taste of the Originals, they won't stop until they've killed them all."

Viv felt her mouth drop open, then she quickly regrouped. "All of my Loups?"

"All of the Originals," Nikoli said. "Your Loups, the Nosferatu and the Chenilles."

Turning to her sisters, she said, "Surely there's a spell we can cast to protect them."

"Spells might save some," Nikoli responded. "But far from all."

Gilly and Evee got to their feet and walked over to Viv. "They've offered to come with us during feeding time. They feel that having all the Originals in one place is exactly what the Cartesians are waiting for."

Viv looked back at Nikoli, her heart now thudding with fear. "All of them?"

He nodded solemnly. "They want all of them."

Swallowing hard, Viv felt she had little choice but to accept their offer, despite how she felt about the earlier attack.

"We leave for the docks at 2:50 a.m.," Gilly said.

"If you are all in agreement, we'll be at the dock then to make certain we don't miss you."

Evee nodded and nudged Viv, who gave a hesitant nod.

"Please be prompt," Evee said.

The three cousins, who were seated, rose and walked over to Nikoli.

"We most certainly will," Ronan said.

After Gilly led the men to the front door and escorted them out, Viv headed for the stairs to stave off any questions from her sisters.

"Wait," Evee called after her.

Viv stopped midstep and looked over at her.

"Grimoires before feeding tomorrow morning, remember."

Viv nodded and hurried up the last few steps.

When she finally made it to her bedroom, she closed the door and rested her back against it for a few seconds, her heart beating like a marching band had taken residence there, her mind whirling in too many directions. Cartesians, all of the Originals, the deaths of her Loups—the clairvoyant vision of Nikoli.

Of all the things that were going to feed or be fed in the next day or two, Viv knew without question that she would be one of them.

Chapter 10

Stepping out of the shower, Nikoli wrapped himself in one of the hotel robes, then headed for the sitting area of one of the adjoining suites they'd been able to score at the Hotel Monteleone.

He appreciated the spaciousness of the suites and the architecture of the old hotel, as much as he appreciated the city. From the moment they'd landed, he'd felt all the energies roiling through New Orleans in a huge wave. It was as if their destination hadn't been the city but a person. You either smothered or fell in love with her.

For Nikoli, it had been love. In more ways than one.

Lucien and Gavril sat on a paisley-upholstered couch in the sitting area, and Ronan in a straight-back chair. All three men wore jeans and were bare-chested.

When they had arrived at the hotel earlier, they

had gorged on a huge dinner. Afterward, Lucien and Gavril claimed the showers, and while waiting his turn, Nikoli had fallen asleep across one of the queen beds. Ronan, who shared a suite with him, had snored softly in the bed next to his.

Thanks to food, sleep and now a shower, Nikoli felt like a new man. Unfortunately, after all they'd experienced since arriving here, he considered that it might take more than feeling like a new man to accomplish this mission.

As if reading his thoughts, Lucien said, "I think we're in over our heads, cuz."

"Yeah, man," Gavril said with a nod. "Like twelve feet over our heads."

Nikoli let out a sigh, went over to the minibar and grabbed a bottle of water. He drank deeply, thinking about what his cousins had just said. He capped the bottle and set it on the counter, then turned to Ronan.

"What do you think?"

Ronan looked at Lucien and Gavril and gave a slight shrug. "I think we just need to strategize. We have three witches responsible for some pretty large sects. Some in the city, some outside of it. Besides, with all that's happened so far, even if we did call for backup, other Benders wouldn't reach us until we'd lost half or all of the Originals. We can't just sit around and wait. We have to establish a plan."

"I agree," Nikoli said.

Lucien tapped the seat of the couch he sat on with a finger. "If we called for backup right now, even if we wind up in the heat of battle before they arrive, at least we'd know the cavalry was on the way."

Nikoli studied him for a moment. "If you keep your

head focused in that direction, we've already lost the mission before we've started. Look how long it took us to get here from New Zealand. Other Benders are in parts of the world unknown to us."

"Maybe," Lucien said with a frown. "But our fathers would know where to locate them."

"If you want to call your daddy and have him bring your little nursemaid along to hold your hand, go right ahead and do that," Nikoli said. "We're grown men, trained Benders, and we need to handle the situation."

"That's harsh, bro," Lucien said.

Nikoli scrubbed a hand over his face. "Didn't mean for it to come out that sarcastic. Look, I'm just as concerned about this situation as the three of you. But if we keep a positive, straightforward mind-set, I think we have a good shot of accomplishing this mission. I know there had to have been generations of Benders before us who faced the same challenge. Maybe not with Originals, but a serious challenge nonetheless. I've never heard of any team of Benders calling in for backup, have you?"

His three cousins shook their heads simultaneously.

"We haven't even fought here yet," Nikoli continued. "I'm not ready to throw in the towel and run to Daddy saying, 'I can't do this, it's too hard.'"

"Yeah, he's right," Gavril said. "It's like Ronan said. We just need to have a strategy, a game plan as to how we're going to take this on."

"Good," Nikoli said. "Now let's look at this. Problem number one is that we have Originals spread throughout the city. At least the Loup Garous have been contained in one compound, which makes it easier."

"The Chenilles," Gavril said, "are spread out in three or four different cemeteries. There's no way we can keep hopping from one to the other. We can't watch them all at one time."

"The Nosferatu are in one place," Lucien said. "That's not really a big help because it gives us yet another place to monitor. You have one North compound, three or four cemeteries, and the catacombs at St. John's. I know my math isn't the best in the world, but the way I figure it, that's at least five locations, possibly six. And there are only four of us. If we split up, how will one of us handle a horde of Cartesians that can suddenly decide to drop from the sky?"

Gavril nodded. "Another problem is, since we have the Originals in separate areas, which will keep us hopping from one place to the other—or separate us so we each taking a territory or two—we won't any time or opportunity to scout for Cartesians *before* they make a hit. We'll just have to wait at our assigned territory for them to appear. We'll all be dealing with surprise attacks."

"Good point," Ronan said. "What do we do about our inability to spread out and search for them? And— side note here—I don't know if any of you noticed, but there are subspecies in the city. Vampires, werewolves—"

"Where did you spot them?" Lucien asked.

"I smelled them the minute we got off the plane," Ronan said.

Nikoli sighed again. Just what they needed. Ronan had the gift of enhanced smell, just like he had the ability to amplify his hearing. If Ronan claimed he smelled vampires and werewolves, you could bet your life they were around.

"I think we need to stay focused on the Originals," Nikoli said. "That's where the Cartesians are going to hit first. They've already tasted first blood, so the subspecies are not going to be a priority."

"So what do you suggest we do?" Lucien asked.

"Split up and take different territories," Nikoli said. "Each of us should pair up with a Triad. They'll help keep their sect in line."

Gavril snorted. "Let me guess, it just so happens that you plan to pair off with Viv, right?"

Lucien tried to hide a smile behind a hand and failed.

"What are you talking about?" Nikoli asked.

"Aw, cuz, come on," Lucien said. "We saw the way you looked at her. I thought you were going to trip over your tongue. You went all mushy-eyed the second you saw her. That woman has you crossed six ways from Sunday."

"Me?" Nikoli said. "What about the three of you? Gavril, you were so far up Gilly's behind, always asking where she was and if she was coming, that a flea couldn't have farted between the two of you. And Lucien and Ronan, the same goes for you two and Evee."

Lucien and Ronan looked at each other, and Nikoli spotted the slightest hint of competition flash between them.

"I've got no problem taking Evee," Lucien said.

"Fine," Nikoli said. "But that either leaves one man out alone, which I highly disapprove of, or Ronan makes one of us a threesome. It's your call, Ronan."

A hint of a grin played around Ronan's lips. "I'll pair with Lucien and Evee."

Nikoli saw Lucien's eyes darken.

"All right," Gavril said. "But I'm not sure about all this. Let's face it, they may be witches and Triads, but they're still women. You get what I'm saying? We have to fight Cartesians and watch out for our own behinds so they don't get chewed up by an Original or a wandering subspecies. Now we're throwing women into the mix. We'll want to protect them. It's going to be hard to stay focused."

Lucien huffed. "Get real, cuz. It's going to be hard for you to focus because they're so beautiful, not because you only want to protect them."

Gavril shrugged. "Well, so? What's the difference? It's still going to be distracting."

The room fell silent for a moment, and Nikoli was sure each man was thinking about the Triad he was attracted to. He wondered if his cousins' fathers had experienced the same challenge.

When Nikoli was twenty, his father had warned him against getting involved with a woman while on a mission. He had told his own story about the time he'd been in France, fighting Cartesians alongside Nikoli's uncles, and how he'd met a woman named Maria. The most beautiful woman in France, he claimed.

She was the daughter of a man in charge of a group of vampires who'd been attacked by the Cartesians. He'd daydreamed and fantasized about being her husband, had even wondered what their children might've looked like. Just thinking about Maria so incessantly had put that group of Benders in danger. To this day, his father still carried the scar left by a Cartesian's claw on his left shoulder.

His father had also warned him to never tell his mother the story or she'd hound him about it until his last breath.

Nikoli and his cousins were born within two blocks of each other, just outside of Chicago, but they hadn't stayed there long. In fact, they didn't stay anywhere for very long. When his father decided it was time to move due to an extended mission, his three brothers and their wives and children moved right along with them. The cousins were homeschooled and watched over closely by their mothers, who worried incessantly about their husbands.

When Nikoli decided at the age of ten that he wanted to be a Bender like his dad, his three cousins jumped on the same train, as well. Now, when Nikoli thought back on it, he wondered how they hadn't given their mothers a heart attack at an early age. The four cousins refused to remain underfoot. They were always sneaking out, exploring new territory, using sticks as if they were scabiors and pretending to kill every Cartesian that ever existed. They were invincible, courageous. They were the Hylands. Just because his father was a Bender, it hadn't meant that Nikoli would automatically inherit the title. A man wasn't born a Bender. It was something he chose to do.

And just because Nikoli chose to be a Bender, it didn't necessarily mean that the dream was going to come to pass. He and his cousins had to go through extensive training, not only from their fathers, but from other Benders. If at any time a Bender thought a trainee was unsuited for mission work, he was ousted immediately, no questions asked, no explanations given.

Luckily, Nikoli and his three cousins had passed their training period with flying colors.

The job wasn't always as glamorous as others assumed. It was dangerous, exhausting and trying work. Although Nikoli had never confessed to his cousins, it had been more than once that he questioned his decision about becoming a Bender. When a man spent his life fighting one Cartesian after another, all the while watching others go about daily life with wives and children, love and companionship, it caused him to struggle with focus.

He had to keep the bigger picture in mind. A Bender's job wasn't just to remove Cartesians. His job was literally to save the world from the monstrosities. Without the Benders, the world, the very universe as they knew it, would be destroyed.

Ronan got to his feet and stretched, breaking Nikoli's reverie.

"You still with us, cousin?" Ronan asked Nikoli. "Caught you daydreaming for a while."

Nikoli grinned. "Busted. I was thinking about when we were kids."

Lucien slapped a hand to his forehead and laughed. "Well, that's sure a side-step from what we were talking about. Don't know what brought that up, but we had some good times back then."

"Yeah," Gavril said, grinning. "I don't know how we survived to reach our thirties. We were hellions."

Ronan laughed, something he rarely did. "Hellions is an understatement," he said. "How we didn't kill somebody or ourselves is beyond me."

Gavril gave a hearty laugh. "Remember the time we built that missile? That big plastic tube with the bottom panel loaded with fireworks?"

Lucien gave Gavril a light punch on the shoulder. "Hell, yeah, I remember. We put Miss Lunenburg's cat, Pansy, in the tube because we needed an astronaut. How we didn't kill that cat when the fireworks went off, I'll never know. My mom grounded me for a month over that little experiment."

Nikoli grinned. "Mine did, too."

Gavril and Ronan chimed in at the same time, "Me, too!"

They all laughed over the memory, and Nikoli let the laughter die away on its own before he signaled a time out. "But back to our previous discussion, where were we?"

"The Triads," Ronan said.

Nikoli snapped a finger. "Right. The witches will help keep their sects fed, subdued and corralled in their assigned territories. We simply do surveillance of each den and watch for the Cartesians."

Ronan cleared his throat. "Cousins, no one's mentioned this, so I'm going to. We've admitted that all of us are attracted to one Triad or another. They are intelligent, beautiful, powerful women. Who wouldn't be attracted to them? But they will be of danger to us, costing us focus. You know all the energy and concentration it takes to properly operate our scabiors, to make certain we're on target. We really need to be honest with one other. If we don't separate ourselves from the Triads emotionally and mentally, we're in serious trouble."

"So what happens if we blow off the Triads and

wind up having a pack of Originals, suddenly looking at us like we're dinner?" Gavril asked.

"That's why we definitely have to partner with the Triads," Nikoli said. "They'll keep an eye on their own while we watch for the Cartesians. Ronan brought the issue out in the open. So let's be fair with ourselves. We have to break off emotionally, mentally from the witches and really concentrate. We have a lot to lose here. We're not talking about just any old mission. These are the Originals. How do you think it will look in the Benders' history books if we arc the generation that allowed them to be destroyed? Now, Viv told me earlier that some of the Chenilles and Nosferatu—also some Loups—work and have chores in the city so they can learn to interact with humans. Some work during the day, others at night. We need to make certain that doesn't happen until we get the Cartesians under control. We have to make certain all of the Originals are kept in their dens. We can't have a bunch of Originals running haphazardly through the city while we're at the compounds and other locations, watching for Cartesians."

"I agree," Ronan said.

"I don't think we'll have a problem convincing the Triads of that," Nikoli said. "Not after what happened today."

Nikoli sat on the arm of the couch and looked from one cousin to the other. "All right, just to make sure we're in agreement. When we meet with the Triads, the game plan we present will be to pair off. Lucien and Ronan with Evee, Gavril with Gilly, and me with Viv. They are to keep their sects in their dens, not allow them to work or tend to other chores outside of their assigned area. Gavril, see if you can talk Gilly into collecting all of her Chenilles into one cemetery. I know Viv had a challenge corralling all of her Loups into one compound, but she managed it. Gilly might be able to accomplish the same, which would make it a hell of a lot easier on everybody. All of the Nosferatu are in one area already, so they're a nonissue. This way, we narrow the territory. All of the Loups in one compound, the Chenilles in one cemetery and the Nosferatu beneath the cathedral. I think this would make things easier to control."

Lucien nodded. "Makes sense."

"Yeah," Gavril said. "I'll convince Gilly to do it."

Nikoli gave him a thumbs-up. "Now remember, cousins. Keep your mind on the job and your dick in your pants. Stay focused and strong."

They all nodded, leaned forward, and all four stacked their right hands on top of the other in agreement.

Nikoli leaned back. "Okay, let's finish dressing and head out there."

Silently the cousins dispersed and went on the hunt for their clothes.

While Ronan went to the bathroom, Nikoli dressed. The silence in their room gave him time to think.

He was already screwed. Somehow, and he didn't think it was by spell but simply by being, Vivienne François had stolen something from him. His heart. Every moment he'd been away from her since this morning, he'd hungered for her, like a man who hadn't been fed in years.

Truth be told, if anybody had a challenge during this mission, Nikoli did.

Chapter 11

Viv had just tucked her Grimoire away when she heard a soft tapping on her bedroom door.

"Yeah?" she called out.

The door creaked open, and Gilly and Evee's heads popped out from around the corner of it.

"You okay?" Evee asked.

Gilly pushed the door open wider, and she and Evee stepped inside, their familiars perched on their shoulders.

"Yeah," Viv said. She walked over to her bed and sat, causing Socrates to meow in protest and move farther up on the bed toward the pillows. "Y'all don't have to babysit me. I read the Grimoire. My mirror's still gray by the way."

"We didn't come to check on that," Gilly said. She sat next to Viv. Evee quickly followed suit. "With everything that happened with your Loups today…" Gilly glanced over at the alarm clock sitting on the nightstand near Viv's bed. "Well…yesterday…I knew you would read it."

Viv plopped her hands in her lap, wove her fingers together and tapped her thumbs against each other. She looked down at her hands. "Sorry I acted like an ass earlier."

Evee put an arm around Viv's shoulder and gave her a quick squeeze. "No apology needed. We understand. I can't imagine what it must have been like, seeing your Loups that way. Having to burn—"

"Can we not talk about that?" Viv said, standing abruptly.

Startled, Elvis chirped and ran from Gilly's right shoulder to her left. Hoot let out a screech, and his head bobbled.

Viv started to pace. "I've been having a hard enough time getting that vision out of my head as it is. All I want to concentrate on now is how to save the rest of our broods."

"And ourselves," Gilly added.

"What do you mean?" Evee asked.

Viv gave Gilly a stern look. Out of the three of them, Viv considered Evee a magnolia among thorns. Gilly carried herself with far more grace than Viv did, but she had a temper like a startled cobra and a mouth to go with it. Evee, on the other hand, had a huge, tender heart and always saw the good in people and situations. Viv and Gilly were usually peeking around corners to find the bad hiding in both.

"She has to know what we're facing," Gilly said,

frowning at Viv. "Leaving her in the dark won't help her defend herself."

Evee slapped her hands against her thighs, and Hoot's head did a one-eighty. "Stop all the twisting and turning of words," she said to Gilly. "Just spit it out. What did you mean when you said 'ourselves'?"

Gilly looked up at Viv, who walked up to Evee.

"Honey, if those Cartesians want the Originals for their power, there might be a chance they'll want us for ours."

Evee's eyes grew wide. "But we're human. Ronan and Lucien said Cartesians hunt those from the netherworld. They said it straight out. So that doesn't include us, right?"

Viv took Evee's hands in hers and immediately caught a vision of her sister injured and bleeding profusely. She wanted to jerk her hands away but knew that would frighten Evee all the more. She tried to offer her sister a small smile, something that might give her a bit of hope, but failed. All she knew to do was make the truth as palatable as possible.

"We really have no idea what those monstrosities will do or what they're capable of when it comes to Triads," Viv said softly. She released Evee's hands and gave her a small kiss on the cheek. "Let's hope for the best and prepare for the worst, okay?"

Evee looked over at Gilly as if for confirmation.

"Right, right," Gilly said. "What she said. Prepare for the worse, just in case, that's all."

Viv rubbed her hands over her face, then asked Gilly, "Were you comfortable with Gavril hovering in your shadow all the time, being up your butt, checking to make sure the Chenilles were safe?"

"He's thorough, that's for sure," Gilly said. "Only had one problem with the guy."

Viv felt anger prickle her spine. "What problem?"

"I couldn't stop staring at him. That's one good-looking hunk of flesh right there. It's distracting."

Evee lowered her head and tried to hide a smile. "Same here. Only I had two of them to stare at."

Gilly and Evee looked up at Viv simultaneously, and Gilly asked, "You?"

"Yeah, Nikoli is easy on the eyes, but I had too much on my plate to worry about his looks."

"Damn, I'm sorry, Viv," Gilly said. "Forget what I said. I'm just an insensitive asshole."

"Yes, you are," Viv said and offered her a little smile. "Now, look, we've got to figure something out. Our broods cover a lot of territory. Even with the Hylands, I don't know how we're going to keep an eye on everybody."

"We could split up," Evee said nervously. "Cover more ground that way. My Nosferatu are already in one place at St. John's, and Viv, you've got all your Loups around the city in the North compound. That narrows the territory we have to watch over a little."

Gilly stood, and Elvis chittered. She blew out a loud breath. "My Chenilles are spread out across three cemeteries. I'm going to have hell to pay with the heads of my packs, but I'll bring them all to Louis 1. It's the closest cemetery to St. John's. But that only puts two of us near each other. Viv, that leaves you out at the North compound alone, and we just can't chance that."

"She wouldn't be alone if we pair up with the Hylands," Evee said.

Viv, who'd been staring out of her bedroom window, listening and mulling over what Gilly and Evee had said, whirled about. "We just met those guys, and you want me to trust them with your lives?"

"What other choice do we have?" Gilly said. "Viv, you've got to at least consider it. I think they're legit. You were right when you said Gavril was in my shadow. He was. But in a good way. Very protective and an absolute gentleman."

"Same for me," Evee said. "I'd feel safe with Lucien and Ronan. Do you have a problem with Nikoli, Viv?"

Viv began pacing again. Yes, she had a problem with Nikoli. Her clairvoyant visions of seeing him and her naked and the fact that she'd treated him like shit. "I really railed on him," she admitted to Evee and Gilly. "Like bad. Even if we decide that pairing up is the way to go, they may not want to. And even if they do, Nikoli might not want to be paired with me." Saying it out loud made Viv's stomach churn.

"As if," Evee said. "He's a man, Viv, not a little boy. I'm sure he understands. And look, there's nothing stopping Ronan from going with you and Nikoli with me and Lucien."

Viv signaled for a time-out. "We'll figure out the Hylands later. One other thing we need to discuss is putting our broods on lock-down. No going to work or running errands. At least until this fiasco is over."

Evee sighed. "My Nosferatu will give me hell about that, but you're right. It's the only way to keep them safe."

"You do realize that if we take away their outside privileges, we're going to have a lot of infighting," Gilly said.

"I know," Viv said. "Boy, do I ever. Remember Milan and Warden?"

"Right," Evee said.

"I don't know why your binding spells didn't work on them," Gilly said. "But if you run into any issues again with jazzed-up alphas, maybe I can run out there and help."

"Thanks," Viv said, but shook her head. "I need to take care of my own. Y'all know we're going to have to talk to the Elders about all that's going on, right? Maybe they'll have some answers as to how we can better handle this situation."

"Guess we should have gone to them yesterday," Gilly said and pursed her lips thoughtfully.

"We'll make a point of seeing them later today," Viv said. "After the feeding."

Gilly and Evee nodded.

"And one other thing," Viv said. "If we do pair up with the Hylands, watch yourself. Remember the Triad curse."

"Yeah, yeah," Gilly said. "Can't marry a human or live intimately with a human. We know." An evil grin spread across her face. "But that curse doesn't say a damn thing about kissing them."

"Gilly…" Viv warned.

Gilly batted a hand at her. "You can't tell me that before you got into a tiff with Nikoli that you didn't want to kiss those luscious lips of his."

Viv waved a dismissive hand and turned back to stare at the window. No way was she going to let on to either of her sisters that she'd wanted to do more than kiss him.

A small shiver ran along her spine as she remembered her vision about Nikoli. The shiver came from a bite of pleasure and a huge gulp of fear. She had no idea what they were in for next. All she had to go on was the vision she'd caught when she'd held Evee's hands.

Sister trumped an X-rated vision, hands down.

Chapter 12

Nikoli's global wrist unit had allowed him to locate the docks without any problem. Fortunately, the streets from the hotel to the dock had been relatively empty, save for an occasional cab and a wandering drunk or two.

Nikoli let instinct guide him through the cool October night to the Françoises' ferry.

"Are you sure this is the right one?" Lucien asked, running a hand through his hair.

Before Nikoli could answer, he heard the lapping of water and saw a shadow move ahead to his right. A gray shadow meshed with the darkness, as no lights illuminated the wharf. He didn't need light to know it was Viv. His body recognized her immediately, which disturbed him.

Back at the house, when Viv had fallen against him and he'd caught her to keep her from smacking onto the floor, he'd inadvertently been swept up in what must have been a clairvoyant scene.

He felt a little ashamed of himself. He should've stood her up more abruptly, disconnected from that vision, but he'd chosen to ride it out with her.

It had taken every ounce of willpower he possessed for him not to physically react to what played out in Viv's mind. In that close proximity to his cousins and the other two sisters, it would have been difficult to hide a boner.

What had been impossible for him, however, was to get the images out of his head. That concerned Nikoli the most. He had to stay focused on this mission. It was too big, too much was at stake for him to be distracted.

He parked the Camaro near the loading area. As he and his cousins walked closer to the pier, the sight of Viv grew clearer in the moonlight. She wore jeans, a white T-shirt and a light denim jacket. Understated attire for one who carried such magnificent beauty.

She walked over to them, hitching her thumbs into the front pockets of her jeans. "Thank you for being on time."

Nikoli nodded.

"Please wait here a moment," she said.

Nikoli watched as Viv walked aboard the ferry and headed for its bow. She stood at the railing, her back to them. He saw her arms drop to her sides, then extend slightly. She formed an O with each hand, her thumbs and forefingers pressing together. She lifted her arms a bit higher.

Nikoli tilted his head and held his breath, a trick he'd learned to increase his ability to hear things at a distance. He listened to Viv chant.

"In shadows formed by moonlit night,
let all but vision remain in sight.
In cover walk thee hand-in-hand,
to my voice—to my voice, my immediate command.
Rocknigh—foring—tramore—naught."

She stood there a few seconds longer, then dropped her arms and turned toward them.

"Where is Evee?" Lucien asked.

"And Gilly?" Gavril asked.

"They'll be here soon," Viv said. "As soon as I make it to the North compound, they'll be following right behind."

"Shouldn't we wait here for them?" Gavril asked.

"No," Viv replied. "You'll come with me." She turned her back to them again, leaned over the railing at the front of the ferry, then threw a hand out, like she was casting dice.

The ferry began to move, much quicker than Nikoli remembered from his last ride. Although he saw the shore on the opposite side of the river, a ferry traveling at its normal speed would've taken fifteen to twenty minutes to reach shore. They were mooring onto the opposite dock in less than five.

As soon as the ferry was secured, Viv hurried over to the pickup parked under the lean-to. The cousins followed her, Nikoli pulling up the rear.

"All of you should be able to fit in here if you squish together," she said. "If you want to stretch out, two of you can ride in the cab, and the other two can hop in the bed of the truck. It's a little cluttered back there, but you're welcome to it."

Nikoli tagged Lucien and motioned for him to follow him into the cab. Gavril and Ronan caught his signal and jumped into the bed of the truck.

Sliding onto the bench seat, Nikoli allowed himself to be sandwiched between Viv and Lucien. The positioning couldn't have been more wrong.

He felt it difficult to breathe, being so close to her. Viv's hair was still braided, and the braid lay over her right shoulder and came to rest in her lap. A black mane of exquisite beauty.

Viv looked around Nikoli to make certain Lucien had closed the passenger door, then peered over her shoulder to check on Gavril and Ronan in the bed of the truck. It was as if she purposely avoided eye contact with him.

Nikoli didn't take offense. After his unintentional walk through her erotic vision, he couldn't blame her. She probably suspected that he had watched.

After slapping the truck into gear, Viv gunned the accelerator and the truck roared off. It was then that Nikoli heard the motor from the ferry start up again. He looked back.

"Is someone else on the ferry?"

"No," Viv said.

"But I know you shut the engine off when we moored. Now it's on again."

"I know."

"Do you have an automatic guiding system on it?" Nikoli asked.

Viv cast a wry smile his way as they bumped along a dirt road. "Um…yep, what you said. It's headed back to pick up Evee's brood."

After five minutes of bouncing and jostling down partially graveled roads, Viv swerved onto another dirt road that led to a giant set of wrought-iron gates. Each iron panel had the initial F planted in its center.

She pulled out a remote from the console of the truck, pressed a button and the gates chugged open. She drove past them and turned into a heavily wooded area.

The path they followed was only wide enough for one vehicle. Tree branches scraped and slapped the sides of her pickup as they barreled forward. The farther they drove, the denser the foliage became and the darker the night. It wasn't until they were completely canopied that Viv turned the headlights on.

Moments later, they bounced into a clearing and she veered left. Her headlights suddenly speared two men standing a few yards away. They appeared to be twice Nikoli's size.

"You have company," Nikoli said.

She nodded. "The one on the left is Jaco, my East pack leader. You've already met him. The one on the right is Aaron, who takes care of the West."

Viv finally pulled the truck to a stop and got out, leaving the engine running. "The four of you stay put until I signal all's clear," she said. Not waiting for a response, Viv closed her door and walked toward the two Loups.

With the headlights still on and the driver's window down, Nikoli watched her tall, slender body move with grace and power. She reminded him of a cougar.

When she came face-to-face with the two men, she tossed her braid over her shoulder so it fell down her back. The tip of it landed between her buttocks, which caused him to shift uncomfortably in his seat. Without prompting, a vision of his hand wrapped in that braid pulling her toward him flashed into his mind. He squeezed his eyes shut a second to block it.

"Those are some big dudes," Lucien said. "Think we're going to have a problem with them?"

Nikoli motioned for him to be silent, then leaned closer to the driver's window to see if he could pick up any of the trio's conversation.

They spoke in low voices, but hearing from great distances was one of Nikoli's specialties, one that had saved his life many times.

"Those men will not harm anyone," Viv said to Jaco and Aaron. "I'll make certain of that."

"But you never bring strangers here," Aaron said.

"Bringing them here was not wise, especially after what happened yesterday," Jaco said. "Terrible idea."

Even from this distance, Nikoli saw something waver over the faces of the two men, their features appearing to undulate. Not drastically, but enough to be noticeable.

He realized he was witnessing two Loups struggling to keep from morphing into their true nature, and it was Viv's presence that kept them in human form. The night was lit with a brilliant three-quarter moon. A time for Loups to howl, feed and mate. He was impressed at the power and confidence with which Viv addressed the Loup Garous. She stood at least five foot seven, but looked to be child-size in the presence of the two men. Yet she seemed to control them effortlessly.

"I see that you have repaired the gate and the fence," Viv said to Jaco and Aaron. "Is the back territory secure?"

"Yes," Jaco said. "You wouldn't have had us tend

to the repairs if you didn't think we could manage by feeding time. Isn't that right?"

"Why are you giving me attitude?" Viv asked.

"I don't like those men here," Jaco said, his voice growing deeper, a soft growl rolling beneath it.

"Like it or not, they are here by my invitation," Viv said. "And you will respect that. Now let's prepare for the feeding. We're already running slightly behind schedule."

With that, the two men turned away and disappeared into a heavy thicket of trees. Once they were out of sight, Viv turned and signaled for Nikoli to turn off the engine of the truck and come meet her.

No sooner were Nikoli and his cousins by her side, than Viv walked over to a large oak tree. She put an arm around it as if she meant to hug the tree, then Nikoli heard the soft click of a latch opening. A six-inch section of tree bark opened like a door. He stepped back to get a better look.

Viv's fingers danced over a panel of buttons inside the door.

A loud whoosh suddenly sounded from a great distance away. It was followed by a rumbling that grew louder with each passing second until Nikoli felt the vibrations from it beneath his feet.

"What is that noise?" Gavril asked.

Viv pointed to a steel fence about seventy feet away. The fence stood over fifteen feet tall and in the moonlight, Nikoli saw that the barbs on top of the fence were tipped in silver.

"If you watch through that opening," Viv said, "just past that small clearing there, you'll see. This compound consists of five hundred acres. I have the

West and East Loup packs cordoned off in the far back acreage. I made the decision to gather all of them in one place so they could be watched together until we sorted through this mess."

"Smart move," Nikoli said.

Viv tossed him a small, shy smile.

The rumbling grew louder, and soon Nikoli spotted the horns of a bull, then another and another. He squinted into the darkness and saw cattle rushing into the compound. That's when he noticed the fence within the fence. It created some sort of shoot that allowed the animals to head in only one direction. He heard the squeal of pigs, the neighing of goats. Hundreds of animals seemed to rush by.

"We feed in order," Viv said to the cousins. "To avoid conflict. Evee's Nosferatu go first since they only feed on the blood." She held up one hand and pointed a finger skyward and said loudly, "Come hither!"

At that command came the sudden braying of cows, squealing of pigs and screaming of goats. Nikoli saw treetops sway off in the distance. Though he couldn't put an eye on any Nosferatu or any of the animals once they'd cleared the shoot, he knew the feeding had begun.

"Is it possible for us to get closer so we can watch the feed?" Nikoli asked Viv.

She looked at him as if he'd grown a second head. "I'm not going to risk your life or endanger the Nosferatu by allowing you inside the compound. We allowed you to come here, so whatever you need to smell, go smell it, but do it from this side of the fence.

You're welcome to investigate the perimeter, but inside the compound is off limits," Viv said with a scowl.

"If the Nosferatu are feeding right now, where is Evee?" Lucien asked.

"And how did they get into this area?" Ronan added. "It certainly wasn't from where we entered. I would've spotted them."

"Just as I have Jaco and Aaron," Viv said. "Evee has two leaders that help her at feeding time. My sister won't cross the river. She's afraid of water."

The information Nikoli had received prior to this mission indicated that Evee controlled the element of water, so he didn't understand her fear of it. He decided against questioning Viv about it.

"So how do you get all of the Nosferatu over here without them being seen?" Ronan asked.

A look of frustration crossed Viv's face. "You have your secrets, we have ours."

Time appeared to jump into fast-forward because it seemed like only minutes later when Nikoli heard a shrill caw and the sound of many crows flying overhead.

Evidently seeing the puzzlement on Nikoli's face, Viv said, "That is Evee calling them back. Now if you'll excuse me, I have to tend to my Loups. They're next."

With no further explanation, Viv unlocked a wide steel gate and slipped through it. She relocked the gate, then disappeared into the forestry.

"I don't like all the secret-secret stuff," Lucien said.

"Me neither," Gavril said.

Nikoli held up a hand. "We're the strangers here. You wouldn't expect us to welcome strangers into our territory with wide-open arms and say, 'Sure, come on in, I'll show you everything we do,' would you?"

"But we're here to help them," Gavril said.

"Then let's help them," Nikoli said. "Once they're through with the feedings, we'll walk the boundaries of the compound from this side of the fence and see if we pick up anything."

"Why do we need to wait until after the feedings?" Ronan asked, then struggled to hold back a yawn. "They won't let us inside the compound anyway, and we don't need them to examine the outside of the territory."

"Be patient, cousin," Nikoli said. "Be patient. We may need them more than you know."

The night grew silent. The bawling, bellowing, screeching, screaming and neighing of the animals had vanished. Now the only sound that echoed to Nikoli's ear was that of gnashing teeth and the sound of mouths chomping on flesh.

It was a difficult sound to process. It sent Nikoli's protection instincts into overdrive. He knew all animals, whether they walked on two legs or four, had to eat to survive. Nature had its own process. But hearing all of it going on at one time made Nikoli feel sorry for the cattle that had to be used to feed so many that haunted the night.

This part of the feeding seemed to take longer than that of the Nosferatu for it was a while before Viv returned.

Once she was back at their side, she lifted a hand in the air, pointed a finger skyward and issued a command. "Come hither!"

The sound that followed was like hordes of hyenas

had infiltrated the compound. Wailing, high-pitched laughter and squawking.

Gilly suddenly appeared out of the brush to their left.

Startled, Gavril swung about, his right hand grappling with a sheath that hung from his belt. Nikoli prayed his cousin's action didn't startle the sisters.

"Whoa there, boss," Gilly said to Gavril. "Is that a gun at your side? A knife?"

"Sorry, no, Abigail," Gavril said. "It's my scabior. We each have one."

Gilly frowned. "You have a what? And let's just cut to the chase. Call me Gilly, will you? Abigail sounds too stuffy."

Gavril smiled. "All right…Gilly."

Nikoli cleared his throat. "Our weapons are called scabiors. We use them to battle the Cartesians. I'll remove mine from its sheath so you can look at it, if you'd like."

When Viv nodded, he reached for the sheath hanging from his belt.

Viv took a step closer to him and Gilly walked over cautiously. Nikoli slowly pulled out the scabior, and laid it out across his left palm. The eight-inch steel rod glistened in the moonlight and the bloodstone at the scabior's tip winked when he turned it just so.

Gilly let out a snort. "That looks like a toy! That's what you use to kill those monstrous beasts you told us about? It looks like the most you'd be able to do with it is poke out your own eye."

Nikoli couldn't help but grin. He loved the openness of the Triads. Although they were more than courteous, they weren't afraid to say what they meant. "I know how it appears, but you'll have to just trust me. It does the job."

"Can I hold it?" Gilly asked.

"No," Nikoli said. "I'm sorry. If it's used in the wrong manner by an untrained hand, you could annihilate everything within this five-hundred-acre compound. It took years of training for us to learn how to use it effectively."

"All right, big whoop," Gilly said with a pout.

The sound of hyenas gave way to the crunching of bones.

"Are the Chenilles in there?" Ronan asked. "Are they making that noise?"

"Yes," Viv answered. "They ingest the marrow from the bones. That's why the different breeds are brought in a specific order. Once all of them have had their fill, we'll either settle them down in their sleeping habitat or send them off to tend to other chores before dawn. The Chenilles and the Loup Garous aren't sensitive to daylight like the Nosferatu. Many of them have jobs that we've assigned them to during the day, so they'd learn to coexist and interact with humans. The same goes for the Nosferatu, only they serve by night. This feeding time is to make certain they are satiated so the potential for an attack on a human is minimized considerably. We've decided, however, to put them all on lock-down until the Cartesians are dealt with."

"Another good call," Nikoli said, impressed with her foresight.

"So is that where Evee is now?" Lucien asked. "Putting her Nosferatu away before dawn? Tucking them in?"

Viv grinned. "Yes, they're being tucked in."

"Will we see Evee again later this morning?" Ronan asked.

Viv gave him a quizzical look, then said, "She'll be dockside, waiting for us when we're done."

"You really have one hell of an operation here," Nikoli said. "Fast and efficient. It's so well organized. I'm impressed."

"Thanks," Gilly said. "You should be. This is a lot of hard work." She looked at Viv. "I'm going to go gather them up now." She took off at a fast pace along the east side of the fence that cordoned off the compound.

Suddenly, Nikoli caught a nostril full of noxious gas and cloves, a sure sign that one or more Cartesians had broken through to their dimension. He took off, following where the scent seemed to lead. It happened to be in the same direction Gilly was headed.

Lucien, Gavril and Ronan immediately took off after him, evidently picking up the scent, as well.

"Wait!" Viv shouted.

Nikoli heard her clap her hands twice. He glanced over his shoulder and saw her hands held out as if signaling for them to stop. Before his brain could register that she was casting a spell, he heard her utter a short incantation. Immediately he and his cousins were brought to an abrupt halt, as if they'd slammed into an invisible barrier.

"No, no!" Nikoli shouted. "Release—release, the Chenilles will be killed if you don't."

Gilly whirled about, her expression one of fear and utter confusion. She looked from Viv to Nikoli, then back to Viv. "Release, Viv! Let them go!"

Viv heeded her sister's request and clapped her

hands twice more. The abrupt dissolution of the barrier caused Nikoli and his cousins to fall to the ground.

Nikoli scrambled quickly back to his feet and took off running, Gilly ahead of him.

"Where do I go?" Gilly shouted. "Viv!"

"Right behind you!" Viv yelled.

"Stay back!" Nikoli warned. "Let us get there first."

"How will you get to them?" Gilly asked, her breath coming in short bursts. "You can't enter the compound this way. The gate's back there!"

Nikoli nearly gagged on the smell of sulfur and cloves. The farther they ran, the thicker the scent became. He stopped suddenly and pointed due north.

In that moment, the sky appeared to split open and four creatures with heads the size of two buffaloes melded together burst through the opening. Their arms were the circumference of a gigantic oak tree. Razor-sharp claws grabbled for Chenilles.

Shrieking laughter filled the night, and Nikoli caught sight of Chenilles running in every direction. Long, lanky bodies, some hairless, some spotted with fur. All of them terrified.

"No!" Viv and Gilly cried in unison, then both yelled out a binding spell. Unfortunately, all it did was appear to piss off the Cartesians for they turned in the sisters' direction.

Fearing Viv and Gilly might be attacked, Nikoli immediately held his scabior out in his right hand as did his cousins, and they aimed the weapons at the Cartesians. Before they could get a bead on them, two more Cartesians appeared, instantly capturing a Chenille apiece. They bit their captives' heads off, then sucked at the necks as if they meant to extract all of the innards, heart and soul.

Gilly screamed, but her voice barely reached an audible volume before Viv was at her side. Both women stood motionless, mouths open, as Nikoli, Lucien, Ronan and Gavril aimed their weapons, gave two quick twists of their wrists, twirled the scabiors between their fingers and took aim again. Bolts of lightning shot from their bloodstones and hit their target.

Nikoli heard the first deafening pop as the lightning bolts hit the Cartesians on their heads and pushed them back to the fourth dimension. Another pop—the fifth dimension. Then the hole in the sky closed up tightly, and they were unable to push them back any farther.

Gilly was on her knees now crying, her hands covering her face. Viv hovered over her, trying to comfort her as best she could.

With the smell of sulfur and cloves fading in the night air, Nikoli and his cousins shoved their scabiors back into their sheaths.

Nikoli walked over to Viv and Gilly. "You two okay?"

They looked at him, dumbfounded.

Nikoli sighed. "I don't think many more explanations are needed about who we are or what we do or what Cartesians are, are there?"

Viv looked up at him. And a tear slid down her cheek. Her world and mind were being torn apart by polar opposites. Her growing need to be near Nikoli, and the desire to run as far away from him and the creatures he fought.

Chapter 13

After the death of the two Chenilles, it had taken some time to calm Gilly down enough so she was able to get the remaining members of her brood across the river, then head home. Viv would've gladly taken on the chore herself, but she had no control over the Chenilles, nor did Evee. Only Gilly. Just as Gilly had no control over her Loups or Evee's Nosferatu.

The ferry had returned for her and the four cousins once Gilly had offloaded city-side. By the time Viv and the men made it across, Evee was standing at the edge of the wharf, looking shaken to the core and about to jump into the water she so feared. Gilly had filled her in on what had happened.

It was then they'd parted ways with the Benders. And Viv, as much as she didn't want to admit it, hated to see Nikoli go. Yes, he was easy on the eyes, that was a given. Only it wasn't his looks that caused her to want him to stay. It was…him. His strength. His touch, as brief as it might have been made her ache for more. And his eyes, the confidence and compassion she saw in them. The softness and hunger she felt for him every time he looked at her. She and Evee had thanked them profusely and agreed to meet up with the men again later that evening at the triplets' home. Benders and Triads were still human, and despite the severity of any situation, a human had to eat and sleep at some point.

When Viv and Evee had finally returned home around 7:45 a.m., they'd found Gilly crying in the kitchen, attempting to make some kind of tea to help calm her nerves. Viv had taken over the task and set a pot of tea brewing with valerian, an herb for overactive nervous systems, passion flower for worry and St. John's wort for depression.

While she poured the tea, Evee had called one of her managers at Bon Appétit to let know she was under the weather and wouldn't be coming in today. Her staff was more than competent enough to handle the café on their own.

The sisters sat at the kitchen table and downed the tea in silence, all three too exhausted and overwrought to talk, much less ask questions or ponder the morning's tragedy. No one was hungry.

Once the herbs kicked in, they'd gone off to their separate bedrooms to sleep. And sleep they did. Viv didn't wake until two o'clock in the afternoon. Gilly and Evee woke shortly thereafter.

They managed to eat some leftover lasagna, then decided it was time to go talk to the Elders before meeting with the Benders that evening. They needed answers from someone they knew and trusted. Someone and someplace safe.

The Elders lived in a two-story Victorian located in the older section of the Garden District, a good distance from the triplets.

The walk there did the three of them good. The afternoon was cool and relatively quiet, save for the occasional ringing of a trolley bell. Mostly older tourists interested in architecture ventured out this way, so there was no bustle or hassle of crowds.

When they reached the house and rang the doorbell, Arabella answered the door, flanked by Vanessa and Taka. Hugs were exchanged, then Arabella led everyone to the dining room. Tea was already steeping and six cups were laid out, along with colorful petit fours shaped like bonnets.

Viv would have preferred a shot of bourbon.

For over an hour and a half, the sisters filled in the Elders on the initial Loup Garou fight, the massacre at the North compound, the arrival of the Benders and the Cartesian attack on Gilly's Chenilles this morning. Viv, Evee and Gilly took turns interrupting one another's conversation, adding details whenever one or the other forgot something.

Everyone, including the Elders, appeared out of breath when the triplets finished.

"So where do we start?" Vanessa asked with a sigh.

"From the beginning," Viv said. "Are you aware of these Benders and the Cartesians?"

Arabella nodded. "I'm familiar with both. Although, I've not had the pleasure to meet a Bender and am fortunate to have never met a Cartesian."

Gilly threw up her hands. "You knew and didn't tell us during our training?"

"I guess we figured your mother or her sisters had told you," Vanessa said. "I mean, you did train under her up until the blessed dear passed on."

"Mother never told us a thing about them," Viv said. "Neither did Aunt Rose or Aunt Madeleine. As soon as Mom passed away, her two sisters high-tailed it to some other country, dumping their responsibilities into our lap."

"Be nice," Taka said to Viv. "You shouldn't talk about your aunts that way."

"She didn't say anything mean," Evee said defensively. "She told the truth. Rose and Madeleine took off right after Mom died. Period. There's no other way to put it."

"Maybe they were just a bit hasty in their departure," Vanessa admitted.

Arabella let out another sigh. "All of that is irrelevant. What's important is what's going on right now." A sad look crossed her face. "I'm sorry we made such a gross assumption. We should have made certain you knew about both. For no other reason than having the knowledge. You see, what we know about the Benders and Cartesians comes from what was handed down to us. It's not firsthand information."

"What do you know about them?" Viv asked.

"As we've been told, the Cartesians have been around since the 1700s."

"Fifteen," Taka corrected. "They've been around since the 1500s."

"Oh, you're right," Arabella said to Taka, then turned to the triplets. "That's about the same time that the Nosferatu, Loup Garous and Chenilles became Triad responsibility."

"What?" Gilly said. "Some Elder back then just woke up one day and decided to make the Triads responsible for them?"

"Oh, dear," Vanessa said, giving Arabella a disconcerted look. "They don't know about that either."

"Know about what?" Viv asked, suddenly realizing that through all of her years as a Triad, she'd evidently missed, intentionally or unintentionally, some crucial parts to the Circle of Sisters story.

Taka sighed. "The Triads are responsible for the Originals because they created them."

"What?" Viv and her sisters said in unison.

Arabella nodded. "I'm afraid so, my dears. Your grandmother, thirty times removed, and her sisters, were responsible for the Originals. They created them out of anger and spite, and you know what our laws say regarding that. It's quite clear. "

Viv, Evee and Gilly stared at each other, dumbstruck. Viv knew that the Triad screw up had been generations ago, and the curse meted out to them fell on their shoulders, as well. But creating the Originals out of anger and spite… That was a major screw-up. They were fortunate any Triad survived after the initial incident.

"But you're wrong about one thing," Taka said to the triplets. "I told you about the Cartesians when you were small."

"I remember that," Evee said. "But it sounded like a story, make believe. You know, like the bogeyman."

"Oh, they are bogeymen, that's for sure," Taka said. "Only very, very real. We've heard stories over the years about how many vampires, werewolves and the like they've killed. The last attack was somewhere in New Zealand, I believe, not that long ago. They've never been able to touch an Original, though. Until now."

"When did the Benders come into play?" Viv asked.

Vanessa lifted her arms and stretched. "From what I understand, not until a century or two later. Is that right, Arabella?"

"Pretty close. It did take quite some time before someone took action. No spell seems to affect Cartesians. Not then or now. It wasn't until a Cartesian massacred a group of humans that churches got involved. They founded the first group of Benders. Sort of like the Knights Templar, only for the netherworld. Of course, the church would have never commissioned such a group for vampires and the like, but once humans became involved, everything changed."

"The Benders who are here told us the Cartesians are only after factions of the netherworld," Viv said. "Because of their powers. They said they weren't interested in humans."

Arabella shrugged, then eyed Viv. "Every group has a wayward son or daughter. Fortunately, that Cartesian's mistake of attacking those humans wound up being to our benefit."

Viv picked at a crumb on the tablecloth, feeling ashamed of herself. Her North pack Loups and Gilly's Chenille were dead because of her big mouth.

"So we can trust these guys?" Evee asked the Elders. "The Benders who are here now, I mean?"

Taka huffed. "You think? After what you witnessed

this morning, you're still wondering if you can trust them?"

Arabella nodded. "Absolutely. You can. I thank the elements and the heavens that they've been sent to you. I would contact other members of the Circle of Sisters for reinforcement if I thought it would do any good. But I'm afraid adding others into the mix would only put more of our own at risk. No one but you can handle the Originals, and no one but the Benders can handle the Cartesians."

"How can anyone expect just the seven of us to battle these creatures all the while protecting our groups?" Gilly asked. "Those sons of bitches just appeared out of thin air."

"The Benders will handle the Cartesians," Vanessa said and took a sip of tea.

"Yeah, we kind of noticed," Viv said. "But we and they can't be everywhere at the same time."

"I'm confident the seven of you will work the situation out," Arabella said.

"You say that like the only thing we have to battle is a hill of ants," Viv said. "I mean no disrespect, Arabella, but if you had witnessed what we did, you'd know how ridiculous that sounds. You'd be wishing for an army, not seven people."

"You know," Taka said, "I just thought of something. Do you think the sorcerers might be able to help in this situation? Maybe they have resources that we don't."

"Have you lost your mind?" Vanessa asked, her back stiffening in her chair. "Those subspecies humanoids are only interested in themselves. When have you ever known a sorcerer to help a witch? They don't. Because they're greedy, selfish ingrates. Don't you dare mention any of this to those three yahoos in the city, Taka. Do you understand?"

"You're not the boss of me," Taka said, lifting her chin.

"No, but I am," Arabella said. "Not one word of anything we've discussed this afternoon shall leave this house. Is *that* understood?"

"I won't say anything," Taka said, casting her eyes downward. "I was just wondering."

"Well, now you don't have to wonder," Vanessa said. She folded her arms across her chest and glared at Taka. "I can't believe you even thought of that."

"At least I'm trying to help find a solution to their problems instead of just sitting like a lump on a log," Taka said.

"The two of you, stop," Arabella said. "We have enough to worry about without both of you acting like five-year-olds." She turned to the triplets. "I'm sorry we don't have more direction to offer you, my dears."

"Can you at least tell me why my spells on Milan and Warden didn't work?" Viv asked. "That's where all of this started. What if it happens again? What if we're out there trying to protect our sects, just like we have been, and the plug gets pulled on our incantations?"

"Your powers didn't leave you at the time they were fighting," Arabella said. "The sexual tension between Stratus and those two alpha males might have weakened them, but it didn't steal them."

"But I told you nothing I did worked," Viv insisted, tapping a finger on the table for emphasis.

Arabella reached over and patted Viv's hand. "Had

you kept a cool, clear head and called upon your elemental guide for assistance, things would be very different right now."

Viv blushed and pulled her hand into her lap. "Look, I know this is all my fault. I'm doing my best to fix it. I can't bring back my dead Loups or Gilly's dead Chenilles, but I—"

Arabella shook her head. "I'm not making accusations, just giving advice. The three of you must stay clearheaded and strong during this time of tribulation. Generations of Triads before you have kept these Cartesians away from the Originals. You have to stick together. Work with the Benders."

"Arabella?" Evee said. "Why are the mirrors in our Grimoires reflecting only gray?"

"That's not a good sign," Taka said with a tsk.

"She didn't ask you," Vanessa said.

Arabella held up a finger, signaling for the two Elders to be silent. "It's gray because the future has become uncertain. The images it reflected before were for the three of you to take heed. To show you what would happen if you shirked your duties. That mirror, like the universe, takes your words seriously. Now what's uncertain is who will survive this ordeal. It may not be a matter of any one of you leaving your duties behind. It may be given pause, wondering if the three of you will survive."

"Shit," Gilly said, then slapped a hand over her mouth. "Sorry, no disrespect meant."

Arabella gave her a half smile. "No worries, dear. I heard that very word and some far worse from your mother's mouth more than once."

"I want to know how their weapons worked when

the Benders used them," Taka said. "We were never given that information before. It would be good to know, something to pass on."

"What?" Gilly said. "You mean in case we don't make it and die?"

"Well, there is that," Taka said.

"Don't be so crass," Vanessa warned, then turned to Gilly. "You're not going to die, dear. We're confident you and the Benders will be the victors in this battle."

"Yeah, yeah," Taka said. "But I still want to know how the scorpions work."

"They call them scabiors," Viv said. "The weapon isn't very big or impressive to look at. Had I seen it in any other setting, I would've thought it was an amateur witch or sorcerer's wand." Viv described the metal rods and how the cousins used them. "The Cartesians seemed to enter the world through a big rip in the sky."

"What did that rip look like?" Taka asked, her eyes bright with curiosity.

"Blacker than any black I've ever seen," Viv said. "But when that lightning bolt hit the Cartesians, it pushed them back into the hole, which seemed to create another hole, one even blacker than the first, behind it, and the Cartesians were pushed even farther back."

"It's called a dimensional rift," Arabella said to Taka. "The hole in the sky that Viv is talking about."

"A dimensional rit," Taka said, dreamy-eyed.

"Rift," Arabella corrected. "If this is something you plan to pass on, make certain you've got the information right. Look what happened with Evette. You told her about Cartesians, and the poor dear thought you were talking about bogeymen."

Taka waved a dismissive hand. "Just a little mis-understanding." She turned to Viv. "What happened after that?"

"I heard two loud pops, then the hole in the sky immediately closed up, taking the Cartesians with it."

"I didn't hear any pop," Gilly said, looking at Viv.

"How could you not? It was so loud."

Gilly shrugged, confusion on her face. "Maybe… I guess… Maybe I was in shock and just didn't hear it."

Vanessa nodded. "Funny thing about shock. It can do strange things to people, even Triads."

"And these Cartesians were as big as they say?" Taka asked.

"Massive," Viv said. "I've never seen a creature with a head or arms that big."

"What was their method of attack?" Taka asked.

"I told you," Viv said. "They came out of nowhere from the rift in the sky."

"No, I mean how did they kill the Chenilles?"

Gilly held up a hand, her brow deeply furrowed. "I don't want to talk about that. It was the most horrible thing I've ever seen."

"I know it must have been a very traumatic ordeal for you, sweet one," Vanessa said. "But for once, Taka is right. Where the Circle of Sisters is concerned, if there is valuable information that may help another sister at another time, we need to be informed."

Gilly put her elbows on the table and looked at Viv. "You can go ahead and tell them, but I don't have to listen." With that, she stuck a forefinger in each of her ears.

Viv looked at Evee. "I didn't give you all the gory details. You sure you want to hear this?"

"Not really, but I have to know what we're facing," Evee said grimly.

Viv nodded and turned to Taka. "The Cartesians bit their heads off. Then they sucked on their necks like they were trying to pull everything inside out. When they finished, all that was left was a rag of flesh."

Taka slapped a hand over her eyes. "I should've never asked. Now I'm going to have nightmares."

"Try living that nightmare," Viv said, then got to her feet. "We need to head back home now. The Benders will be returning this evening. Any further advice?"

Evee and Gilly rose from their chairs and waited for Arabella to speak.

The Elders stood up, and Arabella motioned everyone toward the front door. When they reached it, she touched Viv on the shoulder and looked deeply into her eyes to make sure she had her attention. Then she looked gravely at Gilly and Evee.

"The only other piece of advice I can offer," Arabella said, "is to remember the warnings of your Grimoires. The mirrors may be reflecting gray right now, but they weren't always that way. Remember." She tapped a finger over her heart. "Watch over your hearts and your heads, especially where the Benders are concerned."

Viv held back a groan. Deep inside her, she already knew that where Nikoli was concerned, she was about to screw up again. Big time.

Chapter 14

No sooner had they left the Elders than Viv felt a nervous twitch in her gut. Her mind suddenly filled to overflowing with chaotic images of Chenilles, Nosferatu and Loup Garous clashing into one another, running through the city among humans. Oddly enough, at the same time, she saw Chenilles carefully tucked away in the Louis 1 cemetery, the Nosferatu in the catacombs of St. John's and her Loups in the North compound. The conflicting images didn't make sense.

Viv allowed the twitch in her gut to decide which she should pay attention to.

"Evee, I think you need to check on your Nosferatu," Viv said as they continued walking toward home.

Evee came to a stop and stared at her. "Why? Did you pick up something?"

Viv and Gilly pulled up alongside her.

"Yes," Viv said and explained what she had seen. "It was a conflicting vision. So just to be on the safe side, you should check out your brood."

Gilly blew out a breath. "I'm going to Snaps and let my managers know I'll be out for the evening. Then I'll head to the cemeteries, check on everyone, then start moving those in the City and Lafayette cemeteries to Louis 1."

Viv nodded in agreement. "I'll go to the compound and talk to Aaron and Jaco to make sure things are copacetic."

Gilly gave Viv a wary look. "Are you sure you're telling us everything you saw? I mean, you're not holding back anything to protect us, keep us from freaking out?"

Viv shook her head. "I swear. I've told you everything, as senseless as it sounds. That senselessness is why I'm suggesting we check on our broods."

Without another word, the three sisters parted ways, each heading in a different direction.

When Viv made it to the ferry, she jumped aboard and pushed it to a speed that nearly tipped it starboard. As she flew across the water, Viv couldn't help but remember the last time she'd ridden the ferry.

Nikoli had been with her. The memory caused her to feel his presence beside her, and it sent heat flashing through her body. It frustrated her that no matter how dire the situation, his face always sent a flush to her cheeks. Part of her wanted to meld to him, side by side, never leaving his presence—his scent. Yet the responsible part of her, the side that had a habit of raining on her and her sisters' parade from time to time, knew it best to stay away. Emotionally especially. They couldn't, shouldn't be together.

The first thing Viv spotted when she made it to the front gates of the North compound was Aaron and Jaco arguing, circling each other as if ready to attack.

Viv pulled the old pickup as close as she dared to the Loups, then killed the engine and hopped out.

"What's going on here?" she said to Jaco and Aaron. She had to yell over their arguing. Both were so absorbed in slinging curses at each other that neither of them noticed she'd arrived.

When the two Loups spotted her, they froze, their expressions like two kids who'd been caught with cigarettes behind a woodshed. Both wore jeans and were bare-chested. Their long hair gleamed with sweat, as did their faces and chests.

"We have a situation," Jaco said.

"No, we don't," Aaron said. "They have to be somewhere around here. You didn't check the East section of the North compound yet." Aaron looked back at Viv. "The entire compound hasn't been checked." He jerked his chin at Jaco. "He's too slow."

"If you're so smart and fast," Jaco said to Aaron, "why can't you come up with a clean count on your side of the compound?"

Aaron growled and Viv shouted, "Hold up! Hold up!" She waved her hands and shook her head. "What the hell are you two talking about?"

Jaco stepped toward Viv, his massive bulk towering over her. "We've been through a count twice," he said. "It looks like we have at least fifty Loups missing. Twenty from Aaron's pack and at least thirty of mine."

Viv felt her blood run cold and her eyes narrowed.

"What do you mean by missing? Was there another attack?"

Jaco gave a small shrug. "We found no dead bodies, no blood. They're simply missing. We've been calling out to them, trying to connect with them for at least the last three hours, but no response."

Viv scrubbed her face with her hands. "How long did it take the two of you to get the fence repaired?"

"About an hour and a half," Aaron said, stepping up alongside Jaco. "We worked as fast as we could."

"Could they have escaped before the repairs were completed?" Viv asked.

"Not from my pack," Aaron said. "I didn't bring them over until the fence was secure."

Viv looked at Jaco. He lowered his head.

"If mine did escape while we worked, I'm positive I would have sensed that," Jaco said. "I don't see how...or when." He glanced at Aaron. "Maybe you lost your twenty while en route here. Did you consider that possibility?"

Aaron growled. "Shut your fucking mouth, dog bone. I watch over my pack. You might be able to use a broken fence as your excuse, but I watch over my own."

"Then how the hell do you lose twenty of them?" Jaco snapped.

Viv clapped her hands together hard to get their attention. "Both of you, quit acting like infants. If we have fifty Loup Garous missing and there are no dead bodies or blood, that can only mean one thing. They have to be somewhere in the city." She glared at Jaco. "Did you search every part of this compound?"

"The only section I've not covered yet is the far

East side. I was about to head over there when smart-ass here decided to give me directions on how I should accomplish my search. I know this compound like the back of my hand."

"Then finish searching it," Viv demanded. She turned to Aaron. "I want you to go back into the compound and recount your pack, make certain the first count wasn't an error."

"I didn't miscount," Aaron insisted. "I have twenty missing."

Viv glared at him and said through clenched teeth, "I said go back and recount. We have to get a true picture of what we're dealing with here, and I don't want to work with erroneous information."

Both Loups gave her a quick nod, then made their way into the compound to do as they were ordered.

Feeling like she'd vomit at any moment, Viv got back in her truck and headed to the ranch house. Maybe Charlie, Kale or Bootstrap saw or heard something that would give her a clue as to her missing Loups' whereabouts.

When Viv reached the ranch, she found Charlie hammering on a fence post in the cattle grazing pen. When he spotted Viv, he waved and a smile creased his weathered face. He tipped his cowboy hat up a notch when she drove up beside him and stopped the truck.

"How you doing, Miss Viv?" Charlie asked.

"Fine, Charlie, thanks for asking," Viv lied. No way could she tell Charlie what was really going on. "Where are Bootstrap and Kale?"

"Oh, I sent them out to Abbeville to pick up a truckload of hay bales. Got 'em for a good price from a farmer I know out that way. Even though the boys are gone, I can surely tend to whatever you need help with, Miss Viv."

Viv leaned through the driver's-side window and swiped a hand over her face. "I know I asked you this last time I came out here, Charlie, but I need to ask again. Have you seen or heard anything unusual coming from the back five today?"

"You're meanin' the place you told us we need to stay out of?"

"Yes," Viv said, feeling like a fool talking this way to someone nearly twice her age.

Charlie took off his hat, pulled a bandanna out of his back pocket, then wiped the sweat from his brow. His lips pursed. His brow furrowed. Then Charlie shook his head slowly as he stuck the bandanna back into his pocket and his hat back on his head.

"I ain't seen nothing, but you know, now that you mention it, I heard what kinda sounded like a bunch of coyotes yelping earlier today. I thought it was just a pack of 'em moving through the woods. Didn't see any though. Been keepin' a close eye on the horses and livestock just in case. Better they're out in the woods than here. Other than that, I haven't seen a thing but this ol' fence I've been workin' on."

Charlie tilted his head slightly and studied Viv's face. "No disrespect meant, Miss Viv, but you sure look like you're carrying a bucket full of worry. Are you sure there isn't something I can help you with?"

Viv worked hard at giving Charlie a smile. She wished she had someone else to talk to about the Cartesians, about her Loups, about everything that was going on. And if anyone could keep a secret it was Charlie Zerangue. But she didn't want to chance it.

Knowing him, he would've stormed into the compound to help track her Loups, even if it meant risking his own life.

"Just a lot on my mind, Charlie. But thank you anyway." She pulled the gearshift into Drive and held the brakes for a moment. "You take care. I'll be talking to you again soon, I'm sure."

With that, Viv drove back to the compound where she found Aaron standing by the gate, toeing dirt with his boot. She pulled up next to him.

Aaron looked at her, frowning. "Twenty missing for sure," he said. "I don't know what to say. I don't know where they went or how they got out."

"And you brought your pack here after the fence was repaired, right?"

"Yes. No way I would've let my pack in here if it wasn't secure."

"There has to be a breach in the fence, somewhere," Viv said. "Loups don't simply vanish into thin air. They couldn't have jumped the fence, even if they'd morphed. It's too high. And, if by some freak act of nature one did make a jump that high, the silver tips on the barbs would've skewered the Loup. It would still be up there wailing for help."

Aaron nodded, looking lost for words.

In that moment, Jaco jumped out of the brush and hurried over to Viv. "Entire area searched. My count's the same. Thirty missing."

"Great," Viv said sardonically. "Not only do we have to watch over this compound, but we've got fifty MIA Loups. They could be running around the city for all we know. If we don't find them before feeding time, the gods only know what or whom they'll attack."

Aaron and Jaco simply stared down at her.

"Watch over this territory. Don't take your eyes off it. Stay inside the compound and walk its perimeter. Count and recount your packs to make sure we don't lose more."

They nodded in unison.

Viv slammed a foot on the accelerator and peeled out of the area, heading for the dock.

She had no clue as to how they were going to manage this mess. Although they'd narrowed the territory by putting the Chenilles in one cemetery, her Loups in one compound and the Nosferatu in the catacombs, the plan seemed futile. Now they had to worry about her Loups roaming the city, and the last thing they needed was a whirlwind of public attention. Up until now, she, her sisters and their broods had stayed under the human radar. She feared that luxury had just been shot to hell.

When Viv made it back home, she found Gilly and Evee pacing around the kitchen table. Gilly had obviously been running her hands through her hair because her pixie cut stuck out in little spikes, like antennae. Evee had dark circles under her eyes and they looked swollen, like she'd been crying. The sight of them twisted Viv's stomach into knots.

"What's wrong?" Viv asked.

"I have fifteen Chenilles missing," Gilly said, her eyes suddenly brimming with tears, something uncommon for her.

"And I've got ten Nosferatu gone," Evee said and leaned against the table as if needing the support.

Gilly and Evee looked at Viv.

"I have fifty Loups missing," she said quietly, perplexed by the missing Originals.

"Sweet Mother Earth, no!" Evee said. "Viv, what are we going to do? All of those Originals could be out in the city. They're going to miss feeding time. People will be in danger."

Viv put a finger over each of her eyelids to keep a headache at bay. She shook her head. "I have no damn idea. This is way out of hand. All we can do is take one challenge at a time and deal with it."

"Maybe we should go back and see the Elders. Let them know. Maybe they can help us find them," Evee said, her voice lilting with hope.

"They can't do shit," Gilly said firmly. "We're the only ones who can deal with the Originals. All the Elders would do is fret, talk over one another for an hour and serve us tea. I mean, really. Can you actually see Arabella, Taka and Vanessa running around the city looking for Originals? No. I don't know why we have Elders anyway. They're frigging useless."

"Stop," Viv said, her voice low with anger. "Those women took us under their wing when we had no one. They trained us, worried over us and still do. That's called family. And I don't want to hear you dissing family."

Gilly huffed and looked away.

"Look," Viv said, "the Benders will be here in about forty-five minutes. Maybe they'll have some ideas on what to do."

Evee tapped the table with a finger. "What if… What if we conjured up some kind of repellent spell? Something that would keep the Originals away from humans?"

Viv shrugged. "Might be worth a try. Let's get to our Grimoires before the Benders get here. Maybe we can find something in our books that will allow us to at least manage the missing Originals while we deal with the Cartesians."

Gilly and Evee agreed and the sisters took off for their respective bedrooms.

Viv trudged up the stairs, feeling angry, lonely and more afraid than she'd ever been in her life.

Chapter 15

By the time the Benders returned to the François home at 7:30 p.m., Viv felt wired with worry. The dark pressing up against the windows didn't help.

They sat around an antique dining table that held eight people. An expansive, eighteenth-century crystal chandelier hung overhead. The cousins were dressed all in black, though the shirts were different styles.

Viv wore jeans and a royal blue pullover sweater. Gilly had dressed in white linen pants and a pink, long-sleeved T-shirt, and Evee had chosen jeans with an olive-green button-down blouse. Simple but stunning against her olive complexion and copper-colored eyes.

They'd spent the last five minutes attempting small talk, and it had been halting at best. Even so, just looking across the table at Nikoli made Viv feel like she could breathe for the first time in hours. Something about him calmed her mind and riled her up physically at the same time.

The triplets' situation had worsened since the last time they'd been with the Benders and Viv was ready to push the small talk aside and get on to business. Oddly enough, as dire as things were, having Nikoli here gave her an uncanny sense of hope. No one else, except for her sisters, had ever made her feel that way.

"Things have changed since we parted this morning," Viv said, looking around the table at the cousins. "And not for the better."

"What changed?" Nikoli asked, his expression growing more solemn. "Did you have another attack?"

"It couldn't have been that," Gavril said. "We would've picked up on it."

"Not another attack," Gilly said. "I don't think so anyway."

"What happened?" Nikoli asked.

"I have fifteen Chenilles missing," Gilly said, and her lower lip quivered.

"What?" Gavril said. "Missing from where?"

"They're unaccounted for," Gilly said. "I went to open Snaps this afternoon, told my managers I'd be tied up for the evening, then went to take count at the cemeteries. I'm fifteen short."

"From one cemetery or all three?" Gavril asked.

"All three. Lafayette, St. Louis 1 and City."

Evee leaned into the table. "And I have ten Nosferatu that have gone MIA."

Viv saw the cousins eyeing each other and wondered what messages they were sending.

"I did a head count a few hours ago," Evee said.

"That's when I found out they were gone. The two captains I have in charge at the cathedral had no idea they were missing, saw no one leave the catacombs."

"What about you?" Nikoli asked Viv.

"Jaco and Aaron told me we're at least fifty short. That's from all the compounds. If you remember, I told you I had brought everyone into the North compound. My sisters and I have our own way of calling our groups to us, and we've been calling out to them, trying to connect with them for hours. No response."

Nikoli sat back and folded his arms over his broad chest. "So now we have to add another challenge to the mix. Not only do we have to find a way to protect the Originals, we now have Nosferatu, Chenilles and Loup Garous on the loose. And they won't respond to their mistresses' calls. We have to assume they're roaming free in the city. Definitely not an ideal situation."

"You're not telling us anything we don't already know," Viv said.

"Did you let your Elders know?" Gavil asked. "Any possible solution from them?"

"We haven't told them anything," Gilly said tersely. She glanced at Viv before looking back at Gavril. "There's really nothing they could do. We're the only ones who can handle the Originals. No need to worry them just yet."

"And you can't even feel where your factions might be?" Ronan asked.

"No," Viv said, "which is odd. That's never happened before."

"If you can't feel them," Ronan said, "does that automatically mean they're dead?"

"Not necessarily," Viv said. "I've had a wayward

Loup or two over the years that didn't respond to my call just to be hardheaded. I don't see fifty of them doing that, though."

"All right," Nikoli said. "We simply have to add this to our to-do list. My cousins and I came up with a game plan that we wanted to discuss with you. We think it's pretty solid, but now that we have some Originals missing and we have to assume they're milling around people, we may have to retool that plan."

"What were you considering?" Gilly asked.

"We thought about each one of us pairing off with one of you," Gavril said. "Now, because there are four of us and you're three of you, one of you—well, actually, we decided it would be Evee—would have two Benders with her. For example, Gilly, you and I would take care of the Chenilles. Evee, Lucien and Ronan stand watch over the Nosferatu. And that leaves Viv and Nikoli to tend to the Loup Garou. We also discussed something regarding the Chenilles. If it's possible, we'd like to see them all corralled in one cemetery, the way Viv has her Loups in one compound. That way we wouldn't be running from cemetery to cemetery."

Gilly tilted her head to one side, narrowed her eyes and pursed her lips. "We're five steps ahead of you. We took care of that before you arrived. And we even discussed pairing up with you."

Gavril shot her an admiring look. "That's great. How did you manage to put the Chenilles in one cemetery and not have them kill each other over territory?"

"I trisected the cemetery with a binding spell," Gilly said. Viv saw a blush rise in her cheeks.

"Very well thought out," Nikoli said. "This will be very helpful. We'll only have three places to monitor.

One cemetery for you, Gilly. The cathedral for Evee, and the North compound for Viv."

Viv felt her heart flutter in her chest. "I like the divide and conquer thing, but what do we do about the Originals that are missing?"

"Since we've just found out about it, you'll have to give me a minute to think that through."

"What about having seven Benders instead of four?" Viv asked.

Nikoli's brow furrowed. "I don't understand."

"Well...do you have any more of those scabiors?"

"No," Lucien said. "Each Bender is given a scabior at the time of their training and it stays with them until their death."

"Can you get more?" Viv asked.

"No," Gavril said. "They're not like guns or knives. The way it works is one scabior to one Bender."

"What are you thinking?" Nikoli asked Viv.

"I thought if you had extras, that my sisters and I could use them, as well, to fight Cartesians. It wouldn't be just the four of you. I mean, I'm sure I could handle one. It didn't look that hard. I'd have to get used to that loud popping noise, though. Scared the hell out of me the first time I heard it."

Nikoli stared at her, seemingly frozen. "You heard that sound?"

"Yeah."

Nikoli turned to Gilly. "Did you?"

"No, I never heard a popping anything. But then again, Viv has great hearing. All of us have our own little specialties, you know? Like Viv hears really well and does this partial invisibility thing. I have a strong sense of smell and can astral project. Evee runs really fast, and she can channel and produce illusions. She can do things with water, too. I can do things with fire, and Viv with earth."

"I understand different abilities," Lucien said. "It's the same with us. Nikoli has exceptional hearing, Ronan can smell anything a mile away and Gavril runs faster than a gazelle. As for me, I can jump up five to six feet from a complete standstill."

"Wow," Evee said. "Very impressive." Her copper eyes twinkled with a smile.

Nikoli put a finger to his lips for a moment and the movement sent the scent of him wafting Viv's way. He smelled of soap and musk. So delicious.

He suddenly turned to Viv. "The Triads... I mean, the three of you are human, right?

"Of course we're human," Viv said, slightly taken aback. "We have different talents like the four of you do, but it's kind of like being a prodigy. We simply have the ability to do different things. Why do you question whether we're human?"

"Because until this moment, I've never heard of another human being able to hear that popping sound. Only a Bender."

"Sorry to bust your bubble," Viv said with a shrug.

"What did you see before or at the moment you heard the sound?" Nikoli asked.

"I saw a big, black rip in the sky, like it had been unzipped. Blacker than anything I've ever seen. Then those monstrosities lunged out. When you did whatever you do with your scabior and that bolt of lightning shot out of the bloodstone, hitting the Cartesians right on their heads... Good shot by the way..."

"Thank you."

"I saw the Cartesians fold over in half, like they'd been punched in the stomach. Then I saw them get sucked backward into the hole in the sky. That's when I heard the first pop. There seemed to be an even darker place behind them that pulled them farther back. When they entered that darker space, that's when I heard the second pop. After that, the sky closed up. No more pops." Viv got to her feet. "Now, I hate to break up our little tête-à-tête but the clock's ticking. I need to go check on my Loups. See if anything else has changed."

Everyone at the table stood.

"I'll go with you," Nikoli said.

"I can handle it on my own," Viv insisted. "I've been doing it for years. Look, we have Originals on the loose and Cartesians dropping out of thin air. So what's the verdict? Pair up or spread out so we could cover more territory?"

"You and your sisters can't go out there alone," Nikoli said solemnly.

"Since when?" Viv asked, frowning. "Is there something you haven't told us?"

Nikoli glanced around the table at everyone before settling his eyes back on her. "I haven't even discussed this with my cousins yet because the thought just occurred to me. If the Cartesians, specifically the leader of the Cartesians, is so hell-bent on getting to the Originals, there's a good possibility he might take the three of you out so he can have easier access to your groups. It's like the old saying, if you want to destroy a beehive, you kill the queen. If he destroys the three of you, he has nothing to hold him back from the Originals. You wouldn't be around to protect them."

"Wait," Evee said. "You mean the three of us might be attacked by Cartesians?"

"We've discussed this already, Evee," Viv said, slightly annoyed with her sister and not sure why.

"The thought occurred to me," Nikoli said. "And I think it's a valid concern. We have to assume the worst. Think about it. What would you do if you were in the Cartesians' leader's shoes? You want to conquer every Original because you want their power. Because the ultimate goal is supreme power over the world. Over the universe. What would be the fastest way to accomplish that goal? It would be to get the three of you out of the way, leaving the Originals unprotected. He'd have complete control over all of them."

Evee held a hand to her mouth.

"Shit," Gilly said with a shaky voice. "That makes sense."

Gavril stood military straight and said, "I won't let anything happen to you, Gilly." He looked at Evee and Viv. "To any of you. The three of you will be with one or two of us at all times. We'll get this figured out and taken care of. You have our word."

"But we can only do so much with what we have," Viv said. "That's reality. We have a responsibility to the city to protect the people in it. I can't just sit by the compound and wait for these Cartesians. I have to look for my missing Loups."

"The Nosferatu and Chenilles, too," Gilly added.

"Can you cast a binding spell around the Originals that are missing?" Nikoli asked Viv.

"Each of us did cast a repelling spell, hoping that will keep the missing Originals away from people. But since they're not even responding to our calls, we have no way of knowing if the spells will be effective or not."

Nikoli stroked his beard thoughtfully.

Viv let out a frustrated breath. "We need to figure out a way to secure the Originals we're controlling now. That way we can hunt for the ones that are missing."

"I have an idea," Ronan said, giving voice for the first time since they'd arrived. "I don't know if it will work, but it may be worth a try."

"Speak now, cousin," Lucien said, "or forever hold your peace."

"You remember the fencing around the North compound?"

"Of course," Nikoli said.

"And that big steel corner post not far from the entrance?" Ronan looked at Viv. "Do you have the same kind of poles on the other three corners of the property?"

"It takes more than four poles to hold up that much fencing," Viv said. "There must be at least forty."

"Perfect," Ronan said. "Now, do you have access to any bloodstones?"

"Oh, I have tons of bloodstones out in the work shed behind the house," Gilly said. "I work with a lot of crystals and gems."

"Wonderful," Ronan said.

"What are you thinking?" Nikoli asked him.

"Okay, hear me out before you blow me off, all right?" Ronan said.

"Go," Nikoli said. "Let's hear it."

"What if we set a bloodstone on top of each corner post at the North compound? The posts are steel like our scabiors, and with the bloodstone added, you'd basically have a gigantic scabior. If we had four of them aimed at each other and charged them with our real scabiors, they'd stay charged since no one's able to hold them. With the four posts aimed at the center of the compound, we'd basically be creating a huge electrical canopy over it. That way no Cartesian would be able to drop down into the center of it."

"Hmm," Nikoli said. "I've never heard of that being done before."

"Me neither," Gavril said. "But it sounds plausible."

"How are we going to move those huge, steel posts so they're aimed at each other?" Lucien asked.

"Does it matter if they're bent?" Viv asked. "Like two or three feet from the ground, if they were bent from there and aimed where you want them?"

"I don't think it would make a difference if they're bent rather than hammered at an angle into the ground," Ronan said. "As long as they're aimed toward each other."

"Then the problem's solved," Viv said. "All I have to do is have Jaco and Aaron bend the posts. I don't know if you've ever seen a Loup in action, but the strongest of them can easily bend something like that."

"How do you keep them in the compound if they're that strong?" Lucien asked. "Aren't you afraid they'll escape?"

"One reason," Viv said, "is because the barbs on top of the fence and woven through it are dipped in silver, something none of the Originals can tolerate. And second, I would only have Jaco or Aaron bend those poles. I trust them. They know we're here to take care of them, feed them, protect them from people who would literally kill them for sport."

"So what do you say?" Ronan asked Nikoli. "Think it's worth a shot?"

"You may have something there, cousin. If we can make this happen at the North compound, we might be able to create a version of it around the cemetery where the Chenilles are and in the catacombs. If it works, that would protect the Chenilles, the Nosferatu and Loup Garous, who are already contained, from the Cartesians. That would give us some freedom to look for the ones that are missing and hunt for Cartesians before they figure out a way to get through the containment areas. It'll take longer to secure a cemetery since we're limited on manpower."

"Manpower won't be a problem," Gilly said. "My lead Chenilles can take care of that."

Everyone standing at the table exchanged glances.

"So what do you say?" Viv asked Nikoli. "Do we give this a try or what? Are you confident enough that you can charge those poles with your scabior?"

"No," he said. "As I said, to my knowledge, this has never been done before. I do know that if you aim a scabior at anything and activate it, something will definitely happen. Since we're talking steel and bloodstone, though, and no Bender handling it, it should stay charged. That's only taking into consideration the laws of physics and how the scabior works. My vote is we give it a try."

"I say yes, too," Gilly said.

"Same here," Gavril said.

"I'm in," Lucien added.

"Me, too," Evee chimed in.

Ronan shrugged. "It was my idea so of course I'm for it."

Viv nodded. "Gilly, why don't you and Gavril go take a look at Louis 1. Figure out where we'll set up this rig job. Evee, you can go with Lucien and Ronan to the cathedral to figure out how we'll set up scabiors in the catacombs. I'll collect the supplies we'll need and head to the compound so we can get Jaco and Aaron started on the posts. Let's plan to meet up at the ferry at our regular time, right before feeding. We'll compare notes then."

Everyone except Nikoli shuffled around the table and headed for the foyer. As Viv watched her sisters pair off with their respective Bender and leave the house, she offered a short prayer to the elements, asking for guidance and protection.

Nikoli called out to his cousins. "Stay sharp!" Then he looked at Viv as he continued to speak. "We have to protect what is ours at all costs."

Tonight could change everything. They'd either win or lose everything they'd ever known. He glanced over at Viv. Or treasured.

Chapter 16

Viv bit the inside of her cheek hard. The pain did little to stop her hand from trembling as she closed the front door of her home, sending her sisters and the other three Benders on their way.

Nikoli stood just behind her, which sent a flush throughout her body, and no amount of cheek biting changed that. She scolded herself silently. *You've gotta turn around, stupid. You can't just stand here, staring at the door. He's going to think you're dysfunctional.*

Viv turned to Nikoli, avoiding his eyes. "Okay, supplies. What are we going to need?"

Nikoli ticked a list of items off with his fingers. "Flashlights, bloodstones, rope or cable."

"What's the rope or cable for?"

"Just in case." He grinned. "We'll also need a ladder. My cousins and I are tall, but not tall enough to reach the top of the twenty-foot pole, even if it is at a forty-five degree angle. The bloodstones will need to go on top of each pole."

"We don't have to worry about ladders," Viv said, heading for the kitchen. Nikoli followed closely behind. "My Loups can shimmy up the poles and set the bloodstone wherever I tell them to. The same goes for Gilly's Chenilles and Evee's Nosferatu. Though I'm not sure how we're going to handle the catacombs. Twenty-foot poles and fencing will definitely not fit under the cathedral. There's not much height under there."

"We'll figure something out for the catacombs," Nikoli assured her.

When they reached the kitchen, Viv went to a supply cabinet and pulled out two flashlights. She handed one to him. "It's cloudy tonight. We'll definitely need these. No need to bother with rope or cable here. I've got some in the back of my pickup I keep parked under the lean-to across river."

Nikoli nodded, took the flashlight she handed to him and stuck the long handle of it into his back pocket.

Lucky flashlight.

She hurried out of the kitchen, Nikoli in tow.

When she reached the stairs that led to the second floor, she said to him, "I have a couple of items to get upstairs. If you don't mind, please wait down here. I'll be right back."

"Sure," he said. He placed a hand on the newel post and planted a foot on the bottom step. His eyes bore into hers. "I'll be waiting right here."

Those swirling, stormy gray eyes caused Viv to

nearly trip on her way up the stairs. She had to get her head together.

She entered her bedroom, and Socrates, who'd been stretched out on her bed, confronted her with a loud hiss.

"Why, Vivienne," Socrates said, sarcasm in his tone, "what have you been up to?"

"Too much to go through right now. And besides, I know you, you little sneak. I'm sure you've been creeping and hiding around every corner and already know what's been said and planned. I don't think there's one bit of conversation we've had that you've missed. You know what's going on."

"Oh, I'm not talking about all the Cartesian hullabaloo and scabiors and what not. I'm talking about you and the Bender downstairs. The one who's anxiously awaiting your return. I can feel him, even from here. He's really struggling to keep himself together, you know. You seem to have an odd effect on him." Socrates lifted his head as if to sniff the air. "Hmm. His heart is beating faster, and he's fighting to keep his thoughts on the job. They keep bouncing back to you."

"Shut up already," Viv said and went to her closet.

"You know what you're planning is a stupid idea," Socrates continued. "Someone is going to get hurt or killed."

"I didn't ask for your opinion," Viv said. "I've got all the scoop on how dangerous it is, but I have no choice. My Loups are in danger. So are the Chenilles and Nosferatu. What would you have me do, stay home and play canasta with you?"

Socrates yawned. "You don't even know how to play canasta. I'm just warning you. It's my job." He shook his head rapidly, as if to clear his mind of sleep. "Humans can be so ridiculous at times. Take me for example. I know when to nap, when to eat, I know when to keep my nose out of certain situations so I don't get into trouble. Humans on the other hand eat fat-laden garbage from drive-through windows, carouse most of the night and manage three or four hours of sleep, thinking they'll be productive the following day. And they allow their asses to make decisions for them instead of their heads."

Viv came out of the closet with a satchel and headed for the nightstand on the right side of the bed. "You know I don't eat drive-through food."

"I'm talking about humans in general," Socrates said. "The thinking with your ass part, though, you have down pat."

Ignoring him, Viv opened the top drawer of the nightstand and pulled out a spool of red yarn. She threw it into the satchel.

"What?" Socrates said. "You plan to knit him a sweater?"

"No, Kitty Warhol. It's for emergencies. Holding spell."

"Ah, yes."

"Where are Hoot and Elvis?" Viv asked, suddenly thinking about Evee's and Gilly's familiars. "I haven't seen them around lately."

Socrates yawned again. "That ridiculous bird and rat have been in hiding since this Bender-Cartesian incident started. They have no backbone whatsoever. It's quite embarrassing if you ask me."

Viv waved a dismissive hand at her familiar. "I'm

sure if Gilly or Evee needed Hoot or Elvis, they'd be there for them."

"Maybe," Socrates said and stretched.

"You on the other hand may not be in hiding, but you sure seem pretty chilled considering all that's going on."

"My job has always been to look after you, warn you of impending danger and offer advice, all of which you routinely brush off."

Viv headed for her bedroom door, then stopped and turned to him. "I take your advice into consideration...sometimes."

"My point exactly," Socrates said.

"I said sometimes because most of the time what comes out of your mouth is nonsensical ranting. You have an attitude, cat."

"A familiar mirrors his mistress," Socrates retorted.

Viv blew out a breath. "Whatever. I don't have time to argue with you. I want you to stay here. There's a lot going on, and I don't want you to get hurt. I know you've overheard about the Cartesians and that we're missing some of the Originals. I don't need to be worried about you, so stay put."

"Oh, I plan to," Socrates said. "But if I may...and even if I may not...I will leave you with this one piece of advice, Ms. François."

Viv rolled her eyes. "What?"

"The gentleman who awaits you downstairs..."

"Yes?"

"Be careful, Vivienne." Socrates looked at her solemnly. "Beware of him."

She frowned. "What are you talking about? Is he dangerous?"

"In more ways than you know. He won't harm you physically. In fact, he'll do quite the job of protecting you. It's your heart that concerns me."

"Well, don't let it."

"Vivienne," Socrates warned. "He may be your undoing."

"Yeah, yeah, I know. I remember. I can't marry or live intimately with a human. I don't need to be reminded of that *again*."

Viv left the bedroom, closed the door and hurried down the stairs. She slowed considerably midway down the staircase, when Nikoli swung around the newel post at the bottom step and faced her.

He was breathtakingly handsome. She wanted to jump from the middle of the staircase right into his muscular arms. And she knew without question he'd catch her effortlessly. So strong. So tempting. She'd give up half her Grimoire to taste his full lips.

"Are you all right?" Nikoli called up to her.

His voice startled Viv back into action. She clambered down the stairs. "Sorry. Just thinking about the supplies we need. Wanted to make sure I didn't forget anything upstairs. Now we have to go to the back of the house, to the workshop. That's where Gilly keeps her bloodstones."

Nikoli gave her a small smile, bent at the waist and swept his right hand out like a gallant knight. "After you, milady."

Viv squashed back a groan of desire, then held her breath as she scooted past him. If she had to inhale his scent one more time, all bets were off. She'd strip him naked here and now and have her way with him.

Keeping her eyes focused straight ahead, Viv meandered through the dining room, then into the kitchen and to the back door. She opened it, went down two steps and signaled for him to follow her outside.

The workshop was a thirty-by-forty-foot structure, painted beige with forest-green shutters. Evergreen foliage grew in planters that bordered the two front windows. It looked more like a cottage than a workshop.

They never locked the building, so Viv let herself in and flipped on the light.

She turned to motion to Nikoli and nearly ran into him as he was right at her back. Viv swallowed hard and pointed to the satchel hanging from her right shoulder.

"I'll get the bloodstones," she said hoarsely. "How many do you think we'll need?"

"Four for each holding area. So twelve should do it."

"All right," Viv said. "I'll bring sixteen just in case. You never know. One might break or we may wind up needing extras. Always better to have more than not enough, right?"

Nikoli gave her a sultry look. "I agree. It's always better to have more."

Viv cleared her throat and pushed her way past worktables covered with artist's palettes, paintbrushes, strips of canvas and jars of crystals and dragon's eye that they occasionally used for spells. Gilly was the expert when it came to understanding the properties of every gem and crystal known to man. To Viv, they all looked like pretty rocks.

Beyond the tables, near the back left corner of the cottage, Viv found a large woven basket sitting on the floor. It was filled with the bloodstones. Gilly had either hit a sale or had been hunting them on her own and hit the mother lode.

"Would you mind holding the satchel open while I go through these?" Viv asked Nikoli, who stood at her side.

"Of course." He took the satchel from her shoulder and opened it wide.

Viv squatted near the basket, and Nikoli followed suit. Trying her best not to bump into him, she started rummaging through the bloodstones, choosing the largest in the lot. She might not have been touching Nikoli, but there was no getting past his scent, a mixture of leather, musk and fresh, rain-kissed air. She felt her breath quicken.

What that man did to her should be against the law. No other male had ever affected her this way. A jumble of emotions flip-flopped within her heart and mind. And that wasn't even taking into consideration the physical reaction he caused in her. Her body seemed to disconnect from her brain and simply react to him. She was thankful for the sweater she'd chosen to wear, for she felt her nipples harden.

Viv narrowed her eyes and forced herself to concentrate on the bloodstones, rummaging through the entire basket.

"Are you certain we won't need a ladder?" Nikoli asked.

"Positive." Viv struggled to keep her eyes away from his mouth. So far she'd collected eight fist-size bloodstones. "The ones I put in the satchel are the biggest bloodstones we have. The rest are smaller."

"As long as they're larger than the one on my actual scabior, it should work. It just needs to protrude above the top of the post. By the way, those posts are solid, right?"

"Of course," Viv said. "Any Loup could swipe down a hollow post in a nanosecond."

"I figured as much," Nikoli said. He peered into the satchel, then stuck a hand inside and scrounged about. He glanced up at her. "What's with the yarn?"

"Backup," she said. "For emergencies."

Nikoli grinned. "You know I want to ask what emergency would call for red yarn, but you're a Triad, so I'll leave it at that. Red yarn it is."

Viv couldn't help but smile back at him. He knew when to press and knew when to pull back, the markings of an intelligent man.

She went back to rummaging for bloodstones, chose eight more of the largest remaining stones in the basket and placed them gently into the satchel.

With that done, Viv sat back on her haunches. "I think that's all we'll need. Oh...wait." She swiveled to her right, dropped to her knees and crawled to a small, white cupboard a foot or so away. She opened it and pulled out a pouch that had FIRST AID written across it in red.

She looked back and tossed the pouch over her shoulder to Nikoli. He caught it in midair, then dropped it into the satchel.

"I thought you did your own healing," he said.

"Oh, we do. But having a Band-Aid around never hurts." Viv crawled back over to him, all the while wondering why she just didn't get to her feet and walk out of the workshop.

When she reached him, she sat cross-legged on the floor. She dug through the satchel: bloodstones, flashlight, first aid kit, yarn. "I think we're good," Viv said, chancing a look at his face. Big mistake.

While she'd been taking inventory of the items in the satchel, Nikoli had evidently lowered himself beside her to check out the contents, as well. When she turned to him, they were but a breath apart.

Both of them froze, eyes locked, and in that moment the rest of Viv's world disappeared. All that existed was the scent of him, the brawn of him. His gorgeous face, his silky hair, his Van Dyke that she longed to touch. The only thing either of them had to do was move a fraction of an inch and their lips would meet.

Her body raged with desire. Her mouth went dry, her breathing labored.

Before Viv knew it, not knowing who made the first infinitesimal move, she found her lips on Nikoli's. From the moment they touched, their kiss grew fervent, hungry, familiar. His mouth, his essence, felt like something Viv had never experienced before but had craved, starved for it for an entire lifetime.

She had no thought of the Cartesians or her Loup Garous. Of any mission or plan. All she had on her mind was the feel and taste of Nikoli Hyland. And the feeling that she'd die without more.

Nikoli leaned forward, gently pushing her onto her back. Viv's legs uncrossed naturally.

He sat beside her right hip, never moving his mouth from hers. His hands cupped the sides of her face, stroked her hair. His fingertips ran down the sides of her neck. His tongue probed the inside of her mouth, and she sucked on it greedily, wanting him to explore every inch of her. Wanted his tongue to run down the length of her body and back up again.

Viv had no conscious thought of time or place. They could have been in the middle of a public arena for all she cared. She wrapped a hand around his neck, pulling him down harder against her, and moved her other hand to his chest, feeling the tautness of him, searching for buttons. She found two and quickly unfastened them, her knee brushing against the hardness trapped behind his black jeans.

Finding a third button, Viv fumbled with it, then felt one of his large, strong hands grasp her wrist and gently pull it away. He held her hand against his chest, over his heart, and she felt the maddening beat of it. It matched her own.

Without breaking their kiss, Nikoli moved her hand from his chest to over her head, where he held it against the floor. The fingertips of his free hand roamed down the side of her cheek, traveled down her neck, then lower. Over her sweater, across her left breast. Lower still, until she felt his fingers find their way beneath her sweater.

The softness of his touch drove her mad. She wanted to rip off her clothes and press her naked body against him. She needed to be filled, to be fed.

Nikoli's fingers hesitated over the top of her half-cup bra that barely contained her rock hard nipples. That's when she finally broke their kiss and panted. "Yes—yes."

Viv closed her eyes and arched her back, encouraging him to take more. His fingers found her right nipple, and he rolled it gently between his thumb and forefinger. She groaned loudly, felt her body quiver. She had never been touched so completely. The sensation went beyond flesh on flesh. It reached down to

her core. Viv heard herself begging, pleading, "More…
more."

Nikoli didn't hesitate to oblige. He lowered his
mouth to her nipple, ran his tongue over it, let his
teeth softly scrape over it, and Viv felt her hips rise
and fall. Rise…fall, as if she rode the hardness that
gave claim to his own arousal.

As his lips and tongue worked their magic over
her right breast and nipple, his hand moved to her
left breast, where he found it swollen with passion,
that nipple just as hard as the other. He gently rolled
it between his finger and thumb, then tugged on it—
released it, then ran his thumb over it.

Viv became blind with need. She groaned with desire.

When Nikoli's mouth and tongue moved slowly
across her sternum to her left breast, Viv thought she'd
lose her mind. She desperately needed him inside her.

"More," Viv cried out. "Oh, Nikoli…"

The sound of his name seemed to trigger something
in him, for his fingers traveled quickly down her stomach to the top of her jeans. He unfastened them, and
she felt his fingers work their way inside.

"Yesss," she panted and lifted her hips.

His hand moved lower, his fingers inching their
way beneath her panties. Then finally…finally—his
hand cupped her heat.

Viv groaned loudly and arched her back again. He
lowered his mouth to hers once more, and his tongue
pushed its way into it. It darted in and out of her
mouth. Soon his middle finger dipped into the swollen wetness of her and took on the same rhythm as
his tongue. In…out, his finger reaching to the farthest

depths of her being. Viv felt a wave of pleasure build up inside her. Higher, stronger, and she held her breath, waiting for it to crest and wash over her.

She didn't have to wait long.

With his fingers stroking, probing, pressing deep within her, Nikoli's palm brushed against her swollen nodule of lust, and Viv cried out. His palm brushed against it again, his fingers plunging deeper, and in that moment the tsunami that had been building inside her reached its peak and crashed over her again and again. Her mouth flew open, but she remained wordless—mindless, as the powerful orgasm consumed her.

She finally let out a guttural moan of pleasure so loud it deafened her own ears. Nikoli held still as her body contracted around his finger. The waves of pleasure seemingly endless. Viv shuddered until the waves calmed.

She never felt him remove his hand or refasten her jeans. The next thing that drew her consciousness to here and now was the touch of his hand on her cheek. He kissed her lips, her nose, her eyelids.

When she opened her eyes, he was looking down at her, smiling softly. His eyes never left hers as he straightened her bra and lowered her sweater.

Warm butter seemed to flow through Viv's body, and she didn't want the sensation to ever end. She wanted to stretch like a cat and curl up next to him and sleep. She didn't want to let this moment go. She didn't want the peace she felt within her body and mind to leave.

His hand moved over her lips, and Viv smelled her own passion on his fingers, which sent a flare of heat through her body once more. Nikoli must have sensed it because he drew his hand away and placed it at his side.

He kissed her gently. "You're so beautiful, Vivienne. So much woman." He let out a deep sigh. "We must go now," he whispered and released her hand that he'd locked over her head.

She tugged at him. "But...you..."

"Shhh," he murmured and kissed her again. "There'll be time for that later. Right now we have things to tend to. Come."

Viv wanted to say, "I just did," but kept the comment to herself. She felt as though she'd been left to wander in déjà vu-land. Her premonition the night she'd first met him had been spot on, almost to the exact moves.

She felt light-headed when Nikoli helped her to her feet. He took the satchel and hefted it over his right shoulder.

On wobbly legs, Viv followed him out of the workshop. He closed the door behind them, then took her hand and led her to his Camaro.

"Are you okay?" he asked, opening the car door for her.

"Yes," Viv said softly. The world still looked glossy through her eyes.

He smiled at her, and they loaded into the car and headed for the ferry.

Despite where they were headed and all that faced them, Viv had never felt more alive in her entire life.

Chapter 17

As they drove to the dock where the ferry was moored, Viv found herself wishing the car had a bench seat so she could sit closer to Nikoli. They rode in silence, but she kept her eyes on him as he watched the road. Every so often, he'd cast a look in her direction. At times his expression held the appearance of ultimate satisfaction. Other times, he appeared disconcerted. A confusing combination.

Viv didn't want to think about what had happened in the workshop. She just wanted to feel it. The residual power of it still echoed in her body. If she overthought it, like she did most things, she'd miss out on the simple sensation of pleasure.

It didn't take long, however, for her mind to take the reins and say, *Bitch, what did you just do?* She grimaced at the voice yelling in her head.

What *had* she just done? When Viv thought back on it and tried seeing it through Nikoli's eyes, she imagined him thinking her to be a wanton harlot in heat. Condemnation and embarrassment attempted to override the pleasure she'd tried so desperately to hold on to.

Viv folded her hands in her lap and rolled her shoulders forward. The last thing she'd ever want was for Nikoli to think of her in such a negative way. But there was no way for her to undo what had already been done.

She peered over at Nikoli and caught him watching her with a smile. They'd stopped at a red light at the corner of Toulouse and Dauphine.

"Uh…" Viv said, unsure of how to say what she needed to tell him. "Back there… I mean at the, uh… the workshop. I—I don't know what came over me." She lowered her head and wished for once her hair wasn't pulled back in a braid. Her cheeks felt like they were on fire. "I just wanted to, uh…to say I—I'm sorry. I don't know what—"

Before Viv could finish, she felt Nikoli's hand gently take hold of her chin and turn her face toward him. Holding her there, he steered the car over to the side of the road with his free hand, came to a stop, then shoved the gear into Park.

He turned to her. "Vivienne, don't ever apologize for being who you are. You're one of the most beautiful women I've ever known. Not only physically, but your heart, your mind. I was drawn to you the moment we met. You never need to apologize for your passion. It's refreshing, exhilarating. You're open, not only in what and how you think, but in your sexuality, and you allow your body the freedom to express itself honestly. I lo—appreciate that about you."

"But isn't a woman's body reacting to sex normal?" she asked.

Nikoli arched a brow. "Far from it. Some women, for whatever reason, have trouble letting go. They need to be coaxed to give their body permission to experience sexual pleasure. Others see their sexuality like an old shoe, ready to slip onto anyone's foot."

"Oh," she muttered. "Guess I need to get out more."

He chuckled. "Whatever you do, don't change. And never compare yourself to another woman or think you need to blend in with some fashion group, who, for the most part, can often times come across as fake and vain. Stay just the way you are. You're perfect."

Nikoli glanced over at the windshield for a moment, then turned back to her. "I'm not sorry about what happened, and I don't want you to be. Ever. Okay?"

Seeing the sincerity in his powerful gray eyes, Viv nodded.

"Promise?" He stroked her chin with his thumb, then released it and trailed his fingers down her cheek. "I don't want you to ever regret it."

Viv gave him a small, still-embarrassed smile.

"Good," he said, then turned back to the steering wheel, shifted gears on the car and pulled back onto the street.

They drove in silence for a while. Traffic appeared unusually light and pedestrian traffic even more so. Viv stared out of the passenger window, thinking but not really seeing anything that went by.

"Have you alerted Jaco and Aaron about our arrival?" Nikoli asked.

"No. I never tell them when I'm headed out there. I just show up. That way they don't have time to prep anything or clean up a screw-up before I arrive. Keeps them on their toes."

"Smart lady."

He turned right onto St. Ann Street, then drove down four or five more blocks to Decatur and took another right.

They were still on Decatur headed for the street that led to the wharf when Viv caught sight of something out of the corner of her eye. She squinted to get a better look out the passenger window and spotted a tall, pale figure with a bald head darting into an alleyway between two shotgun houses.

"Stop the car!" she said.

"What's wrong?"

"I think I saw one of Evee's Nosferatu over there." She tapped a finger against the window.

Nikoli quickly pulled the car over to the side of the road, the passenger side wheels climbing the sidewalk.

As soon as he came to a stop, Viv opened her door and jumped out of the car. She heard a rumble of thunder. "Be right back," she said without looking back at Nikoli and took off for the alley.

No lights shown through the windows of the houses on either side of the alley, indicating that either no one was home or the dilapidated buildings had been abandoned.

Having forgotten her flashlight in the truck, Viv squinted into the darkness and slowly made her way to the entrance of the alley. She pressed her back up against clapboard siding and inched her way forward.

Something rustled ahead, and Viv froze, straining

to hear more clearly. The rustle of leaves, like some-one walking through them in short, halting steps. The darkness proved unforgiving. Even squinting, all she saw was more darkness. She wanted to kick herself in the ass for having left the flashlight behind.

When the rustling sound stopped, she started to inch forward again, being careful not to rustle any-thing herself. As she moved, Viv considered a game plan.

She had none.

What the hell was she supposed to do with a Nos-feratu? She had no power over them, just as Evee had no power over her Loups.

Viv contemplated one option. She might not be able to control the Nosferatu, but she could certainly put a boundary spell around herself, keeping the creature away from her. Of course, that plan would only work if it didn't pounce out of the darkness and kill her first.

Suddenly, the rustle of leaves started up again, only louder. Whatever made the noise had managed to get much closer to her, and it now sounded like it was run-ning in her direction. She stood stock-still, holding her breath—holding her ground, still unable to see. What good was there in being a witch if she didn't have in-frared vision or couldn't produce it?

Viv felt a presence drawing closer, faster. She pressed her back firmly against the wall and just when she felt the presence almost on top of her, a beam of light flooded the alley. It blinded her for a moment.

She whipped her head from right to left and saw Nikoli standing with a flashlight in the alley. He aimed the light toward the opposite end of the alley, and she saw, not five feet away from her, a Nosferatu, hunched over with its arm thrown over its eyes.

Man-made light did no harm to the Nosferatu, not like natural sunlight, but she was sure that looking directly into a flashlight beam burned the hell out of its eyes.

The creature's head was bald with one large, bulging vein running from the bridge of its nose to where a hairline should have been. The vein branched off like a tree, spreading across the top of its head. It had large, black eyes, skin like an albino and cauliflower ears. Its fangs weren't its incisors, but its two front teeth. Sharp, needle-like and deadly. Its fingers were twice the length of a normal man's, and its nails, yellow and gnarled, were at least four inches long.

Nikoli lowered the beam of light to the creature's feet, which were bare. Its toes abnormally long and contorted.

The Nosferatu hissed at Viv, threw its arm to its side, then crouched.

She knew it was ready to pounce.

"Get out!" Viv shouted to Nikoli. "Go back to the car!"

The creature hissed again and inched forward awkwardly, seeming uncertain about its next move.

Nikoli didn't budge, and Viv yelled at him again. "Go!"

Remaining where he stood, Nikoli turned the flashlight so the beam once again hit the Nosferatu directly in the eyes, causing it to shrink back and hide its face. "I'm not leaving you here. If I go to the car, you're coming with me."

"This is one of Evee's Nosferatu. I can't leave!"

Viv turned to the creature and shouted out a binding spell.

"Heed my voice, ye creature of night.
I bind thee now from taking flight.
Inside or out, it makes no matter.
Boshnah, morva, benlu, sonah!"

Nikoli moved the light beam to one side, evidently checking on the spell's effect. The creature lurched forward, causing Viv to reflexively drop into a crouch. The beam of light returned once again, searing the Nosferatu's eyes. She might as well have been singing "Mary Had a Little Lamb" for all the good the binding spell did.

The next thing Viv saw was Nikoli running toward her at full speed. He sprang right for the Nosferatu, hitting the creature mid-chest, dropping it to the ground on its back. The flashlight flew back in Viv's direction.

Viv scrambled to her feet, grabbed the flashlight and cried out, "No, Nikoli! It's too strong!"

As she predicted, the Nosferatu freed itself like a snake, slithering out from beneath its captor's grip, and got to its feet before Nikoli had a chance to turn around. The creature grabbed him by the throat and held him up with one hand until Nikoli's feet dangled in the air.

Viv saw Nikoli immediately cross his arms over his chest, draw in a deep breath, then do a half twist in midair, which released him from the Nosferatu's hold. Landing on his feet, Nikoli threw an uppercut, catching the creature under the jaw. Its head snapped back, but the punch did little more than piss it off.

The creature hissed loudly and lunged for him.

Nikoli dropped onto his haunches, then met the Nosferatu lunge for lunge, throwing all of his weight into a punch that landed against the creature's left temple. This time it knocked the Nosferatu back a couple of feet.

Viv knew no spell would stop it and nothing she could say would stop Nikoli from trying to protect her from it. That left her with only one option.

While creature and man struggled for the upper hand, Viv raced to the car, grabbed the red yarn from the satchel, then ran back to the alley.

Holding the spool in one hand, she found the loose end of the yarn, pulled it free and continued to unspool it, estimating the length she'd need.

When she reached eight feet, she mumbled a short cutting incantation, and the eight feet of yarn immediately broke free from the spool. She glanced down the alley, the flashlight still on the ground, casting light and shadows over the fighting creature and Nikoli.

She hurriedly attached one end of the eight-foot piece of yarn to a crevice in the clapboard siding on her right, then pulled the remainder of it across the alley to the house on her left.

With the red yarn stretched across the north end of the alley, she shouted a holding spell.

"Yarn of red, spirits blue,
Hold what's captured firm like glue.
Yarn of red, binding real,
By my command, ye shall be steel.
Steel of gray forged near a river,
Ye shall now become a coil of silver."

Viv grabbed the spool of red yarn and ran at break-neck speed around the house on her left until she reached the south end of the alley. There, she repeated the process with the yarn and issued another holding command.

Now that both ends had been secured, Viv ducked under the clothesline of yarn and yelled at Nikoli, who had just drop kicked the Nosferatu onto its side. "Holding spell!" She pointed to the red yarn. "This way. Hurry!"

He looked puzzled but darted off in her direction. He was only ten feet away from her when the creature flew through the air and pounced on Nikoli's back, dropping him to the ground and knocking the breath out of him.

Without a second thought, Viv ran toward him.

Straddling Nikoli's back, the Nosferatu lifted its head, eyes blind but for the kill, and bared its fangs. It barely had time to lower its chin, much less drop its head to Nikoli's throat before Viv landed a side kick to the creature's face, pitching it off Nikoli's back. Having no time to ask permission, Viv scrambled for the sheath attached to Nikoli's belt and yanked out the scabior.

The creature sprang toward her, fangs bared, and she rammed the handle of the scabior into the Nosferatu's left eye. It fell to the ground, shrieking in pain. Viv pulled out the scabior, which made a sickening *schtuuck* sound and she hurried over to Nikoli, who'd gotten to his feet.

Before the creature regained its footing, Viv grabbed Nikoli's shirt and ran for the end of the alley. She yelled, "Duck!" just before they reached the yarn. She ducked, scabior still in hand, and Nikoli's shirt yanked free of her grasp as he did a duck and roll.

The creature, now flailing mere inches behind them, shrieked like a banshee the moment its body touched the yarn. It screeched in fury, backed away, then ran full speed ahead, back in their direction, one eye glaring at them like a rabid dog, the other leaking thick pus-colored fluid.

Nikoli pulled Viv off to one side, and they both watched as the Nosferatu hit the red yarn at chest level. Smoke rose from the black sarong that covered it, and the rest of its body appeared to flatten as if it had hit a thick pane of glass. The creature screeched in pain and fell onto its back, then rolled from side to side.

Viv signaled for Nikoli to follow her and she hurried off to the car. He matched her step for step.

"Red yarn?" he said after they'd both jumped into the car.

"Holding spell. It won't stop a Nosferatu from attacking, but it'll hold it in place until Evee can send one of her leaders over to collect it."

The car engine roared to life and they were soon speeding down the street, tires screeching.

"Do you have a cell phone?" Nikoli asked, not taking his eyes off the road.

Viv looked at him quizzically. His hair was tousled, his cheeks streaked with dirt and scratches. "No. Do you?"

He shook his head. "We never carry one."

"Why? Electromagnetic field interference?"

"Yep. Screws with the scabiors."

"Same here. Only it messes with our incantations. Throws them off."

"So how are we going to let Evee know about her Nosferatu?" he asked.

Viv tapped her right temple. "I already have." Earlier, when they'd run for the car, Viv had wordlessly issued a yearning spell for Evee, along with coordinates to her Nosferatu.

She leaned her head back against the seat for a moment to catch her breath, then remembered something.

Sitting upright, Viv held out her right hand. "I believe this belongs to you." She handed Nikoli the scabior.

He did a double take from windshield to scabior and reached for his sheath as if to verify it was missing. His expression was one of amazement and disbelief.

Obviously finding his sheath empty, Nikoli took the scabior from her and grimaced at the stickiness on the handle. "How...? When...?"

"Had to borrow it. Nosferatu needed eye surgery," she said. "Sorry about the eye goo on the handle. I didn't have time to clean it.

"I—I..." Nikoli's mouth dropped open, then snapped shut.

Viv smiled and dropped her head back onto the seat and closed her eyes. She was glad Nikoli hadn't been bitten. He would have either died or turned into a similar creature.

And no way would Viv ever have sex with a Nosferatu.

She turned her head and peeked through eyelashes at the gorgeous hunk of man sitting beside her. Besides, she'd already been bitten—by a Bender.

Chapter 18

He'd had fun watching all of the action over the past couple of days, but now he grew bored. It was time to clean house.

It's not that he'd been surprised by the Benders' arrival. He'd expected it. Those four pathetic losers always brought their toys when no one had invited them to play. No matter where he sent his Cartesians, the four fools or others like them—showed up, flipping and twirling their little batons. So they took out a Cartesian or two. No big deal. The size of the army he was building would dwarf any army from the Benders' world. Collectively, they'd certainly be able to handle those four little twerps.

So far, he'd gotten the biggest kick from the death of the Chenilles earlier. It had been as easy as shooting fish in a barrel. Right under their noses. Oh, and the crying Triad—extra icing on the cake.

Sure, now he had to wait until the Carties that the Benders had shot with their batons made their way back to him. When a Cartesian either pushed its way into or had been thrust into other dimensions, it took some time for them to return. Always waiting on a rift.

Always.

Fortunately, his Carties had only been pushed to the fifth dimension. Only one away from him. Their return might take a while, but not centuries. No. Those little baton-twirling majorettes had only shot them two dimensions away from their world. They'd find their way back to him. To their god.

He was a patient leader. They'd be back soon enough to watch the sinking of Atlantis—the Originals—the Triads. His glorious victory.

There were plenty of games to play to occupy his time until then. Not only was he patient, he was ingenious. Who else would have thought to shove some of the Originals out of their dens instead of killing them? Only he had the brains to come up with a plan like that. Which was as it should be. Great leaders thought in great ways.

Missing Nosferatu, Chenilles and Loup Garous kept the Triads running in all directions. Along with those dickless Benders. Distraction. Diversion. Dictator. That was the name of this game.

The one thing a Triad couldn't do was clone herself. How else were they going to hunt for the missing while protecting the cloistered—and themselves? And what could the stupid Benders do with all of that mess flying in every direction? Why, even now they were scurrying about wondering, "Where, oh, where do I stick my baton now?"

He'd show them where to stick it.

This was survival of the fittest, and he was king of that game.

Too often it appeared that humans had no fittest, only mentally and physical challenged nitwits who called themselves leaders. By the time he was ready for them, for the humans, the pickings would be as easy as berries on the vine. He'd crush those berries and serve them up as wine to his Carties.

How did that saying go? As a man thinketh, so shall he be. Or some kind of crap like that. And therein lay the human demise. They blurted out words that had no meaning in them. Blah, blah, yada, yada. See how big my dick is.

He, on the other hand, did and meant what he said. To himself, anyway.

By tonight, or tomorrow at the latest, he'd be well on his way to acquiring the victory he'd been planning, preparing for and dreaming of for centuries. Someone with a lesser mental capacity would probably consider his actions a form of revenge. And if he was honest with himself, and on occasion he was, he'd have to admit that was partially true.

He'd been an innocent bystander, minding his own business, going about his own life, living by his own creed when someone decided, without his permission, to divert his personal journey and make it their own.

Little did they know that their meddling would change the very course of history. For the Originals, whose innocent lives had also been diverted, for the Triads, who, in secret, he'd always coveted, for the world, something they had no business toying with in the first place.

He'd been fortunate over the years, that the meddling few had created multitudes of species that had kept his Cartesians fed and growing in number for centuries. The vampires, whose powers tasted like honey right off the comb. The leprechauns, albeit with lesser strength, held the unique aftertaste of gumdrops stolen from a candy vendor. The werewolves, an acquired taste, like snails and caviar. The djinn, like a strong, heady wine.

Each unique, diverse. His for the choosing. It simply depended on what his palate craved on any particular day. No, those responsible for their existence had no idea just how tasty they were.

Had they not realized, all those centuries ago, that no secret stayed hidden forever? They'd sat, so haughty, filled with false righteousness and self-designated authority, pointing fingers at whom they considered the lowly, and changed the course of lives. All the while, thinking no one would ever know, ever find out. How wrong they had been. How gloriously wrong.

The truth would not only be revealed, it had become his weapon of choice.

He had to admit, however, that he carried a secret of his own. He'd coveted generations of Triads. Often daydreamed of how, once destroyed, their power would taste on his tongue. Sweet? Salty? Or strong and heady, like the finest fruit from a champion winery?

Soon.

He'd find out soon.

Now, though, he had the luxury to play for a while, which he planned to do. The Triads would know more misery, worry, heartache and temptation than they'd ever experienced in their miserable little lives. He'd show them, the wenches who played queen with the Originals like they owned the netherworld. He'd show them exactly who owned and controlled what. Once he'd had his fill of playing with them, he'd slowly savor their destruction.

If he had any regret, it was that he'd never see the Originals or the Triads bow at his feet. On a positive note, however, they would *become* his feet—his arms. His brain and heart. His weaponry for ultimate, universal control.

As for the meddling Benders, he would squash them like bugs. Or simply use them to clean his teeth after he'd snacked on Triads and gorged on Originals.

Chapter 19

Hoisting the satchel onto his right shoulder, Nikoli boarded the ferry and watched Viv at the helm. He held onto the railing, expecting her to rocket across the water as before. Suprisingly, she kept the ferry moving at a slow and easy pace across the muddy river. It gave him time to study her, not that he hadn't already. Every time he saw her, in fact. Nikoli couldn't help it. She fascinated him to the point of distraction.

The cool night air blew tendrils of hair from her head, and the tip of her braid slapped between her buttocks. How he longed to wrap a hand around that braid and pull her toward him—to kiss her, make love to her, make her his own.

Nikoli didn't know whether to be angry with himself for feeling this way and for what happened in the workshop earlier. Or to be excited to know Viv yearned for him as much as he did for her.

Logic snapped at him in his head. *How can you be angry over something that's so completely out of your control?*

Back at the shop, when Viv had turned to him, she'd been so close that he'd felt her breath on his face. In that moment, something more powerful than anything he'd ever experienced overtook him.

Nikoli was far from a teenage boy with raging hormones. As a Bender and in his midthirties, Nikoli rarely, if ever, lost control due to a woman. Granted, he was no saint, but he'd always kept romantic dealings, of which there'd been few, and Bender missions separate. He'd learned from Lucien's and Gavril's mistakes that mixing the two held the potential for disaster. About five years ago, both had been suspended by an Elder Bender for four months for chasing after skirts instead of taking care of business.

Thinking about his cousins, Nikoli wondered how things were going on their end. They didn't have telepathic abilities, nor could they conjure spells in order to communicate. They ran strictly by instinct. He didn't feel that Lucien, Gavril or Ronan were in danger, not from Cartesians or from any Original anyway.

What concerned him was their undeniable attraction to the Triads they had been paired with. Each time he'd seen Gavril stare at Gilly, the man's eyes took on that hound-dog yearning look. Then he had Lucien and Ronan. He sensed both were vying for Evee's attention and was curious as to which one would pull ahead in the race.

Seeing Ronan interested in Evee had Nikoli intrigued. He'd never seen that particular cousin, a very private man, show any outward attraction to any woman. Nikoli knew he dated when they weren't working, but Ronan always kept any and all information about the woman very hush-hush.

Lucien, on the other hand, they often called Butter Man, for rarely did he cross a woman who didn't instantly turn to butter when given his attention.

Not that Evee or Gilly were easy catches by any means. But the truth was none of them should have been trying to win or vie for any of the Triads' attention. They had a serious situation at hand. But who was he to judge? Nikoli had not only crossed the line he always harped on, he'd high-jumped it like a hurdle.

Viv glanced back at Nikoli and smiled at him. Her straight, white teeth, her full, to-die-for lips made his heart and body ache with need.

He returned her smile, knowing full well that, for all intents and purposes, he'd breeched that creed earlier. He'd managed to keep his pants zipped, but that was semantics. His cousins weren't stupid either. If Nikoli had noticed them ogling Gilly and Evee, they must certainly have seen his tongue hanging down to his kneecaps for Viv.

"I know we have a lot to do at the compound," Viv suddenly said to him from over her shoulder. "But I wanted to make this ferry trip slower so you'd have a chance to see the Mississippi. I don't sense any trouble from the compound, so we have a little time."

Nikoli nodded and smiled.

Grinning, Viv motioned with her chin. "Why are you standing so far away?" she asked. "Why don't you come up here, feel the breeze on your face and smell the water? It may be brown and muddy, but the scent is bayou—South Louisiana. The only place you'll catch the scent."

Nikoli watched her, not knowing what to say. If he stayed where he was she might take it as an offense, thinking he didn't want to be near her. Which was the farthest thing from the truth. He wanted, needed to be close. Wanted his arms wrapped around her.

He'd been doing his best to keep some distance between them so he'd have his mind on the mission. But distance hadn't helped that one bit. The mission was crucial, but he didn't want to hurt Viv's feelings. One was just as important to him as the other.

"Come on up," she said again.

This time Nikoli gave in and went to meet her at the bow of the ferry. He hooked his hands onto the railing, tilted his head back and closed his eyes, took a deep breath.

Viv had been right. The water here did have a unique scent. It didn't smell like the Atlantic or Pacific, both of which he'd traveled many times. Although he'd boated across the Gulf of Mexico a time or two, the trips had been far from the coast of Louisiana. Even there the water had looked and smelled different. It was almost as if this water was the core of New Orleans. It had built her, fed her, and had been essential in creating the beauty that was the city.

He glanced over at Viv. "It's beautiful."

She smiled. "Only place like it in the world. I know other bodies of water have white sand and blue-green waters, but those waters and sand seem to suit the cities or countries they surround." She shrugged. "I guess it's different for everyone, water I mean. This—" she waved a hand to indicate the waters below "—is part of home."

Viv's hands came to rest on the top railing, and, unable to stop himself, Nikoli reached over and put one of his hands on top of hers.

She looked down at their hands, then up at him.

"Waters often reflect the nature of the inhabitants who live near it," Nikoli said. "And this is no different." He gave her hand a gentle squeeze. "You are as unique as these waters, Viv. Very different than any woman I've ever met before."

Viv lowered her eyes shyly and said, "Oh, I'm sure you've met tons of women around the world. Beautiful women, sensual women, rich and smart women. Women who don't have baggage like the Triads carry."

Nikoli didn't think it was a good idea to admit to any woman that he had in fact known quite a few, even though Viv had stated it as common knowledge. He knew women well enough to know that responding to the statement in the affirmative carried its own set of problems. With Viv, however, in his heart of hearts, Nikoli wanted nothing but transparency.

"It's true, I've known quite a few women around the world." He took her hand that he'd been holding on to and placed it over his heart, tapped it against his chest. "But trust me when I tell you, despite the number of women or the country they came from or the time I knew them, I've never met anyone as beautiful and unique as you. You're bright, intelligent, strong-willed, yet conscientious and caring."

Viv pursed her lips, cocked her head, gave him a wary look, then laughed. "You've either practiced that line in front of a mirror ten thousand times or you're the best bullshitter on the planet."

"Honestly, I would never tell you anything that wasn't true, Vivienne."

She smiled, then sighed and looked ahead, lifting her head to catch the breeze of the night. "You're pretty special yourself," she said, not looking at him.

Nikoli didn't respond, hoping she'd share more of her feelings.

She did.

"When I first met you and your cousins, I thought this was all bullshit," Viv said. "I mean, we'd never heard of Benders before. But I have to admit, I was immediately attracted to you. All of your cousins are very handsome but there was just something about you that really stuck with me. As hard as I tried, I couldn't help but think of you in a romantic way. There's just something about you that causes an urgent tug inside me. That's never happened to me before, and I don't even know why I'm blabbering on about it. It's a little embarrassing." She looked up at him. "No…it's a lot embarrassing."

"Please don't be embarrassed," Nikoli said. "I've never told any other woman the things I've told you just now. I hope you'll always feel free to tell me what's on your mind."

"Well, now that you mention it…" Viv paused midsentence as they pulled up to the docks across the river. She moored the ferry, made certain it was locked down, then turned to Nikoli. "You know, I've seen the way Gavril looks at Gilly and the way Ronan and Lucien look at Evee. That worries me. You seem stronger, emotionally and mentally, than your cousins, more focused, more able to retain control. I haven't seen your cousins in action, though. If the three of them have gone gaga over my sisters, do you feel confident they can stay focused enough to protect them? To protect the Originals they're responsible for?"

"They wouldn't be with them if I didn't," Nikoli said. Having heard the concern in her voice, he squeezed her hand reassuringly.

She nodded, offered a small smile.

The soft look in her eyes, the fullness of her lips, the hint of dimples when she smiled. She'd drop any man to his knees. Her ability to think quickly on her feet, her confidence when taking charge. Nikoli could've stood staring at her, listing a million reasons why she was special.

It was then Nikoli realized, with some trepidation, that he was falling in love with Ms. Vivienne François.

Chapter 20

By the time they finally reached the North compound, Nikoli drew in a deep breath through his nose. He smelled the faint odor of cloves, residue from the previous Cartesian attack.

All appeared quiet. A little too quiet for his liking. And dark. Clouds had thickened overhead, blanketing the moon and stars. He reached for the flashlight he had stashed in his back pocket, then glanced over his shoulder to Viv, who walked a step or two behind him. She carried the second flashlight and had it aimed at the ground, sweeping the beam from left to right, surveying everything around her closely.

"No new tracks," she said when she caught him looking back at her.

He nodded, then, for no other reason but reassurance, touched the sheath attached to his belt to make certain his scabior was securely inside.

Though he'd never admitted it to Viv, he'd been unnerved when she'd handed it to him in the car. Having someone take the scabior from its sheath without him realizing it felt like an assault. Like someone who'd fallen asleep with two arms, then woke only to discover they now had one. And no clue as to the when, who and how of it all.

Nikoli remembered Viv's attack on the Nosferatu, how she'd jabbed it in the eye. He hadn't known then what weapon she'd used. Only assumed, given that she was a witch, that she had conjured up whatever tool she'd needed. Recalling the fight with the Nosferatu, Nikoli suddenly wanted to slap his own forehead.

He aimed his flashlight at Viv's feet. "I'm sorry," he said. "I forgot to thank you."

"For what?"

"Back there, with the Nosferatu. You saved my life."

She batted a hand in his direction. "I didn't do much really. You handled yourself pretty well."

"Yeah, until he knocked me on my ass. I saw it coming. Its fangs were ready for the kill before I could even catch my breath."

"I'm confident you would've kicked right back, breath or no breath," she said.

"Do you always take compliments and appreciation that well?" He grinned.

Viv smiled back at him. "Okay, all right… You're welcome."

"I owe you one," he said.

She gave him a mischievous look. "Oh, I think we'll run into plenty of opportunities to even the score."

Nikoli couldn't quite define the look that suddenly crossed her face. A little confusion—an undertone of danger—excitement. Simply put, Vivienne François mystified him. Aside from her beauty, her mysterious nature was probably the reason he was so attracted to her in the first place.

He glanced away for a second. He felt he should mention how deeply her taking his scabior without his knowledge had affected him. And he would. But not now. She'd just saved his life for heaven's sake.

"Come this way," Viv said, motioning to him with her flashlight. "Let's check out the tracks Jaco showed us earlier. See if there are any fresh ones near them."

She led him closer to the compound gate, then veered off to the left, about fifty yards. As they walked, Nikoli aimed the beam of his flashlight into the compound. He came to a halt when he spotted two Loup Garous dodging between trees in the dense forest.

He'd never seen a morphed Loup up close before. They amazed him. Their bodies were larger than that of an average werewolf. They had pointed ears, a longer snout and, from what he saw, thicker fur. They ran through brush like lightning, dodging trees, jumping thickets, heading for the back acreage of the compound. Evidently the beam from his flashlight had frightened them, and they sought a safe place to hide. They were so agile and quick, if he would've blinked at the wrong time, he'd have missed them.

"Over here," Viv called, signaling with her light.

When he turned his flashlight toward her, Nikoli

saw her kneel on the ground, her flashlight now poised over a spot in the dirt right in front of her. It was the tracks Jaco had shown her.

You could've seen the tracks from a helicopter. They were that huge, but no surprise to him. Nikoli had seen similar many times before.

"That must've had you scratching your head when you first saw them," he said.

"It scared the shit out of me. I couldn't imagine an animal big enough to create a print this big. I thought it might have been a bear, but Jaco said even the biggest grizzly couldn't have made prints this size. I understand now what he meant."

"Do you see any others?" Nikoli asked. "Anything new nearby? If there are, I might be able to detect their travel pattern from point of entry."

"Nothing near the first ones," Viv said, then aimed her flashlight farther ahead. "We should have a look around the brush up ahead."

Before Nikoli knew it, Viv was on her hands and knees crawling on dirt and grass and swiping her way through a heavy cover of bramble and thickets.

He followed her.

The farther they crawled, the thicker the bramble became and the thicker the grass beneath their hands and feet. Tree branches and foliage lay thick overhead like a canopy. It felt like Mother Nature had cocooned them in her arms. A safe, quiet hideaway.

"Find anything?" he called out to Viv. He had to keep his head turned slightly to the left because right in front of him was her perfectly proportioned, heart-shaped ass, which made crawling all the more uncomfortable for him.

"Not yet."

They crawled a bit farther before he asked, "Have you contacted Jaco and Aaron to let them know we're here? We should get started on those posts."

Viv stopped and peered over her left shoulder at him. "No, I haven't. But I will, soon enough." She turned back and resumed crawling.

When they were about a hundred feet inside the cocoon, Viv stopped again, then turned and sat on the ground. She brushed grass and dust from her jeans. Nikoli pulled up next to her and sat, as well.

"I haven't found any tracks up this way so far," she said. "The brush only gets thicker from here. Before we get tangled up in it, it'd probably be best to head back."

He agreed, but neither of them moved. He made certain to keep the beam from his flashlight away from her face and out of her eyes. Those beautiful, cobalt blue eyes with long, thick lashes. They mesmerized him. So full of expression, so fierce. So intense.

Her face was mere inches from his, and Nikoli heard her breathing become short and shallow. He felt her breath, hot against his face. Her entire body seemed to radiate the same kind of heat. She held an invitation in her eyes, a question, an undeniable hunger.

Nikoli didn't have to be asked twice. He reached for her, behind her, wrapping his hand in the braid of her hair and pulled her close. It was his fantasy unfolding into reality.

The moment their lips touched, his desire for her became an all-consuming inferno. Her lips, her mouth tasted of honeysuckle.

Viv reached for him, weaving her fingers through his hair and pulling him closer. She lowered one of her hands and dug fingernails into his back.

Nikoli marveled at her. An all-or-nothing woman. She gave all to her Loups, all in her kisses, in her passion. Gave her all to anything she wanted or demanded. And she slipped effortlessly from one compulsion to the next as if no distance varied the desire.

Remembering that he'd seen her Loups only moments ago, Nikoli reluctantly removed his lips from hers. "We can't. Not here, not now. Not this way."

Viv groaned and the sound quickly took on the tone of a low growl. She crossed her arms in front of her, grabbed the bottom of her sweater and quickly pulled it up and over her head. Then she reached behind her back and unhooked her bra, letting it drop from her breasts and arms and fall into her lap.

Her breasts were perfect. Full, firm. Her nipples dark and hard.

"Yes," she said, her voice low and husky. "Here. Now. And this way."

Before Nikoli had the chance to respond, she swung her legs about and sat astride his lap. She pressed her body against him, grabbed a handful of his hair and lowered his head down to her breasts.

Where they were and why they were there became lost to Nikoli. He inhaled the delicacy of her skin, her undeniably erotic scent—lilac with an earthy undertone. A scent that would drive any man crazy, making him beg for more.

He cupped her breasts, rolled her nipples between his forefingers and thumbs, tugged on them gently until she threw her head back and moaned with desire.

Nikoli turned his head to her left breast and flicked his tongue over the nipple, nipping at it gently with his teeth. He took his time before turning his attention to her other breast. The heat from her, from between her legs, penetrated his body. A scorching fire that refused to be denied.

Nikoli struggled with not taking her right then and there. Her hands were still tangled in his hair, and she pulled hard, forcing him to look up at her.

"I need you," she murmured. "I need you inside of me." She held on to his hair with one hand and reached down between his legs with the other, searching for the fly on his jeans.

Nikoli gritted his teeth, reached down, grabbed her wrist and held tight. He looked deeply into her eyes. "Not—this—way," he said, his voice low and gravelly.

The smallest of whimpers escaped Viv. "Yes—this—way."

Unable to resist her, Nikoli leaned forward, pushing Viv gently onto her back. She unfurled her legs so her body lay flat on the brush beneath them. Her eyes were bright with hunger and need.

Nikoli swung both of his legs to one side of her and knelt near her waist. He leaned over, put his lips to her right ear, kissed behind it, beneath it and let his tongue slide down her neck. He bit into her flesh ever so gently.

The groan that escaped her sounded animalistic, feral. It injected his own desire with adrenaline that made Nikoli want to rip off the rest of her clothes and shove the hardness throbbing behind his jeans deep within her without any preamble. But this wasn't about him and his needs. Everything was about Vivienne.

He longed to satiate the hunger within her more than he desired the air he breathed.

Lowering his mouth to her breasts again, Nikoli forced himself to slow his pace, take his time as he licked and caressed her breasts. Her moans echoed throughout their cocoon.

He slid his tongue down her sternum to her belly while his fingers worked the button loose on her jeans and lowered the zipper.

As he licked down the length of her belly and back up again, he worked her jeans and panties off one hip, then the other and tugged them off her buttocks. Viv had already kicked off her sneakers and she began working the jeans down lower with her feet until she'd freed herself from pants and panties.

Nikoli didn't have to touch her to know she was wet, swollen and ready. He smelled the sweet musk of her and moaned as he lowered his head to the core of her heat. He pressed the tip of his tongue between the slit that held the fire that raged within her. The heat emanating from her amazed him, devoured him.

As he pushed his tongue in deeper, tasting her sweetness, Viv arched her back and lifted her hips. He knew what she wanted, but he knew what she needed.

He let his nose graze over her clit, and she bucked up against him.

"Yes!" she cried.

Keeping his tongue at her center, he pushed it inside of her slowly. In and out. Lapping up all she had to offer. He purposely stayed away from the swollen nodule that would cause her to explode beneath him.

Not yet.

Viv arched her back again and lifted her hips, a

sure sign that she wanted, needed more. He worked his tongue inside her. In and out. In and out. In. Out.

When Nikoli felt she could bear no more, he quickly replaced his tongue with his right middle finger and covered her swollen pearl of pleasure with his mouth, his tongue flicking over it again and again. His other hand cupped her buttocks, lifting her hips higher and he drove his finger in deeper. Her heat became fluid, flowing out of her body and over his hands. She cried out loudly and shuddered with the violence of her orgasm. He lowered his mouth, dipping his tongue into the hot lava that flowed from her.

When her gasps became short pants, Nikoli sat back on his knees, lowered the zipper of his jeans and released the hardness that had been causing him physical pain for some time. He leaned over her, allowing the tip of it to press against the hot, wet opening of her. He kissed her and she greedily sucked on his lips, nipped them with her teeth, shoved her tongue into his mouth.

Nikoli entered her gently, a fraction of an inch, then pulled back until the tip rested against her heat once more.

Viv released her mouth from his, arched her back, thrust her hips upward, trying to drive the remaining length of him inside her. But he held back.

"More!" she cried, arching her back, her neck.

Slowly, purposely, he lowered himself into her. Each time she thrust her hips up to him, he'd pull back. Only when her buttocks rested in his hand did he push deeper inside her.

He heard his heart pounding in his ears, his body demanding more, feeling ready to implode if he didn't act quickly.

When he could take no more, Nikoli thrust the remaining length of his hardness into her. "Yes!" Viv screamed, then wrapped her legs around his waist, her hips meeting him thrust for thrust.

It took mere seconds before her body shuddered and she cried out with release. She bathed him over and over with sweet, hot lava, her body contracting around him, pulling on him as if she needed the whole of him inside her.

Only then did Nikoli allow his own release. He groaned with the intensity of it, was blinded by it, and he called out her name.

"Vivienne..."

When his own body stopped convulsing, he lay atop her, putting a hand to the ground on either side of her body to minimize his weight. He whispered in her ear. "Vivienne—my Vivienne."

Moments later, she lay in his arms, her head resting against his chest. Nikoli held her tightly, stroked her hair and before he realized what was happening, he found himself silently mouthing the words, *I love you.* Although he hadn't said it out loud, those were words he'd never even considered saying to another woman.

Slightly unnerved by his emotions, he kissed the top of her head. Ever so slowly, his mind and body began to take on the weight of the responsibilities that awaited him. He kissed the top of her head again and was about to tell her it was time to get dressed when he caught the sudden scent of cloves. His arms tightened around her and he sniffed the air to make certain.

Cloves.

He hadn't been mistaken. It held only a hint of sulfur, which meant the Cartesians were working their way into the third dimension through some rift nearby.

Viv pushed away from him abruptly and sat bolt upright. "Cloves," she said.

"You smell it, too?"

"Yes." Viv scrambled for her clothes. Not bothering with her bra, she yanked her sweater over her head and wiggled into her jeans. She grabbed her sneakers and shoved her feet into them.

Nikoli pulled up his zipper and righted the clothes on his own body. When she finished dressing, he got to his hands and knees and crawled quickly toward the opening of their cocoon. Viv followed closely behind.

The closer they got to the opening, the stronger the sulfur scent grew. The smell of cloves became overwhelming, mixing with the sulfur, both growing thicker, heavier by the second.

When Nikoli broke free of the opening, he turned back to Viv. "Stay in there!"

"Screw that," she said and popped out from the opening.

Nikoli didn't have time to argue with her. The smell of the Cartesians was so strong that he knew the rift had already been opened. Lightning streaked across the sky and a clap of thunder shook the ground.

He reached for his scabior and realized it wasn't in its sheath. Shocked, he glanced down to make certain. No scabior.

Puzzled, he looked over at Viv, who stood beside him on the right. No scabior in her hands.

"What the hell," he said. "Viv—"

"I smell it, I smell it!" she cried. "Where are they? What direction?"

Thinking the scabior might have fallen from its sheath when they'd crawled through the cocoon or during the heat of their lovemaking, he shouted at Viv over another clap of thunder. "Stay put! My scabior!"

He quickly ducked back into the cocoon, crawling as fast as he could. The flashlights were still burning brightly inside. Three quarters of the way into the cocoon he found his scabior. Grabbing it, Nikoli put it between his teeth, then hurried back to the opening as fast as his hands and knees would allow.

When he reached the opening, he found Viv standing nearby. He jumped to his feet and spotted a wide, black opening in the sky to his left. He took the scabior from his mouth and held it out in front of him. He heard howling, yipping and roars of fury coming from the Loup Garous inside the compound. Another streak of lightning and Nikoli looked up at the sky. A second rift had formed off to the right, and it yawned open right before his eyes.

"Get behind me," he shouted at Viv over the howling and thunder.

She did as she was told, and he aimed the scabior at the wider of the two rifts above them. He walked slowly to his left, holding the scabior up and out. It only made sense that the slit he was aiming for had been worked over longer by the Cartesians. He was sure this would be where they'd make their first appearance.

He zeroed in on the rift, allowed his breathing to grow shallow. Concentrated.

It was then he heard Viv's loud scream.

Nikoli whirled about just in time to see a Cartesian

hanging out of the smaller rift. It swung its gigantic claws toward them. Viv appeared frozen in place.

With a roar, Nikoli ran, then dove, tackling Viv and dropping her to the ground. But he'd been a second too late for her to go unscathed. The Cartesian's claws swiped across Viv's left arm, shredding her sweater and leaving long gashes in her flesh.

Shaking with fury, Nikoli quickly got to his feet, aimed the scabior, twisted his wrist twice, twirled the scabior between his fingers at the speed of light, then took aim again. A bolt of lightning shot from the bloodstone and hit the Cartesian in the head. It folded over with a high-pitched screech, and its body jerked back into the rift.

Nikoli stood his ground, concentrated, putting all his effort into sending the son of a bitch as far away as he could. If possible, he would've jumped into that hole and beat the bastard into a bloody pulp. He heard a pop, then a second. More high-pitched screeching.

A third pop, then a fourth—fifth. The screeching grew muffled.

Nikoli let his anger rage, wanting to push the electrical charge from the bloodstone farther. He heard a sixth pop, then a seventh. Only then did the second rift in the sky zip close. The first immediately followed suit.

Drawing in a shaky breath and half-dazed, Nikoli looked about for Viv. She wasn't where he had left her.

Panicked, he called out for her, "Vivienne!"

When she didn't respond, he took a step to start hunting the compound for her and tripped over something.

Flailing, Nikoli caught his balance and looked down to see what had been in his way.

It was Viv.

Lying lifelessly on the ground near his feet.

Chapter 21

Startled from a nightmare, Arabella Matthews sat up in bed and glanced at the clock that sat on a nightstand near her bed. It was a little after 11:00 p.m.

The nightmare had been so vivid it was as if she'd been living it right here and now. Arabella rubbed the heel of her hands over her eyes to scrub away sleep. The dream had involved the Triads, she remembered that. Something…something about one of the Triads hurt? No…dying. One of them had been seriously injured and died.

The Benders had been in her dream, as well. Four of them. And they'd been fighting so many Cartesians she couldn't count them all. Huge, terrible beasts with one mission. To kill and conquer.

Arabella remembered that in the nightmare, she'd stood in the midst of the chaos, along with Taka and

Vanessa. Spells. They'd tried so many spells. Binding. Protection. Submission. Nothing worked. Taka screamed. Vanessa cried. She had done both. The dream had felt too real to be a coincidence, which forced Arabella out of bed. She had to let the other two Elders know about it. Something had to be done, although she was clueless as to what.

She walked into Vanessa's room and shook her awake.

"Mmm, stop…" Vanessa said groggily. She opened one eye and peered up at Arabella. "What?" Evidently seeing something in the Elder's expression, Vanessa sat up quickly. "What's wrong? Has there been another attack?"

"I don't think it's happened yet. I had a dream. A nightmare. It felt too real to ignore. We need to gather and discuss it. It's important. You wake Taka. I'll go into the kitchen and get water boiling for tea."

As Vanessa scrambled out of bed, Arabella hurried off to the kitchen, filled the kettle with water and placed it on the stove. As she woke more fully, the dream didn't dissipate. The details remained vivid. Too vivid. It made her anxious and sweaty.

By the time Arabella had set china saucers and cups steeping with chamomile tea on the table, Vanessa came into the kitchen, wearing a white robe over her white, floor-length flannel nightgown. Her silver satin slippers whispered quietly across the hardwood floors.

Taka followed close behind, her white hair sticking up in wild, tangled tufts. She wore gray sweatpants, an orange, flannel hoodie and green socks with yellow smiley faces on her feet.

The two Elders sat at the kitchen table. Small and

circular, it seated four and was where they usually ate breakfast. Arabella needed small, comfortable and familiar. The kitchen table was their usual meeting spot when the three of them needed to discuss Circle of Sisters issues or occurrences in the city that might affect them. Sharing her dream in a larger room would have made her voice echo. Just the thought of that put Arabella's last nerve on edge.

"What's going on?" Taka asked, then yawned. She took a quick sip of tea. "Vanessa said you had a bad dream. Is that why we're meeting?"

"I already told you what happened and why we're here," Vanessa said with a huff. "Don't you ever pay attention?"

Taka rolled her eyes and sipped tea again. "I pay plenty of attention." She turned to Arabella. "You sure your dream wasn't from indigestion? You know, from the pot roast we ate earlier tonight?"

"I'm sure," Arabella said. Before she could get another word in edgewise, Vanessa rapped the table with her knuckles.

"Look here, missy," Vanessa said to Taka. "I cooked that pot roast, and it was quite delicious if I do say so myself."

"A little too much salt if you ask me," Taka said, and rubbed sleep from her right eye.

Arabella held up a hand to silence both of them. "Stop bickering. Yes, I did have a bad dream, Taka. A nightmare. Only I don't think it was just a dream. I feel it was a warning."

"What kind of warning?" Vanessa asked. "What did you see?"

"I saw the Triads in dire straits. One of them was killed."

Taka gasped loudly and her teacup clattered onto its saucer. Tea sloshed over the cup.

"Dead?" she asked. "Not just injured, but dead?"

"My word, how horrible!" Vanessa said and picked up her cup of tea. Her hands trembled so badly, she set the cup back on the saucer, then folded her hands on the table.

"I know," Arabella agreed. "I also saw Originals running through the city. All of them out of control because the Triads were fighting for their own lives. The three of us were in the nightmare, too."

"Including me?" Taka asked, wide-eyed.

Arabella nodded. "It was as if the entire city of New Orleans was in a panic and no matter what we tried, we couldn't affect any change. None of our spells worked, not one incantation. In the dream, it felt like we were…unplugged."

"The dream sort of makes sense when you think about what the Triads told us when they came here," Vanessa said.

"Yeah," Taka agreed. "Things weren't exactly okay. So what do we do? Do you have any ideas at all?" she asked, turning to Arabella.

Arabella sighed. "The only thing I can think of is putting all we've got into one big protection spell. Wrap it around the Triads."

"Hell, we need to wrap it around the city," Taka said.

"What about the Benders?" Vanessa asked. "Should the protection spell include them?"

Arabella pursed her lips thoughtfully. "I'm at a

complete loss when it comes to the Benders," she said. "I don't know if putting a protection spell around them will somehow negate their powers and effectiveness in fighting the Cartesians. And frankly, and sad to say, I don't think I want to take the chance."

"Good point," Taka said.

"They're here to fight the Cartesians," Arabella said. "So we need to trust that they are well equipped to do just that. If they're with the Triads, who will be protected by our spell...hopefully...then there shouldn't be any worry about an Original attacking the Benders."

"Sounds good on paper," Taka said.

"What are you talking about?" Vanessa said to Taka. "Do you see any paper on this table?"

"She's just making a point," Arabella said. "It sounds good as we're talking about it, but having it work is another story."

"Yeah," Taka said. "Another story."

Vanessa rolled her eyes, then said to Arabella. "Let's get started then. What ingredients do you want us to use for this particular spell?"

Arabella aimed her chin at Taka. "You take care of gathering the herbs. We'll need rosemary, sage, thyme, lavender and bay laurel."

"Got it." Taka nodded.

"Vanessa, would you please collect the stones we'll need?"

"Sure," Vanessa said. "Which ones?"

"Amber, to increase the power of the spell, jet, to absorb negative energy, amethyst, to cleanse, blue lace agate for healing, azurite for psychic ability, and clear quartz, which, as you know, is needed for all mani-festation spells."

"But we're not manifesting anything," Vanessa said, looking confused.

"I want this protection spell to be so strong it will seem like a living, breathing organism," Arabella said.

Vanessa nodded. "Got it."

"Now, we'll also need a blend of bergamot, cypress and myrrh oil, along with three candles," Arabella said. "One green candle as it relates to physicality, a yellow one to clear the path for our spell, then purple for spirituality. I'll take care of the oils and candles."

"Okay," Taka said. She pushed away from the table and stood. "Let's get started."

Vanessa took a quick sip of tea, then stood as well and sighed. "I wish we'd put one of those gliding chairs on the staircase so we wouldn't have to walk those steps. The stairs are hell on my knees."

"Mine, too," Taka said. "And my bunions. But the pain'll be worth it. It's for a good cause."

Arabella wished for the gliding chair, as well. She knew what the two Elders meant. They rarely went upstairs anymore due to arthritis, bunions, hip aches and ankle pain.

She hated getting old. That was one slight when it came to the Circle of Sisters' order. From the begin-ning of the order, they were able to conjure spells to heal but not when it came to aging. They believed in allowing nature to take its course, which meant gray-ing hair, creaky joints and sagging body parts that used to be round and perky.

"Once we've gathered our ingredients, we'll come back here and use the kitchen table for the altar," Ara-

bella said. "That way we won't have to keep running...
well, keep going upstairs to check on the burning candles."

As the three Elders moaned and groaned their
way upstairs, Arabella thought about the right words
they'd need for the protection spell. This wouldn't be
a standard "don't touch me" spell. It had to be bigger,
stronger. Their words had as big a part to play in the
conjuring of the spell as the ingredients they were
about to collect.

When they reached the second-floor landing, the
Elders split off in different directions, each headed for
the rooms where specific items were stored.

Thirty minutes later, they stood gathered around
the kitchen table again. Taka cleared away the cups
and saucers, then wiped the table down with a dish-
cloth. Arabella laid out a circular black silk cloth in
the center of the table. Then she placed the green, yellow and purple candles in a triangle along the edges
of the cloth.

Arabella nodded to Vanessa. "Place the stones in a
circle within the triangle of candles. Start at the point,
next to the green one."

"Any specific order?" Vanessa asked.

"Yes, start with the clear quartz, then follow with
the azurite, going clockwise. After the azurite, place
the amber, then jet, followed by blue lace agate and
close the circle with the amethyst."

Vanessa quickly did as she was told, and when her
task was completed, Arabella went over to one of the
kitchen cabinets and removed a stone bowl. She pulled
open a utility drawer and took out a box of matches.

She brought bowl and matches back to the table and placed them in the center of the crystals.

Arabella nodded at Taka. "Put the herbs in the bowl, please."

Taka made quite the show as she dramatically sprinkled sage, rosemary, thyme, lavender and bay laurel into the bowl. She dusted her hands off over the bowl to brush off any herb residue.

Arabella took a bottle from her robe pocket. She opened it and placed three drops of her special blend of bergamot, cypress and myrrh oil on top of the herbs.

The other Elders stood silently as Arabella took the matches, lit the candles, then placed the match onto the herb and oil mixture. Once it began to smolder, she brought the match to her lips, blew it out and flicked the used match into the kitchen sink.

"Let's join hands," Arabella said.

When they were connected, Arabella stared deeply into the smoldering concoction in the stone bowl and said, "Repeat after me… We call upon the elements of life—water, air, fire, earth—to aide us in our quest."

Vanessa and Taka obediently repeated her words.

"Anything or anyone intentionally set on harming the Triads shall be thwarted. And the harm intended for the Triads shall be sent back to thee. We do not accept harm to them. Protection is their shield from all negativity and hatred, from injury and illness. They do not harm others, so others cannot harm them. So we speak this, so shall it be."

The two Elders holding onto Arabella repeated her words verbatim.

Arabella continued, "And we speak a second protection over the Triads. Protection against dark enti-

ties and demons. This shield shall keep out evil. This
shield shall keep out harm. This shield does not allow
demons or negative entities to pass through it. This
shield shall be the Triads' domain, and they alone
determine what is allowed to pass through it. So we
speak this into being, so shall it be."

When Vanessa and Taka completed their repetition,
all three of the Elders sighed.

"It is done," Arabella said.

"What about the people in the city?" Vanessa asked.
"Aren't we going to put a protection spell over them?"

"We can try," Arabella said. "But without knowing
each person, seeing their faces in our mind's eye, it'll
be sort of like tossing confetti in the air. If we specifically blanket the city, that doesn't allow nature to
take its course."

"What do you mean?" Taka asked.

"Tonight, somewhere in this city, people will die.
Either by natural causes or unnatural causes having
nothing to do with the Originals. We can't alter everyone's future. A person's time to die is their time
to die."

"Well, that doesn't seem fair," Taka said. "Doesn't
the same apply to a Triad? If it's their time to die, I
mean?"

"No," Arabella said, a bit uncomfortably. In truth,
Taka was right. But Arabella steeled herself and lifted
her chin. "They belong to the Circle of Sisters. And
we're responsible for them."

"We'll need more supplies if we're going to attempt
a protection spell over the people in the city," Vanessa
said. "I'll get more crystals."

Taka frowned. "Wait a minute. Since when, as Elders, have we ever gone off half-cocked when it came to conjuring spells?"

Both Arabella and Vanessa stared at her, blinking. It was one of the most intelligent questions Taka had asked in some time.

"We're not going off half-cocked," Arabella finally said. "We're only doing the best we know how. We weren't trained to stave off Cartesians and flight-risk Originals. As head Elder, I've simply formulated what makes sense."

Taka pursed her lips, then said, "I know neither one of you want to hear this, but since we're looking at such a serious situation, don't you think we should get some help? Like from someone who knows the city?"

"And who might that be?" Vanessa said warily.

"The sorcerers," Taka said.

Vanessa threw up her hands. "And here I thought her brain had just regained some logical use."

"We can't let the sorcerers know about this," Arabella said. "The last thing we need is Cottle holding everything that's going on over our heads, claiming we're powerless, useless. He already thinks he's a know-it-all."

"What about Shandor or Gunner?" Taka asked.

"Shandor is Cottle's lapdog," Vanessa said. "He'll run to him with the news in a heartbeat."

"Gunner?" Taka asked, her brow furrowing.

"We're not knocking your ideas, dear," Arabella told Taka. "I don't think it's safe to leak word of this, even to Gunner. I might trust him more if he wasn't always around Cottle and Shandor. I don't know what their connection is, but it's disconcerting and doesn't elicit trust, in my opinion. We can, however, contact others within the Circle of Sisters and have them conjure protections spells that will overlap ours."

"Good idea," Vanessa said. "That'll certainly give us some leverage."

Seeing the distraught look on Taka's face, Arabella said, "We've always taken care of our own. We simply can't take the chance that word will get out in the city."

Taka tsked. "Don't you think you're being a bit dramatic?"

"Our sisters weren't being dramatic when they were hung by anti-witch zealots back in the early centuries," Arabella reminded her.

"We'll call more sisters," Vanessa said. "It'll work. You'll see."

Taka scowled at Vanessa. "Are you, like…trying to comfort me?"

Vanessa snorted. "Absolutely not. Simply making a statement."

"I certainly hope our spell, along with those of our other sisters, are effective and in time to save the Triads," Arabella said. "And the people in this city from the Originals. If not, we might all be destroyed."

Taka stared at Arabella, her eyebrows knitting together. "All of us?"

Arabella nodded. "Every last one of us, just like the lynchings our ancestors suffered centuries ago. This could very well start off another witch hunt, another hunt to destroy all of the Originals and their subspecies. And we'd be stuck right in the middle of it all."

Chapter 22

Viv heard someone call her name. She wanted to tell them to hush. Her arm burned like hell, and she didn't feel well. She wanted to sleep.

Suddenly, it felt like a switch flipped on in her brain, and she remembered where she was and about the Cartesian. Her eyes flew open, and she found herself lying flat on her back on the ground. She'd obviously passed out, something she'd never done before.

Gazing up at the sky, Viv saw that the rifts were closed. She sat up, struggled to get to her feet and felt something grab her uninjured arm. She let out a bloodcurdling scream.

"It's me."

She recognized Nikoli's voice.

"It's just me," he said again. "The Cartesian's gone."

Viv was finally able to focus on his face. She reached for him, clung to him and shivered.

He held her close. "It's okay, baby. It's gone."

She pulled away from him, her eyes wide and questioning. "I saw two… There were two holes in the sky. I…I don't understand. You—you were right about the Cartesians coming after us!"

"I think they used the two rifts as a trap," Nikoli said. "To distract us. Have me wonder which one they'd drop down from first." He shook his head. "I don't know for certain. Hell, they could have just as easily dropped down from both. What makes me think it was a trap was they waited for my attention to be focused on the larger rift before the Cartesian dropped out of the other one and attacked you. By the time I saw it, I ran as fast as I could…" He cupped her face with his hands. "God, Viv, you could've been killed."

Even though her arm hurt like hell, she took his face in her hands and kissed him hard. "Thank you. I think we're about even now, so no more close calls, okay?" Her eyes welled up with tears, and she scolded herself. *Don't cry! Don't cry!*

"No more," he said, then helped Viv to her feet. "We need to get you home so I can tend to the wounds on your arm."

She looked down at her arm and saw the sleeve of her sweater. It looked like it had gone through a shredder, and blood oozed from the gashes in her arm.

"On second thought, you may need stitches," Nikoli said. "We should go straight to an emergency room and have a doctor take a look at that."

Viv eyed him. "I'm a Triad, remember? We don't do hospitals and doctors. We heal ourselves with herbs, crystals—shit like that."

The frown on his face deepened. "So can you do a

spell? Have the wounds close up and go away? Make the bleeding stop at least?"

"I'm a Triad, not a stupid vampire." She plucked at a piece of the shredded sweater sleeve. "Can you rip this off? We can use it to wrap the wounds, staunch the bleeding and keep the dirt out until I can tend to it better."

Pursing his lips, Nikoli took hold of the fabric of the sleeve closest to her shoulder and pulled. It ripped at the seam, and he continued to tease it loose all the way around her arm. When the last stitch tore free, Viv carefully tugged the sleeve down her arm and over her hand. She saw three long gashes on her arm. *Don't cry. Don't cry*, she repeated.

She held the material out to him, "Do you mind?"

"Of course not." Nikoli took the material from her and wrapped it around her wounds. "They're bleeding pretty good. In order to stop it, I'm going to have to put a little pressure on the wrap. Tell me if it gets too tight."

Viv nodded and gritted her teeth as he flipped, tugged, then tied the torn sleeve around her injured arm. She couldn't tell how deep the gashes were from all the blood.

When he was done, Nikoli said, "I really think we should go to—"

"Don't think," she said. "You've covered up the wounds nice and tight, so it's all good. I'm not bailing over some little cut."

"They're not so little."

"It's my arm, so I get to call it. They're little." Before he hit her with a retort, Viv spun about on the balls of her feet, cupped her hands around her mouth and let out a loud, long howl, then two sharp barks and another howl. Her voice echoed far into the night, over the din in the compound, the thunder rumbling from every direction.

Viv looked back at Nikoli. He probably thought she'd lost her mind. "I'm calling for Jaco and Aaron. They usually respond right away. I hope they're okay." She waited a couple minutes and was about to send out another come-hither call when the branches of the trees in the thicker part of the forest to her left started to quiver.

Jaco suddenly appeared out of the brush. Standing in human form, he looked haggard and beyond exhausted.

"Where's Aaron?" Viv asked.

Jaco shook his head and shrugged. "He went missing about four hours ago. I don't know where he is."

"You've been dealing with all of the Loups in this compound by yourself?" she asked, stunned.

"Yeah." Jaco looked at the material wrapped around her arm but didn't say anything about it. He looked at her with weary, bloodshot eyes.

Viv felt sorry for her lead Loup and wanted to hug him for his loyalty and commitment to her. But she knew better. No personal contact. Not with the leaders. It would undermine her authority. She drew in a deep breath to clear her head. "There's only one more thing I need to ask you to do, then I'll assign two other Loups to patrol the compound so you can get some rest. We want to try something that might help protect the entire compound from the Cartesians."

Jaco suddenly lifted his head and sniffed. Viv's

body went on alert. Though she still smelled residual clove, she didn't catch anything new.

"What's the matter?" she asked.

Instead of answering, Jaco let his nose lead him to the underbrush, where she and Nikoli had had sex. He leaned over and sniffed deeply, then turned to look at Viv, a steely expression on his face.

"I smell you and..." Jaco sniffed again. "Him." He aimed his chin at Nikoli, who stood a few feet away. "Does that mean that while I've been busting my ass inside that compound, trying to control all the in-fighting, worrying about when the next Cartesians were going to drop out of the sky, the two of you were in there, screwing like rabbits?"

Evidently overhearing Jaco, Nikoli took a step toward him, fury on his face. Viv held up a hand to stop him.

She turned her attention back to Jaco, feeling like she'd just been slapped. She firmed up her stance and kept her eyes hard. "Remember who you're talking to. The Triad who feeds you, who gives you a safe place to roam without fear. The one who protects you from human hunters. What I do is my business, not yours. Tell me, when you find a female in heat, have you ever known me to run up to your den and condemn you for fucking some little bitch in heat while I'm having so many problems elsewhere?"

Jaco's eyes went soft, and he dropped his chin to his chest. "I...I apologize."

"See that it never happens again." Viv forced her voice to remain strong and firm when what she felt was small and ashamed. Jaco was right. "Now, as I was saying, we have a plan, and I need you to do something for me. For this compound and all the Loups. Once you complete the task, I'll assign two other Loups to keep watch until I get back. You need some rest."

"What do you need?" Jaco asked.

"We're going to set something up that we believe will keep the Cartesians from dropping down into the compound. If it works, that'll give me time to search for our missing Loups."

"And if it doesn't?" Jaco asked.

"Back to square one," Viv said. "I wouldn't ask you to do this if I didn't think the plan had potential and knew you were the right Loup to help make it happen."

Jaco squared his shoulders. "What do you want me to do?"

"See that corner fence post?" Viv pointed to the thick steel post that braced one corner of the fencing. "I need you to bend that pole to a forty-five-degree angle so it's pointed at the center of the compound. Start about waist high."

"Why would you have me do that?

Viv gave him a stern look.

"O-okay, no problem. That it?"

"It's a start. Once it's bent, we can take care of the rest. If it works, I'll need you to find the other three poles that square off this property and bend them the same way. All of them need to be pointed to the center of the compound. We're getting ahead of ourselves, though. Let's start with the first. See what happens."

Jaco nodded and scurried off for the first fence post.

Nikoli stood beside her as they watched Jaco stand at the base of the post, hitch up his denim pants, then wrap his arms around the post. He let out a loud "Huh!" and leaned over from the waist. The pole began to bend, creaking in protest. Once it leaned at a forty-five-degree angle, Jaco turned to look at Viv, and she held up a hand, signaling all was good.

She turned to Nikoli. "Do you have the bloodstones?"

"There're in the satchel over there." He pointed to the brown bag sitting on the ground next to the entrance of their hidey hole. "I'll get it."

Once Nikoli had retrieved the satchel, he pulled out one of the larger bloodstones. He held it up, examined it, then scowled.

"What's wrong?" she asked.

"I can't believe I didn't think about how we were going to attach these to the poles. Look at that angle. The stone's going to fall right off."

"No, it won't," Viv said and held out her hands. "May I have it, please?"

Nikoli handed her the bloodstone, and Viv quickly ran her hands all the way around it over and over, all the while muttering a holding spell.

"Stone of blood, spirit anew,
Bind thyself firm like glue.
Stone of blood, binding real,
By my command ye shall meld with steel.
Donda—Lorra."

When she was done, Viv called Jaco over to her and handed him the stone. "I want you to shimmy up the pole you just bent and place this on top of the pole."

"But it'll fall off," Jaco said, giving her a puzzled look. "That pole's at a forty-five."

"Trust me," Viv said. "It'll stay in place."

Jaco jostled the stone in his hand as if studying it,

testing its weight, then shrugged and headed back to the pole.

"You sure this is going to work?" Viv asked Nikoli.

He sidled up to her. "You've already asked me that. Sorry I can't give you a different answer. I really don't know if it's going to work until we try it. Like I said, it's never been done before."

She felt as if someone had just dropped a three-hundred-pound weight on her shoulders. This had to work. She couldn't accept anything but it working because the alternative was unthinkable.

Viv watched as her Loup shimmied up and across the pole one-handed. When he got within arm's reach of the top, he took the bloodstone, then reached under the pole and up and placed the stone directly onto the pole's center. He held on to it, glancing down and over at Viv.

She nodded, and Jaco released the stone.

The bloodstone remained in place as if it belonged there and had always been a part of the pole. A huge smile lit up her Loup's face as he slid down the pole and hurried over to her.

Nikoli, who'd retrieved their flashlights from the brush, aimed a light beam at the top of the pole. "Well, I'll be damned. That's some mojo you've got, lady."

"I know," Viv said. "And by the way, why would you do that to yourself?"

Nikoli looked down at her quizzically. "What?"

"Damn yourself."

He grinned.

Viv returned the smile, then dug through the satchel for three more bloodstones. She'd decided to have Jaco finish the job with the other three poles while they tested the first one. She didn't want him to be around and wind up being disappointed if something went awry.

After finding the largest of the remaining stones, she placed the satchel on the ground. One by one, she rubbed her hands over the stones she'd chosen, chanting over each one in turn.

"Stone of blood, spirit anew,
Bind thyself firm like glue.
Stone of blood, binding real,
By my command ye shall meld with steel.
Donda—Lorra."

"What now?" Jaco said when he returned to her side. "You going to test it?"

"Soon," Viv said. "Take these three stones and find the other three poles. Do the exact same thing you did to that one, okay?"

"Got it."

Viv handed him the stones, wincing from the pain in her arm. "Return to me as soon as you're done."

Jaco nodded and took off, soon disappearing into the forest's brush.

Once he was out of sight, she turned to Nikoli. "Show time."

"Fingers crossed," he said and reached for his scabior. Holding it in his right hand, he turned back to Viv. "Don't look so worried. I have confidence this'll work. Just because something's never been done before, doesn't mean it can't or won't work."

"I know. You're right." Viv offered him a small smile. "Rock on, Magic Man. It's your show now."

She saw his eyes soften. He glanced at the makeshift bandage on her arm, and sorrow flitted across his face.

"Hey, it's all good," Viv said. "Don't beat yourself up. It's just a couple of scratches that'll heal in no time. You're forgetting the big picture. You saved my life, remember? How can you feel bad about that?"

"I don't," Nikoli said. "Your safety means everything to me. It simply hurts me to see you hurting."

Viv was taken aback by the emotion in his voice, the concern in his words and the depth with which his storm cloud–gray eyes studied her.

The wind suddenly picked up and stirred the cool night air. It wafted over her, and she breathed in deeply, appreciating the coolness against her fevered arm. She smelled the air charged with electricity, smelled the rain in its belly. They were in for a gully washer.

"You may want to get started before we get doused. Rain's coming."

"I smell it," Nikoli said and handed her the flashlight, then held out the scabior.

Viv watched in anticipation, but before Nikoli could twitch his wrists one way or the other, Jaco came bursting out of the brush over to her.

He was panting, out of breath. When he reached her side, he leaned over and put his hands on his knees and sucked in a breath. "They're—all—done," he said, each word coming out on the heels of a pant.

"You mean the poles?" Viv asked. "You've already finished them?"

Jaco nodded, sweat streaming down the sides of his face.

"Wow," Nikoli said. "That was fast."

Jaco scowled at him but smiled proudly at Viv. "You told me to return to you when I was done. Is there something else you want me to do?"

"Good job, Jaco," she said. "We're good for now. Go back to your den and get some rest. I'll assign two other Loups to watch the compound before I leave."

"When will you know if this plan you had will work?" he asked. "Having this compound under protection twenty-four-seven would be great."

"We'll know soon," she promised. "I'll give you an update when we find out." Lightning crisscrossed the sky, and Viv cringed reflexively. A loud clap of thunder quickly followed. "Go now before you get stuck in this storm."

Jaco gave her a formal bow from the waist, then hurried away.

Viv glanced over at Nikoli. He already had the scabior aimed at the pole.

A disconcerting thought suddenly struck Viv. "Wait. How are you going to get to the other three poles to charge them? At least two of them are only accessible through the compound."

"We don't have to physically be at those poles to charge them," he said. "This one, like the other three, is aimed at the center of the compound. If I'm able to charge this one, the electromagnetic field will immediately strike the bloodstone directly opposite of it, causing the second one to charge. The two charged poles will form a horizontal crossbeam that will ignite the other two poles."

Viv looked at him in amazement and for the first time since his arrival, she was grateful he was a Bender.

"Ready?" he asked.

"Past ready."

Nikoli spread his feet apart, firming his stance. He aimed the scabior, gave two quick twists of his wrist, then whirled the scabior through his fingers and re-aimed, his brow furrowing.

A bolt of lightning shot from the bloodstone attached to the scabior and hit the bloodstone attached to the pole. The large bloodstone shimmered, and sparks flew from it. Soon the pole began to glow an odd orange color, and she saw it sway slightly.

"You're melting it," she said to Nikoli and bit her bottom lip.

He held up his free hand, signaling her to be silent.

Viv knew he had to concentrate. Although she feared the pole would melt into a huge puddle of molten steel, she had to trust he knew what he was doing.

In that moment, the bloodstone that sat on top of the pole shot out brilliant white light toward the center of the compound. And in a matter of seconds, like dominoes, three additional brilliant lights fell into place, all four linking as they should. Strobing, sparking, lighting up the compound like a football stadium during a game.

"It worked!" Viv shouted and had to work hard not to clap her hands and jump up and down like a five-year-old. "It worked! It worked!" Then, unable to stop herself, she clapped her hands and jumped once. Pain flashed across her arm from the gashes, quickly curbing her enthusiasm.

Nikoli stared up at the lights, his expression one of wonder and amazement. He shook his head slowly as if in disbelief. "Damn, it actually worked." He shoved the scabior back into its sheath.

Viv couldn't help but run to him and reached up to give his neck a hug. Her injured arm slapped her into submission. She threw her good arm around him and gave him a big wet kiss. "You did it! You made it work."

A sharp pain jabbed her injured arm again, and Viv grimaced and drew her good arm back to her side.

They stood side by side, watching as groups of Loups darted among the trees, dodging the light.

Out of nowhere, Jaco suddenly appeared at her side again.

"Where did you come from?" she asked. "I thought you were heading back for your den."

"I have news," Jaco said, glancing up at the lights in the sky, seemingly unimpressed. He looked back at Viv. "When those…things lit up, I was at the north end of the compound, near the back. I found Aaron."

Relieved, Viv looked about and asked, "Where is he? Why isn't he with you?"

The look on Jaco's face caused Viv's stomach to turn sour.

"He's dead," Jaco said.

Viv felt her mouth drop open, and she snapped it shut. "How? Where?"

"I have no idea how," Jaco said. "All I know is there's not much left of him. Found him near the fence out back. I don't know what all these lights are about, but I sure hope that whatever you're doing with them works."

Viv felt her brain struggle to grasp the fact that she'd lost another one of her Loups. This one a pack leader. The three-hundred-pound weight returned to her shoulders. She wanted to sit down. No, lie down. Close her eyes and sleep this nightmare away, then wake up to find things back to normal.

Unable to find any words to comfort Jaco, she watched him walk away. Her shock was too great to call him back.

Nikoli stepped up to her. "I heard," he said. "I'm so sorry."

She turned to him. This time she couldn't tell herself not to cry.

He took hold of her uninjured arm and pulled her in close. He held her head against his chest. She heard the rapid beating of his heart.

Viv remained too dumbstruck to say a word.

"I can't bring him back," Nikoli said. "None of them. But I'll do everything in my power to make certain nothing more happens to you or to the Originals. I'll bring order back to your world. You'll see."

Viv nodded slowly against his chest, wondering which would come first. His order to her world or her own death.

Chapter 23

Assigning two different alphas, Petros and Carlton, to watch over the compound had been tough on Viv. Aaron, her West pack leader, had been with her since she was a child. She still couldn't believe he was gone, that she'd never see him again—his soft brown eyes, his silky black fur and his signature birthmark—a pink ring of flesh around his left nostril.

Her only comfort when issuing the new assignment was knowing she was helping Jaco. He needed time to rest, to heal emotionally and physically. Something she didn't know if she'd ever be able to do.

So much had happened over the last two or three days. Viv couldn't even remember how or when all of this started. How long had it been since things were normal? She wondered if she would ever know times like that again.

Exhaustion beat on her, as did the pain in her arm. She and Nikoli had already crossed by ferry to city-side and were standing beside her truck. Only then did she allow herself time to feel.

"I'm going to miss that big guy," Viv said to Nikoli, fighting off tears.

He rested a hand on her shoulder. "I know you will. You've done a spectacular job caring for the Loup Garou. I don't know of anyone who cares about their charges the way you do. Who loves them the way you do. I'm sure you get frustrated at times. I know I do with my job. But you keep after it. You don't quit."

When she heard the word "quit," a tear slid down Viv's cheek. She quickly brushed it away.

"It's okay to cry," he said.

Viv looked away from him. "No, it's not. There's too much to do. We should let Gilly and Evee and your cousins know that the makeshift scabior worked at the North compound so we can start setting up their territories."

Nikoli tucked a finger under her chin, turning her head so she faced him. "It's a little after midnight already. We told them we'd meet them at the ferry for feeding time. That's only three hours away. Since they're going to meet us here anyway, why don't we use that time to look for your missing Loups?"

Viv drew in a deep breath. She wanted to be every-where at one time. At the compound, looking for her Loups, helping Evee and Gilly look for their lost broods and protecting her sisters.

Her injured arm gave witness to the fact that the Cartesians were out to get them. What Nikoli had said about the leader of the Cartesians probably wanting them out of the way so he could get to the Originals freely had been spot on. They were all under attack. She didn't know where to put herself or know which direction to turn.

Evidently sensing her muddled thoughts, Nikoli tapped her gently on the nose with a finger. "Tell me what it feels like whenever one of your Loups is nearby but you can't see him. How do you sense them? By scent? By sound? By sensation?"

"Sensation," Viv said, not understanding where he was going with the question.

"Okay," he said. "Let's start with that. What does that sensation feel like?"

She thought for a moment, trying to find the words to describe it. "It starts out as a tingle at the base of my spine that works its way up to my neck, then my ears begin to ring."

"Do you feel anything like that now?"

She shook her head. "No. You think if I did that I'd be standing here right now?"

"I know, I know."

"Where are you going with this?" she asked.

"Bear with me. When your Loups are in the compound and not ordered to work—you know, they're simply hanging out, being Loups, going about their own business—what kind of sounds do they make?"

"I don't understand," she glanced over at Nikoli, and he looked deeply into her eyes. "What do you mean by sounds?"

"Think about it," he said. "When you and your sisters are just hanging out, not into any conversation, doing your own things, does Gilly hum to herself? Does Evee whistle a tune?"

"They don't do any of that," she said.

"Okay, but do you get the point I'm trying to make? When your Loups are just hanging out together, what kind of sounds do they make?"

"It depends. Sometimes they growl territorially, sometimes they howl, some bark or yip. A few make a clicking sound with their tongue that I've never quite been able to figure out. Other than that, they're usually quiet."

"Okay, that's a good start." Nikoli released her chin and leaned against the truck, crossing his feet in front of him. He pointed to his left ear. "Whenever I want to hear something more clearly that might be a great distance away, I have this trick I use to amplify the sound of whatever I have a bead on. Maybe if I show you that trick and you try it, it might amplify your ability to feel that sensation you get when you have a Loup that's nearby but out of sight. The reason I asked you about the sounds they make when they're not feeding or given a chore is so I can help you listen for them while you feel. That way the two of us will be like radars, seeking a missile."

Exhausted and hurting and trying to contain the ache in her heart over Aaron's death and frustrated over all she was unable to do, Viv didn't think she could feel one more thing. Still, Nikoli had piqued her curiosity. If there was a way to amplify the sensation, maybe that would help her find the missing Loups.

She turned to him. "Show me how you do it with your hearing."

Nikoli stood upright and patted his chest. "Back up against me. Put your back to my chest."

Viv eyed him suspiciously.

"No funny business. Here." He patted his chest again.

"Okay." Viv turned and backed into him. The moment her body touched his, she felt something spark inside of her, and she quickly squelched it. Something had to be seriously wrong with her for her to react the way she did every time she was near this man. The entire world could be coming to an end—much like hers was now—and she would still want to have sex with him. She couldn't help but wonder if all the hell breaking loose now had something to do with her sleeping with him earlier.

"Hold your arms out a little so I can get my arms around you without hurting your injured arm."

She did as she was told, and felt his hands wrap around her waist and settle over her diaphragm.

"Now, breath in deeply. Take in all the air your lungs can hold."

Viv drew in a deep breath through her nose. She smelled muddy water, gasoline fumes from the city and the rot of street garbage. She held that breath, waiting for Nikoli's instruction.

"While you're holding your breath, think about what the sensation feels like when an out-of-sight Loup is near. Think about it—concentrate on that tingling sensation that starts at your spine and works its way up your neck. Feel the ringing in your ears."

Viv felt herself grow calm under the sound of his voice, her body tuned to her Loups. She focused on the tingling that made its way up her spine, like a hundred spider legs jittering their way up her back.

"Now slowly let out that breath through your

mouth. Release all of it, still thinking about that tingling sensation."

Viv released her breath slowly. As she came to the end of that breath, Nikoli pressed in and up on her diaphragm and another puff of air escaped her lips.

"See?" he said. "There's always a little left over. You need to make sure that entire breath is released. So just when you think you're at the end of it. Push a little harder. There's always a little more." He eased the pressure off her diaphragm and slowly removed his arms from around her waist. He turned her to face him. "That's the trick," he said. "It's all in the breathing, letting the oxygen go all the way to your core, and concentration. Once you tune into that sensation, you can turn slowly left or right, and the sensation will grow stronger, just like sounds grow louder for me, when you're facing in the right direction of the target you're looking for. When I do that, it feels like all of my senses suddenly wake up, especially my hearing. Now, let's try it again, only this time I won't touch you so nothing will distract you."

Viv was a little disappointed she'd be doing this on her own. She liked having his arms around her and having his body pressed against hers made her feel safe.

"Does it make a difference if they're in a location they're supposed to be in, like the compound," Viv asked, "versus them just taking off, nobody knowing where they went or how they got there?"

"It doesn't. They are your Loups. The who, what, when, where and how don't figure into the equation. Remember, it's all about feeling, breathing, concentrating. Don't let all of the other stuff muddle your thoughts. Don't think about why they're not heeding your call. Just feel them."

"What if I can't?"

"At least try it. They are your Loups. It's not like you're trying to zero in on vampires or werewolves whose lives were never a part of yours. Those Loups have been a part of your life since the day you were born. They're part of you. So go ahead, give it a try. See if you pick up anything. Lean against the truck and close your eyes if it'll help you."

Viv felt a little foolish, standing at the end of a dock, near her truck with her eyes closed. You never closed your eyes at night while on the streets of New Orleans. Still, she heeded his advice, leaned against her truck and closed her eyes.

She drew in a deep breath through her nose and held it, the way Nikoli had shown her. She thought about the tingling, prickly sensation she wanted to feel, the spider legs that always started at her spine. She thought about how the spider legs traveled up her spine to the base of her skull. Then the ringing in her ears, almost like an alarm, letting her know a Loup was nearby.

She allowed herself to get lost in that thought and released her breath slowly, still thinking about the spider legs, forcing more breath out of her lungs. Thinking about the tingling up her spine—the ringing in her ears—spider legs.

Viv suddenly froze, holding back what little breath she had left in her lungs. She felt it, tingling at the base of her spine. Only this wasn't in her head. It was for real.

She remembered what Nikoli had said about slowly turning from left to right to see if the sensation grew stronger when she faced one direction versus the other. Keeping her eyes closed, Viv turned slowly to her right. The tingling at the base of her spine remained at a constant, but oddly enough, she felt a different, disconnected tingling in the middle of her back when she faced east.

Feeling her heart rate triple, Viv turned slowly to the left, and the tingling at the base of her spine grew stronger. The one in the center of her back now the constant.

"I feel something, she whispered, afraid to open her eyes. Afraid she might lose the sensation if she did.

"Think about your Loups," Nikoli whispered softly in her ear. "The ones missing. See them in your mind's eye. Let the sensation build. Grab on to it and hold tight, like it's a physical object."

Viv drew in another deep breath and the tingling she felt in the base of her spine grew stronger, more pronounced. So did the one in the center of her back. Two separate places. The tingling didn't inch its way up her spine the way it normally did.

She released her breath and said, "It's still there, only stronger. I feel the tingling in two separate places. It's not crawling up my spine like usual. And they must be stationary because the tingling in both spots doesn't move in any direction. My ears aren't ringing, but I know it has to be them."

Nikoli whispered, "Now let your instincts take those feelings and guide you in the direction of your Loups."

"One's east, the other west," Viv said, already knowing the direction. "I think the ones in the east are a bit farther away because the sensation doesn't get as strong as the one to the west." Viv opened her eyes, pushed away from the truck and faced him. "Now what do I do with that? If we head west, how far do we go?"

"There's only one way to find out," he said. "Hop in the truck. We're heading west."

She didn't argue when Nikoli opened the passenger door for her, helped her inside, then ran around the truck and jumped into the driver's seat. He turned the engine over, lowered the window at his side and set the truck into motion.

"You concentrate on that sensation while I drive," he said. "Tell me when to turn left or right."

"How am I supposed to know which way to turn?"

"Your instincts will tell you and the sensation will confirm it. I'll keep an ear peeled for any of the sounds you said the Loups make when they're together. And considering you heard the pop from the scabior, I'd say your hearing is like radar. So ear alert."

Viv looked out through the windshield but didn't see anything in front of her. She kept her mind's eye focused on her Loups and the sensations in her back.

Ten minutes into the drive, she directed him to head north on St. Peter Street, which brought them through the French Quarter. As they closed in on North Rampart, the tingling at the base of her spine grew stronger, and she knew they were getting closer to some of her Loups.

"Take a right," she said. "Here on Rampart."

Nikoli turned right as she instructed. He drove slowly. There weren't many people out at this hour, not in this part of town. Even the tourists knew to stay clear of this area late at night.

By the time they reached Ursulines, the tingling at the base of her spine was so strong, Viv felt as if a live electrical wire had been placed beneath her skin.

"Take a left, take a left," she demanded, sitting at the edge of her seat.

He did as she asked.

Three blocks later, Viv could barely sit still. They were now at the corner of Treme and St. Philip, one of the most dangerous parts of town. "They're around here. Park, park!"

As soon as Nikoli pulled the truck over to the side of the road and killed the engine, Viv jumped out of the truck, paying little heed to the pain shooting through her injured arm.

She began to walk down Treme, concentrating with all her might, stepping slowly, carefully so as not to lose the radar now so alive in her body.

Viv heard the beep of the automatic lock on the truck, and Nikoli called after her.

"Wait up!"

She didn't want to wait. If she had this tight of a bead on her Loups, she didn't want to take a chance in losing it. Viv kept walking and heard the thud of footsteps running toward her.

When Nikoli reached her side, she saw he had a large coil of guideline cable resting on his shoulder. It was the same type of cable they used to repair the cattle pens back at the ranch. She'd had some left over in the back of her pickup, along with miscellaneous tools from the last repair job Charlie and Bootstrap had done. She meant to bring it to Jaco so he could cordon off a breeding area—something he'd asked for.

"Has anyone ever told you that you can be a little hardheaded at times?" he asked.

"What are you doing with that?" she said.

"Just-in-case supplies." He hefted the coil of cable higher on his shoulder. "Let's go."

She shook her head in bewilderment. "Something feels odd around here," she said, training her eyes straight ahead. "Gangs hang out around here. Drug dealers. They all come out at night but look, the streets are empty. That's unusual." What was even more unusual for Viv was that her clairvoyant abilities seemed to have gone by way of the dodo bird. She may have gained a new radar, but her tried-and-true abilities had somehow fallen asleep.

Nikoli put a hand on her shoulder and held tight to keep her from walking any farther. "Hold up a second. Wait. I hear someone screaming for help. It's really muffled but I hear it."

Viv had been so focused on keeping her radar alive she hadn't heard anything but her own breathing and voice. She tilted her head slightly, strained an ear and finally heard it. The muffled cry of a woman. There was a short scream, then a loud gasp.

Breaking free of Nikoli's grasp, Viv hurried toward the sound. "There," she said, coming to a stop in front of two run-down, shotgun houses. Trash was strewn about their yards, and it looked like the mailboxes had been demolished with a baseball bat.

The woman's voice led them through an alley between the houses into the backyard. There sat an old beat-up sedan, its tires missing. Someone had propped the chassis up with cinder blocks. And three of Viv's missing Loups were beating on the windows of that car, trying to get to the woman trapped inside. The Loups were scraggly and scrawny, like they hadn't eaten in days.

Nikoli squeezed Viv's shoulder and whispered, "If we don't get them away from that woman—"

"The Loups will break the glass, and she'll be toast," Viv finished. "I know."

"Try a holding spell."

She raised an eyebrow at him and whispered, "You're telling me how to do my job?"

He gave her shoulder another little squeeze. "No way. Your ball game."

Viv inched closer to the vehicle, her arms stretched out in front of her, hands up, palms out.

"Heed my voice ye creatures three,
I bind thee now to follow me.
Inside out it makes no matter.
Boshnah, morva, benlu, sonah!"

The three Loups stopped beating on the windows, turned toward Viv and snarled.

"Oh, shit," she said. "It didn't work."

"Yes, it did," Nikoli said. "You got their attention away from the woman in the car."

"Yeah, but now they're going to come after us."

"Perfect." Nikoli removed the cable from his shoulder and held the coil in his right hand. He stuck his bottom lip between his teeth and let out a loud whistle. "This way, you ugly sons of bitches! You want dinner? Come get it."

He quickly turned to Viv. "For once, please, hear me and stay put. I'm going to call them out toward that big metal utility pole over there. Once I get them there, I'm going to use this cable like a lariat and lasso them to that pole."

"When did you suddenly become Roy Rogers?" She stared at him, wondering if there was any limit to the number of talents he possessed.

"Who's Roy Rogers?"

"Never mind. You're talking about taking on three Loups. That's like you trying to take on twenty men. You can't do that alone."

"I don't exactly have a cavalry to call. Look, when I see them running in my direction, I'm going to let them close in just enough to get the cable around them. The idea is to trap them between the cable and that pole. When I toss the cable, you start a holding spell. By the time the cable loops back to me, you'll be done and the cable will be locked to the pole."

"I tried a binding spell, and it didn't work."

"We're talking holding spell with two inanimate objects. It'll work. Don't cause the cable to meld with the pole like you did with the bloodstones back at the compound. Just make it tight enough to hold the Loups until you can get one of your alphas out here to scoop them up."

"Got it," Viv said, amazed once more by his brilliance.

The three Loups howled, then growled. They moved a little closer to Viv and Nikoli, bumping into one another, like they weren't sure whether to leave a sure thing trapped in the car that they'd already been fighting so hard to get to or head for the two humans on foot.

Nikoli stepped away from Viv and walked a few yards away toward the utility pole, whistling for the

Loups as he went. For once, she did as he asked and stayed put.

One of the Loups kept eyeing her, but each time Nikoli whistled, it whipped its head back in his direction.

"Here," Nikoli shouted. "Over here! You want dinner? Come get it."

The Loups rolled their heads from shoulder to shoulder and sniffed the air. They huddled together and as a group moved toward Viv, then lagged left and headed for Nikoli. They moved cautiously, evidently suspecting a trap.

Viv could tell by their actions there wasn't an alpha among them. All three were followers with no leader, so they were unsure of the direction to turn.

Nikoli, who'd finally reached the utility pole whistled louder and let the guideline cable unfurl. It looked to be about eight feet long. Keeping hold of one end, Nikoli whipped the cable with one hand and it whistled through the air like a bullwhip.

Viv watched as the Loups drew closer to Nikoli. She was out of their line of sight. Now they were dealing male to male, and Loups never gave up territory without a fight.

Nikoli suddenly growled at them, mimicking an angry Loup, one ready to fight. The three Loups growled back, and their united voice was deafening. They spread out in an attack formation, ready to encircle their prey. Had there been a fourth Loup, Nikoli would've been screwed. Viv didn't know how on earth he'd handle those three.

The Loups lowered their heads and hunched their shoulders, preparing to spring forward. Viv kept her eyes on them, hoping the woman in the car had had enough sense to get out and run while the Loups were preoccupied with Nikoli.

She'd barely finished that thought when the Loups charged. Nikoli moved behind the pole, letting them draw closer. He seemed to be counting. When the Loups were about fifteen to twenty feet away, he tossed the length of cable out wide, snapping his wrist so the flying end of it would return to him, like a boomerang.

The second Viv saw him release the cable, she yelled quickly:

"Cord of steel, home anew,
Bind thyself, firm like glue.
Cord of steel, binding real,
By my command, ye shall cling to steel!"

The Loups never knew what hit them when the guideline cable looped back to Nikoli. He released his end of the cable, and the thick guidewire caught the Loups from behind and slammed them against the utility pole. The cable held fast and the Loups yelped and howled, struggling to get free.

As much as she hated to, Viv cupped her hands around her mouth and howled for Jaco. She hated to disturb him, but he was the only one she trusted to come and get the three Loups.

From a great distance away, she heard Jaco's response. He'd heard her and understood.

A streak of lightning suddenly lit up the sky, and thunder rolled up behind it. A thunderstorm was about to let loose over their heads. And one thing that kept Viv from connecting with her Loups was a strong electromagnetic field. Lightning the greatest one of all. If they didn't hurry, she'd lose the connection she had with the Loups she'd felt in the East.

She saw Nikoli walking toward her. His hair was tousled, his face weary. Her heart still lunged at the sight of him. The connection she had with him had gotten too far out of hand. Viv wondered if her intimacy with Nikoli had been the reason for Aaron's death, for the missing Loups, for her own attack.

Although he didn't know it, Viv had heard when Nikoli had mouthed, "I love you," as they held each other within the confines of the forest. She wanted so much to say the same but had held her tongue. The curse of the Triad loomed over her like a concrete wall ready to collapse on her head. They could never be together. History had sealed that deal, and she didn't even know the entire story as to why.

It was all her fault. It was she who'd allowed Nikoli too close. Close enough to capture her body and soul. He was human, and she knew better.

It felt like karma had come back to slap her in the face. Viv shook her head, felt her heart drop to her feet. Instinct and conscience told her what had to be done to fix the problem, and the thought made her want to be swallowed up by Mother Earth, never to return.

She had no choice but to face a concrete resolution...

Viv had to let Nikoli Hyland go.

Chapter 24

After the Loups were bound to the metal pole and Jaco was summoned to come and get them, the sky opened up and rain pummeled them from every direction. Lightning flashed across the sky, and thunder rolled along with each flash. Viv felt the vibration of it in her body. The problem with a lightning storm was that the resulting electromagnetic field seemed to short-circuit her ability to sense her Loups and their whereabouts. All she was able to do now was recall the sensation, the spidery-like tingling in the middle of her back that she'd picked up earlier.

The fact that the sensation had been in the middle of her back, told her the remaining missing Loups were somewhere west of where they were.

Viv and Nikoli were already soaked by the time they made it back to the truck. She noticed as he grabbed the steering wheel that his hands and fore-arms were scratched and bruised from handling the cable. She wanted to take each one of his hands and place healing herbs on them, kiss them, soothe them, comfort him. Then she remembered her steely resolve. She had to distance herself from Nikoli.

"Which way?" he asked. "Where do you want me to go next?"

Viv shook her head. "I'm not sure. With this lightning storm, I've lost all tracking sensation. The last time I felt it, I knew one group was west and another east. If you've got that hearing mojo you told me about earlier, we may have to count on that to find the others. Remember, when they're together and not on the hunt, they make yipping sounds or growl and bark. If they're all asleep—or worse, dead—you won't pick up any sound at all."

"Got it," he said.

"Won't it be hard for you to hear anything with all this thunder?" she asked.

Nikoli glanced over at her, and a look of puzzlement flashed across his face. She read it to mean, *Why are you sitting so far away from me?*

Evidently choosing not to address that question, he said, "I can separate the sounds, zero in on the ones that belong to my target."

Thankfully he didn't insist she move closer to him. She didn't know what she would have said if he had. As difficult as it was, she had to keep distance between them. The farther, the better.

"Since we've already hit our target west, it makes sense for us to head east, no? Since that's the direction you felt the other group?"

"That's about all we can do," she said. "Drive east and hope your Superman hearing picks up something."

Nikoli grinned. "Superman, huh?"

She gave him a half smile. "Yeah, well..."

Driving up Esplanade, they continued east until they were out of New Orleans proper. Fifteen minutes later, they came upon a commercial area with warehouses stacked one against the other. The road ended just past the warehouses and right at the Mississippi waterline. Very few security lights illuminated the area.

"I'm not hearing anything," Nikoli said. "But it's pretty dark back here. Good place for them to hide out."

"I have no idea," Viv said. "With all this rain and thunder, I'm not picking up a damn thing."

"All right, unless you want to head across the river, I'm going to get out of the truck and see if I can make a little Superman action happen."

With that, Nikoli parked, killed the engine and got out of the pickup. He squinted against the rain.

Not looking forward to another soaking, Viv reluctantly grabbed the satchel, hooked it over her right shoulder and got out of the truck, as well. She went over to him and concentrated on the rain beating a rhythm on her wounded arm instead of her close proximity to Nikoli.

She watched as he cocked his head to one side and closed his eyes. Viv felt his energy reaching out for a specific sound. They stood there for three or four minutes, soaked to the bone before he said, "I hear something, but it's not howling or yipping. It's like the gnashing of teeth and something being ripped apart. No, wait…"

Viv knew before he said any more that he had honed in on her Loups. The sound he described was the sound of them tearing into a fresh kill.

"I just heard a growl," Nikoli said and pointed ahead, into the dark, water-drenched night. "It's coming from out there, about three to four hundred yards away. I can't make anything out in all this rain. What's out that way?"

"An old, deserted factory," she said. "It's three stories high and has like ninety thousand square feet of space inside. It's been there for as long as I can remember. I think they used to manufacture some kind of oil-field equipment in there." She swiped a hand over her face to rid it of some water. "The company went belly up about twenty years ago. No one's been out there since. No rebuild. Nothing. The owner's just left."

"How can a factory be that far out there when we're standing so close to a shore? The factory would have to be sitting on the water."

"There's a peninsula down that way. It juts out into the water about five hundred yards or so."

"Can we get there by truck?"

"Not unless you want to spend the wee hours of the morning stuck in mud," Viv said. "There's no road or driveway leading to the factory anymore. Just a grass-covered peninsula."

"So we'll hike it," Nikoli said, then got back in the truck to fetch a flashlight before heading off in the direction of the factory.

Viv followed, occasionally swiping water from her face. Her clothes stuck to her body like a second skin, and the braid hanging down her back felt like it weighed twenty pounds.

Now that she was soaked, Viv didn't mind the rain. In fact, she wished it would soak right through to her soul and wash away all she'd done over the past few days, sending it straight to a sewer. Maybe then the world would stop spinning cockeyed, and she'd save the rest of her Loups and be able to protect her sisters from the Cartesians. Maybe if enough water soaked through, it would cleanse her enough so there wouldn't be any more Cartesians. Who knew?

The wind shifted, sending a blast of cool air over Viv's body. She shivered. Okay, so maybe she did mind the rain.

When they finally arrived at the dilapidated factory, Viv saw a heavy chain strung between the handles of two iron front doors. A giant padlock had been attached to the chain, denying entry to anyone without a key. Old buckets and other plastic debris littered what was once a front lawn, and from what she could see in the dark and rain, it looked like every window in the old factory had been shattered with either a rock or pellet gun.

She was relatively certain some of the city's homeless had made this place their permanent residence. She might have been a witch, but the place still creeped her out.

Viv walked around to the side of the massive building with Nikoli at her heels and spotted a side entry door standing slightly ajar. She held a finger to her lips, signaling to Nikoli that they should proceed quietly.

He shifted to one side and peered through the crack

in the side door. "Can't see anything inside," he whispered. "Too dark. I hear the chomping noise, but I can't even make out what's making the sound. Don't know if they're your Loups or not."

"Let me see," Viv said quietly and ducked under his arm. She pressed an eye to the crack in the door. It was so dark inside it felt like she'd pressed her eye up against a black wall. The building held a noxious odor of fresh blood, urine, oil, wet fur and mildew.

The sounds she heard, however, left her little doubt that some or the rest of her missing Loups were inside. She knew the sound of feeding when she heard it. She stood listening for a while, then decided they'd never get anything accomplished just standing out in the rain.

Nikoli must have been thinking the same because he pushed gently against the door. "We're not getting anywhere like this. I'm going in."

The door creaked so loudly when he pushed on it that Viv heard it over the pounding rain and thunder. When it was wide enough, he slipped in sideways. Viv followed right behind.

They stood inside for a moment, letting their eyes adjust to the dark. Viv tapped Nikoli on the back. "Let me have the flashlight." Somewhere between here, the docks and Treme, she'd managed to lose hers.

He handed it to her. "You turn that light on, and they're either going to attack or scatter."

She flicked a finger against his back. "They're my Loups, remember?"

"Yes, ma'am," he said quietly, and she heard the smile in his voice.

Holding her breath, Viv flipped the switch on the flashlight.

In the middle of a vast, oil-stained concrete floor were at least twenty of her Loups, all fighting over what remained of a human body. All that was recognizable was a foot still trapped inside a worn-out sneaker with no laces. The sound of chomping, chewing, snarling echoed loudly through the building. It made her sick to her stomach.

Startled, the Loups huddled, ducking their heads, protecting their eyes from the light. Some of them yelped. A few growled and turned in their direction, faking a pounce. But Viv knew better. None were going to leave dinner behind.

No amount of cable was going to capture this group. Viv blew out a frustrated breath. "How on earth are we going to get all of them back to the compound?" she asked Nikoli.

He swiped a hand through his hair, then his beard. "Any spell come to mind?"

Viv tskcd. "For some reason I can't even hang onto one Loup with a binding spell. What's it going to do with twenty?" Her Grimoire suddenly came to mind, and Viv mentally went through the worn pages she'd read morning after morning for the past fifteen years.

One spell stuck out in her mind, and she considered it. She hadn't attempted this spell before but remembered the word verbatim. She had no idea if it would work or fall flat like her binding spell. But there was only one way for her to find out.

"I'm going to try a teleportation spell," she said. "See if I can get them back to the compound in one fell swoop. I don't know if it's going to work or piss them off. Just saying."

"What can I do to help?" Nikoli asked.

"Watch my back." She handed him the flashlight, and the jittery Loups looked over in their direction, then back at dinner. She knew when they looked over this way, all they saw was a beam of light. But there was no discounting their sense of smell. As soon as they finished the meal they'd already started, the greedy Loups would be looking for more. Since there was little left of their fresh kill, Viv knew she needed to get with the program or get out.

The spell called for Viv to sit on the floor with her legs crossed and her arms on her thighs, hands palm up, and her eyes closed. Not exactly thrilled with the close-your-eyes part, Viv slowly lowered her body so as not to startle the Loups, then finally sat.

With a slow, fluid motion, she sat cross-legged and placed her arms on her thighs, keeping her hands palm up. She glanced one last time at Nikoli, then over at the Loups before closing her eyes. She blocked out the feeding sounds and rain beating against the old structure, the wretched smell of the building. All she allowed in her mind was a vision of her Grimoire. Then she began the spell.

"Par mon commandement,
laissez-vous le corps et l'ame,
a la place mon esprit maintenant.
rapidement se deplace.
Adhon—Fiontan—Uri—Ila!"

After reciting the spell, Viv didn't want to open her eyes and face another disappointment. While she was still in a zen state, Viv repeated the spell, hoping a double whammy would do the trick.

"Par mon commandement,
laissezvous le corps et l'ame,
a la place mon esprit maintenant.
rapidement se deplace.
Adhon—Fiontan—Uri—Ila!"

"They're gone!"

Hearing Nikoli's excited cry, Viv opened her eyes. Every Loup that had been feeding on the human, still smeared across the floor, had vanished into thin air.

"You did it!" Nikoli said and helped Viv to her feet.

Not wanting to get too excited yet, Viv hurried out the side door, into the night, where the pounding rain had turned into a lazy drizzle. She cupped her hands around her mouth and howled for Jaco to confirm the Loups' arrival. She had to howl twice more before she heard his response.

She *had* done it. The Loups were back in the compound! Viv whirled about on the balls of her feet, no longer caring about the pain in her arm. She wanted to fly into Nikoli's arms and celebrate.

No, no more, she reminded herself.

With great effort, Viv kept her demeanor businesslike. "I need to get back to the compound before feeding so I can help Jaco. I'm sure he can use an extra pair of hands." She turned to head back to the truck and heard Nikoli call out.

"No. Not yet."

She turned to face him. "What?"

He motioned to the remains of the person the Loups had been feeding on. "I can't just leave the body here like that. I'm not sure if we should call the police or not."

"We can't call the authorities. That'll start an investigation. The Circle of Sisters will wind up being involved. My own sisters, too. I can't take that chance."

"But what about him—her? They might have family looking for them. Loved ones who are worried sick over their disappearance."

"I have to think about my family, Nikoli. No authorities."

He frowned, looked over at the body, or what remained of it. Then took the flashlight and walked across the length of the building, shining a beam of light into one corner or another.

"What are you doing?" Viv asked.

Instead of responding, Nikoli bent down and picked up an old shovel. The spade was still intact, but the handle was broken and only two feet long.

"I'm going to bury the remains. I know we're running out of time so I'll be quick. We just can't leave that body there to rot."

With that, Nikoli hurried past her and out of the building with his broken shovel. He didn't walk far before he started digging.

Viv watched as he managed to haul up three spades of dirt.

"There's an easier way to get that done," she said.

He looked up at her quizzically, and she motioned for him to step back a few feet. When he was out of the way, Viv held her hands out in front of her in a praying position, silently issued an incantation, then parted her hands like a book. The earth where Nikoli had been digging opened up.

Since there were so few remains left from the body, she'd called for a three-foot-by-three-foot hole, and that was exactly what she got.

Nikoli nodded as if this was a daily routine for them and went back into the factory. He came out moments later with his hands filled with blood and leftover innards. He walked over to the hole and gently placed them inside. When he did it, it was as if someone turned off a faucet in the sky because the rain abruptly stopped.

Nikoli made at least five trips carrying mangled flesh and bone. His last load was the foot still encased in the sneaker. Once that was safely in the hole, he grabbed the broken shovel and started tossing loose dirt into it, burying the remains.

Neither of them spoke as he shoveled dirt over the few remaining pieces of flesh and bits of hair and bone.

When he was about done, Viv took the flashlight and went to the entrance of the factory, where she'd spotted a few old buckets strewn about in the grass. She found one that sat upright and had about six inches of rainwater in it.

She carried the bucket back to Nikoli. He looked inside it, then dipped his hands into the water and washed off the blood and dirt. Viv watched him, her heart full, her mind quiet for the first time in her life.

When he was done washing, Nikoli stood, wiped his hands dry on the back of his pants, then quietly stared into Viv's eyes. She saw hunger in them, not just for her body but for *her*, all of her. It was as great a hunger as she had for him.

Nikoli held out a hand.

Viv took it with trepidation, and they walked away from the factory, hand-in-hand.

She didn't know if accepting his hand—accepting him, had just sealed her fate, but she'd had no choice. It felt like two universal truths had been set into motion from the moment they'd met.

Their hunger for each other existed for a reason.

And, from this day forward, their love, so full—so complete—so satisfying, would never again be denied.

Viv stopped for a moment and turned to Nikoli. Their eyes held, soft, deep, longing. Still holding one of his hands, Viv felt his pulse beat faster and was certain he felt the same from her. She had no idea when or how any of the reprecussions from the Triad curse might come to be. But one thing she knew for sure. The biggest curse of all would be living without him.

Then an intensity she had not seen before brightened Nikoli's eyes, yet his face remained sober. Her heart felt like it wanted to leap from her chest to touch his heart, and he obviously felt the same for his grip tightened on her hand.

And in that moment, as if the universe knitted them together, Viv and Nikoli whispered simunlateously, "I love you."

* * * * *

Need an adrenaline rush from nail-biting tales
(and irresistible males)?

**Check out Harlequin® Intrigue®
and Harlequin® Romantic Suspense books!**

New books available every month!

CONNECT WITH US AT:

Harlequin.com/Community

 Facebook.com/HarlequinBooks

 Twitter.com/HarlequinBooks

 Instagram.com/HarlequinBooks

 Pinterest.com/HarlequinBooks

ReaderService.com

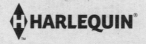

**ROMANCE WHEN
YOU NEED IT**

SGENRE2017

Save $1.00

on the purchase of any

Harlequin® series book.

Available wherever books are sold, including most bookstores, supermarkets, drugstores and discount stores.

Save $1.00

on the purchase of any Harlequin® series book.

Coupon valid until July 31, 2018.
Redeemable at participating retail outlets in the U.S. and Canada only.
Limit one coupon per customer.

52615203

Canadian Retailers: Harlequin Enterprises Limited will pay the face value of this coupon plus 10.25¢ if submitted by customer for this product only. Any other use constitutes fraud. Coupon is nonassignable. Void if taxed, prohibited or restricted by law. Consumer must pay any government taxes. Void if copied. Inmar Promotional Services ("IPS") customers submit coupons and proof of sales to Harlequin Enterprises Limited, PO Box 31000, Scarborough, ON M1R 0E7, Canada. Non-IPS retailer—for reimbursement submit coupons and proof of sales directly to Harlequin Enterprises Limited, Retail Marketing Department, 225 Duncan Mill Rd., Don Mills, ON M3B 3K9, Canada.

U.S. Retailers: Harlequin Enterprises Limited will pay the face value of this coupon plus 8¢ if submitted by customer for this product only. Any other use constitutes fraud. Coupon is nonassignable. Void if taxed, prohibited or restricted by law. Consumer must pay any government taxes. Void if copied. For reimbursement submit coupons and proof of sales directly to Harlequin Enterprises, Ltd 482, NCH Marketing Services, P.O. Box 880001, El Paso, TX 88588-0001, U.S.A. Cash value 1/100 cents.

5 65373 00076 2   (8100)0 12314

® and ™ are trademarks owned and used by the trademark owner and/or its licensee.

© 2018 Harlequin Enterprises Limited

HSCOUP0318

Looking for more satisfying love stories
with community and family at their core?

Check out **Harlequin® Special Edition**
and **Harlequin® Western Romance** books!

New books available every month!

CONNECT WITH US AT:

Harlequin.com/Community

Facebook.com/HarlequinBooks

Twitter.com/HarlequinBooks

Instagram.com/HarlequinBooks

Pinterest.com/HarlequinBooks

ReaderService.com

⬧H HARLEQUIN®
™

**ROMANCE WHEN
YOU NEED IT**

HFGENRE2017R

Want to give in to temptation with
steamy tales of irresistible desire?

Check out **Harlequin® Presents®,
Harlequin® Desire** and
Harlequin® Kimani™ Romance books!

New books available every month!

CONNECT WITH US AT:

Harlequin.com/Community

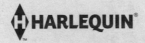

Facebook.com/HarlequinBooks

Twitter.com/HarlequinBooks

Instagram.com/HarlequinBooks

Pinterest.com/HarlequinBooks

ReaderService.com

HARLEQUIN®

**ROMANCE WHEN
YOU NEED IT**

PGENRE2017

Looking for inspiration in tales
of hope, faith and heartfelt romance?

Check out **Love Inspired**®,
Love Inspired® **Suspense** and
Love Inspired® **Historical** books!

New books available every month!

CONNECT WITH US AT:

www.LoveInspired.com

Harlequin.com/Community

 Facebook.com/LoveInspiredBooks

 Twitter.com/LoveInspiredBooks

www.ReaderService.com

Love Inspired®

LIGENRE2017

Love Inspired®

Save $1.00

on the purchase of any
Love Inspired® book.

Available wherever books are sold, including most bookstores, supermarkets, drugstores and discount stores.

Save $1.00

on the purchase of any Love Inspired® book.

Coupon valid until July 31, 2018.
Redeemable at participating retail outlets in the U.S. and Canada only.
Limit one coupon per customer.

52615199

5 65373 00076 2 (8100)0 12313

Canadian Retailers: Harlequin Enterprises Limited will pay the face value of this coupon plus 10.25¢ if submitted by customer for this product only. Any other use constitutes fraud. Coupon is nonassignable. Void if taxed, prohibited or restricted by law. Consumer must pay any government taxes. Void if copied. Inmar Promotional Services ("IPS") customers submit coupons and proof of sales to Harlequin Enterprises Limited, PO Box 31000, Scarborough, ON M1R 0E7, Canada. Non-IPS retailer—for reimbursement submit coupons and proof of sales directly to Harlequin Enterprises Limited, Retail Marketing Department, 225 Duncan Mill Rd., Don Mills, ON M3B 3K9, Canada.

U.S. Retailers: Harlequin Enterprises Limited will pay the face value of this coupon plus 8¢ if submitted by customer for this product only. Any other use constitutes fraud. Coupon is nonassignable. Void if taxed, prohibited or restricted by law. Consumer must pay any government taxes. Void if copied. For reimbursement submit coupons and proof of sales directly to Harlequin Enterprises, Ltd 482, NCH Marketing Services, P.O. Box 880001, El Paso, TX 88588-0001, U.S.A. Cash value 1/100 cents.

® and ™ are trademarks owned and used by the trademark owner and/or its licensee.

© 2018 Harlequin Enterprises Limited

LICOUP0318

Inspirational Romance to
Warm Your Heart and Soul

Join our social communities to connect
with other readers who share your love!

Sign up for the Love Inspired newsletter
at **www.LoveInspired.com** to be the
first to find out about upcoming titles,
special promotions and exclusive content.

CONNECT WITH US AT:

Harlequin.com/Community

 Facebook.com/LoveInspiredBooks

 Twitter.com/LoveInspiredBks

LISOCIAL2017

LOVE
Harlequin
romance?

Join our Harlequin community to share your thoughts and connect with other romance readers!

Be the first to find out about promotions, news, and exclusive content!

Sign up for the Harlequin e-newsletter and download a free book from any series at

www.TryHarlequin.com

CONNECT WITH US AT:

Harlequin.com/Community

 Facebook.com/HarlequinBooks

Twitter.com/HarlequinBooks

Instagram.com/HarlequinBooks

Pinterest.com/HarlequinBooks

ReaderService.com

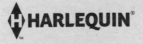 **HARLEQUIN**®

**ROMANCE WHEN
YOU NEED IT**

HSOCIAL2017